continued ...

PRAISE FOR THE
ALLIE BECKSTROM NOVELS

Magic for a Price

"Breathtaking.... Monk is a storyteller extraordinaire."
—*RT Book Reviews*

"The action comes to a blazing crescendo."
—*Gizmo's Reviews*

"Deserves to be savored ... amazing and incredibly satisfying." —A Book Obsession

Magic Without Mercy

"Urban fantasy at its finest.... Every book is packed with action, adventure, humor, battles, romance, drama, and suspense." —*Sacramento Book Review*

"Fast-paced, action-packed, and jammed full of all manner of magical mayhem." —Monsters and Critics

Magic on the Line

"Dark and delicious.... Allie is one of urban fantasy's most entertaining heroines." —*Publishers Weekly* (starred review)

"Allie Beckstrom is one of the best urban fantasy heroines out there." —Fresh Fiction

"An action-packed series." —Night Owl Reviews

Magic on the Hunt

"An absolutely awesome series." —Night Owl Reviews

"Another nonstop adventure." —Romance Reviews Today

Magic at the Gate

"Allie's adventures are gripping and engrossing, with an even, clever mix of humor, love, and brutality."
—*Publishers Weekly*

"A spellbinding story that will keep readers on the edge of their seats." —Romance Reviews Today

Magic on the Storm

"The latest Allie Beckstrom urban fantasy is a terrific entry.... This is a strong tale." —Genre Go Round Reviews

"First-rate urban fantasy entertainment." —Lurv a la Mode

BOOKS BY DEVON MONK

The Broken Magic Series

Hell Bent
Stone Cold

The Allie Beckstrom Series

Magic to the Bone
Magic in the Blood
Magic in the Shadows
Magic on the Storm
Magic at the Gate
Magic on the Hunt
Magic on the Line
Magic Without Mercy
Magic for a Price

The Age of Steam

Dead Iron
Tin Swift
Cold Copper

HOUSE
IMMORTAL

DEVON MONK

A ROC BOOK

ROC
Published by the Penguin Group
Penguin Group (USA) LLC, 375 Hudson Street,
New York, New York 10014

USA | Canada | UK | Ireland | Australia | New Zealand | India | South Africa | China
penguin.com
A Penguin Random House Company

First published by Roc, an imprint of New American Library,
a division of Penguin Group (USA) LLC

First Printing, September 2014

 REGISTERED TRADEMARK — MARCA REGISTRADA

ISBN 978-0-451-46736-2

Printed in the United States of America
10 9 8 7 6 5 4 3 2 1

For my family

ACKNOWLEDGMENTS

Thank you, Anne Sowards, editor extraordinaire, for making all of my books better and this one particularly shiny. Thank you also to my agent, Miriam Kriss, for believing in me every step of the way. Deepest thanks to the many wonderful, skillful people inside of Penguin who have gone above and beyond to support and create this book. My heartfelt gratitude also goes out to the amazing artist Eric Williams, who brought Matilda and her world to such vivid life.

To my crazy, dedicated, and lovely first readers, Dean Woods and Dejsha Knight—thank you both for all that you do on such tight deadlines. I couldn't do this without you. A huge thank-you to my terrific family, one and all. Your support and encouragement mean the world to me. To my husband, Russ, and sons, Kameron and Konner, you are the very best part of my life—thank you for taking this journey with me. I love you.

Finally, my dear readers, thank you for coming along with me into this new world and letting me share Matilda's adventures with you. See you on the other side.

HOUSE
IMMORTAL

1

They named the comet Mercury Star. Not for how brightly it burned, but for the star-shaped hole it punched into the land, and the rich, strange mix of minerals it left behind. —1603
—from the journal of L.U.C.

The way I saw it, a girl needed three things to start a day right: a hot cup of tea, a sturdy pair of boots, and for the feral beast to die the first time she stabbed it in the brain.

"You missed, Matilda," Neds called out from where he was leaning in the cover of trees several yards off.

"No," I said, "I didn't. This one doesn't have a brain to hit. Kind of like a certain farmhand I know." I pulled the knife out of the crocboar's skull and sank it into the thrashing creature's eye before dodging out of the way again.

It lunged at me, three-foot tusks and long snout lined with crocodile teeth slashing a little too close for comfort. Crocboars weren't smart, but they had the teeth, claws, and tough skin to make up for any intelligence they lacked.

"Now you made it mad," Neds said.

"Not helpful." I jumped out of the way and pulled my other knife.

"I've got the tranq gun right here," he said. "And a clear shot."

"No. Wait. I want the meat clean."

Keeping property out here in the scrub meant occasionally trapping and taking down feral beasts before they damaged crops or the domesticated animals. Crocboars weren't good eating, since they were too filled up on the nano that laced the soil of this land. But they made terrific dragon chow.

The beast thrashed some more, ran out of steam, folded down on its knees, and fell over dead.

Just like that.

"Can't get over how quick those things fall," Right Ned said.

"Who are you calling brainless, by the way?" Left Ned grumbled.

I shook the slime off my gloves—crocboars excreted oil—and glanced at Neds.

Most people stared, eyes wide and mouths open, when they first meet Neds. There was good reason for it. Neds had two heads but only the one body, which was never the most normal sort of thing.

Both of him had sandy blond hair cut short and soft blue eyes that gave him an innocent shine, when most times he was anything but. He was clean-cut good-looking, a few inches taller than me, tanned and hard muscled from farm work; something you could tell even though he wore a dark green T-shirt and baggy denim overalls.

He'd left the touring circus and was looking for a job when he saw the ad I'd taken out at the local feed store. I wanted a farmhand to help with the land and the stitched beasts my father, Dr. Case, had left in my keeping.

Especially since my brother, Quinten, hadn't been home in more than three years, something that worried me terribly.

Most people had been scared off by one thing or another in that ad: the hard work, the beasts, or me—a single women holding down her own chunk of land far enough from a city we weren't even covered by House Green, nor were we on the power grid. Neds never complained about any of that. He'd been a fixture on the farm for two years.

"Bring the net over," I said. "We have some dragging to do."

It didn't take us long to throw the net over the beast and tug it tight so the rough hide caught in the rope fiber. That was the easy part. Dragging was the hard part.

I walked over for my rifle, picked it up, and took one last look at the trees and dry summer underbrush around us. Nothing else moved; nothing reared for attack. So that was good.

"Who gets this one?" Right Ned asked, tossing me a rope. "Pony or the leapers?"

"Lizard. I think it's about ready to molt. It should be nice and hungry."

"Just tell me we don't have to boil down scales today and I'm happy," Right Ned said.

I took a length of rope and slung it over my shoulder, and Neds did the same.

"No boiling." We put shoulders to it and dragged the half ton of dead and stink behind us. "But we could have a little fun and scrape a few scales free while it's eating."

"Never have seen the fun in that," Left Ned complained, like he always complained. "But if it pays extra . . ."

"It doesn't. Same pay as every day: food, roof, honest work. And the pleasure of my conversational company."

"Speaking of which," Left Ned said. "Isn't it about time we converse about a raise?"

"When we clear a profit, you'll get your share," I said.

Right Ned slid me a smile, and I grinned back. Left Ned and I had had that conversation daily since they'd wandered up the lane and shook on the terms and job. My answer had never changed, but it didn't stop him from asking.

Lizard wasn't hard to spot since it was approximately the size of a barn and was napping behind the electric fence. It was harmless as long as you didn't move fast around it, didn't look it straight in the eye, and didn't poke it.

"Always meant to ask," Right Ned said. "Where'd the lizard come from? Did your Dad make it too?"

"Yep. Stitched it up piece by piece." We stopped dragging, and Neds and I bent to the task of pulling the net free of the beast.

"What's it all made of?" Right Ned asked.

"Iguana, if you'd believe it," I said. "Of course, bits of other things too—crocodile, kimono. No boars."

"And how do you explain the wings?"

"No idea. Mom said Dad had a whimsical side to his stitchery. Said if he was going to make living creatures, he may as well make them beautiful."

I threw the last of the net off the crocboar and straightened.

The lizard stirred at the commotion and shifted its big shovel-shaped head in our direction.

"You stand on back with the tranquilizer," I said, handing Neds my rifle. "I'll heave this into the corral. Plug it twice if it gets twitchy. Takes a lot to put it down. Are we gold?"

"We're gold," Right Ned said. He stepped back and set my gun down while he pulled his tranq gun.

"You know no one says that anymore," Left Ned said. "Gold isn't what it used to be."

"Gold is just the same as ever," I said. "People aren't what they used to be."

I hefted the front half of the dragon kibble up off the ground, dragged it a little closer to the fence. It was heavy, but I was an uncommonly strong girl. My brother had made sure of that when he'd stitched me together.

"Did you ever ask your father why he stitched a dragon?" Right Ned asked.

"Lizard."

"Four legs, four wings, reptile the size of a house." He raised the tranq gun at Lizard who opened its yellow slitted eyes and then raised its head and rose onto its feet. "Dragon."

"All right, dragon. Who knows? Mom said it was during his scatty years, shaking off his time after he left House White. Maybe just to see if it could be done."

"So your dad gets a pink slip from House Medical and stitches together a dragon?" Right Ned shook his head, admiration in that smile. "Wish I'd met him. He aimed high."

"I don't mind high, but I wish he'd aimed smaller." I heaved the first half of the crocboar over the metal wires. "Then maybe Lizard would go catatonic every couple of months like most stitched creatures of a certain size."

I heaved the other half of the lizard's breakfast over the fence. It landed with a squishy thump.

"And maybe Lizard wouldn't be such a big, smart, pain in the hole to deal with." I stepped away from the fence, but did not turn my back. Lizard was cobra-fast when it caught sight of something it wanted to eat.

"Do you think it could survive on its own, if it were set free?" Right Ned's voice muffled just a bit from holding the gun ready to fire if the fences failed.

"I suppose. Well, maybe not in city. It's never been on dead soil. Large things unstitch there, don't they? Not enough mutant nano to keep them going?"

Left Ned answered, "Can't keep a stitch that big alive in the city. Hard to keep the smaller bits alive unless they are very, very expensive and very, very, well made. It's not because of the soil, though."

"Sure it is," I said. "It's all about the soil. Out here in the scratch, we still have devilry in our dirt. Makes stitched things stay stitched."

"Never thought you were the sort of girl who believed in magic, Tilly," Right Ned said in the tone of a man who clearly did not believe in the stuff but had spent years taking money from people who did.

"Stardust, nanomutations, witchery. Whatever you want to call it, Lizard there is breathing because of it."

Lizard finally got a solid whiff of the dead thing and smacked at the air, sticking out its ropelike tongue to clean first one eye, then the other. It started our way with that half-snake, half-bowlegged-cow waddle that made a person want to point and laugh, except by the time a person got around to doing either of those things, Lizard would be on top of them and they'd be bitten in half.

It opened its big maw and scooped off a third of the beast quick as a hot spoon through ice cream, then lifted its head and swallowed, the lump of meat stuck in its gizzard.

"All right, we're gold," I said, as Lizard made contented *click-huff* sounds. "Looks like it's not going to attack the fence. Or us." I pulled off my gloves and smacked them across my thigh to scrape away the dirt and slime. "So, are you hungry? 'Cause I could eat."

Neds shifted his finger off the trigger, set the safety, and leaned the barrel across his shoulder. "I wouldn't mind a hot breakfast."

"Good." I picked up my rifle and slung it over my shoulder, then headed up the dirt lane toward the old farmhouse. "It's your turn to cook."

Left Ned complained his whole way through it, but he and Right Ned put up a decent egg and potato scramble.

I made sure Grandma had her share of the meal, ate more than my share, then did the dishes as was only fair. Just as I was drying the last plate, there was a knock at the door.

Neds stopped sharpening the machete they called a pocket knife. He glanced at the door, then at me. We didn't get unannounced visitors. Ever.

Our nearest neighbors were five miles off. If they needed anything, they'd tap the wire before stopping by.

Grandma in the corner, didn't seem to notice the knock. She just went right on knitting the twisted wool spooling up off the three pocket-sized sheep that puttered around at her feet. The sheep were another of my dad's stitched critters, built so they grew self-spinning wool. I'd tried to breed them, thinking I could sell them and make a little money for the repairs on the place, but like most stitched things, they were infertile.

I wiped my hands on a kitchen towel and opened the door.

"Are you Matilda Case?" the stranger asked in a voice too calm and nice for someone who was holding his guts in place with one hand.

"I am," I said, even though Neds always told me I shouldn't go around giving people my name without having theirs first. "You're a long way from the cities. Do you need a ride to a hospital?"

The stranger was a couple inches shy of seven feet tall, had a broad sort of face with an arrangement of features that fell into the rustic and handsome category, five o'clock shadow included. His mop of brown hair was shaved close by his ears and finger-combed back off his forehead so that it stuck up a bit—which passed for fashion maybe a hundred years ago.

His shirt, under the gray coat he wore, was high collared, buttoned, and might have once been white. That, along with his dark gray breeches and military boots laced and buckled up to his knees, gave him a distinctly historical sort of look.

Gray clothes meant he was claimed by House Gray, one of the eleven powerful Houses that ruled the modern world's resources, from technology and agriculture straight on up through defense, fuel, medical, and the gods we worshiped. Gray ruled the human resource—all the people in the world, except for those who claimed the twelfth, powerless House: House Brown. Loosely democratic, House Brown was made up of people who lived off the grid, scraping by without the comforts and amenities of the modern world. House Brown was barely recognized by the other Houses.

I was House Brown, but I wore green, Agriculture, when I needed to trade with nearby businesses. No one from House Gray, or any other House, had ever come to my farm.

I had changed out of my filthy hunting clothes into a pair of faded blue overalls and a checkered shirt. It wasn't at all House Brown or House Green compliant, but, then, I'd been off grid and below the radar all my life.

Just the way my brother wanted us to be.

"Unless you're here to sell me something," I said as I leaned the door shut a bit. "In which case I'll just save you what air you've got left and say no, there's no Matilda Case living here."

He didn't smile, but his eyes pulled up a bit at the bottom and something that looked like humor caught fire in them. That's when I noticed the color of his eyes: cinnamon red, like mine when I was injured.

I took a step back, startled, and he took a step forward.

Neds racked a round in the shotgun he'd had propped by his knee and then all of us in the kitchen held perfectly still.

Well, except for Grandma. She just kept on singing her knitting song about sunshine through lace and liberty's death, her fingers slipping yarn into knots, smooth and liquid for a woman of her still-undetermined years.

"Not a single step closer," Left Ned said, his voice always a little colder and meaner than Right Ned's. "You have not been invited into this home."

The stranger looked away from me, and I thought maybe for the first time he noticed that there was a house, a room, and people around us. A whole farm, really: 150 acres tucked back far enough in the rolling hills of Pennsylvania that the nearest fill-up station was thirty miles away.

He certainly noticed Neds—both heads of him. And the gun.

Since Left Ned was talking, I knew he was willing to bleed up the stranger a little more if that's what it took to keep him out of the house.

"I'm looking for a doctor," the stranger said. "Dr. Renault Case."

"He doesn't live here anymore," Right Ned said calmly, everything about his voice the opposite of Left Ned's. "If you need someone to take you to a town doctor, I'd be willing. But there's no medical man here to help you."

The stranger frowned, sending just a hint of lines across his forehead and at the corners of his eyes. "You think I came here for help?"

I nodded toward his gut. "You are bleeding rather strongly."

He looked down. An expression of surprise crossed his face and he shifted his wide fingers, letting a little more blood ooze out, as if just noticing how badly he was injured. If he was in pain—and he should be—he did not show it.

Shock, maybe. Or expensive drugs.

"I didn't come here looking for help from Dr. Case," he said, cinnamon gaze on me, just on me, and the sound of his blood falling with a soft *tip tip tip* on my wooden floor. "I came here to warn him."

"About what?" I asked.

He hesitated.

Left Ned spoke up. "Say it, or get walking."

"His enemies are looking for him. For him and what he's left behind on this property. I come offering protection."

It was a dramatic sort of thing to say, and he had a nice, deep, dramatic sort of voice for it. Chills did that rolling thing over my arms.

But there was only one problem.

"He's dead," I said.

"What?"

"My father, Dr. Case, has been dead for years."

That, more than anything, seemed to take the starch out of him. He exhaled, and it was a wet sound as he tried to get air back in his lungs. I almost reached over to prop him up, afraid he might just pass out and further mess up the clean of my kitchen floor.

He was a big man, but, like I said, I'm strong.

"Are you certain?" he asked.

I'd been twelve years old when the men from House Black, Defense, and House White, Medical, came to the farm. I'd hidden like my father had taught me, up in the rafters of the barn. I'd watched those men kill him. Kill my mother too. I'd watched them search our house and carry out boxes. I'd watched them pick up my parents' bodies, put them in a black van, then use our garden hose to clean up the drive so not even a drop of their blood was left for me to cry over.

My brother had come home from studying the old skills—electrical tinkering, metalwork, analog and digital system repairs—out on the Burnbaums' homestead about three months later. He'd found Mom and Dad gone, and me and Grandma trying to hold the place together. Right then, he'd started his crazy crusade for information and histories that had eventually made him unofficial head of House Brown.

The same crazy crusade that had left me alone on this farm for three years with an addle-minded grandmother, a two-headed farmhand, some impossible creatures, and the communication hub for the scattered, off-grid House Brown folk my brother promised to look after.

My brother might still be alive, but not my parents.

The image of their bodies being carried away flashed behind my eyes again.

"I'm very certain," I whispered to the stranger.

"I . . ." He swallowed hard, shook his head. Didn't look like that helped much. His words came out in a slur. "I thought . . . I should have known. Sooner. We thought . . . all our information. That he lived."

"Neds," I called.

The stranger's eyes rolled up in his head and he folded like someone had punched him in the ribs. I put my hands out to catch him, got hold of his jacket shoulders and pivoted on my heels, throwing my weight to guide him down to the floor without knocking his head too badly.

I crouched next to him. This close, I thought maybe there was something familiar about him.

Neds strolled over. "What are you going to do with him, Tilly?" Right Ned asked.

"I don't know. Check his pockets, will you? See if he has a name. If he's really House Gray, we might have trouble on our hands." I was already pushing his hand to one side so I could get to his wound. It was deep and bad. Might be from a crocboar. Might be from any number of beasts that grew up hungry and mean out on the edges of the property.

I could mend him enough to get him to a hospital hours away in my old truck on these old roads. If he hadn't lost too much blood, he might survive.

I stood. "I need the sewing kit. The medicines."

"Tilly," Right Ned said. "I don't think that will work."

I was already halfway across the kitchen toward the bathroom, where I kept all the supplies for taking care of Neds and Grandma.

"Tilly," Left Ned snapped. "Stop and listen, woman."

I did not like being bossed around by that man. Either of them. I turned.

Neds hunkered next to the stranger, his shotgun in easy reach on the floor beside him, his shoulders angled so the shirt stretched at the seams. He'd pushed the man's jacket sleeve back to reveal his arm up to his elbow.

Stitches. The man had a thick line of charcoal gray stitches ringing his entire forearm. Not medical stitches, not medical thread. Life stitches, like mine.

I instinctively held my own hands out, turning them so they caught the light. Thin silver stitches crossed my palms and circled my thumbs, making the gold-brown of my skin look a little darker. Just as those same silver stitches tracked paths across my arms and my legs, and curved up my stomach, my breasts, and around one shoulder. Just as stitches traced my left ear to the curve of my jaw and ran a line across my neck. I kept my hair free to cover them up. If I wore gloves and long-sleeved shirts and pants, no one knew I was made like this.

Made of bits.

Not quite human.

Stitched like my father's other illegal creations.

The only other people in the world who were stitched were the galvanized. Warriors, historians, counselors — they were prized and owned by the heads of the Houses. Rumors said they were owned against their will and put on display in the fights during the annual Gathering of Peace, and any other politically influenced event. Owning a galvanized was proof of the House's wealth and power. Rumors said they were the reason the Houses were no longer at war with each other, because the galvanized refused to be involved in House-to-House conflict.

Rumors also said they were immortal.

The galvanized began as a medical curiosity, then went on to become oddities, supersoldiers, historians, while remaining technological and medical guinea pigs. Tired of being owned and used, the galvanized walked away from the Houses. It became known as the Uprising, and once people saw that the galvanized refused to follow House rules, they too defected from House control.

The Uprising saw thousands of people fleeing from multigeneration debt to the Houses and forming their own House — House Brown — which they intended to run democratically as a loose collective of people unhappy with House demands and injustices.

The galvanized stood with them. In an attempt to kill House Brown and its promise of freedom, the other Houses banded together to wage war on House Brown, vowing it would never be recognized as a legitimate House. Years of guerilla resistance and war nearly brought the world's system of resource management crashing down. The Houses finally agreed to a peace treaty drawn up by the galvanized.

House Brown would have no voice in world affairs or the affairs of Houses, but they would be left alone. In exchange, the galvanized would return to the Houses; give up their rights to be considered human; and become servants, slaves, and subjects once again.

The galvanized had agreed to those terms. No one knew why.

I'd never once in my life met a person stitched like me. Until this man. This stranger bleeding on my floor.

"You'll need the other thread," Right Ned said. "Hospital out here won't know what to do with him, or with us for having him."

I was nodding but my body seemed far away. "He's . . . he's . . . like me. I thought galvanized were different. Immortal and perfect."

"He's hurt." Neds strolled over to me.

He touched me only in the most urgent of times.

Contact for him, he had told me, was an intimate sort of thing. He knew an awful lot about a person if he put his hands on their skin for too long. He said he respected me too much to do that, to know things about me I wouldn't want him to know.

But he touched me now, his warm fingers brushing oh so lightly across my palms.

It was a strange enough occurrence, it snapped me right out of my drift.

"You'll need the medical supplies at the pump house," Right Ned said again, his blue gaze searching to see if I was listening. "Your father's supplies."

I glanced between him and Left Ned, who seemed a little disgusted. But, then, Left Ned was always a little disgusted when he touched me. Right Ned never let that show. Right Ned never made me feel like I should be ashamed of what kind of things I was made up of.

"I'll be back quick," I said. "Watch him. Watch Grandma.

And make up the spare bed. Clean sheets are in the linen drawers."

I jogged out the door, wanting to move, to be away from that stranger and the questions he had brought into my kitchen. What enemies? How close were they? And which House did he belong to exactly?

The sun pushed up over the tree line. The birds couldn't seem to sing enough about it, but there was no heat to the day yet. I jogged down through the trees, down past the ramble of blackberries until the rush of the stream outsang the birds.

The pump house was a long stone building set beside the stream. It generated electricity for the farm and the computers and other off-the-grid equipment we used for communication and for keeping our place out of sight. It pumped fresh water up to the house and out to the water troughs in the field and barn for the beasts.

On the inside—or, rather, the underside—was my father's workshop that my brother had forbidden me to enter when we were young.

That moratorium had lasted one week before I picked the lock, hacked the code, and let myself in. He hadn't found out about my frequent visits to the lab for almost a year, and by then, I knew the secrets of the place better, even, than he did.

I pushed open the door and stepped into the cool dark and damp. I didn't bother switching on the light. I knew exactly which stone in the back wall to pull free to expose the lever for the hatch.

I pulled that lever, the sensors within it accepting my fingerprint signature. The floorboards lifted, revealing wooden stairs. I hurried down those and flipped the light switch.

Bulbs popped on, burning with such cool intensity, I closed my eyes and counted to three before opening them again.

This steel room beneath the wood and stone and dust

of the pump house looked like it belonged in a space-ship.

Every wall was covered with steel and burnished to a soft shine, drawers and shelves built from ceiling to floor. Some of those drawers were locked in such ways, I'd never been able to open them. Others I never wanted to open again.

In the center of the room was an empty metal table wide enough for two people to lie on it side-by-side. The floor was carved and burned with symbols, lines, and fig-ures that made my head hurt if I stared at them too long.

I'd asked Quinten what the symbols represented, but he just shook his head and said he hadn't figured it out yet. Some of the things on the farm were old. Older even than Dad's research and experiments. Maybe older than Grandma. Dad had never explained them and the rec-ords were seized by the Houses back when Dad had been killed.

Mysteries at my feet, and all around.

I strode to the drawers, counted three in from the cor-ner and pulled on the smooth, cold handle.

Inside were a dozen master spools of thread, each filled with glassy silver strands of different thickness. *Fi-lum Vitae*, or life thread. It was my dad's concoction, made of the minerals and organic matter that filtered from the soil and river to spin out here—nanowitchery and devilry included.

Next to the threaded spools were empty wooden bob-bins. I hooked the heaviest threads into the notch of two bobbins.

I pressed my thumb on the button on the side of the drawer, engaging the machinery. Bobbins spun, filling with thread from the master spools. As soon as the bob-bins were fat I let go of the button and a diamond-edged blade cut the threads.

I put the bobbins in my pocket and gathered up a sheet of needles, surgical scissors, and clamps.

Most of my knowledge of how to use my father's medical supplies was taught to me by Quinten, the genius that he was, whose hand at stitchery was even finer than Dad's. Over the years he'd left for months at a time, leaving me to repair the beasts Dad had pieced together. Leaving me, sometimes, to repair myself.

I was human—I ate, drank, laughed, and cried. I'd grown from a baby to a girl. Then I'd gotten sick and almost died.

Quinten had spoken of it only once over a bottle of moonshine he'd gotten for repairing the Phersons' radio. When I'd almost died, I'd been eight, and he'd been thirteen. He'd stolen me out of bed when Mom and Dad weren't looking, and with that genius mind of his, he'd done . . . something to me.

Made it so my memories, my soul, and all the *me* of me were picked up and transplanted into the sleeping mind of one of Dad's hidden experiments: a stitched-together girl child who had been sleeping for a couple hundred years.

Dad had been furious. Mom had been horrified. But shortly thereafter, my original body failed and my stitched body survived.

With me in it.

I was our biggest secret: the real monster the outside world would tear apart if found.

So, yes, I was human. But I wasn't *only* human, since the sleeping girl's body was a remnant from a failed experiment that had happened so long ago, she'd been forgotten. Dad had smuggled her out when he left House White.

Good thing for me that he did.

I shut off the light, jogged the stairs, closed the hatch, and traded the dampness and memories for the warming light of day.

The whine of a drone engine high above made me walk a little faster.

That wasn't good. The farm wasn't on any of the flight

paths of low-level crafts or drones. We were a pocket of nowhere surrounded by the bustling cities of everywhere.

I knew it wasn't a coincidence to hear an engine up in the blue above me today, of all days.

Whoever this man was, he had troubles following him. Which meant I needed to get him patched up and off my property before those old enemies of my father became new enemies of mine.

2

HOUSE ORANGE

Slater Orange preferred to walk, taking the long, narrow hallway and stairs down fourteen flights, deep into the earth. House Orange, Minerals, controlled the mineral resources in the world, and he had been the head of that house for seventy years.

Over those years, he had refined the treaties and deals held between his House and all the others to his benefit. Minerals were, after all, limited and desired. That scarcity placed his House firmly in the highest ranking among Houses, though there were those who saw themselves as above him.

But all the deals he had secured had not given him the one thing he desired: immortality.

His body, which appeared to be only forty years old, was nearly one hundred. The youth treatments developed by House White, Medical, and House Yellow, Technology, had stalled the advancement of age for him, and for most of the heads of Houses.

But it could not stall the disease that had been eating away at his body for decades.

Death ended all mortal men. This was a truth even the heads of Houses could not bribe, innovate, or deal away.

But not all men were mortal. The galvanized, six men and six women, were more than three hundred years old. Nothing short of violently destroying their brains could kill them. There had been extensive experiments on the first galvanized to prove out that theory. Arms and legs could be removed, organs destroyed, but the brains of these twelve strange people remained active, their bodies easily repaired, stitched together, and made whole.

It had made them unholy terrors on the battlefield—foes that never fell and never forgot.

And it had made them the thing he most wanted to tear apart to understand.

He had assumed Dr. Renault Case and his wife would know why the galvanized were immortal. That question had been the center of Dr. Case's research when he was at House White. But the capture of the Cases had not gone according to plan. They'd been killed, and the brightest minds had confirmed that their research seemed to be nothing but nonsense full of antiquated theories and abandoned experiments.

His hope of applying the galvanized technique to his own failing body had ended with them.

Until three years ago, when the existence of an intelligent and overly curious man by the name of Quinten Case had been brought to his attention.

Slater Orange reached the bottom of the stairs and paused, pulling the cuffs of his silk shirt straight beneath his copper brocade vest and burnt orange frock jacket, and then adjusting the ascot at his neck. He was, after all, civilized.

Today he and his House would offer a deal he knew Mr. Case would not refuse.

He pulled a silk cloth out of his pocket and dabbed away the sweat that slicked the top of his lip. Better Quinten Case think this just another day in the long string of days that had constituted nearly three years of employment.

Better he not know today would be the day everything in his life changed.

Assured his personage was in order, he walked the softly padded hall down to the huge library and research room that served as a place of study for Mr. Case.

He held up his hand, and a door-sized section of the wall faded from sight.

"Good day, Mr. Case." Slater stepped into the room. "How are you?"

Quinten Case was a lean man in his thirties with a mop of messy brown hair and a tightly trimmed beard and mustache. His eyes were glints of navy blue that missed no detail. He'd been contracting himself out from House Gray, People, to a variety of Houses, and had landed in the possession of House Silver, Vice, before being loaned to House Orange in lieu of a large debt between House Silver and House Orange.

He was a brilliant, restless man. Perhaps even more brilliant than his father. Slater Orange knew Quinten had agreed to be loaned to House Orange only in the hopes of gaining access to his data, as he had found a way to gain access to the data at each House where he had worked.

Slater believed he was looking for his father's research. And he had made sure he found it.

"I am well enough, Your Eminence," Quinten Case answered from where he was pacing in front of a shelf full of rare books.

The chair by the false window that displayed any view in the world was pushed to one side, the window blank. The table that had always been covered in books, papers, and recording devices—not that the frustrating Mr. Case had ever taken a single note in all the time he'd been here—was cleared and dust free.

"My contract with you has been fulfilled," Quinten said. "More than fulfilled by months now, as I've been trying to explain to your servants. My three years are over. I have organized your research library. I have scoured every entry for the information you wanted. There is no data that indicates the galvanized experiment can be replicated. I am sorry not to have found more encouraging results. I will be taking my leave."

"Will you?" Slater Orange asked with zero interest. "And where do you think you will go?"

"Back to House Gray, of course."

"Such an interesting choice."

"I wouldn't think so," he said. "It is the House that has legal claim to me."

Slater almost smiled at him bringing up the legality of his ownership. The Houses were the law, and the law was whatever they desired it to be.

"While you have been looking through my records, Mr. Case," Slater said, "I have been looking through yours. Not the records of your service to House Gray. Older, hidden things."

Quinten was still pacing, pacing. No expression on his face, no pause in his step. He was a caged thing that had finally spotted the open door. He wanted out. But he knew if he rushed his keeper, he would never be granted freedom.

"I have found something very precious to you. Something you hid away on a farm. Do you know what that is, my dear Mr. Case? Do you know *who* it is?"

Ah, there. Quinten faltered just slightly in his pacing, the surprise catching at his feet.

"I see that you do," Slater went on. "Would you like to know how I discovered the creature you built, that lovely young girl?"

"I don't know what you're talking about," Quinten said. "I do know I have a right to contact House Gray."

Slater ignored him. "Your mother believed she could get information out to someone who cared, all those years ago before they died. She believed there would be other people at other Houses willing to take her side. To save her husband. To save her. And, yes, to save the abomination they had been so intent to keep a secret all these years. A stitched daughter.

"She said nothing of you, her only natural son," Slater continued. "I have spent months wondering over that. Perhaps you have spent years wondering why your mother would send out a distress message and not mention you."

That finally made Quinten stop pacing. He turned and pressed his fingers to his lips, gathering his thoughts.

"I am a man of some intelligence, Your Eminence," he said. "Unless I am allowed to see this message you speak of, I have no opinion on it whatsoever. I respectfully request contact with House Gray."

"There is nothing House Gray can do for you, Mr. Case," Slater Orange said. "I own you now. And with the press of a finger, I can send forces out to capture that young woman you built."

"I respectfully request contact with House Gray," he repeated.

"Let me make my intentions very clear," Slater Orange said. "I will go to extremes to tear that lovely young girl apart slowly and brutally until I see what makes her tick.

"Or . . ." He lifted the cloth to pat the sweat at his lip, just once. "You can tell me what you know. What have you found in your father's research? Better still: how did you make that girl galvanized? Is she immortal or is she nothing more than a toy doll, slowly unwinding?"

Quinten shifted his shoulders a fraction and curled his hands at his sides. He might be a scholarly man, but he had spent most of his life out in the unclaimed lands, scratching out his survival day by day. He was a resourceful man, and maybe just a bit wild.

"I have served my contract," he said. "You will release me now or allow me contact with House Gray."

It was all he said. A curse of sorts. A defiance.

"Ah, now, Mr. Case. You know I can't do that. What I can do is kill her while you watch."

Quinten didn't even blink, nor did his breathing change. He had probably already worked through the outcome of this meeting. An outcome that would not be in his favor.

Slater needed that young stitched girl alive. If Quinten refused to give him the information on how to create a galvanized body, then she was the only person in the world who had been stitched in modern times. A blueprint. A beginning of his forever.

She was his chance at immortality. A chance he must take before his body gave in to the disease even his best doctors had run out of solutions for.

She was his last chance to cheat death.

"Now," Slater Orange said. "Let us negotiate your life and the life of that poor, helpless creature."

3

Settlers cleared that land, staked their farms, built their homes. They did not know a dead comet lay beneath their soil until they dug up its grave and discovered what it had left behind.—*1712*

—from the journal of L.U.C.

I jogged across the porch and into my kitchen. Neds and the stranger were gone, leaving behind a good-sized puddle of blood on the floor.

Grandma still sat in the corner, knitting away, the little sheep, Clotho, Lachesis, and Atropos, having curled up to sleep at her feet. She was singing about sawbones at the grave and hope begging for mercy's gun. For a sweet old gal, she sure did have a bloody taste in music.

"Where's Neds?" I asked as I dug in the cupboard and pulled out the jar of scale jelly.

She blinked watery eyes and lowered her knitting—still the same cream-colored scarf she'd been working on for months. It was near long enough to wrap a person head to foot with a good yard or so left over, but she insisted it wasn't long enough yet.

"Which Ned, dear?" she asked.

"Both of them."

"I think he was moving that dead body that came to visit," she said. "Don't know why a body would want to die on the kitchen floor. Bedroom floor, maybe. Or porch. Wouldn't be too bad to die on the porch, would it? If you could see the sky."

"He's not dead," I said. I hoped.

"Oh, that's good." She glanced around the room, then whispered, "Is he a ghost come to haunt? All these years later, I have my regrets. Of course, we all do."

"Not a ghost either, so no need to regret anything, Grandma. Just sit here. I'll be right back."

That was about as much sense as I could get out of her these days. Sometimes she'd clear up and every word out of her mouth was right on target. But most the time she was wrapped in that aging mind of hers, singing that one bloody song, living those old, regretful memories, while fingers counted off her remaining time in loops and stitches.

"Don't step in the blood on the floor, though," I said as I headed out of the room. "I'll mop it up in a second."

She went back to her knitting and song again. "Coated with blood, knife cut to the bone, filling the cup that peace drank alone . . ."

There was a time when her hush-little-baby tune was about Papa buying mockingbirds and golden rings. Now it was verse after verse of sadness and pain.

I didn't know how much she remembered of my parents being killed. She'd never spoken a word about my father or mother in fourteen years. But she'd never been the same since, really. I suppose neither of us had.

The spare room was next to Neds' room, which used to be my father's office.

Grandma and I bedded on the other side of the house—I in my parents' master bedroom; she in the room that used to be mine when I was a girl.

The entire upper floor of the house was empty and dusty and had enough space we could put up a traveling sideshow if we wanted. That space had come in handy now and then, when we'd hosted House Brown families on the move who had lost their stakes to the creep of cities or had their farms swallowed up by House claims.

It was part of why I kept Quinten's communication network going. Those of us in House Brown were nomads, living on the fringe, unwilling to buckle to the rules and regulations of the other Houses. Unwilling to give up our lives and freedom because the rich and powerful decided to tell us how to live.

House Brown had no voice among the other Houses. Which meant we had only each other to count on for our safety and needs. Clear and fast communication was vital for the survival of thousands. I wasn't the only communication hub in the world—there were four others—but I was the only one in North America. And if the Houses found out what I was doing here, found our network and equipment in the basement, they'd shut us down and put thousands of people at risk.

Which was why I needed to get this galvanized man off my land, pronto.

I caught up with Neds in the hall. He'd hooked his arms under the stranger's shoulders and was walking backward toward the spare room, sweating hard as he dragged the man.

"You change the sheets?" I picked up the man's boots, helping to carry him. He weighed twice what I expected. No wonder Neds were sweating.

"Yes," Right Ned grunted. "Did you get everything?"

"I think so. Brought some bandaging just in case. And the jelly. It did good for me when the pony put a hole in me last year."

Neds stopped next to the bed, which had an old quilt and blanket pulled all the way down to the footboard and fresh, fold-creased sheets stretched out across it.

"Ready?" Left Ned said. "Lift on three."

I nodded.

"One, two, three." Neds lifted and swung the top half of the stranger, while I did the same for his bottom half.

The springs creaked and moaned under the man's weight, and the mattress sagged alarmingly. But the frame was hardwood and held up.

"Feet hang over pretty bad," I noted. I got busy unlacing and unbuckling his boots—a good, sturdy pair that had seen years of wear and repair. I tugged those off and dropped them to the floor.

Right Ned wiped at his sweaty bangs, then tucked thumbs into the tool loops on the sides of his overalls. "You need anything else? Water and rags for the blood maybe?"

"Water's a good idea. A bucket should do. Then maybe some help lifting him if I have to wrap the bandage all the way around his middle."

"He shouldn't be here," Left Ned said. "House Gray. Probably a spy. Or worse."

"Isn't your say," Right Ned replied. "This is Tilly's house. Her decision."

I turned away from setting the supplies on the nightstand to find Neds standing right behind me.

Left Ned was scowling and obviously working to keep his opinion to himself. Right Ned raised one eyebrow, and I grinned at the spark of humor in his soft blue eyes.

I didn't know how that man could stand Left Ned's attitude sometimes. But they were brothers. What else could he do?

"Do you think there's something dangerous about our visitor?" I asked. Neds had more worldly experience than I, since he'd been in and out of the big cities and traveled for most of his life. "Seeing as how he's unarmed and unconscious," I added.

"Go ahead," Left Ned said, "joke about it. But he's trouble. Galvanized trouble."

"It's fine," Right Ned said. "Nothing about him you can't handle. We've seen you take down crocboars barehanded."

"You should have kicked him out on his heels, not dragged him in here and bedded him down like a lost puppy," Left Ned muttered. "He's a stranger."

"I take in lots of strangers," I said. "Plus, he's wounded. A Case always tends to those who are hurt. Even if he was my sworn enemy, I'd patch him up before kicking him to the crocs."

"We know that's your way, Tilly," Right Ned said. "And we respect it. Don't we?" he said to Left Ned.

"No, *we* don't," Left Ned said. "Too much kindness will just get you trouble. And that"—he jerked his thumb over his shoulder toward the bed—"is already too much trouble."

Right Ned rolled his eyes. "We'll get the water. Be right back."

I knew Left Ned was right. Sometimes it was better for all involved just to let a wounded thing lie. Sometimes kindness only reaped a bitter harvest.

But the man had come to warn my father. He'd come to help him, quite possibly at the risk of receiving that wound he now suffered. If for nothing more than his stated intentions, I felt he deserved to be mended.

And quickly, before he drew unwanted attention to my property.

Neds, probably Right Ned, had pushed the curtain back from the window, letting the daylight in to cheer the place.

From here I could see the row of oak trees stretched out on either side of it, all the way down the two miles before it ended at the old highway no one used anymore now that the cities were connected by freeways, sky, and tubes.

I pushed my hair out of my eyes. Grandma said my hair was the color of maple syrup and beautiful. I just thought it was bouncy and got in the way too much. I turned back to the supplies.

Thread, needles, scissors, clamps, plain cotton, and bandages. Regular disinfectants didn't work on me, and I'd guessed they might not work on him either, which was why I'd brought a small jar of scale jelly. It looked like fruit jelly, a nice amber yellow of peach or tangerines boiled with sugar. But it was not eating jelly at all.

It was boiled-down lizard scales. When Neds had taken some of it down to the feed and seed just to see if they had ever seen the stuff, the owner had no idea what it was made of.

Dr. Smith, who'd been buying wormer for his goats that day, took an awfully strong interest in it, and said it didn't look, smell, or feel like any medicine he'd ever used to patch up people or animals. He'd volunteered to run it through his lab to see what made it up.

Luckily, the Neds aren't the sort who trust easily. They'd told the doctor no, laughed it off as just a single near-empty jar they'd found down by the old nuclear power plant at Clark's River, and come on home.

We didn't know why it worked on me—maybe it was a stitched thing. It did nothing at all for the Neds. But as long as it worked, I was happy for it and did my best to keep a supply stocked.

"You're lucky I was a nosy and willful child," I said as I rolled up the sleeves of my checkered shirt. "Even luckier Quinten answered my questions. Well, most of them, anyway. Let's get to patching that gash of yours."

I braced my knees against the box spring and lifted him a bit, then tugged off his jacket sleeve by sleeve.

I put him down as easy as I could, but it must not have been that easy. He moaned a little, and his eyes rolled under the lids.

"Now I'm going to take off your shirt," I said in a friendly voice. I wasn't sure if he could hear me, but I didn't want him to wake up fighting. I'm strong, but preferred not to stitch up a wound while ducking a fist.

His hands, covered in half-dried blood, were twice the size of mine. And the rest of him matched that proportion.

Not much could knock me out cold, but I figured if he clocked me, I'd be seeing stars.

"I'm starting here with your sleeves." I made sure all the cuff buttons were undone, then leaned over him. "Rolling up the right sleeve, my friend." My fingers brushed against the ridge of stitches that circled his forearm.

I'd never touched another person life-stitched like me. Never touched a man, unless the few times I'd patched up Neds' cuts counted. My father, then brother, had insisted I stay hidden. Said if I let any other person find out I was stitched, they'd come to kill me, kill us all—land, beasts, and every last Case included.

So I didn't have the experience with men that other woman my age had. I had long ago accepted that was just the way it would be.

Unless I found someone whom I could trust with my secret. Whom I could trust with my life.

And that only happened in fairy tales.

Gently, I dragged one finger along the stitches on the man's arm again. It wasn't a horrible feeling; it wasn't frightening or odd.

Being stitched was evidence of a mending, an overcoming of pain. Our scars were proof that we were strong enough to keep living.

I carefully slid the button at the top of his collar through the hole. His collar loosened. He caught his breath just slightly as my knuckle brushed the bare skin of his neck.

I didn't think the galvanized had much feeling. Just in case I was causing him pain, I decided to keep talking.

"My farmhand says you're trouble. I hope you prove him wrong and see that I'm just here trying to help you."

I thumbed the next button open. "So just stay still. I'll try to be gentle."

I hadn't put my hands on this much of a man, well, ever. I was trying not to get distracted by it, but couldn't help but let my imagination wander over him a bit.

I undid the rest of his buttons, then assessed the situation of his torn-up undershirt. Seemed a shame to cut up a man's shirt, but it already had a slash through the front from whatever sharp edge he'd gotten into an argument with.

Didn't look like a crocboar did it. Too clean, and he had too many of his guts still on the inside.

I tugged his undershirt up out of his pants, exposing just an inch or two of his bare stomach above his belt. His skin was a shade lighter than his hands, several shades lighter than my skin.

No stitches at his belt line, just smooth ridges of muscles.

I took up the scissors and cut along the seam of his undershirt, holding the material in one hand away from his skin. Even at rest, he had a body of a fighter: muscular arms, chest, stomach, and thighs. I knew the galvanized fought for show, but I'd always suspected it was just for show.

I was wrong.

"Hold still. I'd hate to stab something important." I slid the scissors under the narrow strap over his shoulders. Snipped, blew a breath to get my hair out of my eyes, stretched across his chest, and cut the other shoulder free.

I folded the material down and away to one side, leaving him bare beneath me.

Stitches ran from the muscles of his left shoulder, crossed with another set over his well-defined chest to make an X over his heart. The stitches continued over the tight muscles of his stomach, skirted the edge of his wound, and ticked down across the muscle ridge above his left hip bone. Three thinner lines of stitches tracked from the center of his chest and buried in the knotted muscles across his right ribs.

Other stitches ringed his right shoulder, elbow, wrist, and ring finger.

I'd seen Neds shirtless once when he'd gone swimming in the creek. He was put together in a pleasant, natural sort of way: skin and muscles all the same smoothness, tone, and stretch, making a well-built man who happened to brace a bit wide at the upper back and shoulders to make room for both heads.

But still, even with the unusual number of heads Neds possessed, he was all one body. Organic. Natural.

This man was not natural. It did not mean he was ugly. Quite the opposite.

The stitching joined pieces that were not quite the same color as the rest of him; a little too light as if some of his skin never quite took to sunlight, and in other places a little too dark, with muscles and scar tissue bunching thick beneath. The work it took to make him, to piece him together, was amazing. As fine as anything I'd seen my dad or brother do, even though his thread was much thicker than mine.

"I understand there are only twelve of you in the world—galvanized. But I have no idea why you'd come out to my land. Did you know my father? Do you know his enemies? Your stitches are gray. Does that mean House Gray still claims you, or are you on the run?"

I reached for a cloth to clean the blood from his wound. "Were you in an accident, or put together for a purpose? There must be a point to it, to you. You must have a story." I brushed the cloth gently along the smear of blood on his stomach.

His breathing let go and he gasped. I looked down at his face.

Into eyes red as banked coals.

4

It was called Mercury Fever, and like the California gold rush before it, brought hundreds to the little town, searching for a fortune in the dirt and hills. But the promise of mercury also attracted men of the sciences: mad men with mad plans. — 1869
— *from the journal of L.U.C.*

He didn't blink, didn't look away from my eyes.

I'd seen crazy before. I'd seen beasts mad with pain, and I'd been the one who put them in that pain.

They looked a lot like the man lying in the bed below me.

"You are *safe*," I said. "You are in my guest room in my home. I am just about to sew up your injury."

For too many tumbling beats of my heart, I thought for sure he had forgotten how to understand the language. There didn't seem to be a lot of sanity left in him, just a raw, mindless anger.

I licked my lips and tried out a soft smile even while logic was telling me best thing would be to back up nice and slow and find my shotgun.

"These are scissors." I lifted them so the sunlight could catch them in gold. "I'm just going to put them over—"

The floorboards creaked.

His hands shot out viper-fast, wrapped around my wrists, and yanked me down against him as he shoved back with his heels and pushed both of us off the bed.

I'm a strong girl, but along with speed, that man had monstrous brute force. He was on his feet and I was too, as he manhandled me over to the corner of the room.

"Whoa, hold on," I said. "Simmer it down. We're all friends here. We're all friends."

He planted his back against the wall, seeking a defensive position. My back was against him and the heat of his blood soaked through my overalls and cotton shirt, trickling down toward my belt.

He'd yanked the scissors out of my hand with that grab and roll he'd just done off the bed. He held them hidden, tucked by his thigh, while his other arm hung over my shoulder and across my chest, keeping me still.

I could hurt him. He was in his stocking feet and I had on steel-toed boots, not to mention I knew how to throw a wicked elbow. I wasn't afraid to aim for the parts of him that would hurt the most—including his wound.

"You came here to me," I said. "I'm trying to tend your injury. Which would be a lot easier if you'd get back into bed."

"Told you he was trouble," Left Ned said in a cold, cold voice. He stood in the doorway, a wooden bucket of water in one hand, an old Glock 20 in the other. The gun was aimed our way.

"I've got this under control," I said. "He's just spooked is all. Might better unspook without that gun pointed at him."

Neds had once told me they controlled opposite sides of the body, so Left Ned was primarily right-handed, and Right Ned was left-handed. That meant Left Ned had his finger on the trigger.

Didn't seem likely we'd get out of this without him putting more holes in the stranger.

"Tilly," Right Ned said, "you can't see his face." He

nodded slightly. "I'm pretty sure you don't have this under control."

"Do not," the man said in a voice so low, it was almost a growl, "come closer, or you will swim in your own blood, shortlife."

Both the Neds' eyebrows went up.

All right. Maybe I didn't have my thumb quite as tight on the situation as I'd like, but language like that was not allowed in my house.

"Easy," I said. "No one needs to swim in anything. You don't want to hurt us. We don't want to hurt you." That might have sounded more convincing if one of us weren't pointing a gun at his head. "And I'd appreciate it if you stowed your bigotry."

He said something in a language I didn't understand. Russian, maybe? I was passable with French and Spanish, but Quinten had always handled Russian. Still, it didn't sound like a bygones-be-bygones sort of speech.

"What's his name?" I asked Right Ned. "Did you find anything in his pockets? An identification card of some sort?"

"No. There isn't even a label on his jacket."

"You're gonna let her go, big man," Left Ned said. "Or I'll blow you full of so many holes, you'll be recycled for spare parts."

Death threats. Sure, that'd make him relax.

"Ned Harris," I said. "I'll have none of that kind of talk in front of our guest."

"The stitch is crazy," Left Ned said. "And there isn't any mending you can do to fix crazy. He should be taken down before he hurts someone, Matilda Case."

At the sound of my name, the man behind me jerked. I expected the scissors to fly from his hand toward Neds, but instead his arm around my shoulder loosened and he released me.

"Case?" he said as if he'd just remembered where he was. He inhaled, his breath hard and wet—who knew what kind of damage rolling off the bed had done to his existing wounds—and his posture straightened. The scissors fell to the floor with a *clunk*.

Suddenly I wasn't standing against him at all.

"Step to the side, Tilly," Left Ned said, the gun still trained up and to my right a bit, aimed at what I supposed was the man's head.

Right Ned nodded slightly, a silent plea for me to clear away for the shot.

Instead, I turned and faced the man.

He slumped against the wall, both hands at his side, his stomach dripping with blood and showing far too much of his insides. His color had gone chalk gray, with green shaded in the hollows of his cheeks and around his lips. Eyes that just a moment before had burned sharp were now as dull as cold ash.

"I'm sorry," he said. "Please. Forgive my manners. Your hospitality has been . . . has been more than kind . . ."

"You got that right," Left Ned said. "Now we've run all out of hospitable."

The slosh of the water bucket hitting the floor startled me. I glanced over my shoulder just in time to see Right Ned with another gun in his hand.

It occurred to me that my hired hand was packing an awful lot of heat around the farm. I had a brief moment to wonder if Neds had even more artillery stashed in his overalls before Right Ned squeezed the trigger.

Instinct made me duck. Good thing too. That gun was aimed straight away at me, as much at me, as at the man.

The projectile dart hit the big man square in the chest. He frowned, looked at the yellow feather sticking out of his skin, then slid down the wall, out cold.

"I cannot believe you just— Put the guns down!" I said.

"It's a tranquilizer," Right Ned said.

"Now. Down. Both of them," I said. "We do not shoot our guests. Honestly, I don't know what's gotten into those heads of yours."

"Sense," Left Ned said. "He was holding you hostage.

You understand that, Matilda? How dangerous a thing he is? How powerful? *Galvanized.*" He spit.

"What in the—? Since when do you have an opinion on the galvanized? Do you know him? Know something about him I don't know? Because now would be a good time to share."

Grandma peeked around the corner of the door. "There you are, dear. Is it time to go? The men are outside," she said. "Men in cars."

Left Ned swore soft enough Grandma wouldn't hear him, but I threw him a mind-your-manners look anyway.

"What kind of cars, Grandma?" I walked over to lead her out of the room, and noticed the blood on my hands.

"White, dear."

"White?" Right Ned said, surprised.

"Did you call them?" I asked.

"You know I wouldn't. But White's Medical, and he's hurt. We could hand him over."

So House White must have been tracking the unconscious guy.

"Is he House White?" I asked, wishing I'd kept up with this sort of House information. "Running from House Gray?" Yes, I was the communication hub for House Brown. We tracked where the Houses were taking over land, drone paths, and resource dumps. We also handled seed exchanges; goods bartered; and even kept a books, recipe, and repair exchange. None of those things involved keeping track of the galvanized.

"I don't think so," Right Ned said. "I think he's House Gray."

I ran through what I knew of House Gray's and White's current standing. Didn't think they were at odds any more than usual. Maybe they were working together to reclaim him? Or maybe House Gray had loaned his services to House White?

I was beginning to think Neds were wrong. This man wasn't trouble. He was a lot of trouble.

"I'll go see what they want," I said. "Neds, get him in

bed. Hide the guns and everything else, in case they search. Do not kill him. Understand? That man is not to be killed. If they want him and get surly about it, they'll get him alive."

"We should hand him over now," Left Ned said.

"No."

I had no love in me for House White. I remember too well what my dad had said about them, how they had turned against their own scientists to sell the youth and other regeneration techniques only to the rich. How Kiana White, head of that House, had used medical advancements as bargaining chips to increase her own wealth, while common citizens were denied medical treatments. There was rumor she had even used medical advancements as biological weapons to secure her place in the House rankings.

In my memories, I still heard Dad waking in the night, screaming from the nightmares of his time among them and the things they had made him do.

Right Ned reached over and took the gun from his right hand. "Understood," he said. Left Ned cussed, but didn't fight him about it.

"Grandma," I said. "You can come along with me, all right?"

"It's time, isn't it? Finally time to go?"

I dipped my hands in the water bucket Neds had brought in. "Not far. Just the living room." I took her gently by the elbow.

"I thought we had somewhere to be," she said.

"We do. The living room. All you need to do is knit."

"Aren't you smart?" she said.

"I like to think so."

"What about the sheep, dear? We'll need the sheep."

"Did you leave them in the kitchen?"

"Did I leave who where?"

Okay, that wasn't going to work.

I guided her over to the once-proud, now-thread-worn couch.

"You get comfortable right here," I said. "I'll get you the sheep."

I lifted the edge of the curtain and peeked out. Grandma was almost right about our visitors. There were two cars—both white—and a box van, also white but armored up with plate metal and reinforced glass that looked strong enough to keep the lid on a fission bomb. The wheels were heavy enough to get them through what passed for roads out here, and likely easily switched out for the smoother, more modernized highways.

There was a driver in each car, both men, and one woman driver in the van. The van had a male passenger too.

The sheep would have to wait. House White would be on my porch and through my door any minute.

Not going to happen.

I pulled a sweater off the hook by the door and tugged my sleeves down as low as they would go, then untied my hair so it would fall to hide my stitches.

It had been a long time since I'd faced a city dweller. I just hoped all the blockers we had in place held.

I opened the door and strode outside.

Too late, I realized I'd forgotten my gloves. Stupid. If they were smart—and since they were flying Medical, I figured they weren't dumb—they'd notice the stitches along my thumbs and palms.

I quickly shoved my hands into the pocket of my overalls, and swore there'd be no reason to take them out again as long as I was in their presence.

I strolled out to the edge of the porch and stood at the top of the stair.

Two women stepped out of the passenger's sides of the cars.

"Are you the property owner?" The first woman asked. Her voice was strong but it was not kind.

She was tall and thin as a stem, her black curly hair forced back into smooth waves. Dressed in a white jacket and slacks, she gave me the overall impression of someone who enjoyed announcing terminal prognosis to patients.

The vehicles were fully equipped with scanners, probes, and recording devices, new enough to not only catch every move I made, but also to sift through the house for signs of life and pull up our vital signs and House registry.

I didn't know what other sorts of detecting devices the people might have on them.

Quinten had built blockers for just these sorts of technological advancements and updated them every time he came home. I'd been scrupulous in keeping them maintained. Neds had pitched in too; he was handy with tech. Upgrading had been one of the first things he'd done, taking several trips into the city to get the newest and best improvements for us.

If she scanned the house for life, it should read three people: just me, Neds, and Grandma, unless I set it to read otherwise.

Grandma and I both read human, even though that was stretching the truth on my account. But Neds threw weird vital readings from being the sort of man he was, so anything a little out of sorts could be blamed on him.

"I'm not the property owner," I said. "I just help out here." I lied like it was my second nature, which I supposed it was. I couldn't just go hide up in the barn when trouble came walking, like I had when I was a child. And stabbing intruders in the eye worked only for the dumber sort of creatures that roamed my property.

Now that I was an adult, I did my hiding in plain sight and tried to keep the stabbing to a minimum.

"Old Grandmother Case owns the place," I said.

"You work for her?" The second woman asked.

She was stern lady's opposite. Short and generously rounded at the hip and bust, her white came in a knee-length dress, stockings, shoes, and the jacket of their official uniform. Her hair was also white and cut so it cupped just beneath her ears.

All together it made her look cute and harmless. Except for the gun on her hip.

Since when did Medical make house calls with guns? Since when did Medical make house calls at all? They didn't come out into the dirt, and it showed. They were tightly uncomfortable with the raw and wild of the place.

"Yes," I said, putting on the cheerful. "I help in the kitchen and keep the place clean."

They hadn't moved more than a few paces away from their cars. Probably thought I had a gun trained on them.

I didn't, but I liked that they might think I did.

"What House are you?" the taller woman asked. "Gray? Your ... appearance is not up to code." She gave me a scathing once-over, like I was wearing dead animals instead of relatively clean denim and wool.

Color. It was the cover by which a book was judged.

Each House was in charge of a world resource and took a color as its own. Gray was people and the management of them. I supposed caring for the elderly fell under that House, which meant I should say yes.

Only I didn't have a stitch of gray on me.

This was one of those moments when I regretted being lazy about wearing colors. When I made a trip to town, I greened myself up from head to boot. Green was the House in charge of agriculture, and got me fewer looks and questions. My neighbors—though distant— believe me to be claimed by that House, and I didn't see any reason to tell them otherwise. If White had been asking around, they'd already know that.

Luckily I had on green socks.

I shifted my leg forward and tugged up my trousers with my hands still in my pocket, flashing socks. "House Green. Sorry for the confusion. Got so dirty I had to dig into some clothing left behind by the previous residents a couple generations ago."

That wasn't much of a lie. The shirt I was wearing had been my mom's. Plain cotton with tiny red check against a white background. She had worked lace on the collar and here and there stitched little white hearts between the checks.

I'd nearly worn the shirt out for the love of it.

"Do you also work the land for the elder Case?" the shorter woman asked, tapping something into her palm, though I didn't see a screen there.

"Yes. I plant and harvest so she has winter stores. She donates a portion to the church too, of course. I have records if you care to see them."

"No. That's not why we're here," the taller woman said. "We're looking for a man. Has anyone been by in the past day? Do be aware we are recording, and your statement can be used in proceedings against you."

That last bit about recording and proceedings was common enough knowledge, I was surprised she said it. Then I realized she had to say it because of the gravity of the situation.

They had lost a man. From the look of the van, he was a very dangerous man they wanted locked up and transported. From her statement, it was also very important they find him.

Galvanized. Now I really wished I'd paid more attention to House politics and which galvanized was where and doing what.

What I needed right now was a handy lie. I wasn't going to tell them he was sleeping off elephant tranquilizer in the nursery.

"Sure, sure. I understand you're recording," I said with a smile I did not feel. "But we haven't had visitors in ages."

"So you are saying there is no man in this house? On this property?"

"No stranger," I said. Then I laughed a little. As long as I kept smiling, I could usually hide how angry and scared I was. Right up until I decided fists, and the throwing of them, was the solution.

"My boyfriend, Ned." I bit my lip and looked coyly over my shoulder, like he was half-naked back there. "He's here too. Helps out on the farm."

"Sugarpookum," Ned said right on cue, as if we'd practiced this ruse a hundred times. Which we hadn't.

And also: *sugarpookum*?

"Is someone out there?" He pushed on past the screen door, still wearing the green shirt and overalls he'd had on since this morning. He'd tied a big old stripe of purple on each arm—indicating he was in hope of one day being transferred to House Violet to live a life dedicated to faith.

Ha! I'd like to see faith try to angel up that devil boy. Both of them.

Left Ned chewed on an apple, while Right Ned gave a big, innocent, blue-eyed smile.

One thing about Neds: he was dollar sharp at making people think what he wanted them to think. A far better faker and actor than I was.

"I thought I heard company," Right Ned said with what sounded like real delight. Right Ned was the better liar of the two, a personality conundrum that had not escaped my notice, since generally he was also the nicer of the two.

"Isn't this a blessed day? Sugarpookum, you can't just leave them out here in the drive. Bring them in and offer them up some of the Lord's tea. Would you like some tea made fresh from God's bounty?"

The medicals, faced with a bucket load of country manners coming from a two-headed man bent on converting his life to religion, were caught flat-footed.

Their shared look of disgust was so good, I wished I could put it in a jar and keep it on the mantel.

"I was going to, but hadn't had the chance is all, bumblebug," I said.

Left Ned choked on the apple, which gave me no end of pleasure. Two could play the pet-name game.

"Why don't you come on in?" I said picking up Ned's lie. "We'd love to have you. Bumblebug has been reading scripture and talked my ear off." I rolled my eyes and smiled. "I'm sure he'd love new people to share his devotions with. Especially if any of you have leanings toward House Violet."

Neds walked up next to me and slipped his arm around my waist, tucking his hand over my pocket and expertly avoiding even the briefest contact with my skin. Like I said, he did not enjoy touching me.

"I surely would enjoy the company," he said. "There's so much of God's love to share with you."

The taller woman glanced at her palm and then at Neds.

I held my smile and breath. *Please let it read three humans. Please.*

"Thank you," she said. "We can't stay. If you see a stranger in this area, do not engage with him. Please call Medical immediately."

"We'll do that," I said.

The two women started back to the cars, and I resisted the urge to run into the house, bolt the door, and grab my gun.

"Why do you want him?" Left Ned asked. "Is he dangerous?"

I could have kicked him in the shins for that. That last thing we needed was for them to linger.

The tall woman stopped, one hand on the car door, which was open so I could see the stripe of black down the side of it.

Black and White?

"He is very dangerous," she said, answering only one of his questions.

I casually stepped on Neds' foot, putting a little weight on it so he would shut the hell up. Black meant Defense. Black meant weapons and security. Black was the color of the men who had killed my dad and mom.

He didn't know that because I'd never told him. I didn't talk much about my parents to anyone.

"We'll keep the door locked and our eyes open," I said. "If we see him, we'll call."

I tugged on Neds' tool loop so he would turn with me toward the house. Left Ned opened his mouth to ask another question. Probably one that would tip her off. Probably one that would get us searched, jailed, and killed; my property seized, claimed, burned; my grandmother locked away; and vital communication for House Brown shut down.

So I did what any woman half-scared and half-fuming out of her mind would do to shut him up: I wrapped my arms around him and kissed the man.

5

One mad man, the scientist Alveré Remi Case,
began building his tower. It would take him
two years to construct the laboratory beneath
it. Two years before the great machine he
dubbed Wings of Mercury was poised to alter
time. — 1908

— from the journal of L.U.C.

It wasn't a long kiss, just a peck on Right Ned's cheek.
Still, contact wasn't a thing between us except in emergencies.

I counted this as an emergency.

The kiss had the desired effect. Left Ned shut his
mouth in surprise.

Luckily, Right Ned was a quick thinker.

"Uh . . ." he said, the word coming out a little strangled. Then, louder for the medicals, "If you'll excuse us,
please. Do have a nice day."

He wrapped his arm around my shoulder and walked
me into the living room.

"Well," Right Ned said. "Well."

"What in the devil's blue was that?" Left Ned demanded.

I crossed over to the window to see if our company
was moving on yet.

"That was me keeping your big mouth shut," I said as

medicals drove away. "You of all people know how it is with the Houses. Rule number one: don't ask questions. Asking questions gets you noticed, and getting noticed leads to rule number two: don't get noticed."

"How about rule number three?" Left Ned said. "Don't kiss a man when he's told you he doesn't like to touch things like you?"

He was angry. Trying to get a fight out of me.

"It was an emergency. But, yes. I made a mistake," I said calmly. "It wasn't right of me to do that to you. I'm sorry."

"You kissed me," he sputtered.

"You were about to tell Medical about the stranger."

He shut his mouth and rethought his answer. I was not wrong. Both of us knew it.

"Medical already knows he's here," Left Ned said. "The second you let him into your kitchen it was already too late to hide him."

"No," Right Ned cut in. "I don't think House White knows he's here. They would have just shot us to get to him. The blockers were up. I think we're sunny side for now." He tugged the purple strips off his arms. "No need to apologize, Matilda," he said. "We understand why you did it."

Right Ned hadn't looked at me once since we'd come into the room. But he did now.

He was hurt. Maybe because I'd fought with his brother, but more likely because I'd kissed him. The idea of making Right Ned feel bad made my guts twist.

"Ned," I said to him, "I'm sorry about what I did out there."

"Don't be." There was no forgiveness in his eyes. Just a calm sort of anger that I'd never seen before. "You were trying to keep the things you care about safe. I get that."

Lord, the boy knew how to make soft words sting.

"Not at the cost of our friendship," I said. "Are we settled?"

Right Ned nodded curtly. "We're settled."

Why didn't I believe him?

"I'll go check Lizard and the beasts, then," Right Ned said. "Make sure House White didn't detour out into any of the fields."

"No," a voice said from the hallway. "We need to leave now."

"Black hell," Left Ned swore.

Right Ned gave me the same startled look I was giving him. That had been enough tranquilizer to drop Lizard for a day. It should keep an average person out for two. But not, apparently, the galvanized.

He stepped out of the shadows, shoulders nearly touching each side of the hall, head tipped down so his hair curled toward his eyes. Pale and sweating, he looked like something that had woken up dead in the middle of the road and gone wandering in a daze.

"Good to see you're awake," I said. "But you shouldn't be out of bed. I haven't had the chance to sew you up proper."

"I know how to use a needle." He had his jacket on, his arm tucked against his gut, his eyes still that troubling pain-red.

I glanced at Neds. He had backed into the room to stand closer to me, just the way he did when we got caught unawares by a mutated feral patrolling the edge of the property. Except he didn't have his tranq gun, and I didn't have my knives.

"We have no time," the man said. "We must go, Matilda Case."

He had a sincere and commanding way about him, like he was used to saying things and having folk follow without question or comment.

Yeah, about that: I'd never been much of a follower.

"No."

He frowned and his whole body straightened, as if he'd never heard that word before.

"No?"

"You walked into my house, wounded. I'll see that you're patched up before anyone goes anywhere. And don't bother arguing. You won't win."

He slid a look over to Neds, who were standing off to one side and behind me now, as if expecting the man to charge at any minute. I didn't think he got much support from Neds.

"Do you know who I am?" the stranger asked me.

"I do not. Well, galvanized, obviously. You can tell me more while I look at your wound. Neds, would you get the jelly, please? Here." I pointed at a chair. "Have a sit so I can take a look at your gut."

The man hesitated, paused there in the hallway.

I raised one eyebrow, my finger still pointing.

"If you don't want to sit, you might as well walk out that door. Medical's just left but a minute or two ago. I suppose they'll patch you up. Unless they're the ones who put that hole in you."

He exhaled on a held breath and wiped his free hand over his face, pausing to scratch at the stubble on the side of his jaw. He finally strolled over and sat in the chair across from Grandma, who was humming to herself and paying no attention to what was happening around her.

Neds started off down the hall for the jelly.

"The sooner you leave, the better it will be for all of us," Left Ned muttered as they left. Right Ned hushed him.

"I came here on a matter of some urgency," the man said. "To take your father to safety."

"I'm pretty sure the grave is as safe as man can get."

He flattened both hands on his thighs, elbows out, studying me. "What House are you claimed by, Matilda? This is a farm, so I assume the farm is claimed by House Green?"

He said it like he might have the power to do the claiming. Which he didn't.

"How many questions do I have to answer before you tell me your name?" I asked.

"Abraham," he said. "Seventh." He waited for me to react to that, as if his name alone should mean something to me. But I didn't keep track of galvanized, as they mostly didn't affect me or mine.

"Good to meet you, Abraham. That there is Neds."

Neds walked in and tossed me the jar of scale jelly, which I caught. "And that's Grandma Case. This"—I lifted the jar—"is the jelly that will keep your insides from rotting out."

I nudged the footstool with my boot until it was in front of his chair.

"What is it?"

"You don't want to know," Right Ned said quietly.

"Old family recipe." I sat on the stool and unscrewed the ring on the jar. "Who sent you goose chasing anyway?"

"Looking for your father?"

I nodded.

"We had information."

"We?" Neds asked.

"My House."

"And what House is that?" I pulled the lid off the jelly and dug in my pocket for a cloth to use with it. No cloth. Fingers would have to do.

"House Gray," he said.

"Since when," Left Ned asked, "does House Gray send a stitch . . ."

Abraham pulled shoulders back so he could turn a glare at the man.

". . . to comb the scrub for people?"

"What other House should look for people?" Abraham asked.

Neds shrugged. "There's nothing worth your time here," Left Ned said.

"House and name," Abraham ordered.

"Brown," Right Ned said before Left Ned could answer. "Harris. There still isn't anything here that involves House Gray."

"You are claimed by House Brown?"

"I've filed the papers," Right Ned said.

"When?"

"Recently," Left Ned said.

"Filing papers to claim House Brown is the same as signing away all your rights, all your benefits, pay, and legal voice with any other House," Abraham noted.

"Wasn't always like that, was it?" Left Ned said. "If you galvanized had stood with House Brown instead of selling out for the bribes and dirty deals the other Houses offered you—"

"All right," I said, "you two can break up that old argument. Let's take care of the current wounds before you decide to give each other new ones. Jacket off so I can get to the cut."

Abraham tipped his head, considering me.

"There are people who believe your father is alive, Matilda Case. It won't take them long to come looking for him. And when they find you, unclaimed, they will take you. Without asking. Without giving you a choice in the matter. They will own you."

"That doesn't sound pleasant," I said.

"It won't be. The longer we stay here, the less time you'll have to run."

"Who said I was running?" I nodded at his jacket, which he still hadn't removed. "Off with it."

"Do you understand who is looking for your father? House Medical, Defense, Technology, Mineral, Faith, Power." He ticked off half the Houses. "They won't stop until they find something here."

"What I don't understand is who got everyone hunting for a dead man. My father's not here. There's nothing to find."

Just then the three sheep trotted in from the kitchen, making their tiny little *baaa* sounds.

Abraham opened his mouth, closed it, and watched the sheep patter over to Grandma. She noticed them too, and cooed at them happily, then lifted each up into her lap, where they settled like round, wooly cats.

He opened his mouth again and it took him a second or two to put words in it. "Who stitched those?"

"My dad. He had a knack for nonsense."

"What are they for?"

"Wool, mostly. Grows outrageously quick and keeps us in hats and sweaters. Now, are you going to take off your jacket, as I asked, or do I have to do it for you?"

"The faster you comply, the better," Right Ned said. "She gets prickly when crossed."

"I get prickly when people are bleeding on my furniture. We tend you, and *then* we tend the mess that's following you. In that order. Understand?"

My tone must have finally gotten through.

He unbuttoned his jacket.

"Do you have a price on your head, Mr. Seventh?" I asked.

He paused in the unbuttoning, glancing at Neds, who shrugged.

A smile tugged the corners of Abraham's lips. I didn't like being laughed at, but the smile did a world of good for his face. "It's just Abraham."

"All right," I said. "Abraham, is there a price on your head?"

He pulled his jacket open but did not take it all the way off. He hadn't bothered putting on his bloody shirts, although he'd wrapped his belly in bandaging. Not enough cotton, though. In the short time he'd been wearing it, the blood had soaked through.

"Not on my head, no," he said. "I am secured, claimed."

"Stitch out in the hedge?" Left Ned said. "That's not secured. You deserted House, didn't you? It's why you're busted open and looking for a peace offering to take back to your top man. It's why White is out beating the sticks looking for you."

"Watch your step, Mr. Harris," Abraham warned amiably. "My House stands with me and my actions. Does yours stand with you?"

"No fighting in the house," I said. "You don't like each

other. We've established that." I pulled the bandage knot apart and let the wrap fall loosely around his waist. "So, you're not a criminal. Are you on the run? A slave?"

"I am galvanized," he said in a soft tone that told me neither if that was a good thing nor a bad thing.

I dipped my fingertips into the jelly and the humming warmth of it resonated up through me. It had to do with the chemical makeup of the stuff, the blend of strange minerals and warped nanos natural to this land. The mutant beasts ate it out of the vegetation and rodents. When we fed Lizard, those minerals and odd tech filtered into its scales, which we harvested and boiled down to make the jelly.

"What does that mean, galvanized? I mean, I can see the thread that holds you together, but I don't know much more about you." I meant it to be small talk. But he took so long to answer, I glanced up at him.

"It is how I was made," he said in the way someone would explain that rain came from the sky. "Built piece by piece. Stitched," he said, "like you." He nodded toward my wrist, where the stitches shone a faint silver at the edge of my sweater.

"We aren't the same," I said.

"Oh?"

I don't know why I'd said that. The last thing I needed was to point out that I was different. I glanced up into his eyes. He was waiting, patient as starlight.

"I just mean you're something of a celebrity, aren't you?"

"Yes. All of us are. Except you." He said it as if I would fill in my story, tell him how I'd been made and why I'd been hiding out all these years. I had no intention of telling him anything more about me.

"So, there's more than one of you . . . of galvanized?" I latched onto safer ground in the conversation.

"Twelve." He held my gaze. "Thirteen now."

"I don't count myself as galvanized." I reached out with a large glob of jelly on my fingertips. "Lots of people go under a doctor's needle and thread. I'm just like anyone else who's been mended. This might hurt a bit."

"It won't," he said. "Nothing does."

I didn't care how tough he talked. This was going to sting.

I slathered the jelly against his wound carefully but firmly enough that it would hold to his skin and sink in between the stitches.

He pushed back and up out of that chair like I'd set him on fire. Took three steps away and pressed one wide palm over the stitches.

"What is that?"

"Jelly," I said, slow enough for a three-year-old.

I held up the jar again, and the scent of licorice and lemon that masked the heavy antiseptic tang wafted through the air.

"I felt it."

I raised my eyebrows. "Right. I told you it would sting."

He looked over at Neds. "I *felt* it," he repeated.

"Maybe if you didn't have a breezeway open to your spine, you wouldn't," Left Ned said.

"You do not understand." He took those same three steps back to me.

I stood up from the stool because I wasn't the kind of gal who took a direct confrontation sitting down.

"Galvanized don't feel pain or pleasure."

He pressed his thumb down to the last knuckle into his wound until blood oozed out. He didn't wince, his pupils didn't dilate, his breathing didn't change. He was either a very good actor or he really didn't feel that wound.

"Stop that." I slapped his hands away from the cut. He sucked in a quick breath. "You're wasting jelly and making the cut worse."

He caught at my hand, held it as if my touch was infecting him with sensation. "What are you doing?" This time he sounded genuinely spooked. "What are you doing to me? How are you doing this to me?"

"I am trying to bandage your injury. And you are the worst patient I've ever tended."

Neds snorted.

"So how about you hold still for a straight sixty and stop getting in my way?"

"What are you?" he asked.

Funny; not too long ago, he'd been pretty certain what I was.

"Irritated," I said, "so hush and let me work."

He hushed and stood still.

I finished with the jelly while he stayed on his feet, then tied the wraps back in place, doing my best not to actually come in contact with his skin. Every time I did, he flinched and his breathing changed. It was worrisome.

"You still haven't told me who started this," I said, giving the cloth one last tug. "Who told you my father was alive?"

The sound of engines seared across the sky.

It had been years since a drone flew over, and just today I'd heard two.

Also worrisome.

Abraham's cinnamon gaze shifted across the smooth white of the ceiling as if he could track the aircraft through it.

"Devil rut 'em," Right Ned whispered. "Tilly, you and I should talk."

"Are those drones looking for my home?" I asked calmly as I screwed the lid back on the jar. My heart was beating too hard. "Are they looking for my father?"

"Yes." He drew his eyes down from the ceiling and held my gaze. Not panicked—he was waiting for me to make a decision.

"Did you send the drones here? Did you do this to me and mine?"

"I came to warn your father. To take him to shelter and safety. If you come with me, I will offer you and yours the same."

"And if I don't?"

"First passes are surveyor drones to lock onto me and gauge your level of technology and defenses. The next drones will be equipped with codes to break whatever blockers you have. They'll look for people, animals, legal and illegal possessions and resources. They will send out ground troops.

"If any of the other Houses have drones in the area, this activity will be noticed. And if they find you unclaimed or your papers out of order, they will not offer you shelter. They will sell you and your land to the highest bidder. And your grandmother . . ."

He spread his hands wide. He didn't have to finish that sentence. I knew what they'd do to an old lady who had marbles clacking in her brain. They'd lock her up in the wards, where they'd look after her until they decided to put her out of her misery.

I pressed my lips together, thinking fast. I needed to keep Grandma safe. I needed to keep the beasts on the property safe and the network for House Brown clear and away from other House influence, from other House claims.

Quinten had made me promise to stay hidden.

I'd tried. But hiding wouldn't keep anyone safe this time.

"Son of a sin hole," I said quietly. "All right. Can you call the drones off?"

"I can."

"I need a week to set things in order."

"I can't give you a week."

"I have responsibilities, Abraham. It will take me a week to settle everything enough to come with you."

"What?" Left Ned said. "Matilda, we can run on our own. We don't have to make a deal with a stitch just because he got here before the other Houses that wanted to claim you. You don't know nearly enough about him to just take his word as truth."

Abraham didn't argue with that. He waited like a man who was used to being judged. Like a man who knew his own sins and had come to peace with them.

"Who told you my father was alive?" I asked him quietly again. "I need to know that, at the very least."

He didn't look away, didn't pay attention to Neds, who were cussing up a storm now.

I expected him to tell me it was my brother, Quinten, who had somehow sent him out this way. I expected him to tell me my brother was in trouble and I needed to go bail him out of it.

That was not what he said.

"Your mother," he said softly, "Edith Case. She told us to look for your father here. She told you you would be here too."

6

*With a startling, unexpected comet burning in
the sky, Alveré Case triggered the Wings of
Mercury. A great bell rang out across the land.
And death answered the call. —1910*
                —from the journal of L.U.C.

My mother was dead. I'd seen her killed, seen her and
my father hauled off, taken away. I'd been young,
but I knew they hadn't been breathing, hadn't been moving at all. I'd seen the blood the men in black hosed away.

"How long?" I finally asked.

Abraham frowned. "Since what?"

"How long can you keep the drones away from my
property?"

I couldn't deal with the question of my mother. Not
yet. There was too much pain around the idea of it.

"Two days at the longest," he said, maybe surprised
that I hadn't asked about my mom. "We will be able to
do more if we return to my House. House Gray has some
clout over the transfer and claim of the population. If
you are officially claimed by us, by Gray, we can hold this
land under our protection. It should keep the other
Houses away from it."

"Medical and Defense too?" I asked. "Does Gray
have clout enough to keep both of those Houses away
from here?"

He nodded. "We should."

"Since when does Gray let a *thing* like a galvanized speak for it?" Left Ned asked.

Abraham didn't look over at Neds. He just opened and closed his hands, like he was imagining a neck—or two—there to wring.

"Galvanized are given the right to speak for a House at the House's discretion," he said calmly. "Would you like to challenge my authority, Mr. Harris?"

"Matilda," Right Ned said. "You do not have to go with him. You do not have to sell yourself to a House. We can find somewhere else to hold out until this blows over."

"I don't even know what *this* is," I said. "The Houses are looking for my father, who is dead. They think my mother told them he's alive, but she's dead too.

"And now, somehow, I'm property that's going to go to the highest bidder? I don't think so. Let me settle things here, Abraham. Then I'll travel to the city and meet you there."

"No. That's not how it's going to happen," he said.

"No? I'm sorry. You might speak for House Gray, but you do not speak for me."

"I'm not leaving without you."

He advanced on me.

I advanced right back. "I'm not leaving *with* you."

He looked like he was going to yell, but clenched his teeth. "Rent me a room."

"What?"

"I want a room. For two days while you get your affairs in order. How much?"

"I said I'd patch you up, not open a boarding house."

"How. Much?"

Neds stood just out of the man's line of vision. Right Ned shook his head while Left Ned drew a finger across his throat in the "kill him" gesture.

"You couldn't afford it," I said.

"You don't know what I'm willing to pay."

There was a fire in his eyes. Some of it was anger, yes. But there was a glint of something else. Amusement. He was getting a kick out of arguing with me, of trying to make me bend to his authority.

Not going to happen.

If he wanted to pay, he'd have to pay big.

"Are you carrying gold?" I asked sweetly.

He frowned.

"No? Silver? Lead? Copper?" I made big, innocent eyes at him. "A girl out in the brush doesn't need credit chits, Mr. House Gray. What do you have in your pockets that's worth my hospitality?"

One of the Neds coughed, and I realized that could have been taken in a very different manner.

Abraham flashed me a wicked smile.

"Don't flatter yourself," I said before he opened his mouth, even though a rush of heat stung my cheeks.

He didn't say anything for a long moment. He didn't have to. We'd searched his pockets. They were empty. But his eyes still burned with delight. He thought he had something I'd want. Something that would make me let him stay here.

"Information," he said.

"I don't need information, Mr. House Gray."

"Abraham," he corrected. "Are you sure about that? I have access to more information than you could glean from ten lifetimes out here, Dumpster-diving data off hacked lines."

"Dumpster-diving?" Left Ned started.

"What kind of information?" I asked.

Here it was, his chance to give me something that would help House Brown, since he must have assumed I was lying about being part of House Green.

It was also my chance to see how he had sized me up. What sort of woman did he think I was? What did he think was important to me?

His eyes wandered over my body slowly, from feet all the way up to my eyes. I resisted the urge to fold my arms, turn around, scowl. I didn't like being seen—had spent a life working very hard to stay hidden.

And this man was in the middle of my living room, uncovering every detail of me.

"I don't suppose fashion would interest you?"

Really? I gave him a chance to tell me what he thinks of me, and he takes a dig at my choice of clothing?

I strode over to the door. "No," I said. "It wouldn't. Call off the drones. I'll see you in a couple weeks. Goodbye."

"You heard the lady," Left Ned said. "Get moving."

"Your brother," Abraham said. "Quinten."

Nothing could still me faster.

"I know where he is. Where he was last seen."

"Is he alive?" I asked before I could stop myself.

Dammit. He'd seen right through me. Probably knew all along that I had a brother. Knew that he'd been missing and I'd been worrying.

He nodded. "I will tell you where he has been. I will tell you what we know of your mother's message. I will tell you . . . I will answer *anything* you ask of me. For two days. Then you come with me to House Gray, where we will settle your House claim and the claim on your land before someone comes out here and offers you no choice."

"You call this a choice?" Left Ned said. "How about we pick up our weapons and give you a choice of dying here or walking off our property and dying there?"

"You said my father's enemies wanted to find me," I said, ignoring Neds. "Do you know that for sure? Do you know who they are?"

"Your mother's message was unclear. I'll tell you what I know if you come with me now, or if you let me stay and come with me in two days."

It meant he'd be underfoot. Two days on the farm, getting in my way, getting in my business, uncovering the secrets I'd spent a lifetime hiding. The Lizard, for example. There was no way to hide that stitched monster.

But I couldn't just run off with him blind and leave Grandma and Neds behind to try to deal with House Brown—or, worse, to be harmed if House Gray did not keep their word and this land was seized and burned.

If I was going to negotiate with House Gray for my land, my family, and my House, then two days of grilling him for information might give me something I could use for leverage.

"You'll call off the drones," I said.

"Yes."

"You'll answer anything I ask, truthfully."

"Yes."

"And you'll stay out of my way."

"If you wish."

Not quite a yes, but close enough.

"All right. Two days. You can have the room down the hall. I'll give you a change of sheets and you're welcome to a portion of the meals. Don't bother my grandmother, and otherwise keep your hands to yourself. Neds and I carry weapons, and we aren't shy about using them. Agreed?"

I strolled over, held out my hand.

He wrapped his huge hand around mine, warm and calloused, his eyes widening for just a moment at our contact before he nodded.

"Agreed," he said.

"Neds," I said, "please help Grandma settle in for her nap."

"And where are you going to be?" Right Ned asked.

"Watching our guest hold up his end of the bargain."

Neds got moving and shepherded an already-drowsing Grandma down the opposite hall to her room, the little sheep trotting behind them.

Left Ned threw me a couple pointed looks that made it clear he thought I'd gone insane.

Maybe he was right. Maybe I had.

"Do you need something to call off the drones?" I walked past Abraham and headed into the kitchen.

There was still a pool of blood that needed to be cleaned up.

"Satellite link? Data bounce? Smoke signals?"

His boots fell in muffled thuds as he followed me.

"Just an open sky."

"Right that way," I pointed at the kitchen door where he'd first arrived. "Watch the mess on the floor."

I turned the water on the sink, pulled a couple of heavy rags out of the drawer, and tossed them under the faucet. Cleaning up blood was best done with a lot of hot water and soap.

"Let me help you with that," Abraham said. He hadn't even walked into the room yet. I couldn't tell if that look on his face was guilt or worry.

"Just call off the drones. You aren't the first man to bleed on my floor." I offered up a smile and that seemed enough to get him on his way and out the door.

I wrung out the rags and watched him out the side window. He held up his left palm and jabbed at it, like he was punching in a code.

Huh. Maybe that was why he didn't have anything in his pockets. He was coded into the network with flesh and bone.

He let his hand drop and tipped his head up to search the sky.

Yes, I was staring. He inhaled, his shoulders shifting a little, and closed his eyes. The afternoon sunlight poured over him, glowing up his skin while bringing those life stitches into stark contrast.

The wind pushed his hair around a bit, giving me a good, long look at him.

His face in semiprofile was god-awful handsome: strong nose and cheekbones, square jaw and mouth that relaxed into a slight frown. The lines around his eyes eased a bit as he took another deep breath, absorbing the warmth of the day. I wondered if it was pain that had put the lines at his eyes and across his forehead.

I'd seen the fighter's muscles covered by the bandages

wrapped around his middle and his heavy gray coat. But the way he was standing now turned my mind away from how dangerous he might be. If he'd wanted to, I supposed he could have overpowered Neds, maybe even overpowered me. But he'd talked to get his point across, and though he was annoyed by it, he'd done what I wanted and given me some time to settle things here.

It was . . . well, nicer than I'd been treated by anyone in House before.

Galvanized. I'd heard a lot about them, but had never met one. So far he had caught my full attention.

He took a third deep breath, and this time I inhaled with him and exhaled, letting that breath take away the fear that knotted like a fist in my chest. Fear that I had made the wrong choice bringing him into my house. Fear that I shouldn't have agreed to let him stay. Fear that my brother was hurt, or, worse, and that I'd just sealed a deal that would take away my land and fail the people of House Brown.

For just that one breath, I didn't worry about all the things I should be taking care of.

I just watched him.

He opened his eyes, then turned to look at me.

Crap.

I quickly looked away and poured some soap into the sink, agitating it to get the bubbles to rise.

Had he seen me staring at him?

Probably.

The real question was: why did I feel so embarrassed about it? It wasn't like he knew what I was thinking about him.

Right?

I squared my shoulders and pretended like I couldn't feel his gaze on me. Pretended that I didn't know he was laughing at me.

By the time he strolled back into the kitchen, I was on my knees, halfway through cleaning up the blood.

"Drones are called off. You got your two days," he said.

"All right, then. Clean sheets are in the hall closet. Put the soiled ones on the floor in your room and I'll take care of them." I stood and carried the two rags sopping with soap and blood over to the empty side of the big sink.

"I could lend a hand," he said.

"No need." I wrung out the rags, then sloshed them in the hot-water side of the sink, soap almost up to my elbows.

A little bell set in the corner of the ceiling rang out like a chime stirred by a hard wind. Out in the barn, another, deeper bell rang, and I knew there was another bell even farther out on the edge of the property that gave one low knell.

Someone in House Brown was calling. Someone needed my help.

"What's that?" Abraham asked.

I turned, the two rags in my hands. "On second thought, I could use your help." I deposited the soapy rags in his hands. "Wipe up as much blood as you can. There's a box of sodium peroxide powder here." I plucked the box out from beneath the sink. "After the blood's up, sprinkle this over the stain, but don't inhale the dust."

"I know how to clean up blood."

"Good!" I gave him a wide smile. "I'll leave you to it."

I wiped my hands on a towel and strode out of the kitchen, through the living room, down past Grandma's room and my room, to the narrow door that led to the basement.

It was locked, keyed to open for my fingerprints and for Neds', Quinten's, and Grandma's.

I glanced down the hall before opening the door. Abraham stood at the end of the hall, watching me.

"Better get on it," I said. "Terrible mess, that floor." I

tugged open the door and shut it firmly behind me. Waited there, listening for his boots, but I didn't hear him come down the hall, didn't hear him put his hand on the door latch.

Good enough.

Stairs led me down to the communication hub for House Brown.

When I was young, the basement was a wonderland to me. Filled with copper, wood, and brass mingled with slick plastic and shining silver and glass. The room glittered with a dizzying display of dials, levers, buttons, screens, and wires. I had dedicated three months to learning what every toggle, gauge, and system could do.

Quinten had taken Dad's antiquated short-wave collection and expanded it until we could tap into every sort of data stream ever made. It was why we were now the hub for House Brown. Some of the House Brown communities had current tech and could bounce data from here to Jupiter if they wanted to.

But the majority of the people in House Brown weren't that advanced. Still, it didn't take much to put up a tower and send some kind of a signal.

Quinten had made sure we had the equipment to receive even the weakest signals here, loud and clear.

The main station to the right was Quinten's. He usually sat in the leather office chair in front of the monitors that stacked from floor to ceiling, maps and radar and other vital tracking systems available at a glance.

I preferred the antique hutch off to one side that held analog radio equipment, a telegraph key, and a sweet little laptop Quinten had linked into our entire network.

The laptop screen was blinking in time with several other screens and buttons in the room. I glanced over at the maps. Signal was coming in from Nevada. The Fesslers' land.

I tapped the code into the laptop, flicked on the video, and sent a reply.

Almost immediately, Braiden Fessler—head of the desert homestead of about fifty—snapped onto the screen above the hutch.

He was somewhere between seventy and ninety, his dark skin cooked down by years in the sun until it was a deep mahogany of wrinkles and creases. He wore a tattered, billed cap over his large ears, and his white hair curled down in sideburns to join with a pointed beard.

"Matilda, we need your help. There's heavy equipment moving our way, about thirty miles out. Is there someone you can call to stop this? Is there a way to jam their work orders?"

"It's not that easy," I said. "Did survey drones pass over?"

"About a year ago. Didn't think much of it."

"But nothing recently? No indication you'd been scouted by a House?"

"Nothing."

My fingers glided over the screen, accessing roads, House Brown locations, and nearby cities.

"You're sure they're headed your way?"

"A few of us rode out that way to see what was what. It's a line of earth movers, Matilda. Drills, cranes. I think they're coming to tear down our village and set up a geothermal plant."

I nodded, thinking furiously. That made sense. It could be House Orange, out to throw down a mining operation, but all the records and scans we could tap into indicated there was nothing valuable beneath the Fesslers' parched soil.

There was, however, a strong natural heat source—geothermal—that could be rigged up as a power generator to supplement the nearest city.

"What are we going to do, Matilda?" Braiden asked. "We have children here—babies. There's nowhere else for us. This is our home. Our land."

"They're thirty miles out?" I asked.

"Yes."

I flipped to the satellite feed, got a lock, and pulled up the eastern edge of Nevada.

"I see them. About twenty vehicles." I dialed it in, couldn't see any colors or House markings. "Don't know who's behind it. But I'll find out. Let me track this as far as I can. If we know which House is moving your way and why—"

"We know why," he said.

"No, we suspect they want the thermal. But it could be other things they're coming for. Mining. Waste dump. Data hub."

His dark eyes watered, but he nodded. "When will you know? When will you tell us how to stop them?"

He wanted hope and assurances I did not have to offer.

"The equipment is big and slow moving. I'll have something by tomorrow morning. Just hold through the night. If there's no way to stop them . . ."

"No," he said, cutting me off. "We have run enough. We have been pushed away from green fields and safe hollows. We have escaped the slavery of our generations to the Houses. We will not leave our land. Not this time."

I'd heard that before. So many people in House Brown were tired of running. They wanted to stand and fight, even if that meant losing everything.

"I'll do what I can to find a solution," I said. "In the meantime, I want you to tell everyone to pack a bag."

"But—"

"Mr. Fessler, please," I said, raising my voice just a bit. "We'll do everything we can to find a way to turn them back. But if we fail, I want your word that you will not put your childrens' lives in danger. I want your word that you'll tell their mothers and fathers to run. I want your word that you'll go with them."

"Of course," he said, dropping his gaze.

"Good," I said. "Give me the evening and night. I'll contact you in the morning. Call me if the situation changes in any way."

He nodded and reached forward, ending our link.

I sat there a moment, not breathing.

I'd handled situations like this dozens of times since Quinten had left, but it was never easy. Sometimes we won and got information out soon enough to either shut down the House operation or at least warn House Brown people enough in advance that they could take their valuables and run.

Sometimes we lost.

The odds were never on House Brown's side. But that didn't mean any of us were about to stop fighting.

7

The government's army buried the dead. Hundreds of men, women, and children planted in mass graves at the foot of Alveré Case's tower. The newspapers reported a smallpox outbreak. The newspapers lied.—1910
—from the journal of L.U.C.

The door opened and boots started down the stairs. I'd been living with Neds long enough to know the cadence of his stride.

"Tilly?" he said, ducking the low beam before stepping into the cluttered main room. "I heard the bell."

"It's the Fesslers' place."

"Nevada? Middle of the desert?" Right Ned asked.

I nodded, pulling the maps up across the screens and monitors over Quinten's station. "Heavy equipment headed their way about thirty miles out. Braiden's worried. He wants to stand or die."

"Stupid," Left Ned said. "I say run and live any day. Why are they a House target? There's nothing out there except sand and grit."

"Geothermal, maybe?" I scooted my chair back and walked over to study the screens. "Wasn't there something about the coal shipments being diverted from Big Vegas?"

"Couple months back?" Right Ned said.

"I think so. Check the reports, will you?"

Neds got busy running through hot data—information we'd flagged as important—House movements, rumors of developments or advancements, failures in supply lines.

Sometimes we could make sense of it, like when House Yellow, Technology, built a manufacturing facility right next to the gold-mining operation. They'd won ten years of the mine's proceeds from some kind of in-House settlement with House Orange. Welton Yellow had built the facility to test, improve, and maintain the clever new technologies he developed to dig gold out of the dirt, technology that doubled the mine's production. A technology Welton Yellow refused to share with any of House Orange's other mining sites.

Sometimes we just flagged things that might come in handy—weather changes, crop failure or excess, drone movement, and the like.

"I don't like him," Right Ned said as he scrolled through the last six months or so of data.

"Abraham?"

"I understand you had to patch him up."

I waited for his question. For the reason he'd come down here.

"Just." He looked up from my laptop, where he'd sat to shuffle through information. "Why?"

"I don't know." I wiped the screens and pulled up secondary satellite and ground views. "You know how I am with hurt things."

"He's not a thing, Matilda," Right Ned said. "He's a galvanized tied to a House. Eyes and ears and mouth straight to the head of his House. Whatever he knows, they know."

"What was I supposed to do? Feed him to Lizard?"

"Now you're thinking," Left Ned said.

"Look." I turned and leaned my hip against the curved bank of keyboards beneath the screens. "I know he's trouble. I know I'm in deep here with my promise to go with him. But there was a drone locked onto him. They already know our house is here and our farm. And while I can claim House Brown, I'm not so sure I have rights. Human rights."

Right Ned looked away from the screen. "You're human, Matilda. As much as I am."

"No, I'm not. Have you ever read through the treatise that ended the galvanized Uprising?"

"The great betrayal?" Left Ned said.

"Yes. When the galvanized left House Brown and let other Houses claim them. They negotiated peace between the houses and for human rights."

"Haven't read the treatise, but I know what's in it," Left Ned said. "They bargained for House Brown to have no voice in the world, no resources. Left us alone to fend for ourselves."

"They bargained for humans—all humans, whether of normal configuration or mutated, compromised, or engineered—to have rights. Longlifes and shortlifes, every shape, sort, and size," I said.

"The right to food, shelter, work, and dignity. The right to earn credit and pay off debt. A way to leave other Houses and become House Brown, if they desire. A way out of indentured servitude to the other Houses."

"And?" Right Ned said. He wasn't as loud about his dislike of Abraham, but it was clear he didn't care for him either.

"In exchange, the galvanized gave up the right to be classified as human. They are owned by the Houses. And if I'm like them . . . if I'm galvanized . . ."

"You're not like them," Left Ned said.

But Right Ned gave me a level look. "Didn't they do anything to preserve their rights?"

"Let's just say humans got the better end of the deal."

Right Ned closed his eyes for a moment, anger or maybe just disappointment creasing his forehead. Then he opened his eyes.

"You can still run, Tilly. We can hold him off and you can go."

I'd be lying if I said I hadn't thought about it. I'd be lying if I didn't admit to being terrified of going into the city with Abraham.

"Quinten hasn't been home for three years," I said softly. "Three. He's never been gone more than a year at a time. I know you don't know him, but he's not like that. He'd be home if he could be. And since he isn't, I'm assuming he's hurt or trapped or mixed up in something he can't get out of. So no matter if it isn't safe or smart or the thing I *should* do, I'm going to find out what Abraham knows about my brother."

"And your mother?" Right Ned asked.

"Yes. And who these 'enemies' of my father are. You are going to stay here and look after things—Grandma, House Brown, the beasts."

Their eyebrows notched up, and they both gave me the same blank look.

"No," Right Ned said. "We're not. We are coming with you."

"Why in the world would you do that?"

"Because," Left Ned said.

Right Ned ticked one eyebrow in agreement.

"That's not even a reason," I said. "Let's just track down who's trying to wipe out the Fesslers. We can argue this out later."

I turned back to the screens, and so did they.

An hour later, the only thing I'd gotten out of the data was a headache. I stood away from Quinten's chair and stretched. Neds didn't look up from the laptop.

"You done?" Right Ned asked.

"Need to check on Grandma. Oh, and I'll feed the beasts tonight." I started toward the stairs.

"I do believe it's your turn to cook," Right Ned said.

Damn. He was right. "Let's switch. I'll cook tomorrow."

"Why?"

"Did you find anything yet that will help the Fesslers?"

He leaned back in the chair so Right Ned could glance over at me. "No."

"Neither did I. But there's an untapped database upstairs scrubbing my kitchen floor. He said he'd answer anything I asked."

"You're going to ask him who's out to crush our little desert community?"

"In a roundabout way, yes."

"He's not on our side, Tilly."

"I don't need him to be on our side. I just need him to talk." I climbed the stairs, pulled the door open, and almost yelped.

Abraham was right there, leaning on the wall across from the door, arms folded over his chest.

"Evening," he said, that quick gaze of his soaking in every detail of the shadows behind me.

"Hey." I stepped out and latched the door shut as quick as I could. "Are you done with the cleanup?"

"For a while now."

"Well, then. I'll see to getting you those sheets."

"What's in the basement?"

"Storage. Dust. You know." I strode down the hall and waved my hand over my shoulder. "Basement things."

"A locked door can't keep me out."

"What are you going to do—break it down?"

"I'm assuming you'd shoot me if I did."

"You are an intelligent man, Mr. House Gray."

"Abraham."

"Let's go see about those sheets."

He followed me through the living room and into the opposite hallway, past Neds' room to his room at the end.

The door was open.

Everything in the room was cleaned, dusted, and rearranged.

"So I see you changed the sheets. And the room," I said.

"I got bored."

"You prefer the bed on the opposite wall?"

"I prefer the bookshelf in the lower left corner of the room, and the ceiling fan not to be hanging over my head while I sleep."

"OCD?"

"Feng shui."

"Is it contagious?"

"Hardly anyone gets it."

"All right." I glanced out the window. I'd lost a little time down in the basement; the evening light was just starting to fall.

"Is there a problem?" he asked.

"Not a problem. Night's coming on soon. Since my farmhand is—"

"In the basement burying bodies?"

"—busy, I wondered if you'd give me a hand with the beasts."

"You keep farm animals?"

"Something like that," I said. "You don't mind getting a little dirty with me, do you?"

The corner of his mouth quirked up.

Heat flashed across my cheeks again. Why did I keep saying things like that?

"Looking forward to it," he murmured. "It's been too long since I got dirty."

It was suddenly too hot in the room. No, it was suddenly too hot in my skin.

"I need to check on Grandma," I said. "I'll meet you outside."

I turned and scuttled out of there as fast as I could. Took me no time to walk down to Grandma's room, knock softly on her door, and let myself in. She was sitting in her rocking chair by the window, humming to herself and petting one of the little sheep in her lap.

I took a moment to breathe away my blush. "Everything all right, Grandma?"

"Is it time for us to go now?" she asked.

"No, we're not going anywhere. Well, I'm going out to feed the beasts. Do you need me to bring you something?"

"I'm just fine," she said. "You go on with that man."

"Abraham?"

"That's the one. House Gray. Good man, always such a good man."

"Always? Do you know him, Grandma? Do you know Abraham?"

She had tipped her head and was staring out the window and humming again, as if I didn't exist.

Her lucid moments were getting fewer and shorter. I knew she wouldn't live forever, but things like this chiseled away at my heart. "Okay," I said with the brightest tone I could muster. "I'll see you soon. Neds are downstairs if you need him."

My room was right next door, and I ducked in, plucked up my heavier coat, and shrugged it on as I made my way down the hall.

Abraham was waiting in the living room.

"You have a strange sense of direction, Mr. House Gray," I said. "The out-of-doors is out that door."

"Abraham," he said absently. "After you." He opened the door to the front porch, waiting for me.

I walked past him. I didn't wait to see if he was following as I headed over to the shed and my old Chevy truck.

"Didn't know anyone still used these things," Abraham said.

"A motor vehicle?" I swung into the driver's seat. "You didn't get here out here on foot, did you?"

He settled into the passenger's seat. "My car's parked just off your property. I meant pickup trucks. They haven't been on the assembly line for a century."

"We make do with what we have." I turned the key

and eight cylinders coughed to life, growling happily once it got the rust out.

The sound of it put a smile on his face, even though he shook his head in the way people do when they're remembering fond things.

"Are you really over three hundred years old?" I asked.

"I'm galvanized."

"Is that a yes?" I released the clutch and eased the truck down the rutted dirt road.

"I was born in 1880."

That made him three hundred and thirty years old. He didn't look a day over thirty. "Wow."

"What year were you born?" he asked.

"Twenty-one eighty-four."

He laughed. I glanced away from the road to see what that looked like on him. It looked good. He laughed with his whole body, head tipped back, eyes curved tight, mouth open in a big smile, as if nothing in him hurt.

If he weren't laughing about my age, I might even join in.

"You're not twenty-six," he chuckled.

I slapped his arm. "Yes. I am."

He jerked and all the laughter was gone. "That . . . hurt."

"You bet it did."

"It shouldn't."

"Why? Because I'm a girl?"

"No, because I'm galvanized. And so are you. We don't feel pain. We don't feel physical sensation."

"Speak for yourself. I feel."

"Do you?"

"Of course I do. And obviously you do too."

"I feel *you*," he said quietly.

"Me?'

"You. Only you."

There was heat behind his words, but it wasn't anger. It was the kind of heat that made me want to reach over and kiss him to see what that would be like. To see if that would be enough to end this fire he had set off in me.

Steady now, I told myself. The only thing I was going to use him for was information. All the rest of the needs and feelings he stirred up inside me weren't important.

Which would be fine, if I believed it.

8

The town was abandoned, erased from the maps. They tore the tower down and hushed and hid the records. Only twelve people had survived the experiment when the great bell rang out. They hushed and hid them too.—1911

—from the journal of L.U.C.

I took the corner along the fence. Lizard would be quickest to check on since we'd just fed it this morning. Then we'd go to Pony, the leapers, then the chickens by the barn.

"How do you walk around if you can't feel?" I killed the engine and hopped out into the grass. Yes, I should be asking him a dozen more important things, but I just couldn't seem to let this go.

"A man can get used to all manners of things given enough time." He got out of the truck, shut the door, and walked around. "I have an awareness of my body. Distant, muffled. In extreme circumstances I can feel pain."

"Getting your guts cut open isn't extreme enough for you?"

"No. Is that mountain breathing?"

Lizard was napping in the middle of the field, its belly swollen with crocboar.

"Sleeping. I understand that galvanized are a collection of folk who went comatose and survived some kind of disaster a while ago."

"Nineteen ten."

"All right, a long while ago." I opened the box where the fence controller was housed. "What I don't understand is how that made you immortal."

"No one understands it. It can't be duplicated, and the records of the disaster are sketchy at best. There was an experiment, the Wings of Mercury, that seems to be the crux of the event."

"Never heard of it," I said.

"The name of the project is all that survived. Well, and us."

"So, you're saying if you had a heart attack, or if someone cut off your head . . ."

"My awareness, my memories, remain trapped in my brain."

"And if someone shot you in the brain? Blew all your gray matter to bits?"

"Sufficiently damaged, my brain would fail. If my body survived, a new brain could be transplanted into my body, though there are complications with galvanized metabolism that would burn out a nongalvanized brain within a few years. It isn't theory. They have been . . . thorough in their tests over the years."

"Who?"

"Scientists, doctors, torturers." He shrugged.

"Torturers?"

"It's been a long life, Ms. Case."

"Matilda," I corrected.

He smiled.

Dammit. He'd done that on purpose.

I checked the wires, battery, and ground to the fence. All gold.

"What does it eat?" he asked.

He was staring off at Lizard, his right arm snug against his gut, even though I supposed he couldn't feel the pain from that wound. Must have been habit and instinct to keep pressure on it.

"Feral critters. We get mutant beasts out here. Something in the soil, I think."

"Ever had that tested?"

"The soil?" I closed up the controller box and started back to the truck. "Why would I? As long as I can grow food and drink the water, I don't care what's in it."

"Also, testing would draw attention to your farm."

"A girl likes her privacy."

"I checked the records."

"So?" I got back in the truck. He followed.

"This place isn't registered House Green. You're House Brown, aren't you?"

I didn't want to answer that. I'd rather he assume I was House Green, and therefore had legal voice and House influence behind me.

I started the engine and gave it some gas. The big engine roared. "Hold on. Road gets a little bumpy here," I said over the noise.

He held on as I took the road hot, rattling over holes and ditches.

When I pulled up alongside the field where Pony was pastured, I had made up my mind. If he had really checked the records, he already knew only Grandma was registered House Green.

"Look." I turned off the engine. "There are things I'd rather not discuss with you, and I suppose there are things you'd rather not discuss with me. But I need information to help some people I know."

"House Brown people?"

"Friends."

"All right," he said. "Friends. What do you need to know?"

"Which House is moving heavy equipment into the middle of the Nevada desert."

"That's . . . specific."

I got out of the truck and walked around to the back. "Not far from Red Butte."

"What kind of equipment?"

"Looks like digging. Drilling."

"Looks like?"

I pulled two pitchforks out of the back of the truck. "No marks on the trucks. No colors." I tossed him a pitchfork, and he caught it like he'd been working a farm for years.

"What's out there? Minerals? Water?" he asked.

"I think geothermal."

"That falls under House Red, Power."

I ducked the fence, started off toward the hay chute down the field a bit. "Keep an eye out for Pony. It's a little skittish, so mind the horn."

He scanned the field as we walked.

"Do you know if House Red is tapping geothermal?" I asked.

"It's possible. There was a shift in House Red a year ago. Aranda Red stepped up and her father stepped down. She's been acquiring unclaimed land faster than any other House."

A geothermal claim would secure that land as House Red without much of a peep from other Houses. Which meant there was no conflicting House to call upon to stop this. The Fesslers' homestead would be demolished.

There had to be a way to stop them.

"Pony, I presume?" Abraham nodded toward the beast that stepped out from beneath the old apple tree.

Pony was made from parts, just like all Dad's beasts. The hind of it was zebra, the middle, neck, and head of it horse, and the four chunky legs were bison.

I didn't know where the horn came from, but it sat the center of its flat forehead just like a unicorn in a storybook. Altogether it wasn't that bad-looking.

It whickered, but didn't come any closer to us.

"Who made it?" he asked.

"My dad."

I stopped by the chute. Neds and I had gotten tired of dragging feed out here in the winter, so we'd built a two-story shed, the top of which held a couple dozen bales of hay—or enough to keep the pony happy for half a month, if needed. It burned through a lot more feed than a horse would.

"He stitched it?"

"Piece by piece."

"The lizard too?"

"He had a restless head and hands full of ideas. Stand that side of the chute. We'll need eight bales down and broken." I pulled the chain. Pulleys got the track moving, and bales of hay lined up nice and smoothly in a row, coming down the ramp to *thunk* at our feet.

"And the horn?"

"No idea."

I picked up the first bale, carried it a few yards away from the chute, dropped it, then pulled my knife and cut through the twine.

The pony trotted out away from the tree, then back, unsettled by the commotion.

Abraham had stayed at the chute and was stacking the bales as they fell to keep them from clogging up the system. "What does it do?"

"Mostly? Eat hay. But it can pull or plow if I need it to."

I rested my hands on my hips and studied him. He moved with a steady grace of a man used to hard work and content in it. The wind caught at the collar of his coat and stirred his hair, pushing it into his eyes as he bent, pulled, twisted, stacked. He looked like he could do this sunup to moon down.

"You've done this before, haven't you?"

He glanced over his shoulder and gave me a smile that made me hold my breath from the joy in it.

"Once or twice."

"Well, well. City boy's lived out in the scratch. Were you a farmer or stitcher?"

"Back when I lived in the scratch, there wasn't such a

thing as a stitcher. I owned a cherry orchard, raised some livestock and such."

The bales had stopped falling and the track stilled. He picked up one of the 150-pound bales like it was made of air. "Your turn to answer my question."

"About?" I strolled over, hefted another bale, and carried it to the feed spot.

Pony was walking our way slowly, head down, sniffing the ground.

"Who made you? How long have you been out here hiding?"

"I was born to my mother and father."

"In that body?" he nodded at me as he walked back for another bale.

Weird question for most folk. But, I suppose, not for him and me.

"I really am twenty-six," I said sidestepping the body question. "Do you know where my brother is?"

He dropped another bale, glanced over at Pony, who was nibbling at grass just a few feet away from us. "He claimed House Gray several years ago and requested positions among the histories and libraries in other Houses."

"What does that mean?"

"He's House Gray, and works in one-year contracts for other Houses. The last House he worked for was House Silver."

"Vice?" Silver was the House that dealt with entertainment, drugs, sex, and any other pleasure humanity could think up.

I cut the string on the last bale. "Has he been in contact with you?"

"That's difficult to answer."

"*Yes* or *no* should work." I stabbed a few flakes of hay off the bale and tossed them to one side, inhaling the sweet, dusty green scent as it drifted up from around my boots.

Pony made another soft sound, easing a little closer.

"Yes."

"But?"

He was silent as he broke open another bale.

"But?" I repeated waving the pitchfork his way.

"Your brother has a certain . . . intensity," he said eyeing the tines of my pitchfork. "It seems to run in the family. The last few messages from him have lacked that."

"Can messages be forged?"

"This is the modern age, Matilda. Everything can be forged." He scooped up a handful of hay, then walked slowly toward Pony, his hands low.

I set the tines in the ground and leaned one elbow on the handle. "And my mother's message?"

"We didn't wait to disprove it. I left the moment it came over the transom. Before any other House could intercept it."

"So it might not be real?"

He stopped an arm's length from Pony and held out the hay. Pony nibbled at dirt, trying not to look interested even though its eye was locked on his offering.

"Might not. And yet here you are," he said. "Just as she said. And here is your farm—your father's farm. Just as she said. As real as can be."

Pony raised its head, and Abraham leaned away from the horn and lifted his hand so Pony could wrap its lips around the hay. He ran his other hand down Pony's neck.

The man looked as comfortable out here as a frog in a puddle.

"Could I see it?" I asked. "My mother's message?" It came out a little softer than I'd meant.

The look that crossed his face—kindness and regret— was more than I knew how to deal with.

"Or not," I said. "It's fine. This is enough for Pony. Let's go."

I strode to the truck, tossed the pitchfork in the back, and got behind the wheel.

Abraham gave Pony one more pat, then propped the

pitchfork over his shoulder and sauntered back to the truck. He put the pitchfork in the back and got in.

"I'll show you her message," he said. "When we get to House Gray. I promise."

"Thank you." I started the engine and drove through the falling dusk.

By the time we made it to the pond where the leapers liked to nest, I'd accepted that my mother's message was something I'd have to face.

Her death wasn't a new truth, but hope had sharpened the edges of it again.

What worried me more was my brother. If the latest messages from him had been forged, who had forged them and why? And, more importantly, where was he?

Abraham had been silent on the drive, a courtesy I appreciated.

"You can stay in the truck," I said. "I'll handle the leapers."

He opened the door and got out of the truck anyway.

"So far I've seen a dragon and unicorn," he said. "Leapers brings all kinds of thoughts to mind."

"They're just pond crawlers."

I retrieved a bag of apples out of the back of the truck. Leapers didn't need apples to survive, but they were intelligent, determined little things that would stray far and wide for fruit.

I opened the bag and tossed an apple into the brackish pond.

Abraham leaned against the truck, searching the shadows.

"Up," I suggested.

He looked up at the trees that overhung the water.

A rattle of leaves was all that announced the leapers.

I tossed another apple into the pond.

"Spiders?" he asked.

"Not quite."

The leapers lived up to their name and came hopping

out of the trees and into the pond with fist-sized splashes. They wrapped their little tentacles around the apples, which were bigger than them.

"Octopuses? Tree octopuses?"

"They aren't supposed to climb trees, but one of them figured out where the fruit was, and, well." I shrugged.

"Your father stitched little land octopuses?" he asked.

"Oh, these aren't his. Or at least I don't think so. These have been here as long as any of us can remember. Mutated. Teeth. Poison."

"With a taste for apples?"

"Yes. And they will go miles to find them. Which, in turn, gets them killed and us blamed. Our neighbors don't much appreciate it when they swarm a tree and scuttle off with all the best fruit."

"Why don't you get rid of them?"

I shrugged. "They're not doing any harm. Well, not much. They are poisonous, so it's not like you want them crawling up your legs. But they're kind of cute." I grinned as one of the leapers landed on an apple and fell off. It draped a greenish tentacle over the fruit, hugging it like it had just found a lost friend.

Most of the little monsters found an apple to hug and bob along with. I finished throwing the rest of the fruit in there. It should keep them out of the neighbors' crops for a month.

"That's a lot of apples," he said.

"Just being practical. If I'm going into the city with you, I want things tied down here so it's not chaos when I come back."

He made a *hm* sound.

"What?" I wadded up the burlap bag and tucked it under the pitchforks in the truck.

"I can't guarantee you'll be back here any time soon." He got into the truck. I got in too.

"I don't need your guarantee. I can negotiate my own life, thank you."

"You'll be claimed by House Gray."

The lights on the old truck cut a watery yellow swath through the creeping dusk as we made our way to the barn.

"Yes. And I'm sure House Gray will want me to do ... something for them." I glanced over at him, looking for a clue as to what they might want me for.

"Something," he agreed.

Not helpful. Okay. Fine. "After I do that, I'll come back here. Home. Where I belong."

"You're galvanized. You belong to a House."

"I have a House."

"House Brown? That loosely connected group of drifters, failures, and malcontents doesn't count."

"You fought for those malcontents once, Mr. House Gray."

"I've never stopped," he said. "I just know when to change tactics. Do you understand that out of all the experiments, trials, and advances over the past two centuries *no one* has succeeded in creating a new galvanized?"

"Well, there's me."

"Yes. There's you. Unregistered, un-Housed—and Brown doesn't count," he said before I could argue. "Until this morning, unknown to any of us. If you are made different enough to feel, then an awful lot of people will go to extremes to find out just what makes you tick."

"What, like showing up on my doorstep, bleeding and claiming I need protection on nothing but a message from a long-dead parent? Didn't think I was all that special."

"I didn't say she was alive. Just that we had a message from her. And *rare* is the term I'd use."

"Well, *rare* doesn't mean I'm going to roll over and let a House tell me what to do. I stand with Brown."

He grit his back teeth together so hard, the muscle at his jaw popped out.

I pulled up in front of the barn, which was set just a short ways off from the house, and wondered if he was the yelling type.

"How many friends?" Abraham asked, not yelling.

"Are malcontents?"

"How many of your friends are in the path of the heavy equipment?"

"A dozen families," I said.

"Tell them to pack and leave. It's the safest thing to do."

"They won't listen. It's their land and they intend to stay."

"How far out are the machines?"

"Thirty miles. There's still time."

"For what?"

I licked dust off my bottom lip. "Neds have reminded me that you are not on our side, Mr. House Gray. The deal was for you to answer my questions, not the other way around."

"Neds don't know me."

"Neither do I."

He said something under his breath in that language I didn't understand, pushed open the door, and started pacing.

I walked over to the fence attached to the barn and let myself into the pen.

"Do you want my help?" he finally asked.

"Will it mean I owe you a favor?"

"It means I can buy your friends some time."

"They don't want time. They want their homes."

He leaned his elbows against the top of the fence, his boot hooked up on the lowest rail, as he stared at the chickens running around at my feet. He looked comfortable in that pose, natural to this kind of life, and handsome enough that needful fire spread out through me again.

What was wrong with me? We had just been arguing. I shouldn't be thinking about what his touch would feel like, about what his lips would feel like against my skin.

Irritated. That's how he made me feel. I ignored him and my own body and everything else about today that was driving me mad, and checked the automatic grain feeder instead.

"Those aren't chickens," he said after a bit.

"They're part chicken."

"And part lizard?"

"Lizard neck and tail. Bat wings." I tested the water trough, and then shooed away the hissing flock so I could unlatch the gate.

"Mythology would call them cockatrice," he noted.

"Fancy. We call them chickens."

"It's the Fesslers' place, is it?" he said.

That stopped my breathing for a second.

"How do you know the Fesslers?"

"As you pointed out, the galvanized began House Brown. I knew old Gertie Fessler. She claimed a patch of desert around those parts. If her descendants are anything like her, they are pigheaded and devil-tempered. And you're right. They'd rather stand ground and die."

"That's nice to hear," I said.

"What?"

"That I'm right."

A smile crept up the corners of his mouth. "About the Fesslers."

"About everything."

"Odds are against you there."

"I've never been afraid of playing the odds, Mr. House Gray. Now let's go get some dinner."

9

The first to fall under the scientist's knife was a man who had survived the Wings of Mercury. When he, the undead, took his first breath, they knew the experiment had not failed completely. —1914
—from the journal of L.U.C.

We left the truck where it was and walked up to the house. My feet had been running these paths since I was just a child, and I knew every bend and rock and rise.

Abraham didn't have the same luck. But for a man who insisted he couldn't feel his feet—or any other part of him—he did a remarkably good job of not stumbling.

We stomped mud off our boots before letting ourselves into the kitchen.

The light was turned down low, but a loaf of fresh-cut bread and a pot of roast and vegetables were left on the table, along with a note.

"Secret admirer?" Abraham turned to wash his hands in the sink.

I picked up the note. "Farmhand."

"Uh-huh."

"What romantic-nonsense age did you come from where a note has to be from an admirer? Wait—don't answer that, Mr. 1492."

He chuckled. "Did he quit?"

"Neds wouldn't quit on a note. He just said Grandma turned in for the night and so did he."

"That all?" He dried his hands on the towel, watching me.

It wasn't all. Neds had also said he didn't know what had taken us so long to feed the animals, nor what else we might have been doing. Plus, he said he hadn't found anything useful in the basement. Which meant we had a big fat zero for ideas on how to stop House Red.

"That's all." I crumpled the note and shoved it in my pocket. "Make yourself a sandwich. I'll put on water for tea."

I traded places with him, washed my hands, and filled the pot with water before placing it on the stove. We cooked with electricity, since the pump house generated more than enough for our small farm.

Abraham wasn't shy about putting a sandwich together. He sat at the table and was a few bites into it by the time I put down two mugs and poured water over the mint and chamomile.

I made a sandwich and sat at the table with a sigh.

"Rough day?" he asked, piling some vegetables on his plate.

"I've had worse. Much worse." I took a bite and rolled my eyes at the flavor that burst through my mouth. Neds could cook, and even simple meals were a feast when he put his mind to it.

And he had cooked to impress tonight.

"For instance?" he pressed, already making up a second sandwich.

"Well, nobody died today. That's a plus. How's your wound?"

He swallowed tea and nodded. "Better than it should be. I don't suppose you'd sell me some of that jelly?"

"You couldn't afford it, Mr. House Gray."

"I bet I could."

"You mean your House could. It's not nice of you to promise fortunes that aren't yours."

"I never said I was nice," he said. "And I never promise anything I can't deliver. Even though House Gray claims me—"

"Owns you," I corrected over my tea.

"—I am my own man. I can make my own promises and I can keep them."

"You're working awfully hard to make me trust you."

"Is it working?" he asked.

"Here's an idea," I said. "Why don't you go back to House Gray and tell them there's nothing out here but brush and dirt, and there's no reason for any other House or my father's old enemies to come looking?"

"Even if I did that, it wouldn't change things. By now the other Houses have obtained your mother's message. Old enemies might be the least of your worries."

"Ominous, Mr. House Gray." I pushed the last bite of my sandwich in my mouth and dusted my hands.

"Are you allergic to it?" he asked.

"What?"

"Saying my name."

I paused over my tea. He was watching me, taking in the details of me again, like I was a photo fading all too quickly before his eyes.

"First names seem too friendly, since I've only known you for a day. You laughed at me when I called you Mr. Seventh." I shrugged.

"Vail," he said.

"What?"

"It's my true last name. Though I'd prefer you didn't use it around company or strangers."

"Why not? Are you ashamed of it?"

He sat back, shook his head. "I forget how young you are, Matilda. That"—he held up one hand before I could defend myself—"isn't a slight. It's just . . ." He glanced over my shoulder, staring at the nothing in the shadows there. "Abraham Vail is a name from a life lived long ago." His gaze shifted back to me. "It was a good life. And it is a good name."

"All right," I said. "Mr. Vail. I hope you don't mind my manners, but I'm going to turn in early too."

We finished eating. Abraham cleared the dishes, and I put the roast and veggies away in the cold box and wrapped the bread so it wouldn't go stale.

"Nice job on the floor, by the way," I said as we walked into the living room.

"You're welcome," he said. "It's been . . . interesting. Good night, Miss Case." He gave me a nod that was almost a bow, then walked down to his room.

Yes, I stared after him. I was having a hard time remembering he wasn't on our side, wasn't to be trusted. Especially since he hadn't done anything untrustworthy all day.

Well, he'd showed up with drones tagging his location. But he'd called them off and had been mostly reasonable. If you didn't count the whole thing about me having to leave my family home and get claimed by a House if I didn't want to lose everything I'd spent my life fighting for.

I sighed and scrubbed my fingers over my scalp. I was tired, but took a second and peeked into Grandma's room. She was sleeping, the little sheep snuggled around her, that ridiculously long scarf she'd been knitting draped over the foot of the bed like a wooly coverlet.

Down the hall, Abraham's door closed with a *click*.

Grandma was sleeping, Neds were sulking, and I had a stranger who was the eyes and ears of one of the most powerful ruling organizations in the world bedding down in the spare room.

Not to mention fifty people out in the desert counting on me to save their homes.

I'd catch a couple hours of sleep, then head back down to the basement and see if I couldn't dig up a miracle.

I stripped out of my coat, my overalls, and my shirt, leaving them all in a pile on the willow chair in the corner of the room. I needed a shower, and tromped off to take one in the little bathroom on this side of the hall.

I didn't linger in the hot water, but instead scrubbed the dirt and dried blood off me, then toweled off quick. I pulled on a tank top and a pair of shorts and walked down to my room and crawled under my covers, shivering a little from the cool sheets.

Three deep breaths was all I got before the bell rang out. Not just one little jingle like earlier today; this was nonstop clanging.

Something was going very wrong with someone in House Brown.

I kicked out of my covers and ran for the basement door.

Neds were already running up from the basement—he must have decided to sleep on the cot down there tonight. He flicked the alarm off, but was breathing a little hard at the top of the stairs.

"It's the Fesslers," Right Ned said.

"What happened?"

Abraham was right behind me—still in his breeches—but barefoot and shirtless.

"This isn't your concern," Left Ned said, pulling on the door so Abraham couldn't see behind him.

"What happened?" I asked again.

"They've sent air support. They're being bombed."

Oh, shit. "Are they running? Are they evacuating?"

"No."

"Let me talk to them," Abraham said.

"Step back," Left Ned warned.

"Can you stop it?" I asked. "Can you call them off? Call off the bombing?"

"Yes."

"Bullshit," Right Ned said.

"Do it," I said to Abraham.

"Matilda," Left Ned warned.

"He's doing it."

Neds moved out of the way, and I ran down the stairs, Abraham then Neds behind me.

Abraham pulled up short at the bottom of the stairs. "Hell's hooks. This is beautiful . . ."

"What do you need?" I stood between my workstation and Quinten's, the screens and equipment stacked around and above me.

"Do you have a slip link?"

"Yes. Here." I held the earpiece out for him.

He took half a second to scan the equipment we had rigged up, took the piece, slipped it over his ear, and tapped into the old keyboard, his fingers flying.

"Get me coordinates," he said.

"Do it!" I called to Neds as I patched into every line I had for the Fessler compound. "Pick up, pick up, pick up," I chanted through clenched teeth.

The monitors were locked on the compound, which was a mess of fire and smoke in the dark of night. I didn't see anyone moving around down there, which didn't mean they were dead, but didn't mean they were alive either.

"This is Abraham Seventh of House Gray," he said into the microphone, while keying in a string a codes that I wished I had time to memorize. "You are to cease your activities immediately. This contract is canceled until further notice. Abort."

The old cell line clicked to life and a voice picked up. "Matilda?" It was Braiden Fessler.

"Get out of there, Braiden. Now."

"This is our home."

"If you don't run, it's going to be your grave."

An explosion rattled through the connection.

"Where will we go?" he yelled. "There is nothing for us."

I snapped my fingers, and Neds came over to join me at the feeds. We'd worked together enough that I didn't even have to tell him to pull up the closest, safest homesteads that would shelter the Fessler crew.

"Got it," Right Ned said. "Pocket of Rubies is just to the west of them, and looking for more hands. They could shelter there."

"Braiden?" I said, "are you still with me?"

Nothing but static. All the screens locked, blinked down to black, then powered up again.

"What the hell?" I said. Our system had never faltered. Never.

A man's face came into focus on the screen, too large at first, then pulling away as if he were adjusting a camera to catch his image. He was in his late fifties, with salt-and-pepper curly hair and small, wire-rimmed glasses perched on his round nose beneath thick eyebrows. His skin was fair, his eyes small and bright, and from the scruffy beard and mustache, he looked like he hadn't shaved in a day or two.

"This is Oscar Gray," he said in a pleasant tenor. "Abraham, would you care to explain why you used House authority—without my approval—to cancel the manpower contract with House Red?"

Dammit all. The last thing we needed was another House getting involved. And we certainly didn't need the head of House Gray involved.

Abraham had taken off the earpiece and walked around to stand in front of the main screen next to me. Neds took care to step off into the shadows where he wouldn't be seen. But it was too late for me, so I just stood my ground.

"There is a settlement in the line of their construction," Abraham said.

Oscar frowned. "Are you sure? There are no records of House registration."

"House Brown," he said.

Oscar took a deep breath and closed his eyes. "Abraham . . ."

"Children," Abraham said. "Families."

Oscar nodded. "How many?"

"Fifty people. They can be relocated."

"Why aren't they already relocated? I'm sure notice was served, surveys were done."

"They can be out of there in three days," Abraham said.

Neds, in the shadows, swore softly.

"I can't give them three days. They have tonight."

"Thank you," Abraham said.

Oscar pointed one thick finger at the monitor. "You've put me in a uncomfortable position. Aranda Red is just looking for a reason to give my brother support, and you've handed her a breach of contract. She'll roast me alive."

"Maybe not," Abraham said. "They were running night crews. We agreed to provide the manpower only for day construction, if I'm not mistaken."

Oscar's eyebrows ticked up. "You're never mistaken, but I'll look into it. It's not much of a reason to cancel all the workforce for House Red in North America, but it's something."

"All the workforce?" I asked. "It's only one small construction site."

I knew Oscar had seen me when he'd first patched into our systems. But now he turned so he was addressing just me.

"You must be the daughter, Case."

"I am," I said, because, seriously? There was no hiding now.

"Abraham can explain it to you," he said absently, "but if we are to pull entire crews off a job at a moment's notice, we must suspend all workers on all contracts with that particular House until the matter is satisfactorily resolved."

"I didn't know," I said.

"Of course you didn't." He gave me a small smile. "Abraham, on the other hand, knew full well."

"Children, Oscar," Abraham repeated.

"I know, I know." Oscar waved his hand. "I'll take care of Aranda. In return," he said with a nod toward me, "you and Ms. Case will return to Gray Towers immediately, please."

"I can't leave yet—" I started.

"Miss Case," he said firmly. "You must leave immediately. We've just involved ourselves in a contract dispute with House Red on your behalf, if I'm not mistaken?"

Abraham didn't say anything and neither did I.

In a milder tone, Oscar went on. "Every House will notice the contract dispute. It will take them seconds to trace it back to me, to Abraham, and then to our sudden interest in your property, and finally to you.

"If you are not here to sign papers with me or with another House, you, your property, and everything on it, including, I am to assume, the advanced and unregistered communication system we are at this moment conversing on, will be forcibly acquired."

"But the land doesn't belong to me," I said. "It belongs to my grandmother and she's human. House Green."

"Forcibly acquired," he repeated. "I am sorry. This must all be happening rather quickly for you. But this is the safest course of action for all of you, including your grandmother. Abraham, bring Ms. Case here. Immediately. I'll see what I can do to clean up this mess you've made."

"Thank you," Abraham said.

Oscar smiled briefly, then the screens went black, flickered, and snapped back with the feeds they were usually plugged into.

"Fuck it to hell," Right Ned said.

Pretty much my sentiments.

"Matilda?" Braiden's voice called out over the line.

"I'm here. Are you okay?"

"The bombing stopped," he said. "The sky is quiet. They're gone."

"Good. Now listen to me. I had to call in favors with House Gray to stop them."

"Oh, God, no."

"Which means I owe them repayment. You are to leave the compound tonight."

"But—"

"Right. Now. Pack up the kids and head over to Pocket of Rubies. We're letting them know you're coming their way." I glanced over at Neds, who was already putting in the call to the girls at Pocket of Rubies. "Do you have vehicles and supplies to make it?"

"We do," he said quietly.

"Go. And hand me over to your boy, Thad."

There was a pause, then Thad's baritone answered. "Thank you," he said. "I don't know what you did, but thank you."

"I traded favors with House Gray."

Into his shocked silence, I said, "Your father doesn't want to leave. But this is only a temporary reprieve. Promise me you will get yourself, your families, and your pigheaded father out of there tonight."

"The girls are happy to put them up," Right Neds said.

"Pocket of Rubies is ready to take you in," I said. "They're good people."

"I know," he said. "I know. We'll be packed and out of here in an hour, I promise. And Matilda . . . I'm so sorry about House Gray."

"Just get somewhere safe and we're gold."

"Our homes?"

"Take a few pictures. You won't ever be back."

"All right," he said quietly. Then, stronger: "We'll be fine. May the earth rise to your feet."

"And the wind to your back," I replied, finishing the old House Brown blessing.

I broke the feed and pressed my cold fingers over my eyes, swallowing back the mix of fear and anger and sorrow. They had lost their land. Just like I was going to lose mine.

I stood there long enough, Abraham had time to walk through the room, quietly inventorying all of our equipment, all of our secrets.

There was nothing standing in the way of House Gray shutting us down. Like Neds had said, Abraham was galvanized—the ears, eyes, and mouth of his House. Whatever he knew, his boss, Oscar, must have known.

I pushed away my fears. I had a situation to handle and there was no time for crying. I set the main system back out of emergency status. "I'll need a few minutes to pack my bag."

Left Ned swore.

"Tilly," Right Ned said.

"I want you to stay here with Grandma."

"No."

I glared at both of him.

"Wherever he's taking you"—Left Ned stabbed a finger in Abraham's direction—"we're going."

"You could bring your grandmother." Abraham patted the short-wave radio receiver fondly and strolled over to the telegraph station, bending to study the straight key's setup.

"This is her land and home," I said. "Going in city would be too much of a shock. As long as the land is safe, she stays here."

"The land will be safe when you claim a House," Abraham said.

"I'll hold you to that," I said.

"I'm not staying with her," Left Ned said again.

"Fine. I'll call Boston Sue. Go get your gear."

Neds gave Abraham one last hard look, then walked up the stairs, leaving the door open at the top.

"Listen," I said after Neds were out of earshot. "That was very kind of you, to put your House on the line for the Fesslers. I understand what kind of a risk that is. Thank you."

"It was the right thing to do." His gaze wandered over the room, and a longing softened his eyes before he looked back at me.

It was almost like he missed all this rebel-underground living.

"Not bad for out in the scrub, right?" I said.

"It's impressive," he said, "I'll give you that."

He walked over to a flat, underlit table in the corner. "I recognize all the equipment except this."

He didn't touch the table, but the white light beneath it cast his face in a ghostly glow, shadows from the gears and swinging hands slipping angles across his face.

"What is it?" he asked.

"Something my brother was working on."

"It's a countdown clock?"

"Is it?" I walked over and stared at the confusion of brass gears and needles that spun slowly in clear oil.

"I can't make out the markers," he said. "But it is either almost at the end or almost at the beginning of its cycle. Your brother didn't mention what it was?"

"He always had some pet project he was working on down here."

"Hm. Maybe we'll get a chance to ask him soon." He cleared his throat. "I'll be waiting outside. I'll give you some time to say good-bye."

Abraham walked up the stairs, leaving me behind with the impossible task of saying good-bye to my land, my grandmother, and my home.

10

They were not human, not exactly so. Raised from the edge of death, the twelve men and women who had survived the mad man's experiment were rebuilt, piece by piece, until they were stronger than any human. Perfect for the war effort. Built for it. And sent into battle for their country. — 1941
                              — from the journal of L.U.C.

Boston Sue was my nearest, paranoid, highly armed neighbor lady. I rang her up on the landline, and she answered on the vid.

"Bo," I said, shifting so I was in view of the camera. "I need a favor."

Bo was a large woman, with dozens of neat, thin black braids that draped around to fall in loops at either side of her pierced and decorated ears. Her eyes were deep set and dark and missed nothing. Her skin was darker than mine and so smooth and unstitched, it was like she was carved of the softest clay.

She was probably twenty or so years older than me and wore a gun the way most women wore purses — as a deadly accessory. Today's little number was a semiautomatic, nestled in the folds of her brown and green tie-dyed dress.

"You heard the drones pass over?" Bo asked.

"I heard them," I said. "It's trouble I kicked up."

"Trouble?"

"House trouble."

"Tilly, what did you do that requires drones flying over our privacy?"

"Better you don't know. But I do have a favor to ask," I said. "Can you come stay with Grandma for a few weeks? I promise I'll get in touch after a day or so."

"Sure, sure," she said. "Anything you need, baby sweet."

"The beasts are fed and should be fine for a couple weeks. Neds are going with me."

"Don't tell me any more. Simple is better. Take care of yourself and come home safe, you hear?"

"Promise."

"How can I reach you?" she asked.

"I'll take the walkie-talkie. You know how to reach me."

"I do, I do. Good luck, Matilda."

"Thank you." I ended the link then tromped up the stairs, turning off the light before I shut the door behind me.

Time to say good-bye to Grandma.

"Grandma?" I said, pushing open her door and turning on the table lamp. "I'm going to be gone for a little while."

"It's today?" Grandma asked.

"Yes, it is," I said. "I'm taking a trip."

She sat up, and the sheep tumbled down the quilt. I saved one from going off the edge, tucked it in the crook of my arm, and rubbed its soft little ears.

"You aren't going looking like that, are you, dear?" she asked.

I realized I was still in a tank top and shorts. Great. I'd been mostly naked in front of Abraham. Well, I guess that made us even.

"I'll change and pack a bag," I said. "But I'll be back in to say good-bye, okay?"

"Yes, yes," she said. "Get your things."

I dropped the sheep on her bed. All three of them panicked in a circle, then wedged themselves headfirst into her pillow.

I hurried to my room and pulled on a soft tan tank top and shrugged into my favorite shirt—a green military with cutoff sleeves that had been Quinten's. I slipped into khaki pants, then wrapped my gun belt around my hips and holstered my old Colt revolver. Yes, I was going into a city, but I was not going unarmed.

My coat hung over the back of the old willow chair next to my bookshelf. I put my coat on, then dug around my dresser top, looking for where I'd left my fake ID chit.

Found it, stuck it in my pocket. *What else?* I spun a slow circle, taking in, maybe for the last time, all the things I could call my own. Books, the little circus animals Neds had carved for me, a string of glass beads looped across my mother's lace curtains, my bed with the down coverlet.

A change of clothes seemed practical, so I pulled an old canvas duffel out of my closet and shoved in a pair of jeans, underwear, a shirt, a sweater, socks, and, just in case, I threw in a spare of each. Then some extra bullets, my hunting knives, and the ancient modified walkie-talkie I'd brought up from the basement. Just for good luck, I added in a silver charm bracelet that had been my mother's, and a couple of packets of seeds I'd been saving.

Good enough.

I slung the duffel over my shoulder and turned to leave.

"You aren't going into town looking like that, are you, dear?" Grandma stood in the doorway of my room.

She must have thought she was going with me, and had dressed in a dark walking skirt, sensible shoes, and a warm sweater over her lacy pink blouse.

I took her by the arm and guided her down the hallway a bit, back to her room.

"This will be fine, I promise. It doesn't matter what I look like."

"Oh, my dear child," she said. "It all matters. Very much. This is our chance to make things right." She caught at my hand and pulled me the rest of the way into her room, tugging me over to her bed.

"We don't have time, Grandma," I said.

"We always have time," she insisted. "We are Cases, after all." For a little thing, she had a strong grip. "Now, let's see to getting you properly outfitted. You are going to the city, aren't you?"

"Yes. But you aren't. You'll be staying here."

"I see," she said.

"Do you know what's happening?"

"Not at all."

"I'm going to find Quinten and make sure our property is registered so we can keep it. I might have to . . . take a job with a House in the city for a while. Bo's going to stay here with you. She should be here in a couple minutes. I promise I'll call."

She pulled the ridiculously long cream scarf off her bed. I couldn't tell if she was listening to me.

"Here you are," she said. "All the spare seconds I could find." She draped the scarf around my neck three times and it still dragged the floor.

"Grandma."

"Let's loosen this a bit and get another round in." She tugged and wrapped, and I let her.

This might be the last time I saw her for a long time.

"This is your special scarf," I said.

"Yes, and that is why I am giving it to you." She stopped fussing with the scarf and placed her palms against my cheeks.

"You are so unexpected," she said. "A miracle and hope. Your parents loved you dearly. Do you know that?"

I nodded, surprised. She never spoke of Mom and Dad.

"This will not be easy to do. But I think you are the key, Matilda. You can change our future. Don't be afraid to do what you know is right, no matter what that stubborn brother of yours says."

"What do you mean, I'm a key?" I was totally lost. I had no idea what she was talking about.

"Do you understand what this scarf holds? What the wool can give it?"

"Time?"

"Time," she agreed.

When I was younger, she told me that the little sheep had a way of attracting wasted moments sort of like dry air attracts static electricity. She believed those fragments of time were caught in the thread that made the scarf.

And while it all sounded like a load of hooey to me, I did have a dragon that could distill the healing properties of nano in its scales. There might be some truth to what she said.

"I've given you as much time as I can. If you need it, when you need it," she corrected, patting the scarf again, "pull the stitches out."

"All right," I said, humoring her. "Thank you, Grandma." I gave her a big hug, and she squeezed me back.

"Good luck, my dear." She turned and stooped a bit to shoo the sheep back toward her rocking chair by the window. Then she picked up her needles, and with the sheep at her feet, cast on new stitches, as if I wasn't even in the room with her.

"Good-bye," I said softly. I left. Picked up my rifle in the kitchen and threw two large jars of jelly, a couple of good needles, and the spools of life thread into my duffel, then I was out the door.

Neds were already at the barn with the truck. The engine was running, and he leaned on the open passenger's door.

Abraham stood a slight distance away from him and the truck, staring at the night sky.

"Problem?" I asked.

"A sky dark enough for stars," he said. "I miss that."

"Where did you leave your car?" I asked as I got in the truck.

Neds hadn't gotten in yet. He was giving Abraham a double-barreled glare.

There probably wasn't room enough in the cab of the truck for all of us.

Abraham must have figured that out. He stepped up into the truck bed, the springs dipping under his weight. He leaned toward my open window. "Just down the north road. I'll let you know where to turn off."

I nodded at him in my side-view mirror, and he settled himself, scanning the sky. I hoped he really was looking for stars and not satellites or drones or some other thing up there that could blast my land apart.

I drove along the pasture to where the rutted trail met up with a slightly less rutted lane.

"You're going to trust him?" Left Ned asked over the rattle and rumble.

"He's offered us protection. I'm not trusting him. I plan to read the fine print."

"Other Houses would take you in," Right Ned said.

"I don't want any House to take me in. I don't want to be owned or claimed. And if there's any way out of it, I'll take it. But there is something bigger than me to protect: House Brown. If they destroy that communication hub, a lot of people are going to suffer."

"And if they find your father's beasts?" He lowered his voice, "And the pump house?"

I nodded. Illegal, all of it. Especially the technology in the pump house. "Quinten will be jailed. Grandma too. The land will get stripped. And I'll lose . . . everything."

"You'll lose everything if you claim House Gray," Left Ned said. "You're something new, Matilda. Valuable. A modern galvanized. That House will use you as a bargaining chip to get what they want."

"I am not a thing. And I am no one's chip."

After a short silence: "We should have sent him packing," Right Ned said.

"Well, we didn't."

Left Ned grunted. "You should never have taken a stranger in."

"Really?" I glanced at him. "I trusted you, a stranger, when you first came walking up my property. Gave you a job with no references—remember? Even though you weren't claimed by a House and weren't carrying papers."

He winced, and I caught the slight smile from Right Ned.

Maybe that would be the last of that.

The road switched from rutted dirt to cow-swallowing potholes between patches of pavement. Took some concentration to keep us wheels down until Abraham signaled where he was parked.

"There's something you should know," Right Ned said. "Back when he first showed up. When I touched him, I saw something."

"A vision?"

He shrugged one shoulder. In all the time Neds had been on the farm, he hadn't ever told me, specifically, what he saw when he touched another person.

"I get, I see . . ." He shook his head, as if there were no words to explain it all.

"A person's fear, guilt, regret," Left Ned picked up. "The thing they want to hide. The truth of what they are. That man is not a good man."

"That man," Right Ned said, "has not *been* a good man. I don't know what his moral standing is now."

"What, exactly, did you see?" I asked.

"Him," Right Ned said. "Younger, unstitched. He was locked behind bars, breathing steadily with a gun in his hand. Blood pooled out from the other side of the bars where another man in a uniform—law enforcement from way back—lay in a heap, dead. He shot a lawman. He's a criminal, Matilda."

I nodded. I should be surprised, but, well, the galvanized had organized an uprising and almost overthrown the Houses. Breaking the law hadn't seemed to concern them then either.

"You said he was unstitched? So the vision you saw was from a long time ago when he was just a human. That's more than three hundred years ago. Long before the Restructure. People change."

When the whole world went through the Restructure back in the early-2100s, everything changed. Corporations, countries, powers, joined together to grapple with overpopulation, dwindling resources, and the growing unrest that would have set the world into a crippling worldwide war.

Well, that's the way the historians wrote it. What most folks whispered was that a few rich families and a few powerful corporations got together and made some deals, drew lines in the monetary sand, erased a few political borders, and staked their claim in wide-reaching resource management worldwide.

The Restructure didn't go over well with most people the first ten years or so. After twenty years, people had forgotten the way things used to be. After fifty, only crazy fringers and the occasional charismatic criminal brought up the idea that things should go back to the way they had been—individual countries monitoring and monetizing their resources.

In the old world, you lived in a country you claimed as your own.

In the new world, it didn't matter where you lived. You were claimed by a House—one of the eleven main powers in the world—or chose the twelfth, nearly powerless House Brown. You worked for them, and, in return, they provided for you.

That was the sales pitch anyway.

"Yeah, well, he's not people," Left Ned said. "And back when he *was*, he killed in cold blood. What do you think about that, Matilda?"

I thought Abraham was a very dangerous man. But I'd thought that since I'd met him.

"I think I'll stand and face this problem straight on. I'm done hiding."

Abraham pounded on the back window. I slowed down a bit and glanced at him in my rearview. He pointed to the left. "Turn here," he shouted over the wind.

No road, no pull-off, just a break between the trees where a few had fallen in the windstorm we'd had last winter.

I pulled over onto the shoulder of the road, headlights revealing the glint of metal—his car tucked back under the trees.

The truck dipped and sprang back on its shocks as Abraham jumped out of the bed.

"Here." He strode off into the brush.

I killed the engine and pulled the keys.

"You could still go back," Right Ned said, staring out into the darkness. "We could run. On our own terms. Our own way."

"We could," I said. "But I have a brother to save, a property to keep, and all the people in House Brown to protect. You don't have to follow me, Ned. As a matter of fact, it might be smarter that you don't."

Right Ned gave me the ghost of a smile. "I ain't ever been the smartest man."

Left Ned swore quietly.

I gave them both a smile.

I got out of the truck, hefted my duffel, and shouldered my rifle, then walked over to Abraham's car.

Abraham had disappeared inside the driver's side of the big gray hunk of curves and creases. The car looked like it was made of gray silk ironed and pressed into shape, no seams except where the doors slid aside.

Compared to the rusty old lump of my truck, it was smooth as moonlight on water.

I took the front passenger's side, and Neds got in back.

Abraham's fingerprint shut and locked all the doors, then started the engine, which caused a bunch of lights to flash but made no sound.

In seconds, we were out on the road with no sense of contact with the pavement. I didn't think we were flying, but the thing had good enough suspension we might as well have been.

Abraham took the thirty-mile-an-hour road at over a hundred. Darkness rushed past the windows. Within fifteen minutes, we were so far off my property, I wouldn't be able to walk back without stopping for the night.

Make that two.

"How long until we get there?" I asked.

"Fifteen minutes until we hit a transfer tunnel. After that, half an hour or so," Abraham said.

"Chicago?" Right Ned asked.

"Yes."

I wondered how my farmhand had known that.

None of us said anything more. After a few minutes, the car veered to the right, and a *clank* rang out from beneath the tires. The ramp locked on to carry us to the tunnel.

I'd only ridden the speed tubes once: a very short trip between our place and North Carolina that would have taken several hours on the road, but was over in a matter of minutes in the elevated tubes. I had been frightened at the time, because Quinten had said it was an emergency trip to buy some things we needed.

Although we'd done more than that.

We'd met someone, one of Dad's partners at House White, I think, though he'd carefully worn gray to indicate a human-service position as he helped us with our shopping. Even as a child, I'd thought that strange.

Quinten was more than capable of doing his own shopping, strange city or not, emergency or not. And the man we met never said his name.

Even more telling: Quinten never spoke of him again.

I was pretty sure we took home an extra box in our

shopping bags that we hadn't bought off any store shelf. A box the man had slipped into our bags.

When I was older and thought about it, I wondered why the man looked so much like my brother, although older and sadder. Their eyes were the same, and something about the curve of their chins and shape of forehead had made them similar.

I remembered the older man had patted Quinten's shoulder once, while I ate my first gelato.

He may have been an uncle. I'd never asked. It was just one brief afternoon in a child's life. I'd been more interested in the vanilla on my spoon than the family I'd never see again.

"Almost there," Abraham said, as he finished inputting our destination, our business, our passenger list, and, of course, the credits to pay for the ride.

Then that dizzying sense of being off the ground while simultaneously rising at a steep angle hit my stomach and head as the pod and car was launched.

There was no sense at all that we were moving, but the readouts were green. We were bulleting at about 350 miles an hour over land, straight into a mess of questions in a world I knew nothing about.

And there was no turning back.

11

HOUSE ORANGE

He preferred to keep his hands clean. Nails short and smooth, palms soft and pink. Slater Orange had the resources to limit how much of the world's dirt and grime came into contact with him. On the rare occasion when he touched something soiled, he pulled on gloves spun of silk and dyed the color of the setting sun.

This was such an occasion.

Slater Orange strolled into the sterilized chamber, pressing his gloves securely down into the webbing between each finger. The repetition of doing so, of donning the barrier between himself and the filth of the world, was methodical and comforting.

His surgeons waited for him, the hand-picked men and women he had employed—at great cost and no small amount of subterfuge—for the last five years. They stood, stiff-backed and at attention against the operating table behind them. The grim piles of their most recent failures cluttered the corners of the room.

"And here it is," Slater said, pacing in front of the six brilliant doctors, his footsteps punctuating his words. "The day of your reckoning, after five long years. The end of your contracts. You may show me your progress."

They parted, stepping aside like a curtain on pulleys to reveal the table behind them. A body, a man, lay stitched together with the finest black thread, wires fed into his shaved skull, tubes taped to his arms and snaking into his mouth, chest, heart.

Interesting.

"You may speak." His stride slowed as a predator's might when sighting prey.

The lead surgeon was a narrow-faced woman whose dark eyes showed no hint of human emotion. "The body lives, Your Excellency. The brain is no longer viable."

"You are telling me you have failed in this task I set before you? A task you assured me you could complete?"

The words hung in the air and drew beads of sweat across every doctor's forehead.

"We have failed, Excellency," the lead surgeon agreed.

"Such a pity," Slater said. "Are you sure there are no other avenues you can explore?"

This time it was a man who answered. "We have exhausted every report, every theory, every experiment. We have pored through all documentation collected in the world. Whatever it is that made the galvanized survive, whatever it is that makes them immortal, we cannot duplicate it with our present technology and knowledge."

Slater folded his hands carefully behind him. "How unfortunate. However, your efforts have not gone unnoticed. Your debt to me and to House Orange is paid. You are freed of your contract."

He could sense their relief like an exhale.

Except for the lead surgeon. She stared at him, waiting. No hope, no trust in her eyes.

She was, after all, a very intelligent woman.

A pity he couldn't use her for something more.

Slater turned and paced toward the door. "Thank you, one and all. You have been very useful."

He stepped through the door. It locked behind him.

A small button was hidden in the wall just outside the

door. He pressed his finger against it, triggering the gas that filled the room and killed them all, quickly, silently, and without a mess.

A pity they had not been more useful.

He paced down the hall and tugged off his gloves, finger by finger. Five years of failure was still a success in one manner: he now knew there was only one way forward.

If he wanted to live forever, if he wanted to change the world so that he alone ruled, he must force Quinten Case to pick up a needle and thread.

To stitch him, as he had stitched the girl, Matilda.

He tucked his gloves into his overcoat and then slipped the silk kerchief from his pocket. He wiped away the new blood from the corner of his mouth.

He would need to press Mr. Case into service soon. Before there was no time left for him.

12

Their cobbled, monstrous appearance clothed human needs and desires that even torture and experimentation could not destroy. Heroes in war, they returned to a world in which they had no place.—1945
         —from the journal of L.U.C.

"So do we walk right into House Gray?" I asked after we'd been traveling in the speed tube for a while.

"No. First we will meet with a friend of mine who helped me find you," Abraham said.

"Who's your friend?" I said to keep the conversation going. Sure, my mind was made up about going into the city and claiming a House, but my stomach was fluttering with nerves. This time, right here in this car, might be my last moments of real freedom.

Abraham glanced over at me. "Robert Twelfth."

Right Ned, in the backseat, jerked at that name.

"Isn't he galvanized?" I asked.

"Yes."

"Since when did he go House Gray?" Left Ned asked.

"He didn't. He is claimed by House Minerals and works very . . . closely with the top of that House, Slater Orange."

"What does House Orange have to do with you finding Matilda?" Right Ned asked.

Abraham shook his head. "Nothing. Robert is meeting us as a favor to me."

Right Ned whistled softly. "If he's going behind his House to smuggle an unclaimed galvanized into an opposing House, then you must be very good friends."

"For more than one lifetime," Abraham said.

Immortality—everyone wanted that, right? From the sound of his voice, the answer was somewhere in the not-really zone.

A chime rang out in the car, and then the scenery faded to reveal the tube's internal walls and flat blue-white lighting. Our vehicle slowed and stopped, though it wasn't until the vacuum released that I felt the clack and rattle of machinery moving our capsule out of the arrival port and onto the line of other vehicles waiting to take the ramps into the city.

The front of the tube opened onto a lit street cornered by blocky skyscrapers. More buildings marched off in lines on either side of us, clogging up the horizon.

I had many kinds of computers. I had books. I'd seen cities. But there was nothing I could see that made this city different from any other. Abraham could have taken us anywhere.

"Chicago?" I asked.

"Yes." Abraham started the engine and took the ramp down to the street that was filling with cars rolling down the other dozen unloading ramps.

I craned and dipped my head, peering down dim alleys draped with drying cloths and wooden crates and tables with people hunched over them.

Even though it was still dark out, every street was filled with cars, bicycles, and people tangled in a mess of movement that didn't seem to be getting anyone anywhere.

I'd never seen so many people hurrying in great, clotted crowds, each wearing a dominant House color with stripes of secondary colors on their arms or legs, striding in and out of buildings, across intersections, and climbing stairs to the skyways, where they became silhouettes: caged like birds against the sky.

It was enormous, and so crowded and overfull it felt small, busy, and constricting. I was suddenly glad for the generous space inside the car, for the luxury of not being pressed against the endless crowds and rush.

Abraham drove the streets with the sort of familiarity that made me wonder if he had lived here for most of his life. Or one of his lives, at least.

"Thing I don't follow," Left Ned said, "is how a stitch from House Mineral is going to help us."

"She needs to remain off the loop for as long as possible," Abraham said. "So you," he said to me, "have a chance to choose a House before anyone lays claim to you."

"Anyone except House Gray?" I asked.

A brief smile played across his lips. "We aren't above stacking the odds in our favor."

"Is that how your House operates? Cheating?"

He glanced over at me, possession in his gaze. "We are willing to do anything it takes. When we see what we want."

"And have you?" I said. "Seen a *thing* you want?"

He narrowed his eyes. "Is that what you think? That I, of all people, see you as inhuman?"

"I don't know what you think."

He tipped his head down so that my gaze was caught by his. "I think you are a stubborn, strong, clever woman. I think you are frightened—"

"Hey, now," I interrupted.

"—as any reasonable person should be in this situation," he said right over my protest. "And I think you are fierce, loyal, and kind. Very much," he said slowly, to give his words weight, "the sort of woman I'd want."

Oh. That hadn't been the answer I was expecting. Heat stroked up my neck and cheek. I was having a hard time thinking over all the noise in my head.

Had he just told me he wanted me? That he had feelings for me?

"What are you offering?" I asked. "Exactly."

"My House is offering you protection," he said, nicely dodging my real question.

"Maybe I don't want your House's protection. Maybe I want freedom."

He shook his head. "You are galvanized, Matilda. Freedom is the one thing we'll never have."

He turned the car and we rolled through an impossibly crowded street, then into what appeared to be a concrete gully.

"But what I can give you is choices," he finally said. "Robert is helping me achieve that."

"The same Robert who is keeping secrets from his own House?" Left Ned asked. "Sounds trustworthy."

"Houses rise and fall, Mr. Harris," Abraham said. "Galvanized stand forever."

Ahead of us was another blocky building, old enough and disused enough the concrete had peeled away to reveal snags of bricks beneath.

The building straddled the gully, creating a tunnel that Abraham drove into. The only light was from the streets around us, stabbing through the iron grille windows. He drove up a slight incline to a second level that opened onto a working machinery garage, though the equipment and workbenches were all silent and empty.

He turned off the engine and twisted back to me as he opened his door. "Please stay here a moment."

He got out and straightened his bloody jacket as if adjusting a tuxedo, then strolled a short distance to the green metal door in front of us.

"How much of this do you understand?" I asked Neds.

"Which part?" Right Ned asked. "The driving into a trap or the agreeing to drive with a complete stranger into a trap?"

"The Houses suddenly wanting me and my property?"

"*Now* you ask me my opinion?" Left Ned said.

"Now I'm terrified I made the wrong choice. Talk to me, Harris."

Left Ned rolled his eyes, then refused to look at me.

"There's been talk," Right Ned said. "In the bar in town. Something big's been brewing for months now. House Blue has some kind of announcement at the gathering. Maybe they were tipped off to you and your property. Maybe they think they can own you."

"That doesn't make sense. I'm not big news."

"A living, modern, feeling galvanized?" Left Ned said. "There isn't a House that wouldn't do what it took to possess you."

"Why?"

"What I've been saying," Right Ned interrupted, "is you are not safe here. Not in this city. Not with this House. We should go. While we still can."

"Where? What House is better than Gray?"

"I don't know."

He wasn't telling me everything. I just couldn't figure was what he was trying to hide from me.

The green door opened and a man stepped out to greet Abraham. He was nearly a foot shorter than Abraham and bald, with narrow features and a short beard and mustache.

Abraham was built like the sort of man who could pull a tree out of the ground with his bare hands. The other man was whippet thin and bird sharp. He wore an orange long-sleeved shirt and brown slacks.

They spoke for a moment, then shook hands, and embraced in a brief hug.

"Do you know him?" I asked.

"Robert Twelfth," Left Ned said.

"Galvanized?"

"You can't tell?"

From here I didn't see any stitching on him. From here, I'd think he was standard human like Neds. Well, not like Neds, but not stitched.

Then the two of them started toward the car, and the

light hit Robert just right. A line of orange stitching zippered from his right eyebrow up his forehead and over his skull.

Galvanized. Pieced together just like me. Just like Abraham.

"Tired of sitting around," Left Ned said. He opened the door, got out.

"Great." I grabbed my duffel and rifle, then followed him.

The stale, warm air of the building swallowed me whole after the cool interior of the car. It was a lot hotter and damper here than back on the farm, and smelled of grease and rust and salt.

"Robert Twelfth," Abraham said as he walked our way, "may I introduce you to Neds Harris, and Miss Matilda Case."

Robert walked over to Neds and offered his hand, which Neds shook. "Pleasant meeting you both," he said. "Welcome to the city. May your stay be memorable."

Neds' shoulders took on that tightness that meant he was touching something he didn't want to touch, seeing something he didn't want to see.

"Thanks," Right Ned said.

"And Miss Case." Robert walked over to me, his smile both curious and kind. "It is such an honor to meet you, sister." He gave a short bow and then held out his hand for me.

"Sister?" I took his hand, which was warm and strong. His eyes went wide at that contact.

"I felt that," he said as he rubbed the fingers of one hand into his palm. "Your hand. I felt your hand. How . . . why did I feel you?"

I shook my head, filled with my own unanswerable questions. I glanced at Abraham and Neds, but they were no help.

"I felt her too," Abraham said. "She doesn't appear to know why."

It sounded like an accusation.

They both stood there a second and gave me twin looks of puzzlement and maybe a little hunger.

Awkward.

"So, you don't feel anything either, Robert Twelfth?" I asked.

"Please, just Rob," he corrected with another smile. "Do you?"

"I felt that handshake," I hedged.

"Time is against us," Abraham said. "We need to go. Apologies, Rob."

"No need, Bram. Anything. Anytime," Robert said. "I'll see you at the games, then?"

"Wouldn't miss it," Abraham said. "You owe me money."

"No, I'm pretty sure I won that square."

"You stole it."

"You were drinking maybe a little," Robert suggested.

"You were stealing maybe a little," Abraham said.

"Wasn't I just?" Robert grinned.

They patted each other on the shoulder, and Robert handed Abraham a thin band that he snapped in place over his wrist.

"Be careful," I heard Abraham whisper. Then he walked toward the green door and Robert strode toward the car. "This way, please," Abraham said.

Robert got in the car, started the engine, and drove away.

"I'd always thought House Gray had a little more class than this," Left Ned said. "Empty garages and hidden back doors."

Abraham pressed the wristband into the scanner above the latch and the door swung open. "If you'd rather, you are welcome to walk up to the front door, Mr. Harris."

"No, this is fine," I said, throwing Neds a look. "The quicker we get there, the quicker things can be put in order." And the quicker I could find out where my brother was, and how I was going to keep myself, my grandmother, and my property safe.

Also, how I was going to bargain for my freedom.

Right Ned gave me another look that made it clear he was sure I'd lost my mind.

I was beginning to think he was right.

"Just this way," Abraham waited, holding the door open.

"Said the spider to the flies," Left Ned muttered.

I hesitated. It looked like a trap. It felt like a trap.

"Please," Abraham said, "I'll answer any question you have as soon as we're on the other side of this door. This garage isn't safe for long."

So I stepped through the door, holding my breath and questions for the time being.

13

HOUSE ORANGE

He preferred to wait until his captive looked up. It was power, eye contact. And once that contact was made, the power became his.

"Ah," Slater Orange said, looking into Quinten's sharp blue eyes, "perhaps we can come to an agreement today."

He wiped the silken cloth over his forehead, mopping the perspiration there. Then he pressed the cloth along its edges between his fingers, folding and folding again, until he tucked it into his breast pocket.

Quinten remained in the library, with access only to the small sleeping area and bathroom behind the door to the left. He was pacing, always pacing, his hands folded behind his back.

"This." Slater Orange held up the slim translucent screen. He was not wearing gloves. There was no need for them. The blood he was about to draw wouldn't stain his flesh.

"Your freedom," he said.

Quinten's gaze ticked to the screen, then away. "I want contact with House Gray. There is nothing more I will do, nothing more I will say, until that human and legal right is fulfilled."

"All these years," Slater Orange said, "I had assumed galvanized was a process that could be duplicated. Given enough time, enough medical and technical advancement, any body part could be grown, transplanted, replaced.

"But every body part ages . . . and the brain especially suffers, falters, fails. You must understand, Mr. Case, it is not just a new body that I desire. It is immortality. Forever in one body, with a brain that will never degrade."

"I am not a doctor," Quinten said. "I cannot help you with such things."

"You are a genius, resourceful, willing to build with what you have on hand. Just as you built your sister, Matilda."

Quinten did not stop pacing.

"But you had good parts to start with, didn't you?" Slater said. "A body that had been forgotten, hidden, stored away. A brain that had slept for three hundred years instead of waking as all the other galvanized awoke. Your sister began, as all galvanized began: a human who survived the Wings of Mercury."

Quinten stopped. Turned, folded his arms across his chest, and gave him a bored stare. "I demand contact with House Gray."

Slater Orange held up the slim screen again. "I can only assume that you found a way to transfer her personality, memories, and self into that blank brain. Or perhaps the brain was not blank. Perhaps you cleared away the original personality so that your sister's mind, thoughts, and awareness could be implanted unimpeded. What I do know is that the brain she now lives within was changed by that secret experiment centuries ago. I also assume that if a sniper sent a bullet into her brain or heart that she might survive it, that she would not bleed out and die. Shall we see if my assumptions are correct?"

The screen flickered and split, both images focused on the interior of an abandoned building. In that building were four people: Abraham Seventh of House Gray, Robert Twelfth of House Orange, a mutant with two heads, and Matilda Case.

"A single word from me and the triggers will be pulled."

"It's a recording," Quinten said, studying the time stamp at the top of the screen.

"It is not. Shall I prove it to you in blood?"

Matilda crossed the warehouse and hesitated outside of the green door.

Both sniper scopes followed her movements without pause, holding a narrow bead on the side and back of her head.

"Make your decision now," Slater Orange said. "Agree to follow my orders, or I will kill your sister. Five, four, three, two . . ."

"Don't," Quinten growled. "Don't shoot. Don't shoot her." He took a deep, shaking breath and clenched his hands into fists. "What do you want?"

"Your hands, your knowledge, your stitches. I will provide the body, and you will imprint my memories, my thoughts, my mind into the brain. Into a galvanized: a house immortal."

Not a twitch from the man, though Slater saw that he was sweating now. Good. He was listening. He was hurting.

"If you do so, I will release you."

"You think I believe that?" Quinten asked.

"I think you have no other option."

Quinten nodded, a rusty sort of motion.

"I need to hear that one word," Slater said softly. "Your agreement. That you will make me galvanized. Tell me yes, Mr. Case."

Quinten's gaze did not move from his sister on the screen. "Yes," he whispered.

And he had won.

"I am pleased you have finally agreed to our working relationship," Slater said. "Please understand that there will be a gun trained on your sister every moment until your release. If I do not contact the gunmen frequently with the correct code words, they will shoot."

He tapped the back of the screen and it faded to gray.

"Now then," Slater said. "I will provide the galvanized body. Will you need more than one?"

"No," he said quietly.

"I will send someone in a few hours to take you to the operating room. In that time, please compile a list of any other equipment you may need. After you have acquainted yourself with my resources, we shall make history together, you and I."

14

*Classified as property, the undead dozen were
owned and used in secret. That was the world's
first mistake. — 1963*
  — from the journal of L.U.C.

I shouldered my way through the green door with my
duffel and rifle. It wasn't a room on the other side but,
rather, a large well-lit elevator.

"Garage isn't safe from what? Spying?" Left Ned said.
He stepped through the door, and I moved out of the
way to make room for him to enter. "Why do Houses
have to spy on every inch of soil?"

Abraham paused before stepping in. He frowned and
scanned the empty warehouse, his gaze flicking to the
shadows and corners as if he knew we were being
watched.

"Problem?" I asked.

"Not if we move." He shut the door and pressed the
wristband into a scanner on the wall. I felt that vacuum-
release drop of an elevator kicking in. The elevator came
to a rest with a slight hop and the door opened.

It all happened so quickly, I hadn't even had a chance
to ask who he thought would be spying on us.

On the other side of the open door stood a man. I'd
seen him once before, on the screens in my basement.
Oscar Gray was about my height, blocky built beneath

layers of shirts, a knee-length jacket, and scarves. His curly black hair was streaked with gray, his eyebrows thick on his affable, round face that carried a few lines at his forehead and the edges of his eyes. He appeared friendly, kind.

He tipped his head up to peer at us through the slim gray-lensed glasses perched on his nose.

"Ah, here you are. Good. I am so glad you could all come. Please, come in, come in, and welcome. We have a lot of ground to cover and not enough time, I'm afraid."

Abraham stepped out of the elevator and leaned his arm across the door, holding it open.

"I don't believe we've met officially," I said offering my hand. "I'm Matilda Case. Pleased to meet you."

Neds hissed in a breath, and Abraham coughed to cover a laugh.

Oscar just smiled wider. "Wonderful to meet you, Matilda," he said. "Just wonderful." He took my hand in one of his and then placed his other one over the top of mine.

His hands were warm and smooth, and very human.

"My name is Oscar. Oscar Gray, head of House Gray."

Top man of House Gray. Ultimate manager of humans as resources.

Humans like my brother, like Neds.

But not me. Even so, I was a little starstruck and nervous. This man was one of the eleven most powerful people in the world. People I'd spent my life avoiding at all cost. Oscar Gray turned and strolled into the luxuriously appointed place, his hands clasped together in front of him. "Would you like some tea? Abraham, could you call for refreshments, please?"

The clean, quiet, and beautifully lit room showed sparks of colored art and tasteful gray furnishings amid the soft gray carpet and soothing gray walls.

"You don't have to bother," I said.

"It's no bother. I enjoy company, and you are my guests. Please make yourselves comfortable."

Okay. This wasn't what I'd been expecting out of one of the most powerful people in the world. Kindness to strangers? Seemed a bit below his pay grade.

I wanted to like him for that, but no matter how much the Neds argued otherwise, I really didn't fall into trust with every stranger who sashayed through my life. I needed Oscar Gray to do some things for me, and I knew he wanted something in exchange.

Probably me and my life.

Abraham strode across the room and exited the door on the far left.

I strolled over to the huge curve of windows that fanned out to look over the city.

The elevator hadn't taken us down, or maybe it had, but we had also gone way, way up. We were on top of a skyscraper looking over one of the original old cities: Chicago.

I'd been surrounded by familiar horizons for all my life. The spread of buildings and tubes and roads and aircraft and lights out there in the not-quite-dark was dizzying.

It was also the highest off the ground I'd been without getting pine needles in my hair.

"Do please have a seat, Mr. Harris," Oscar Gray said.

I turned. Neds finally shook out of his shock and stepped into the room.

He was moving like the whole place was made of holy eggshells.

The man had nerves made of cast iron. It might have been funny to see him so rattled, but, then, nothing about my life was funny right now.

"Thank you kindly for your offer," Right Ned said with formality I'd never heard out of him, "but I don't believe I belong here, Your Eminence."

Eminence? I shot him a look, but he was not joking. Not one bit.

Oscar opened his hand toward the couch. "Nonsense. Please. Relax and have a seat. Are you hungry? I could have food brought up."

"No, thank you, sir," Right Ned said. "I'm fine."

"Good. Good. Although the cookies are not to be missed."

Neds walked over to the couch, Right Ned throwing me a startled look. He obviously felt as out of place as I did here on top of the world.

"Miss Case?" Oscar Gray said.

"Yes?" I moved away from the window.

"You could rest your weapon here, if you'd like." He pointed to the coffee table in the middle of the couches and chairs. His eyes were the twinkly kind that made one think he laughed a lot.

"Thank you." I did just that and sat on the couch across from Neds. Oscar Gray took the chair with his back to the windows.

"I would like to apologize for my manner of invitation," he said.

"What invitation?" I asked.

"Abraham. I sent him, rather abruptly I'm afraid, to get ahead of other forces zeroing in on you. It is certainly not an official way of conducting business, but time was of the essence. I hoped he would convince you and your father to come and meet with me so we could speak in person. Perhaps your father had second thoughts and stayed behind?"

"My father is dead," I said.

"Ah," he said. "I'm sorry for your loss. We had thought he was with you."

"Abraham said his enemies are looking for him," I said. "Do you know who those enemies are?"

"I'm afraid so."

Abraham strolled into the room. Behind him was a short, brisk woman in a gray turtleneck and slacks, her black hair slicked back into a severe bun. She carried a tray with thin, beautiful glasses of iced tea and a platter of perfectly round butter-brown cookies.

Her curious eyes missed nothing.

"Thank you, Elwa," Oscar said as he took a glass of

tea and a cookie. He slurped the top inch or so off the tea and then popped an entire cookie in his mouth.

Elwa carried the tray over to Neds and finally me.

I took the remaining glass of tea but not a cookie. I was too worried to eat.

"You are safe," Elwa said so quietly, I almost didn't hear her.

I gave her a brief smile.

My safe was so far away from here.

Abraham moved over and stood behind Oscar, his hands folded loosely at his back in the stance of a man long used to standing guard. I wondered if that wound was bothering him.

"I would like to know who would want to hurt my father," I said. "And I wonder if I might see the message my mother sent."

"We can show you the message. Abraham, be sure that happens, please. As for your father's enemies, it is a complicated answer," Oscar said. "Do you know what kind of work your father used to do?"

Neds glanced at me. He didn't like when I offered up my name to people. I knew he didn't want me to tell a head of a House anything about my father's past.

"He didn't leave many records behind about it," I said truthfully.

"He was claimed by House White—Medical." Oscar took a drink of tea, thinking. "A brilliant man, your father. He had a degree in experimental physics, although he spent his career in Medical. It was a quiet career. Unremarkable in nearly every way. Until he quit and traded *down* for House Green. Suddenly, his career was remarkable."

"Remarkable?" I asked.

"No person of his status trades down, Matilda. No one. That"—he lifted his eyebrows—"made it a remarkable thing. A remarkable thing that drew notice."

"Didn't he serve out his contract with House White?" I asked.

"Yes, he served his time. But when a man who has the kind of information your father had and the mind your father had leaves to another House, it is a concern. Foremost to Kiana White of House White. She was not amused that one of her premier physicists jumped houses to go farming, then dropped out of sight for years. She was even less amused when rumor of his continued research—research that should have belonged to White—surfaced."

"What research?" I asked.

"You, Matilda." He didn't say it unkindly, but just the same, goose bumps rolled down my arms and spine and my stomach clenched.

"I'm not research," I said with more conviction than I felt. "I'm his daughter."

"You are much more than that," Oscar said. "You are what his enemies are looking for. You are what Kiana White would like to claim as her property. A successful attempt at immortality. Forever young."

"People can't own people," I said.

He sipped his tea and studied me a moment.

"Galvanized are not recognized as people," he said. "They are not naturals."

And there it was, straight out of the head of a House. I wasn't a person. I was a thing.

Funny; I felt like a person. I loved and cried and laughed like a person. But hearing it out of his mouth made it more true in some way. Made it more real.

"I still have rights," I said.

He tipped his head. "Mostly true. The first galvanized stitched together and reawakened were little more than laboratory experiments. It wasn't until the process was improved that scientists realized galvanized may have retained the mental and emotional capabilities of a human being. Before then, galvanized were nothing more than locks on death's door that scientists hoped to pick.

"Then there was the fall and the Restructure. During those dark times, the galvanized broke free of their keepers and led an uprising against the Houses, declaring themselves nonhuman and above the law. They almost succeeded in changing the world. They did succeed in branding themselves as nonhuman.

"You can imagine the fear that spread when it became known that the galvanized feel no pain, can replace injured body parts, and never die. They were seen as killing machines, as alien. Monsters. To be burned, crushed, and killed.

"The Houses joined together to pursue the destruction of the galvanized and all those in House Brown who followed them.

"In exchange for mercy for the civilians who had taken up their fight, the galvanized agreed to treaties and terms of surrender. The laws were already in place: galvanized were not considered human. They are a biological and technological result of an experiment.

"I think it's a ridiculous distinction, but the fear of galvanized cut too deeply and bled too long for too many people. Powerful people. The heads of Houses still wear vials of Shelley dust."

I shook my head. "Shelley dust?"

"It burns through stitches. While it won't kill a galvanized, it will cause the limbs, connections, and internal organs to fall apart. Grisly stuff. Distasteful and inhumane."

Abraham hadn't said a word throughout this. He just stood expressionless, staring at the far wall. But I knew he'd been there, been through all these events Oscar Gray related like they were dry text in a history book.

"So House White thinks they own me because my dad worked for them and I'm stitched?"

There was more. I knew the body my brother had transferred my mind into was once stored at House White laboratories. And if House White knew that, then they were right—they owned my body.

My stomach rolled. It was a horrifying thought.

"They believe any experiment that has a basis in the

work he did in House White is their property. So, yes, they believe they own you."

"He didn't make me," I said.

"Til . . ." Right Ned warned softly.

"Oh?" Oscar frowned. "We thought. I thought." He glanced back at Abraham, who was still staring at the far wall.

"Who made you, then?" Oscar asked.

"My brother."

"Quinten? Quinten Case?"

"Yes."

"That is . . ." He closed his eyes, and pulled off his glasses. He rubbed at the bridge of his nose. "This is much more serious that I thought. If I'd known your brother could create galvanized, I never would have allowed him placement at other Houses. Has he told anyone? Did he have friends, people he would confide in?"

"No one in the Houses," I said.

"That's something," he said. "And before the Houses find that I have brought you here and lay claim to you—especially House White—let me give you some choices."

House White had been at my doorstep just a few hours ago. I broke out in a cold sweat at how close I had been to being discovered. I'd thought I was protecting Abraham by lying to them, but it had been more than that. My life had been on the line.

"Are you all right?" Oscar asked. "You've gone rather pale."

I leaned forward and placed my glass next to my rifle. If I'd had a shred less control, I'd just pick up the gun, wave it around threateningly, and leave.

Instead, I leaned back and folded my cold fingers in my lap.

"I'm fine," I said. "What choices?"

"I want to offer you the wing of House Gray. Our strength and protection."

"You can be clear with me, Mr. Gray. You want to own

me. Buy me before anyone else does." I said calmly. "I come at a very high price. One." I held up a finger.

Abraham, behind Oscar, gave me an incredulous look.

"I want my brother's freedom. Two." I ticked up another finger, noting that Neds had gone a little pale in the corner of my vision. "I want my land's exclusion in House bargaining. And three"—I pointed at another finger—"I want House Brown's voice to be recognized."

No one said anything. No one moved.

Oscar studied me for a long moment. Then he pushed up out of the chair in a rustle of coats and scarves and cloth. "Come with me, and we can draw up the contracts."

Neds and I both started to stand.

"Just you, Miss Case," he said.

"Beg your pardon, sir," Right Ned started.

"We'll return in a moment, Mr. Harris." Then to Abraham, "Please stay here and see that Mr. Harris is comfortable."

Right Ned shook his head, telling me not to go.

I pulled my shoulders back. "It's fine," I said. "I'll be back."

"I'll be right here," Right Ned said.

Abraham gave me the strangest look. "You made a list of demands?"

"Why wouldn't I? You did when you gave up your freedom."

He shook his head, a smile spreading across his mouth. "Go," he said. "Unless keeping the head of House Gray waiting is part of your strategy?"

Right. I went.

Oscar had already outpaced me by half the room and waved his hand at the far wall. The wall dissolved, revealing a hallway there, which he continued on down.

I hesitated. If that had been a real wall, it could close again behind me. Close with only Oscar's hand as the key.

"You aren't my prisoner," Oscar called back. He glanced back. "You can leave anytime you wish, but my office is back this way."

"I am just not used to putting my life or fate in the hands of others," I said, striding down the hall.

"Only the most faithful or naïve are," Oscar said. "This way."

I wondered if the Shelley dust really could tear a person like me apart. I wondered if Oscar kept it in his office.

My knives were in my duffel, out by the elevator door, and my rifle was on the coffee table, but I still had my revolver on my hip. That was some comfort.

I followed.

Oscar stopped in front of two beautiful wooden doors. He lifted his hand, and even though I didn't see it, a scanner must have read who he was. Then, just like that, the two doors swung inward silently.

"Not many people are invited to this room," he said as he walked in and waved for me to follow. "But I felt it important that you understand very clearly what you are entering into with House Gray, and what we can offer you."

"That's kind. Thank you." I stepped in behind him and the doors closed with a locking *snick*.

Photos, some old film style, others hovering in 3D hologram, others carved into life-sized flesh-realistic portraits, scattered across every wall in the place, which was otherwise furnished by a desk with a chair on either side.

"This is a histories room," Oscar said. "Not the only one I have, but every House keeps one wherever they do business. In this room are some of my ancestors," he nodded toward a picture of a petite woman with sharp eyes and black hair slicked back into curls behind her ears. "These rooms hold records, diaries, and knowledge of the House, its doings and agreements during a House head's lifetime. Only the heads are able to access every detail of the histories.

"My histories are here also, of course. All the data and

knowledge I have gathered in my time of ruling House Gray."

He walked over to the wall at my right and stopped in front of a hologram and flesh-real carvings of a boy, a young man, and a middle-aged man who all had his eyes, his short nose, his curly black hair.

Next to each image of him was another boy and young man. He was taller than Oscar, thinner and younger, though his jet-black hair had the same curl. His clean pale face was long and smooth, scrubbed as if the world had never touched it. Not a wrinkle, not a freckle, not a single smudge of life seemed to have impressed upon him. While Oscar's eyes tended to catch light and invite a smile, the other man's eyes were dark, piercing, and utterly remorseless.

"Who is that next to you?" I asked.

He winced. "My brother, Hollis. Second in line to rule the House."

"The brother Aranda Red is supporting?"

"The brother many Houses believe should displace me."

"Why?"

"They don't like me, nor my fondness for a balanced power among Houses and freedoms for the people we employ."

"And why do you have all of these histories here?"

"They stand as witness, record, proof. Connected to primary and secondary sources, they create redundancy and open records for other House history rooms to access, if need be. This is a room of record for legal and contractual matters."

It looked like a room full of dead people staring at me.

I crossed my arms and rubbed my palms down them to settle the roll of chills prickling there.

Oscar glanced at me and tipped his head to one side. "Are you *cold*?"

"No, just . . ." I nodded to the wall of people in front of us. "This is something I've never seen before. It's a bit . . ." I shrugged.

"You're frightened?" Now he sounded surprised.

"Not so much that as disquieted. These pictures aren't connected to living folk, are they?"

"No."

"It's just that all these people staring at me is, well, uncomfortable."

"And your arms? Why are you rubbing them?"

I stopped, unrolled my arms from each other, and stuck my hands in my overshirt pockets. "Just goose bumps."

"Just . . . ?" Oscar slicked his hand over the curls on top of his head, then held up one finger, asking me to stay quiet.

He waved his hand at the far wall behind the desk, and once again part of the wall disappeared, revealing a bank of floating screens. Images flickered there: the room where Neds sat, the inside of the elevator, a street that might be another entrance to this place, and about thirty other locations I did not recognize. Some of the screens were images of empty rooms, but most of them had people in them.

People who were working, talking, eating, sleeping.

The screen that showed the interior of this room was paused.

Oscar flipped through images by waving his fingertips in the air, and all the screens froze.

"Now," he said in a hurry as if time was counting down. "There will be no record of this. No one but you and I will know that this conversation has happened. I have even turned off the receivers and recorders within the Gray histories."

"Histories?"

"All the . . ." He pointed at the nearest portrait that stared blankly, and, thankfully, no longer at me. It too was frozen.

"Are you allowed to do that?" I asked. "I thought this was important for legal reasons."

He chuckled. "I *am* House Gray. Of course I can do

that. We need the histories; they contain backup copies of backup copies of information, conversations, DNA, and everything from the last two hundred years or so. A House is only as strong as its history. But every House needs its privacy. And, trust me, every House takes it."

He sat on the edge of the desk and pressed his hands together, palm to palm, in a prayer position, his fingers tipped to his chin. "Goose bumps. Here. Just now. Has that ever happened to you before?"

"Being spooked?"

"No. Well, yes. Have you experienced goose bumps, tingles, cold—that sort of thing?"

"Are you're asking me if I can feel?"

"Yes."

Right. Abraham and the other galvanized, Robert, had been surprised about that too.

"Yes," I said. "I can feel . . . everything."

Oscar shook his head, his fingers still steepled by his lips. "I didn't know."

"How could you?" I said quietly.

"Do you understand how unusual that is, Matilda Case? How unusual you are? You are the first, the breakthrough. Your brother has discovered immortality without the loss of sensation, heart, or mind."

"I might not be immortal," I said. "We don't really know that, do we?"

"There are ways to find out. Do you remember your reawakening?"

"Yes, I think I do."

"Do you remember when that happened?"

"Are you asking how old I am?"

"Yes."

"I am twenty-six."

"Amazing," he said. "Simply amazing. Your brother is brilliant."

"Speaking of Quinten, I want to know where he is, which House he is working for, and I want his debt resolved so that he is free to return home. I know you think you can claim me, but you should know that I won't be much use to you if I'm treated like property."

"I agree," he said.

That stopped my tirade before I even got started.

"I want my land protected, my grandmother safe."

"Yes, and House Brown to hold a voice in the world. All good things to ask for. But if I am to take action on your behalf, we will have to come to an agreement. A legal, signed contract."

"Monsters have the right to sign contracts?"

His eyes narrowed, but a small smile tugged the corners of his mouth. "I've met a lot of monsters in my time, and most of them were very fond of contracts. But I don't see you as a monster. I see you as a woman who cares about her family and home."

Here I was, being asked to trust a stranger. Again. Only this time I was signing my life away.

But what other choice did I have?

"What other choice do I have?" I asked.

"You could contact the Houses you would prefer to be claimed by. I am sure they would take you in immediately. If the House that claimed you decided you were property worth selling, you might be traded to another House."

"Would I have any say about that?"

"No."

"And what about my property? Grandma?"

"It would depend on the House and how they thought they could best profit from owning what you own."

Harsh. But I knew it was true.

"What are you offering?" I asked. "What do you get out of owning me?"

"There. Very good. That is exactly the question you should ask. It is, fairly, the question you should always ask when dealing with any of the Houses. None of us, not a one, do anything unconsidered. Remember that, Matilda Case.

"I won't go into details, since a few hundred years'

worth of politics and history is a tiresome subject. But the short of it: I am offering you protection. From the other Houses, from contractual changes, from harm. You, your grandmother, and of course your brother will all be claimed by House Gray. Mr. Harris too, if they desire. The land will transfer to House Gray, but stewardship will remain in your family's hands for the next ten generations, at which time a new contract can be negotiated."

"Why would you do that?" I asked.

He nodded, again approving my question.

"I have spent a very long life in service to, and being serviced by, people. It has given me an ... extraordinary appreciation for the human condition. Our flaws, our strengths, and our inextinguishable capability for generosity and goodness. Over all these years of seeing the very worst of people, it is the very best that holds court in my mind.

"I am not immortal. I age—slowly—but I am much older than I appear. The end of my time is coming. Not soon. But it will come. This House, and all the people in the world, will be the responsibility of some other man or woman.

"While I am still the man in charge, I will follow my own moral compass.

"You are a desired commodity, Miss Case. Every House will want to possess you. If you freely choose the protection of my house, I will pay a hefty stipend to all the other Houses. If that is done quickly enough, it will seal Gray's legal ownership of you."

"Ownership," I said, suddenly wanting to sit down and catch my breath even though I hadn't been doing anything but standing there, listening to him tell me how my life, my today, and my tomorrow, had just shattered into something I couldn't recognize.

"Legally, yes," he said. "However, I will sign a moral contract with you, just as I have signed one with Abraham. You will be recognized as under my employ, and you will be afforded all services, considerations, and benefits any human under my employ is given."

"So if I say yes, you own me. And you own whatever it is that makes me what I am. The right to research me? To experiment on me?"

"Excellent question!" He clapped his hands together. "Yes and no. As the head of House Gray, I can, conceivably, do anything to anyone. There is no law other than my law within the House and its people. But the contract will state that any and all procedures will be done with your unforced, explicit consent, witnessed by three neutral parties."

"Neutral parties? Do those exist? You just told me that all people fall under House Gray and you're the law here."

"Yes, but some of those people, most of them, actually, work for other Houses. Among the eighteen billion on this earth, many take vows to stand neutral for all sorts of legal proceedings."

"They can't be bribed? Blackmailed?"

"I won't say it doesn't happen, but it is quickly and violently shut down. We Houses make the rules, and we take steps to see that those rules are followed."

He was offering to take me and Grandma in, along with Quinten, to save my property, and to let us keep our property, which would let us keep House Brown connected and strong. And he would do it all without putting me under the knife to find out what stitched me together.

"What about House Brown's voice?" I asked.

"One world-altering step at a time," he said. "That is a longer battle. But I will sign contracts and begin programs and legislation to see that House Brown can gain recognition."

Not exactly a yes.

"If I don't accept?"

"I'll do what I can for you. But the Houses are powerful. If enough of them join together against House

Gray, they will make it . . . difficult to act in your favor, since galvanized don't technically fall under human laws, and therefore don't fall under my jurisdiction. I'm sorry," he added. "It is the way of it."

"I still don't know what you get out of this."

He smiled, lines pressing out from beneath his glasses. "You give me your allegiance and you give me your help."

"Help for what?"

"Taking my brother out of the line of House Gray rulership."

15

They were urban myth—the immortal crea-
tures living among us. Killing machines that
were sent to depose governments and dicta-
tors. But they were not a myth.—1990
                    —from the journal of L.U.C.

"You have gotten the wrong idea about me, Mr.
Gray," I said. "I am not an assassin."

"I don't think you're an assassin," he said calmly.

"I'm not going to kill your brother."

"I don't want you to kill my brother."

"You just told me to take him out of the picture."

"Wars aren't always won with bullets, Miss Case." He tipped his head, waiting to see if I'd ask the next question.

"All right," I said. "How is your war won?"

"Through your allegiance to House Gray, and to me, in particular," he said with a smile. "This unrest my brother has engineered is just enough to depose my position. I would rather serve out my years and pass the House into more stable hands than those of my brother."

I pushed my hair back from my face. "I'm sorry," I said, "I'm sure this all makes sense, but it's late and I've had a long day. I still don't understand what you want."

"I want you to agree to ten years, signed to me. Not to

House Gray, but to me, Oscar Gray, so long as I am head of House Gray."

"You want me to become your personal slave?"

"Not at all. I want your allegiance." He pressed his fingertips against his mouth, then lowered his hands and crossed his arms. "House rulership is a messy combination of in-house and out-of-house support and politicking. The perception of power is almost as important as power itself. If you claim me as House Gray, it will prove that I am powerful. It will also secure my position as the only House to discover a modern galvanized.

"I will be the only House besides House Blue to have more than one galvanized on my payroll. That will silence those who think me incompetent, end the lies my brother has been spreading, and prove—clearly—that I am the one who should remain in this position."

"So, owning me solves your problems?"

He chuckled. "Not at all. My problems are endless. After all, I am the man in charge of managing the most difficult of resources: humans." He tipped his head to glance over his glasses. "Also, I'd prefer if you didn't think of it as ownership, because it won't be."

"Galvanized have no human rights," I said. "How would you prefer I think of it?"

"As a job, Miss Case. I'll draw up a contract. You'll agree to ten years of service to me and my House, with a renewal option at the end of the decade. I will employ you, and in so doing will give you credit, housing, and the rights afforded to any human under my charge."

It was a generous offer. Far more than I expected.

If I could believe he'd go through with it.

I was prepared to bargain for my brother's freedom, my grandmother's safety, my property's protection, and House Brown's voice.

I had not expected I would be offered anything for me, personally, in the deal.

Certainly not human rights for a monster.

Of course, it wasn't that much of a bargain. Just this

morning I'd had all the freedom I'd wanted. If I refused to sign, I could still run and hide like Neds thought I should.

I looked around the room, at all the shiny, smooth technology and the world power that I knew it controlled. If I left House Gray, he'd find me. He'd have every eye of every human in the world looking for me.

Even people claiming House Brown had been known to work deals on the side with the other, legitimized Houses.

It was a lot to take in. More possibilities and unknowns than I wanted to deal with. I didn't even know why his brother accused him of being incompetent. Maybe he was incompetent, and throwing my fate in with his was suicide.

"How much time do I have to decide? To decide all of this?"

"Not long." He exhaled, nodding as if he could hear my thoughts. "It is a lot to weigh and balance. And as you said, you've had a very long day. I think a few hours of sleep might be in order for both of us. You can give me your answer in the morning."

He stood away from the desk, walked around behind it, and pulled out a single sheet of real paper. He glanced at it, then turned it around on the desk.

"Take your time reading through this. If you have questions on the terms, I'd be happy to answer them. I am going to turn all the recording devices back on now, so . . ." He nodded.

I picked up the paper. It was a contract for ten years' employment and allegiance to House Gray. It appeared to be straightforward, but I wanted sleep and a clear head before I made up my mind.

Oscar did something to make all the portraits in the room seem more lifelike. I guess that meant our conversation was being recorded again.

"I will talk to you in the morning," Oscar said. "Rest well. Abraham will show you to your room."

"Thank you," I said.

Right on cue, Abraham opened the door. "Miss Case. This way."

I left the room, and Abraham fell into step beside me.

"Are you all right?" he asked.

"Peaches and sunshine."

"If you'd like to talk—"

"All I want is a shower and a bed. I am tired and, no matter how we cut it, I'm about to become someone else's property. It has damaged my cheer."

"I know this is hard. . . ."

"Do you?" I stopped so I could scowl at him. "Do you know what it's like to lose everything you have? Everything you love because people are going to die if you don't surrender?"

"Yes," he said, a steady darkness in his calm eyes. "I do. I was the first to sign away my rights to end the Uprising. I was the first to shoulder the yoke of being declared nonhuman so others could be free. I know very well that pain."

"Well, it's new to me," I said. "And it hurts like hell."

"I'm sorry, Matilda."

"Tell me it gets better. That the years of being someone else's property makes it easier. That you don't care about the life you had, the freedom, the happiness."

He stood there silently, his jaw clenched.

"Gold," I said, all the tired of the day swallowing me in a smothering wave. "Isn't that just gold."

I started down the hallway, which opened into the sitting room where Neds were standing near the door.

"We leaving?" he asked hopefully.

"We're sleeping," I said.

Left Ned swore.

"Rooms are this way," Abraham said.

I picked up my duffel and my rifle and followed through another wide, well-lit hallway with even more rooms and halls and alcoves reaching off from it.

"Mr. Harris," Abraham said. "This will be your room." He stopped and opened a door to the left.

It was a lovely, modern-looking suite that probably cost three times what I paid Neds in a year.

"And where's Matilda sleeping?" Right Ned asked.

"Just down the hall."

"Get some shut-eye," I said. "I'll see you in the morning."

"Tilly . . ."

"It can wait," I said. "But I promise, you and I will talk. Room's this way?" I started walking, and Abraham followed.

He opened a door on the right.

I sucked in a breath, caught off my footing by its extravagance. Every room I'd been in was tastefully underdecorated. But this room was nearly the size of my entire house, and completely packed with fineries and luxurious fabrics, fripperies and art.

I'd never seen a place so well appointed.

"This is too much," I said. "Much too much. I'd be more comfortable with something less fussy. Like a broom closet."

"All the broom closets are full," he said. "Of brooms. There are no less-fussy rooms to put you in. And for . . . everything . . . this is not too much."

"Is there a shower?"

He didn't step into the room, but pointed over my shoulder. "Bedroom is through that door. Shower there. I'll be out in the main area. If you need anything, let me know."

"You wouldn't happen to have a time machine? So I can go back and ignore you knocking on my kitchen door, and this"—I waved at the room around me as I stepped in—"would never have happened."

He made a *tsk* sound through his teeth. "I'm afraid the time machine is on back order."

"Of course it is." I sighed and walked toward the bathroom. "Good night, Abraham Vail."

"Good night, Matilda Case."

I heard the door close.

The room was silent in a way I'd never experienced. No wind across the roof, no birdsong sinking through the walls, no creaking and settling of old wood or ticking of bugs.

Silent as death.

I didn't like it.

The bathroom was big enough Lizard could sleep in it, and there were all manners of tubs, benches, nozzles, showerheads, and spigots set among the marble and silver and glass. It smelled of sweet soap and lime blossoms.

I shut the door behind me, then bent, unlaced my boots, set them off to one side, and shucked out of my clothes.

I turned on the water to let it warm up the marble shower. I opened my duffel and pulled out my pajamas, pushing the scarf Grandma had given me to one side.

Speaking of time machine. She had said the little sheep attracted time and stored it in their wool. I glanced around the room. I didn't see any cameras, although there was probably some kind of recording device here.

This seemed like a good chance to give Grandma's theory a whirl, here alone, where I wouldn't feel stupid when it didn't work. I gathered the scarf up onto the bench where I was sitting, found the knot at the end of it, and took a second or two to loosen it with my fingernails.

The clock on the wall was an old-fashioned model, ticking away with a second hand. I kept my eye on the second hand, and tugged on the yarn, pulling a stitch.

Nothing.

Well, that was disappointing.

Just for kicks, I ripped out an entire row of stitches.

The second hand stopped.

I was still breathing; my heart was beating.

But the hand on the clock paused and the shower stilled, every drop of water frozen. I counted three seconds.

Then the clock ticked, and the water fell in a rush so loud and sudden, I jumped.

Holy handbasket. I stared at the scarf. A small, logical part of my mind insisted I had imagined it. Maybe I was seeing only what I wanted to see.

So I tried it again, this time pulling out row after row. The clock stopped, the shower stopped, and while everything around me had seemed still and quiet before, there was an underwater weight to the stillness now.

I stood with the scarf in my hand and touched the spray of water. The droplets pushed away from my fingers but did not fall. I could move, I could pick up something and put it down, but the world was frozen in place.

And then time started up again, water rushing, clock ticking, the stillness just stillness.

Prickly heat rolled over my skin. That was all kinds of unnerving. It made me itchy.

I tucked the scarf carefully back into the duffel and brushed my palms together like there was dirt there.

Okay. I could stop time.

Maybe. If it worked again the next time I pulled on the yarn. And there was no reason to think it wouldn't. Except that stopping time was impossible.

It wasn't a time machine—the hands on the clock hadn't rolled backward. But that scarf did seem to be a pause button of sorts.

Grandma had been right. The sheep somehow caught up bits of time in their wool.

I wondered if my dad had intended for that to happen, or if tinkering with sheep DNA, plus the wild nanos mutating in the soil, had had unintended consequence on the little critters.

And how had Grandma discovered it?

Well, it didn't matter. Having a little time in my pocket might come in very handy.

I stepped into the shower and let the strong, hot spray of water tumble over me to wash away the dirt, sweat and worries of the day.

16

No one imagined the fall would happen so quickly. The world balanced on a fragile tipping point for years. Then, suddenly, everything collapsed. Food supply, water supply, economic and political engines, loyalties and borders. And from the ashes of that fall, the Houses rose. —2090
—from the journal of L.U.C.

I woke with a start and sat up, pushing my back to the wall before remembering I wasn't home. I was at House Gray in the cavernous, pitch-black bedroom.

Something had pulled me out of sleep. A sound. I didn't sense another person in the room, didn't hear breathing or movement. Then a soft electronic chime at the bottom of the bed rang out three quick beeps.

"Bo," I said as I fumbled at the table next to the bed, hoping to hit a light. Finally touched something that set off a yellow glow around the ceiling.

I bent over my legs and dragged my duffel from the foot of the bed across the acre of quilt toward me.

I dug out the old walkie-talkie and pressed the receiver, hoping the signal would hold.

"Tilly?" Bo's voice crackled over the line.

"I'm here. Is there something wrong? Is Grandma all right?"

"She's fine and everything's fine," Bo said. "I wanted to make sure you're doing all right. You seemed in a rush when you left. It's a lot of trouble with a House, isn't it?"

"Yes. But it's not more than I can handle."

"Which House is it, baby sweet?"

That was a strange question. "I thought you said the less you knew, the better it would be."

"I changed my mind. If something happens to you and you need help, someone should know where you were last at."

"If something goes wrong, you could be held on charges of aiding and abetting, and a long list of other crimes. You know that, Bo. This isn't a smart move. This isn't like you at all."

"Fine," she snapped. "Blame a woman for caring."

I rubbed my eyes. "I don't blame you. I just think it's better if you don't know . . . any of what I'm tangled up in right now."

"But you'll call? Soon?"

I had never heard her sound so needy.

"What's really wrong, Bo?"

"Nothing, nothing," she said in a rush. "I'm just worried, is all. You call me if you need anything. Anything at all."

"I will," I said. "Thanks. Give Grandma a hug for me."

"Will do."

The line went silent and I stared at the walkie-talkie before putting it back in the duffel. I didn't know what Bo's problem was. She'd been a nice enough neighbor, but had always been more than happy to keep her distance from anyone else and the problems they might be involved in.

Why did she want to know which House I was dealing with?

A soft knock on the door got me out of bed. I smoothed back my hair as I left the bedroom. I crossed the spacious living area, then opened the main door. Neds stood there, wearing his overalls, jacket, boots, and bad attitude.

"So, did you make a deal with these devils?" Right Ned asked quietly.

"I haven't done anything yet. But I don't see how I can get out of it. Oscar said he'd help find my brother and keep Grandma and the land safe."

"And what are you giving him in trade?"

"He wants me to sign a ten-year contract with House Gray. Before you argue about it, I have people to look after. There's no one but me standing between this world and the one I belong in."

Left Ned sniffed. "We weren't arguing."

"You're doing fine," Right Ned said softly. "Making hard choices on your feet." He nodded. "Just wish you'd asked us for input. We like . . ." He stopped, tucked his hands into his pockets, and looked over at a blank spot on the wall. Then: "You know we want what's best for you and your grandma and the farm. It's been a home to us too. And it's not like we've never had to deal with a House. We understand the experience."

"Would have liked it if you spoke up earlier," I said.

"We did," Right Ned said. "But the second Abraham walked over your doorstep, you were done hearing us."

"That's not true. I'm listening right now."

"A lot of people are listening right now," Right Ned said quietly. "How about we go get a coffee?"

"Where?"

"Out," Right Ned said. "Let me take you out for a cup. So we can talk."

He seemed sincere and Left Ned seem annoyed, so basically they were acting normal.

I wondered if I should check in with someone—tell Abraham we were leaving, or let Oscar know he could find me down the street.

No. I'd spent too much of my life making decisions on my own to stop and get a committee vote for coffee.

"I'll meet you by the elevator. I have to get dressed and grab my coat."

I did just that, and slung my duffel over my shoulder.

The rifle would have to remain behind, but I hesitated over the handgun. I dropped it into my duffel.

I could hold my own in a fight, but sometimes the presence of a gun went a long way in making sure that fight never happened.

I shrugged into my coat as I strode down the hall, a little surprised no one had stopped us yet. The big windows in the main room showed the darkness of night hadn't cleared yet. It was very early morning and the sun wouldn't rise for about an hour.

Here and there across the city, little winks of light glittered in strings, streets and buildings cupping the glow.

Neds waited for me by the elevator door.

"We can just go out the way we came in?" I whispered.

"Unless you're under House arrest. Are you under House arrest?" Right Ned asked.

"I don't think so."

"Then we can go," Left Ned said.

Right Ned held his hand out to the open elevator door while I walked in. He waved at whatever camera was watching us from the room, got in the elevator, and pushed the button for ground level.

"I'd understand if you want nothing to do with this trouble," I said.

He stared up at the line of buttons as they lit, one by one. "You don't think I took the job on the farm because I thought it was boring, did you?"

"Not a lot of excitement in planting and cleaning up after critters," I said.

"A dragon, a unicorn, pocket sheep, those things in the pond . . ."

"The leapers."

". . . the leapers, and the flock of cockatrice out back. Unusual. When I first saw the place, it crossed my mind it might be a little trouble."

"Like me."

"Like you." Right Ned shrugged. "I know I can walk

out. We both know. And you don't see us leaving, do you?"

"No," I said, "I don't suppose I do."

The elevator let out a sweet little bell sound and the doors opened wide.

Neds stepped out, and I was right on his heels. I'd expected some kind of shine and neon out here, but it appeared we were in an older neighborhood, or one that had been restyled to appear older.

That slight claustrophobia of buildings stacked too close to one another and looming over me was bumped up a notch by the crisscross of wires that created a net just a few feet over our heads. Above that, several elevated tube lines arced off between the buildings, and a zigzag of stairs and multilevel sidewalks were broken up by narrow doors and small, dusty windows.

Just because there wasn't a lot of neon didn't mean things weren't glowing. Windows, doorways, the edges of the sidewalks sent off yellow-and-amber light.

More than enough light to reveal the crowds of people moving over the street. Some strolled, others jogged and wove through the knot of bodies, each wearing a main House color on his or her torso, some embellishing clothing with stripes or designs in other colors.

But the thing I hadn't noticed from my brief view of the city in the car was how many people were wearing bright-colored thread worked like stitches around their wrists, or, for some, across their faces.

"Are all those people stitched?" I asked.

Left Ned snorted.

"No," Right Ned said. "It's a fashion. A sort of removable tattoo."

"Stitches?"

"People like the galvanized." He started down the sidewalk. "See them as heroes, as stars. Wear their colors, follow their fashion decisions, put on fake stitches. That sort of thing."

I turned around to get my bearings. The elevator door

behind us looked like every other narrow closed door around us, except that the the dust-colored stone above it was carved with the word GRAY.

Good enough. I was pretty sure I could find that if I needed to.

"This way, tourist," Left Ned said.

"Have you been here before?" I jogged a little to catch his stride.

"A couple times."

"Wow."

"Not that impressive. You see one city, you see them all."

"Not you. That." I pointed at the image of Abraham and another man—a galvanized—both wearing breeches and no shirts and glaring at each other like they were about to throw punches. Abraham's dark gray stitches looked like barbed wire dug into his skin and muscles. The other man's skin was darker than mine, and the thick red stitches that crossed his body looked like they were made out of fire.

"What's so 'wow'?" Right Ned asked.

"To start with, they're the size of a building. Also"—I nodded—"half-naked, so that's not bad."

He shook his head. "It's an advertisement for their showdown at the gathering. These things are all over the place."

He waved, and I glanced around, looking for more half-naked pictures. "Oh?"

He was right. Lots of pictures of Abraham and the other galvanized who, according to the fliers, screens, and slides, was Loy Ninth of House Red. But they were not the only galvanized on display. A wide variety of women and men, in modern clothing or historical looks, and all with stitches clearly enhanced, filled the advertisements, shop windows, and more.

It was weird to think the galvanized were celebrities when, in actuality, they were little more than property and a show of power for the House that owned them.

"Coffee?" Right Ned was saying. "Just follow that little cup symbol. See there?" He pointed at a small red cup painted on corners of buildings, sides of stairs, or the sidewalk itself. "That will take you to food if you're not plugged in. If you're plugged in . . ." He shrugged.

"What happens if you're plugged in?" I asked.

"Then the city's riding in your noggin and it will tell you anything you want to know."

"Bothersome," I noted. "Are you plugged?"

"Nope. Doesn't work as well on me."

Probably because of the way he was made up. I studied the other people on the street. Tall, short, all shades of colors found in nature, and plenty of colors not found in nature, most everyone seemed to be of a standard makeup: one head, two arms, two legs.

A few folk were wrapped in wires or things that flashed and glittered in ways that reminded me of lightning and stars, neon flashes here and there in the fold of clothing, and, of course, the stitches.

Other folk were stretched out thin one way or another, or bulked up unexpectedly in the shoulder, hip, or torso, tampered with to fulfill fads and fashions.

Some of those differences were just natural; others were obviously engineered. I noted that the best-dressed people most closely adhered to the human norm, except it was an exaggerated norm—so youthful and perfectly slick, they looked like they were plastic: too perfect to breathe.

Quite a few gazes turned toward Neds, and from the scowls and occasional curse, they disapproved of his presence.

Yes, it bothered me. Wasn't nothing wrong with those boys.

If I didn't have my hands in my coat pocket and my hair down, they'd realize I was the odd one here, the unnatural, the monster.

Or would they see me as a celebrity too?

"How far?" I asked, staring up at a slow-moving

screen that blocked out the sky and flashed the invigorating qualities of something that was making a woman shed her clothing.

"Just— Move, Tilly!" Right Ned, or, heck, maybe Left Ned grabbed my arm and dragged me up against the nearest building.

I, belatedly, noticed that everyone else on the street had pressed to one side and were standing still.

"What?" I whispered.

"Don't talk, don't ask questions, and don't draw attention," Left Ned said.

I tipped my head down like everyone else, and snuck a look up the street. I expected some sort of police force or parade to be cruising down the narrow road.

What I was not expecting was a very large, very tall, very rough-featured man walking down the sidewalk with a slimmer, shorter man next to him.

The big guy must clock in at seven feet tall. His skin was bloodless white, his hair white, his eyes red. A tight white beard scruffed his blocky jaw, and, even from this distance, I could see thick yellow stitches cutting across his forehead, temple, cheek, jaw, and neck.

He wore an undertaker's coat: long, black, and silent as a wing. The inside of that coat was a searing yellow, glimpsed in quick flashes with each long stride he took.

Galvanized.

The crowed murmured in excitement. A flash of lights began, photos snapping away, but the galvanized did not slow.

The man next to him looked about thirty and was eating popcorn out of a bag. His hair was dark brown, parted down the middle, and cut ragged over his eyebrows and ears. His skin was closer to beige than his companion's, but he didn't look like he'd spent any time in the sun. He wore a long-sleeved dark yellow shirt with a flying frog painted across the front of it, a heavy metal flask on a chain around his neck, and jeans and running shoes with mismatched laces.

"Who's that?" I whispered to Neds.

"Foster First and Welton Yellow," Left Ned whispered back.

The head of House Yellow, Technology, and his galvanized.

As they passed, some people went back to walking, jogging, getting to where they were going. But even more remained, although they held back as if there was a bubble, a space around the two men that no one seemed willing to encroach upon.

I kept my head down, not wanting to draw attention.

I heard the big guy's boots against concrete and wondered if they'd iron shod his shoes from the noise of it. Either that, or he was incredibly heavy.

Thunk, thunk, thunk.

Then . . . nothing.

I glanced up. Into the limpid, heavy-lidded brown eyes of the man in the yellow frog shirt.

"And hello, Miss Case," Welton Yellow said. "Popcorn?"

17

The history books called the dark years the Restructure. But those who lived through it knew death, famine, war, and disease. The Houses claimed ownership of the twelve stitched soldiers, and used them to destroy anyone who stood against their rule. That was the world's second mistake. —2095
—from the journal of L.U.C.

I had no idea what to do.

So I made sure my wrist stitches didn't show under my coat cuff and took a small handful of popcorn. Salty. Crisp. "Thank you."

More pictures flashed while Welton plucked up a couple kernels, popped them in his mouth, and chewed, watching me the entire time.

The people around us were starting to squirm. I knew the feeling.

He turned his attention to Neds.

"How about you? Popcorn?" He held out the bag, shook it a little.

"No, thank you, sir," Left Ned said.

"Nice night for a walk, isn't it?" the head of House Yellow said. "Or morning, I suppose."

"Yes, sir, it is," Right Ned said.

"The two of you are going to make it a short, quiet

walk, don't you think?" The man crunched through another handful of popcorn, then smiled. He looked like a cat that had just tipped over a bird's nest.

"Yes, sir," Left Ned said.

"Good. Enjoy yourself." He took a few steps, the hulking undertaker next to him moving right along with him as if caught in his gravitational pull. Then Welton Yellow paused and glanced back at us. "Coffee's not bad at the Jangle, I'm to understand."

"Thank you, sir," Right Ned said again.

The crowd moved in closer to Foster First, who—much to my surprise—posed for a few pictures with people before Welton indicated they should leave. A hole opened in the crowd for their passing like water flowing around a bubble of air.

"Son of a whore," Left Ned exhaled.

"What? What did that mean?"

"Walk. I don't like the attention we're getting," Right Ned said.

I took in the mood of the people around us. A lot of scowls, a few rude gestures.

"Get out of the way, shortlife," a man said as he shoved past us.

In the past, people who were born nonstandard, like Neds, didn't live as long as a more standard configured human. That changed as more and more people were born nonstandard and medical science advanced to deal with the mutations. But the derogatory *shortlife* had stuck.

I hated it.

I expected Neds to take offense with both fists, but he just tugged me back into the stream of pedestrians, up a flight of stairs with metal railing on either side, then switched back onto the second-level sidewalk to another flight of stairs.

"Why was the head of a House on the street before sunrise, eating popcorn?" I asked. "Come on. Doesn't he have better things to do with his time?"

"Yes," Right Ned said, "I'm sure he does. And I don't like that walking this street when you and I just happen to be out for coffee is what he decided to do."

"He couldn't have known we were going to be here," I said. "We didn't know we were going to be here until a couple minutes ago."

"He is technology," Right Ned said. "He knows everything."

If House Gray had cameras pointed at a hundred different locations—probably a hundred times more than what I'd seen, then the House that controlled technology must have a camera and every other kind of recording or sensing device connected to everything throughout the entire world.

"Okay. So he saw us leave the elevator, heard us talking about coffee, and came out to see us for himself. Why?"

"One guess," Left Ned said.

"Me?" I said.

He nodded. "You're still uncontracted. That means you can be claimed. With and without your consent."

"He could have claimed me?"

Both Neds nodded.

"Hell. Should we go back?" I asked.

"No. He told us where he expected us to be: at the Jangle. And that we should make it short," Right Ned said. "I say we do just that, so as not to kick up any more attention."

"Is he friends with House Gray?"

Left Ned shook his head slightly, and Right Ned answered, "Hard to keep up. And with the gathering in just a few days, loyalties are bound to shift. But I think he and Gray are on speaking terms."

"Might be Gray noticed us missing, called in a favor, and asked him to put eyes on you," Left Ned said.

A woman wasn't watching where she was going, and ran into me.

"Careful, now," I said, reaching out for her arms while she clutched at my coat to keep from falling.

"Watch it," Neds said.

"Sorry, sorry," she mumbled. She pushed past me, but not before slipping a piece of paper in my palm.

I glanced down at the paper, then back at her. She was hurrying away from me, but extended two fingers and tapped them twice to her ear.

Two fingers, two taps: House Brown.

"Keep walking," I said.

We blended back into the press of people, and I turned over the paper.

Fesslers safe and accounted for. Pocket of Rubies.

I grinned and stuffed the note into my coat.

"What was that about?" Neds asked, not looking at me.

"Brown."

"News?"

"Fesslers made it."

"Good," Right Ned said. "That's one thing going our way. Café's up here."

The red burn of neon twisted into the word JANGLE cut through the darkness. It was about a block ahead.

"You have any idea why the head of a House would come to look for me and not just send an employee?" I asked.

"Welton's never played by the rules," Left Ned said. "He's too young—real years—to be a head of a House, but he's an off-the-charts genius. Him talking to us was a statement of his intent. Don't think other Houses didn't see what he did. Tracked you down in seconds, and stood right in front of you. Could have taken you if he wanted with that mountainous clunk, Foster First, at his side. But he didn't."

"And?" I asked.

"And," Right Ned said, "that means he honors House Gray's claim to you and your choice in the matter. Yellow is backing Gray's right to protect you and your property."

"Foster First," I said.

"Number is the order in which they were brought back to life. Foster was the first."

"Right," I said, remembering that tidbit of history. "And Abraham was the seventh. Robert with House Orange was the twelfth—the last."

"Except for you," Left Ned said.

"Unlucky thirteen." I grimaced. "I think I'll stick to Case. Do you think the numbers act as a ranking, giving one galvanized seniority over the other, or power over the other?"

Neds shrugged. "I don't keep company with their kind," Left Ned said.

"Except for me," I said.

And here, Right Ned smiled while Left Ned rolled his eyes.

"Except for you." Right Ned opened the door to the café.

It was crowded here too, booths along one wall filled with people, the row of small square tables down the middle of the place nearly hidden by the people standing around them, and the curved bar elbow to elbow with even more customers.

The architecture of the place was at least a century old, maybe two, lots of chrome and bright red and black and white in the place. Music played from the speakers visible in the corners of the curved ceiling, and metal-blade fans that looked like old airplane props rotated lazily down the length of the room.

It smelled of coffee and salt and chocolate. My stomach rumbled.

"Here." Neds tugged me toward the only open spot: a table to the side and behind an ancient jukebox filled with disks and brightly lit buttons with words stamped into them.

We sat on either side of the tiny table, and Neds pressed three buttons in the tabletop, ordering our drinks.

"I don't think we have much privacy here," Right Ned said, "but there's no place private in a city when the Houses have you targeted. I think you should go home, Tilly. Back to the farm. I think we should all go back.

Leave the city before the rest of the Houses get too curious about you and yours."

"I think it's too late for that," I said. "Someone has my brother, probably captive. I can't walk away from that, from him."

"You can't walk *toward* him either. We don't even know where he is."

"Someone knows," I said. "And I plan to find out."

A short woman with curly black hair and a terrific smile pushed through the crowd like a hot knife through butter, stopping at our table.

"Three coffees, black with everything on the side." She slid a tray onto the table. Three small cups filled with rich, steaming coffee sat on the tray, with an assortment of powders, creams, and little cubes arranged around them. "Anything else?"

"That's all. Thanks." Neds pulled a credit chit from his pocket.

Some people still used paper money and metal coin, since it was the safest from embezzlement, but most found it easier to just keep all the comings and goings of expenses linked up to the chit.

She took the chit, scanned it with a small device she wore on the inside of her wrist, gave us a smile, and was off.

"I need to tell you something," Right Ned said. "About Robert Twelfth."

"All right." I dropped four sugar cubes in my coffee and stirred.

"When I shook his hand, I . . ." Right Ned looked away.

"The vision thing?"

"He was a boy, unstitched, maybe fourteen. Climbed down a well and was trying to climb back up. Cold from falling down too many times. His father's gun that he shouldn't have been playing with, shouldn't have let fall in the well, was tucked in his belt.

"He yelled at the sky, but there was a bell ringing out so loud no one could hear him."

Left Ned picked up one of the cups and took a drink. He preferred it black.

Right Ned added in a dollop of cream and didn't look at me as he stirred it. "It isn't like the images we see from other people," he said quietly enough, I might have thought he was talking to his other half. "There was a desperation in it. A drive to survive, to live. No matter the cost."

"Abraham's was the same," Left Ned said. "Survive. No matter the cost."

"It's strange," they said together.

And that, hearing them both come to the same conclusion at the same time, was so unusual it gave me chills.

"What kind of strange?" I asked.

"There's something too similar about their memories."

"Well, not a lot of people are more than three hundred years old. Think it's that?"

"No." They both drank coffee, then Right Ned sighed. "It's almost as if both memories happened on the same day. Maybe at the same time. That bell Robert Twelfth heard ringing out . . . I think I heard it in Abraham's memory too."

"It's unnatural," Left Ned said.

"Did you hear bells when you first touched me?"

"Yes," they said.

"The same damn bell," Left Ned finished.

I didn't know what to say about old memories and visions. The body my brother had implanted my thoughts, personality, and awareness into had a healthy, viable brain that had lingered so long in a vegetative state, the personality had been wiped clean. All my memories were my own, and I'd never heard voices or felt the presence of anyone else in the body with me. Still, it was pretty clear the body I was stitched into wasn't just some random forgotten experiment.

Abraham had said galvanized brains, if uninjured, were immortal and would continue living even if separated from the galvanized body. He had said their thoughts and personality remained. So what could have happened to this girl to send her into a coma she never woke up from?

That question was disturbing, but I wasn't as spooked about it as my farmhand seemed to be.

"If you settle on what it is that bothers you about the visions, I want to know," I said. "But until then, do you have any contacts that might help us find my brother?"

"I know some people," Right Ned started. "People who could make you disappear if you wanted." He said it very quietly, cautiously. As if it were something he should not be sharing.

"I can't. Not yet, anyway. Maybe when I get my brother free, and my land clear, and Grandma safe . . ."

"It would need to be now, Tilly," he said. "Right now. We leave from here and are never seen again. You should say yes."

They were both wearing the same expression—a mix of dead seriousness and maybe just an edge of fear. They knew something they weren't saying. Probably knew a lot of things they weren't saying.

"Tell me everything you know. I can't make a decision that would leave Grandma and my brother stranded without something solid to go on."

The door to the diner opened.

Three men in black jackets, black hats, and dark glasses walked in, scanned the shop, and moved to either side of the door, guarding it.

Left Ned glanced that way. "Too late, I think."

Right Ned was still looking at me. "They work for House Black. And they're looking for you."

House Black. The House that had killed my parents. Maybe even the House that still held my brother.

"I got this," I said, just before swallowing down the last of my coffee. "I've wanted to settle something with House Black for a long time."

I made my way through the crowd toward them. Neds

cussed, and then I heard them move away from the table and head after me.

None of the three appeared to be the head of House Black nor a galvanized, although that was just a guess. Two of the three men stood stock-still, staring forward, and one turned his head to watch my approach.

So I guessed he was the boss here.

I walked right up to him, stood out of arm's reach, which wasn't all that easy with the jostle and bump of people around us, trying to get in and out the door he stood next to.

"Are you here to see me?" I asked.

He tipped his head just a fraction, but I couldn't see his eyes behind those dark glasses. I could, however, tell that those glasses were recording everything I said.

"Matilda Case?" he asked in a flat tone.

"You can go back and tell the head of your House that he owes me a blood debt," I said.

"Come with us." He grabbed my wrist.

I stepped to one side, twisted my palm open and down. Punched his arm hard enough to break it. He growled, dropped my wrist, and took a step back.

I can hold my own in a fight. When a girl sees her parents dragged away, she throws herself into self-defense training for pretty much the rest of her life. Plus, I'd had to wrestle Lizard down more than once, and hunting feral creatures before breakfast was sort of a daily ritual.

But this wasn't a feral creature in front of me. This was a man.

I pulled my gun, finger curled against the trigger, before he had a chance to grab for me a second time.

"Don't try it," I said. "I don't know you well enough to want you dead, but I am not afraid of sending you to the hospital to rethink your line of work."

If those glasses of his were any good, he already knew I had a gun. Just in case, I lifted it enough he saw it for sure.

So did his two buddies, who had taken a step toward us, and paused.

"Step back and step out of here. Tell your boss he has a debt to settle with me." I thumbed back the hammer on the gun, which was old enough to make a very satisfying *clack*ing sound.

The two goons shifted their weight just slightly, suddenly more in the mood for a fight. I supposed they could pull the city down around my ears if they wanted to.

Too bad I didn't care.

The boss man's mouth twitched. He had a broken arm and hadn't more than grunted about it. I was glad I had the gun.

"I don't follow your orders, girl," he snarled. "You will come with us. Now."

The door behind him opened wide. A rush of chilly air whisked through the steamy café and cooled the sweat covering my skin.

"Gentlemen," Abraham said, his low voice both carrying over and silencing the crowd, "you now have the full attention of House Gray."

18

*It may have been the horror of so many inno-
cent deaths. It may have been the human spark
that still burned in the twelve that brought
them together in secret. —2098*
—from the journals of L.U.C.

The men from House Black glanced at Abraham, and
their anger was palatable.

"Fucking stitch," the man who had grabbed for me
muttered so quietly, I almost didn't hear it even though
everyone in the place was silent.

Abraham heard it. His eyes tightened and his fist
snapped out, faster than I could track, slamming into the
man's shoulder. The audible *crack* of a bone shattering
filled the room, accompanied by the man's scream.

Even the silence got silent.

Abraham pushed his forearm under the wounded man's
neck and lifted until the guy was on his toes, struggling
to breathe. In Abraham's other hand was a huge knife,
which he flicked, taking off the man's left ear.

I supposed the guy might have been yelling if he had
air to yell with.

"You will show me proper respect, citizen, and you
will extend that respect to this woman." Abraham sounded
like he was giving a polite lecture on manners while the

man gasped and bled. "She is under House Gray protection."

My stomach knotted.

Abraham was destruction held down by a thin pin. If the men from House Black wanted a fight, someone was going to be dead by the end of it.

It wouldn't be Abraham.

"I am here to see that her well-being is intact," he continued. "Have you damaged her, citizen Black?"

"That was not my intent," he gasped.

"Understood. Now take your House Black business elsewhere before we have any other misunderstandings." Abraham leaned back and lowered the man to his feet. The men from House Black all shifted as if they expected him to throw another punch.

Instead, Abraham opened the door, walked through it, and held it open. Two of the men stepped up and supported the injured guy as they made their way through the door and past Abraham.

Everyone in and just outside the café had decided they didn't need to use the door. Though I didn't think it possible, the crowd inside had pulled back a bit to give all of us a little breathing room.

"You are insane," Right Ned said quietly after the men were well on their way down the street. "No one picks a fight with Defense in a coffee shop."

"Yeah, well," I said, releasing the hammer on the gun and tucking it away in my duffel again. "They picked a fight with me when they killed my parents."

I turned and Neds, both of them, were grinning.

"What?" I asked.

"You," Right Ned said. "Rebel. Always have been."

"Don't forget it," I said.

"Like I could," Right Ned said with a grin.

I stepped outside. Pulled up short.

Abraham was blocking my way, scowling.

"Are you done?" he asked.

The crowd around us moved slower than before, a few people taking pictures of us.

Well, of Abraham.

Dressed in a light gray shirt and dark gray pants tucked into heavy boots, he made for a striking figure. Powerful, dangerous. Someone who stood out in a crowd without trying. He wore his sleeves rolled up so the stitching on his arms and wrists clearly showed, and his collar was unbuttoned just enough that the line that began under the edge of his stubbled jaw could be seen.

He was making it very clear to anyone watching exactly who and what he was: galvanized.

I was staring and didn't care. It was hard to look away from the truth of him. He carried his scars, his pain, and the weight of hard years with a strength that radiated outward. It was primal, sensual, raw. And barely controlled. I couldn't seem to look away. I didn't want to look away.

Something about him caught a fire in me. I licked my bottom lip as heat stretched and filled my body and thoughts. Then my imagination took over and stripped him out of his clothes, just like when he'd been wounded back on the farm. Except in my little fantasy, I was naked and he wasn't bleeding. He was shirtless and pantless, and I was the one lying on the bed as he lowered himself down . . .

One of the Neds kicked my boot with his foot.

"I had clothes on," I blurted.

Abraham's eyebrow twitched up.

"Mental," Left Ned muttered.

"Say yes." Right Ned said through clenched teeth.

Right.

I was standing on a sidewalk, lots of people watching. And recording. I should probably say something.

"All right," I said, even though I couldn't remember what Abraham had asked me. "Sure. Yes. Thank you." That should cover all the bases.

Abraham's stony expression did not change. "Come with me."

I fell into step just behind Abraham, blushing so hard,

my ears hurt. The crowd ahead and beside us cleared out just like when Welton Yellow and his galvanized, Foster, had walked the street.

No one asked us to pose for pictures. Probably because Abraham had just cut off someone's ear.

The Neds next to me seemed uncomfortable with all the attention.

Abraham kept a brisk enough pace that it didn't take long before we were down the stairs across the sidewalk and at the elevator door. Abraham opened the door with a key, waited for us to enter, and then stepped in behind us. The door shut silently.

"Never," he said, staring over the top of my head at the wall behind me, his eyes burning red, "do that again."

"Go for coffee?" I asked.

His eyes ticked down to meet my gaze. Smoldered. "Leave without telling us. Without telling me."

I pressed my shoulders against the wall behind me and met that anger with a steady stare. "It was just coffee."

"No, it was not just coffee. You drew the attention of two Houses, who intercepted you, and four more who didn't. In less than half an hour. Next time you want to go somewhere . . . Tell. Me."

"So you can follow me?"

"So I, and House Gray, can run interference before you break someone else's arm or start another in-House war," he snarled.

Right. That.

"He got grabby, I pushed him. *You* destroyed his shoulder."

"And cut off his ear," Right Ned added.

"You." Abraham's voice rose. "Claimed a blood debt with House Black."

I shoved my shoulders off the wall and stood up in front of him, toe-to-toe, my hands on my hips.

"They killed my parents. Walked into my house, murdered them, and dragged away the bodies. They owe me more than a debt."

So much for cooling down. Anger radiated from every inch of him.

"House Gray can't fight every wrong that's happened in your life," he said. "First House Red; now House Black. Who else are you going to turn against us?"

"Us? I'm sorry," I almost shouted, "but you seem to think that I've signed a contract and claimed House Gray. You seem to think that I *want* to be owned. I don't need a House to fight my battles, Mr. Vail. And I don't need you to do so either. Have I made myself clear?"

He narrowed his eyes, nostrils flaring. I thought for sure he'd explode. But when he spoke it was barely above a whisper.

"I am very, very clear about you, Matilda Case. And how foolish you are being."

The elevator stopped and the door opened with a cheerful *ping*.

I was locked in a glaring contest. There was no chance in Hades I'd be the one who looked away first.

Luckily, someone else broke the tension.

"Abraham," Oscar Gray said. "So good of you to return. We have a guest."

Abraham's eyes flicked up over my shoulder, and his mouth set in a hard line.

I couldn't help it. I turned and looked.

Oscar stood with his back to the wide expanse of windows.

Next to him stood a man dressed all in black. Black shirt, black slacks, black belt, and shiny shoes.

From the way he held himself with equal poise next to Oscar, and the fact that there was a stern, black-stitched man standing behind him, I knew who he must be: John Black, the head of House Black.

19

HOUSE ORANGE

He preferred to be obeyed. The arrogance of the galvanized, Robert Twelfth, had always been a fault in the creature.

Perhaps it was because Robert was the last galvanized stitched together and shocked alive. It had the fortune of receiving the most advanced technological and medical support. Perhaps it even thought of itself as human.

Slater Orange had owned several of the galvanized over the years. Robert Twelfth had been the least willing to obey him.

It was distasteful. Something he had punished it for repeatedly.

Still, the creature had been useful to him and his House in many ways over the years. And now it would be extremely useful to him one last time.

Robert Twelfth stepped into the small, tastefully appointed chamber. It paused just inside the door, hands at its side, eyes cast downward, as was appropriate. "You called for me, Excellency?"

Slater sat behind a desk and regarded the creature for a moment. Robert Twelfth was not his choice in bodies. Too small, bald, and sharp edged.

But it was a strong body. And it was immortal.

That last quality that made it the most desirable of all.

"How many years are left in your contract with House Orange, Robert Twelfth?"

"Thirty-one years, seven months, and two days, Excellency," it said without hesitation.

"Are you aware there is a clause in the contract that will allow me, at my discretion, to release you from your contract with House Orange at an earlier time if I so choose?"

"Yes, Excellency," it said.

"I have decided to amend that clause. To redefine your role in House Orange."

Robert Twelfth didn't say anything, but Slater could see that its breathing changed. Not speeding up from fear; it was suddenly slow and even, as if Robert Twelfth was readying for torture or a fight.

A wasted effort. This would be a battle it couldn't win.

"Are you not curious as to your new post within the House, Robert Twelfth?" he asked.

"I am here to serve," it answered woodenly.

"Yes," Slater said, "you are. Good, then. Come with me, please." He stood out of the chair, hiding how much effort it took to do so.

The doctors had said the virus had accelerated. It would kill him within weeks, even with the hourly doses of medicine he took. Without the hourly doses, the virus would kill him within days.

Slater had stopped taking the medicine three hours ago. From how quickly his strength had deteriorated, he believed his doctors were correct in their prognosis.

"Attend me," he said as he walked through the door at the back of the room.

The galvanized followed him.

They proceeded down a long, clean hallway to the room at the end. A room he had not allowed Robert Twelfth to enter before.

Slater triggered the door to open just long enough for them to both step through before it closed and locked behind them.

No computerized equipment or beeping machines cluttered the room, though such equipment could be at hand in seconds. Instead the room was filled with strange devices made of copper, wire, bolt, and leather.

It looked like a madman's laboratory.

Or a torture chamber.

These were the things taken from Dr. Case's home. These were the designs meticulously sketched in his research.

These were the things that Quinten had used to make a girl immortal, and these things would now make him immortal.

Two clean tables with restraining straps draped off the sides, lay waiting in the center of the room. An array of lights and a spread of medical equipment that was a collision of low and high technology spread out across clean trays.

"Today you will be undergoing modifications," Slater said, holding his gloved hand out toward one of the tables.

Robert Twelfth hesitated.

"You will serve House Orange without question or pause," Slater said. "I assure you no permanent harm will come to you, as is law by contract and seal."

The galvanized made eye contact this time, hatred hooded there.

Slater met its gaze, waiting. His was the only power in this room.

Finally, the creature walked over to the table and lay down upon it. "What is it you want of me?"

"I want you to relax, Robert Twelfth. And when you wake, your purpose will be clear to you."

Slater knew the galvanized couldn't feel pain. But that didn't mean it couldn't feel fear. The light sheen of sweat that covered its forehead betrayed its seeming calm.

"You may come in now, Mr. Case."

Robert flinched at the name. A curious reaction.

Slater watched the galvanized for any other reaction as Quinten Case entered the room, but he didn't flinch, didn't blink.

Quinten wore clean clothes but not sterile scrubs. He had insisted that the kind of operation he was going to perform wouldn't spill blood.

Slater did not believe him, of course. But to ensure that the procedure went according to his wishes, he had arranged for a small motivational offering to be on display.

Quinten Case walked over to the table and secured the galvanized's wrists, feet, and torso with straps even a monster like it could not break.

The galvanized and the man made eye contact, but they did not speak to each other. They both understood the price they would pay for stepping out of line.

"The injection," Slater ordered.

Quinten Case selected a syringe from the table and inserted the tip of it into the galvanized's neck. "I'm sorry," he whispered. He thumbed down the plunger.

Robert Twelfth's eyes rolled up in his head and he went limp. Unconscious.

"Now, Mr. Case," Slater began. "You will note that your sister is still within my grasp."

The wall behind Slater faded to display a screen.

Slater enjoyed watching the man struggle to close down his reactions to what he saw there.

His sister, Matilda Case, was standing in a room with the heads of House Gray and House Black, a mutant, and two galvanized. The screen showed the scene from three angles, as the scopes of guns followed the slightest shift of her every move.

"When you are done," Slater said softly, "when you are successful in transferring my mind into the galvanized body, I will give those gunmen the code to stand down. It is a word only they and I know. If you try to kill me, your sister will die. If you try to stop me, your sister will die. If you are unsuccessful in transferring my mind, memories, and thoughts into that galvanized brain, your sister will die.

"And then you will die. Now begin." Slater drew off

his jacket and placed it neatly on a low table. He then lay on top of the table and clasped his hands across his ribs.

The body would be his, a house immortal. Death would be cheated. And then he would have all the time he needed to take rulership of this House and the others.

A man's voice repeated a message, the words making little sense: *Orange, hidden enemy,* and coordinates. And then the words were gone, and so was his memory of them.

The exhaled hush of mechanical equipment cycling, a soft ticking, and the clink of metal against metal woke Slater Orange. He opened his eyes.

He was lying on an operating table, staring up at the ceiling and lights pocketed there. But he could not feel a thing. Could not feel his body, his face, his own heart beating.

He inhaled. Panic, sharp and sour, coated the back of his throat. What had Quinten Case done to him? Had he paralyzed him? Had the transference failed? Was he dying?

Hot rage surged through him. That, at least, he could feel. If Quinten had failed, then he and his stitched sister would die.

Slater would make them suffer all the way to hell.

"The disorientation should pass soon." Quinten stood to one side of Slater, near enough he could see him. His face was an impassive mask. He held a syringe in one hand and a bone saw in the other.

"The paralysis is temporary. Speech will return first." Quinten's gaze flicked up, as if reading a clock or some other machine across the room. "Now," he said. "I've done what you wanted. You have your new body. Call off your gunmen."

A bone saw. Quinten was a clever man. If Slater didn't speak the word and call his men away from Matilda Case, Quinten would saw off Slater's head.

And the horror of it? Slater would not die. He would

be trapped, bodiless, his thoughts suspended in a brain that never degraded.

In his desire to be discreet about this operation, this crime he was committing, Slater had disabled all recording devices. There were no men standing by to kill the clever Quinten Case.

"She . . ." Slater wheezed. He inhaled, exhaled again. It was strange not to feel anything. But that was the coin paid for immortality.

He had known galvanized couldn't feel, but the reality of occupying a body that had no sensation was far more overwhelming than he had expected.

"She is alive," he said. The dissonance of hearing his words come out in another's voice sent fear crawling over him. Madness scratched at the edge of his mind.

"Call off your snipers," Quinten said again. "And let me speak to her. That will be the only proof I will believe."

Slater ran his tongue across his teeth. Clumsy. Each body part was too thick, disjointed, and miles away from his control.

But he would learn to control this awkward vessel. He would make it his own. And then he would claim the head of House Orange again—the first immortal to seat such power. After that, he would take the world.

"*Gòu,*" Slater commanded through a direct link triggered for just that one word.

Quinten Case glanced at the screen. The tightness at the edge of his eyes relaxed as the gunmen responded to the command by standing down.

"Now," Quinten said, pressing the bone saw against Slater's throat. "You will open a direct line to House Gray so I can speak to my sister."

"That was not our agreement." Speaking was easier now, and even though he couldn't feel his extremities, he had a sense of where they were and how they would respond to him.

"We didn't have an agreement," Quinten snapped.

"Not since the day my employment became imprisonment. Your communication system is locked. Unlock it."

Slater pulled both hands flat to his sides and pushed himself up to sitting. There was power in this body. Strength he had not felt in decades.

Vertigo spun the room, but quickly passed.

Quinten had not pulled the saw through his neck.

Slater smiled. "You cannot kill me. It is not just my communications that are locked. It is my entire estate. But you knew that, didn't you?"

He had endured the pain of his own ruined flesh for decades. Having no sensation was so much better than being in constant pain.

"A brilliant man would have tried to break the codes, would have attempted escape. And you are a brilliant man, Quinten Case."

"What I am," Quinten said, "is a man who refuses to wear anyone's leash. And what you are is a man who put his life in my hands. That was a very foolish decision."

"A calculated risk," Slater said. "I don't fear you, Mr. Case." He stood off the table, one hand still gripping the edge of it for balance. This body was shorter, but much, much stronger than Slater had ever been in his life.

"I am not done with you yet," Slater said. "I know you have been scouring the Houses, looking for information on the Wings of Mercury, that lost experiment from more than two centuries ago. And I know you have found most of it. Most. There is more, a book of drawings and notes that once belonged to your grandmother, Lara Unger Case. The key to time."

Quinten Case tried not to let his surprise show.

"Yes," Slater said. "I know about the experiment. I know that in 1910, a scientist by the name of Case tried to stop time. I know the experiment failed and that it killed everyone within a fifty-mile radius. Except for twelve"—he tipped his head—"thirteen people, who fell into comas. Those thirteen survived the break in time and went on to become the galvanized. Immortal."

"And I know you, Mr. Case, are unnaturally curious about what happened that day. What I do not know is why."

"You will never know why if you don't release me."

"That is not possible," Slater said. "We could both gain by helping each other."

Quinten tightened his grip on the saw. "Only one of us will live long enough to gain anything from that experiment."

"The galvanized do not die."

"Not yet," Quinten said. "But time will collect its due sooner than you think." He tipped the syringe, thumb on the plunger. "Release me. Now."

Slater Orange spoke one word: *"Shandian."*

Electricity cut through the room in lightning strikes. It knocked out Quinten, who crumpled to the floor, twitching, and then lay still.

Fast, brutal, effective, and gone without a trace. It left Slater undamaged. Electricity could not harm galvanized. It was in their lifeblood. It, or some dark form of it, had given the galvanized life and reawakened them from their state of nonliving.

Slater made his way carefully over to the table where his old body lay. He considered it for a moment or two. He was surprised to feel anger at no longer owning it, anger at having been diminished in power even as he had gained physical prowess.

Galvanized were not human. But he refused to be thought of as property.

First, the body of Slater Orange must be transferred to a private, secure room, and left there to die. He had already taken care of the paperwork and contracts that would leave him, now Robert Twelfth, in charge of House Orange.

Slater walked to the door, gaining balance and confidence with each step. He would wash and dress and prepare himself to become the first immortal to rule.

20

When the Houses discovered the undead sol-
diers' secret meetings, they were punished and
tortured for treason and collusion. That was
the last mistake the world made. —2099
                    —from the journals of L.U.C.

That man standing in front of me, the head of House
Black, was the man who had sent people to murder
my parents.

He might be the one who was holding my brother.
Which meant he might be here to release him. Or to try
to take me.

"Matilda Case." Oscar motioned for me to step out of
the elevator, which I did. "May I introduce to you John
Black, head of House Black?"

"It's a pleasure to meet you, Miss Case." John Black
said with an accent that made me think of warmer cli-
mate.

He was taller than Oscar, built like a bulldog, and appeared to be in his early sixties. His brown hair was
dusted with gray, cut short, and receding at the temples.
A mustache curved downward to the edges of his mouth
beneath a nose that looked like it'd been on the wrong
side of a fist more than once.

The lines on his face and the hound-weary set of his
eyes gave him the look of a man who drank his pain.

"Morning," I said.

I glanced at Oscar for a clue. Was House Black here to negotiate my brother's release? Or was this about my morning coffee and bone breaking?

The galvanized man who stood behind John Black frowned at me. The black stitches that speared across his tawny skin through his eyebrow and all the way down his cheek, jaw, and neck, did nothing to distract from his intensity and good looks. His hair and beard were shaved to a shadow, making his angular features and ocean-green eyes pantherlike.

He had on a short-sleeved black T-shirt, which showed the stitching on his muscular arms.

I couldn't tell if he was angry at me or just angry in general.

"Perhaps you could give us a little privacy, Mr. Harris?" Oscar asked.

Neds looked at me.

It was sweet of him to wait to see if I said it was okay. I nodded. No need to get him into any more of my trouble.

"Of course," Right Ned said. "Good day, Excellencies." He strode toward the suites.

"So, this is the new galvanized." John Black strolled toward me, his galvanized walking beside him.

Abraham had also left the elevator and stood a respectful distance to my right, about midpoint between Oscar and me. I wasn't the best at reading body language on a person—give me a wild critter, and I could tell exactly what was going through its brain—but Abraham didn't seem worried about this man or the galvanized with him.

"How old did you say you were?" John Black asked.

"I didn't, sir."

He stopped and the galvanized—Buck, that was his name—flicked a look to Abraham, who gave a slight shrug. Buck went back to frowning at me.

"No," John Black said. "You didn't, did you? So I'm asking you now. How old are you, Matilda Case?"

"Twenty-six, sir."

"Since your reawakening?"

Oscar, who was still standing by the window, answered, "She's twenty-six and apparently wasn't reawakened like the others."

"Are you strong?" John Black asked.

"Would you like me to show you how strong I am?" I offered, maybe with a little too much challenge. Okay, with a lot too much challenge.

Abraham quickly stepped forward. "If I may, Your Excellencies?"

He never spoke that formally around Oscar, but apparently when there was another House in the room, he pulled out all his manners.

"Continue, Abraham," Oscar said.

"I would be happy to test Matilda's strength, reflexes, and other measures that prove her as galvanized."

What? Was the man picking a fight with me?

I glared at him. He glared right back.

Oh, this was so on.

"Will that satisfy you?" Oscar asked John Black.

"It will."

"Good," Oscar said. "We will meet you in the training hall."

Abraham gave both men a shallow bow. They turned and walked down the hall that led to Oscar's office, Buck following behind.

"Matilda." Abraham strode past the elevator and took a cleverly hidden staircase beside it.

I assumed I was supposed to follow so I did.

Abraham stormed down two gray carpeted flights of stairs. I kept my gaze on my feet and my hand on the metal railing as we descended. A test of strength and reflexes seemed pretty straightforward. But I didn't know what those other measures he mentioned would be.

Abraham pulled up short on the next landing. I threw my hand up, palm slapping against his chest to keep from running into him with a full-body press.

Not that I'd mind getting him in a full-body press.

Yes, I was still thinking those kinds of things about him.

"This is not the time to be foolish," he said.

Apparently he was not thinking those kinds of things about me.

"Again with calling me a fool. You know that's no way to sweet-talk a girl."

"I understand you have history with House Black," he said.

"No. I have *murder* and dead parents with House Black."

"Matilda." He wiped his hand over his face. "Listen to me." He took a step backward so there was room between us. "You need to know what's going to happen. Right now."

"All right." I crossed my arms and leaned my hip against the rail. "I'm listening."

"This is more than a test of strength. They are going to be watching you so they can bid on you."

"House Gray and House Black?" I asked.

"Every House. By the time we enter that room, the head of every House will be present in some manner. And since you haven't signed on with House Gray, you will have no say in who claims you."

"What? No. Why did you do this? Why did you tell them you would test me?"

"It was either that or have House Black claim you with no display."

"He can do that?"

"Currently? Yes. After the gathering, some debts between our Houses will fall away. But right now, Black has more power than Gray."

"I am not working for Black. Not ever."

"Black might not win the bid," he said. "There are other Houses that have more power. Blue, for certain. Perhaps Yellow."

"No," I said. "My life isn't going to be taken away from me by a *perhaps*." I turned and jogged up the stairs.

"Where are you going?"

"The contract is in my room."

"You're expected. We're expected. In the training hall."

"Well, they'll have to expect me a little late."

I had put an entire flight between us before I heard him cuss quietly, then pound up the stairs after me.

"This is a stupid idea," Abraham snarled as we jogged across the living room area. "A foolish, foolish move."

"I thought you wanted me in House Gray." I opened the door and rushed into the ridiculously fancy suite. I stopped, turned a slow circle.

Where had I left the contract?

"What?" he asked.

"Give me a second." I jogged into the bedroom.

"Did you lose the contract? Tell me you didn't lose the contract."

"I didn't lose it. It's here." I threw the covers off the bed, then pushed them aside so I could search the floor. Nothing.

"Matilda, you are *killing* me," he said from the door-way. "We have to go. Now."

"Just a second."

"There are no more seconds," he said.

"Oh!" I snapped my fingers. "Hold on." I pulled the duffel off my shoulder and opened it, dragging out the scarf.

"What–"

I yanked on the thread, stitches slipping away, freezing time and muffling the world with a heavy silence. Abraham was frozen in place, his mouth still open.

I carried the scarf with me and continued to pull on stitches as I searched for the piece of paper. Finally found it, a third of the scarf later, on the desk in the sitting area.

I gathered scarf and thread in one hand and quickly signed the bottom of the agreement.

"Thank you, Grandma," I whispered. The silence lifted, the world buzzed back to life and time picked up again.

"—are you," Abraham said from the other room. "Fuck." He strode through the door. The look on his face made me laugh.

"How did you do that?"

"Do what?"

"Disappear?"

"I didn't disappear. I walked right past you. And found the contract." I held up the paper to prove it. "I'm quicker than I look. Don't forget it."

"You signed?"

I glanced down at the paper, the reality of what I'd done sinking in. "Um. Yes. I did. Ten years." The last came out too soft.

I'd just given away a decade of my life.

Abraham was suddenly in front of me. "Matilda?" He touched my shoulders, then drew his palms down to grip my upper arms. His hands were hot as furnaces.

I felt like I'd been swallowed in ice.

"We need to go."

I was too frozen to move.

"We really need to go," he said a second or two later when I still hadn't moved.

I heard him, I was just stuck on the reality of what I'd just done.

His hands shifted, sliding up and up until the heels of his hands were braced beneath my jaw, his fingers spread back into my hair, his thumbs stroking the corners of my lips gently.

"Matilda?" he said softly as he lowered his head to mine, his eyes shifting to gaze at my lips, then back to my eyes.

He was going to kiss me.

That realization came with a collision of feelings and wants and things I didn't know how to define. That realization also came with a heartbeat that pounded heat through my veins and unfroze me. I melted into his touch, wanting that kiss more than anything else.

"Y-yes?" I breathed.

His lips were almost on mine. His body bent over me, closer, closer. I thought I'd burst for want.

I held my breath and closed my eyes.

His fingers squeezed the back of my neck, gentle and possessive.

"If you make me late," he murmured, his breath warm across my mouth, "I will throttle you."

Wait. *What?*

My eyes snapped open.

He drew away so quickly a cold breeze whisked over my skin.

By the time I pulled my thoughts together, he was already out the door.

His voice floated back to me. "Move, Matilda. We're late."

That was it? No kiss? What was wrong with that man? He was sending off more mixed signals than a three-armed traffic cop.

I stuffed the scarf back in my duffel, zipped it tight, and tucked it under the desk.

"You know what you are, Mr. Vail?" I said, storming out after him.

"In a hurry?" he answered.

"A coward."

"Is that so?"

He was already a set of stairs ahead of me. I pounded down them to catch up. "Yes. A man makes a move like that, he follows through."

"And what makes you think I won't?"

"Men like you are all talk and no tango."

He paused in front of a metal door, his hand on the

latch. "How would you know?" He yanked on the door and held it open, blocking my passage with the bulk of his body, a smug smile on his face. "You've never met a man like me."

Yeah, well, he hadn't ever met a woman like me either.

I pushed by him and stepped on his foot hard enough, he winced and sucked in a surprised breath.

Galvanized didn't feel pain. But the galvanized that I'd touched had felt me.

That was to my advantage in this fight. Working the farm with the beasts and ferals meant I was no stranger to bruises and breaks. I was used to pain.

Abraham Seventh had been practically numb for nearly three hundred years. Maybe it was time to see if he remembered how to take the hurt.

The training hall stretched across the entire floor of the building and was beautiful in its simplicity. Light wooden floors soaked up the sunlight pouring in through the huge windows overlooking the city, while white and wood panels separated the space into smaller areas.

Oscar Gray sat on the other side of the training mat that filled a quarter of the space. John Black sat next to him, and Buck stood at his back. The white panels behind them were filled with images of very pretty, very young people, each wearing a distinct color.

The heads of the Houses. Well, seven of them, and one blank screen that held the symbol of House Gold, Money, which probably had a committee listening in.

I took a minute to gawk at faces I'd seen on only scratchy feeds, displayed here in such clear rendering, it was as if they were really in the room with us.

Troi Blue, Water, didn't look a day over twenty. She wore a plunging pale blue dress that rippled against her midnight-dark skin. Her hair was glossy black and fell in gorgeous waves around her shoulders, and her features were soft and perfect. She held herself like royalty, a ruler, superior to all others.

Feye Green, Agriculture, was almost her opposite. Small and slight, she was ghost white and doll-faced. Her pale yellow hair formed a kinky mane that only made her look smaller and more fragile. She was moonlight, and even the pale green of her sweater threatened to swallow her.

"Matilda Case," Oscar was saying. Introducing me, I thought.

I was catching only about half of it, too nervous about all the eyes of all the world's power on me.

I had promised Quinten I would stay hidden.

So much for that.

Gideon Violet, Faith, paced while Oscar talked, his corporate-style plum suit almost old-fashioned, his tie loose, his steel-gray hair making what may have been a handsome face sad and old.

"Newly awakened, newly discovered," Oscar went on.

The other two women were Kiana White, Medical, and Aranda Red, Power. Aranda Red wore her dark hair short and slicked into points at each temple. She had the coloring of a woman who avoided the sun. Her lips were bloodred, her eyebrows and lashes darkened and arched. She looked at me with a slight smile, calculating, predatory. I wondered if her smile would contain fangs.

Kiana White wore her honey-brown hair pulled back loosely, giving her friendly face a golden glow. Her slightly tilted, catlike eyes glittered with curiosity and she sat forward, taking in every detail. She wore a soft white blouse tucked into tailored white trousers, and an air of composure far beyond her apparent twenty-five-year-old looks.

"Today," Oscar said, "she has agreed to prove herself galvanized. Abraham Seventh will assist in the display of her skills."

There were only two other faces up there on screens. Welton Yellow, Technology who was still wearing the yellow frog shirt and half-lidded eyes, but must have finished his popcorn, and a man with short white hair and dark glasses, wearing a silver sweater.

White hair would be Reeves Silver, Vice. He looked like a betting man and had on his poker face.

"Abraham Seventh, Miss Matilda Case," Oscar continued. "Please step onto the mats. We are ready for you to begin."

"No more talk," Abraham said quietly as he walked past me, barefoot. "Let's tango."

He bowed to the Houses, then turned and bowed toward me.

"Hold on," I said. "Excellencies." I gave them a nod, then turned. I took off my boots, shrugged out of my coat.

I'd never felt so naked.

He might be strong, but I was fast. He might be a better fighter, but I didn't have a half-healed gut wound.

I drew my hands over my hair and tied it into a knot at the back of my head, then turned to the mat.

I bowed to Abraham, mostly because I was already feeling a little guilty for what I was about to do to him.

He stepped out onto the mat. So did I.

He swung at my head, his fist big enough to knock a hole the size of Bangkok through the wall.

I ducked, threw a punch toward his neck. His hands blocked upward . . .

. . . and that's when I kicked him as hard as I could in the balls.

He buckled and slammed down on his knees with a groan.

I stepped behind him and clamped my hand on the side of his neck. I didn't know how long the sensation of touch remained after I let go, so it seemed safer to just hold on.

"This auction is over," I said to the Houses. "I am off the block. I've chosen House Gray and signed the contract with them. I'm sure there are medical tests I could pass to settle the matter of being galvanized."

Welton Yellow burst out laughing. The other Houses appeared angry and annoyed.

Buck still stood behind John Black, but his gaze flicked between Abraham and me, then settled on me with a new sort of caution.

"House Gray," Troi Blue said. "Have you brought us here to mock us?"

"No, House Blue, I have not," Oscar said. "The galvanized did not consult with me in this regard."

"Is it true?" John Black asked. "Did you sign a contract?"

"Yes." I let go of Abraham and immediately got out of his reach. I wasn't dumb. "I brought it with me, if you need to see it."

"Stop speaking," Troi Blue snapped. "Until spoken to."

I pressed my lips together to keep from telling her off. This wasn't an argument I could win by being angry. This was a situation that would work out in my favor only if the contract I signed held, and if Oscar and the other Houses agreed that we had a deal.

"You have to admit it was fun," Welton Yellow said. "Thank you, Oscar Gray, for today's entertainment. I concede your claim to the galvanized Matilda Thirteenth, as long as the contract is witnessed and she indeed proves to be galvanized."

"House Yellow," Troi Blue said. "You overstep."

"No, I don't believe I do," Welton said. "Who else wants to bid for a creature that can't be bought? I'd rather not display my wealth, nor favors."

"Conceded," Gideon Violet of Faith said. His screen winked out.

"What House did it claim before coming to you?" Feye Green asked.

"None," Oscar said smoothly. "She was without House."

"Unbelievable," Aranda Red said. "And how is it you found her, Oscar Gray?"

"Accidentally," Oscar said.

Her eyes flashed. She wanted him to say more, to tell her where my home was and what had tipped him off, but Oscar, bless the man, remained cheerfully silent.

"Let's see the contract," John Black said. "Matilda, bring it to me."

Abraham had gotten up off his knees, a sheen of sweat over his stony face. He stood between me and Oscar and refused to make eye contact.

I walked over to my coat and dug through the folds to the inner pocket where I'd stashed the paper.

Abraham took it from me before I'd gotten halfway across the mat and handed it to Oscar.

Oscar tapped something on the side of his wrist, and each of the Houses now had an image of the paper in their hands. Oscar handed John Black the original.

"So witnessed." John Black shook his head. "I have some matters to go over with you, Oscar Gray," he said.

"Of course. You are welcome to stay." Oscar looked up at the screens.

So did I. Only Welton Yellow was grinning, a lazy cat smile. "Good day, all," he said. Then his screen winked out.

Kiana White, Medical, spoke. "Well. That was very interesting. Oscar Gray, will you accept a technician from House White to confirm Matilda Thirteenth as officially galvanized?"

"That would be fine, Kiana White," Oscar said.

"I'll send someone immediately." Her screen flickered out.

Aranda Red scowled and said nothing before her screen went blank.

Troi Blue raised her chin. "This display of power and trickery does not sit well with me, House Gray. We will speak more of this at the gathering." She snapped her fingers, and her screen went blank.

That left only Reeves Silver, Vice, on the screen. "Welcome to the fold, Matilda Case," he said coolly. Then even he was gone.

The room went silent.

After a moment, Oscar cleared his throat. "Well. We have some things to go over, don't we, John? Would you join me in my office?"

The two of them left the room. Buck threw Abraham an explain-later look before following behind.

21

The twelve refused to stay hidden, secret. They refused to be property. Together the galvanized stood against the world and declared war upon the Houses. —2099
—from the journals of L.U.C.

"**D**on't you need to go with Oscar?" I asked.

Abraham took a deep breath and his eyes, when he finally turned to look at me, were cinnamon red again. Maybe pain. Most likely anger. "You have a special skill of stirring up trouble. Do you know that?"

"I was trying to untrouble the trouble," I objected. "I signed the contract. I, um . . . ended the fight quick."

"About that," he said. "Dirty move, Tilly."

It was the first time he'd used my nickname. I liked the sound of it from him.

"Yeah, well. I never said I was any good at the tango either." I picked up my coat and boots. "I suppose someone will let me know my penance?"

"It shouldn't be too severe," he said.

I was joking.

He was not.

"They might just write off the whole thing to you being excited and new and untrained. Tomorrow, though, we'll see that you're trained for the gathering."

"Two things," I said. "Which part of all this am I hoping they'll write off?"

"Your attitude, breaking rules, breaking arms, breaking protocol, and telling off the heads of the Houses. Not the best start for a galvanized." He should sound angry about all that. Hell, he should be angry at me for dropping him to his knees. But he just looked . . . I don't know . . . impressed.

"And the training?" I started up the stairs, and Abraham's footsteps were soon echoing behind mine.

"You haven't heard of it?" he said with overly casual interest.

"Has to do with the gathering?"

"Yes. The annual event where all the Houses gather and pose and position for who will wield the most power in the next year. It used to be a time when grievances against the Houses could be heard, but a three-day gathering isn't nearly long enough to hear all of that. Systems and courts and procedures were put into place to address complaints on an ongoing basis, which allowed the gathering to devolve into a bragging match."

"What do they brag about?"

"Who had higher profits, gained more assets, had a breakthrough in technology or some other advancement. And, of course, who looks the youngest."

"Really?"

"It's become the big race. Youth—or the appearance of it, at least—is a House obsession. The younger the heads of Houses appear to be, the more power they wield. Staying young takes a lot of money, time, and deals between Houses."

"Oscar doesn't look all that young. Neither does John Black."

"Oscar hasn't ever bothered with vanity. John Black prefers people to underestimate him."

"All right, so who's the youngest?"

"It's a toss-up between Troi Blue, Feye Green, and Aranda Red."

"What about Welton Yellow?"

"He's about as old as he looks."

"Oh. So how old are Blue, Green, and Red?"

"Just over a hundred."

"It's a strange world you live in, Abraham Seventh."

"You have a dragon in your backyard."

"It's a lizard."

"A lizard with wings."

"Okay, so that's a little odd. Why do I have to train for the gathering?"

"Galvanized represent their Houses. If there are House disputes, galvanized may be used to settle the issue."

"Settle?"

"Fight."

"Wonderful." We were out of the stairwell and across the sitting room now. "Is that what those posters of you and Loy Ninth were about on the street?"

"No."

I looked over my shoulder. "Just no?"

He lifted an eyebrow. "The gathering isn't the only time we are on display."

"Okay," I said, not knowing what else to say. "Should I mention we talked to Welton Yellow when we went for coffee?"

"We know. He's a friend of our House. He sent you to that coffee shop so I could pick you up. We thought it was public enough no other House would make a move on you, and we thought it was crowded enough you wouldn't do something stupid. Missed that by a moon."

"Hey, now. I was handling it just fine before you showed up."

He raised one eyebrow. "Broken arm and a revolver. A *revolver*, Matilda? You're a couple centuries out-of-date in your choice of weapons."

"I like that revolver. You'd be surprised what a chunk of lead and gunpowder can do to even out a situation."

"No," he said, "actually, I wouldn't be surprised."

"It's not illegal to own a revolver."

"Neither is it illegal to own a canon. Not a lot of people lug them into a crowded metropolis."

"Well, I hadn't planned to be walking around in a crowded metropolis. Then you showed up on my doorstep, all good-looking and bleeding and . . ."

We were in front of my door now. He stepped up and draped his hand on the door above me. Leaned in just a fraction shy of intimate distance. Close enough I could feel the heat of him, smell the warm notes of the cologne he wore.

"Good-looking and what?" he asked with a burr in his voice that gave me shivers.

"And I couldn't leave you bleeding."

"For that, I should thank you." He moved just a half inch closer, his mouth opening slightly on a smile. "Thoroughly," he added. Then, "Unfortunately, I have other pressing matters to attend." He reached behind me and was skillful enough that we didn't even touch as he opened the door. He leaned back so I wouldn't fall through it by accident and pointed at the room.

"I do hope you will refrain from running out for another cup of coffee or starting an in-House war for the next few hours."

I released the breath I'd been holding and tried to get my heartbeat under control. The man did such things to me. Stirred my thoughts and need without even a single touch.

"Sure," I said, trying not to sound hot or bothered. "For the next few hours anyway." I smiled innocently.

He paused, studying my lips, my eyes, and I found myself wondering if he was going to touch me, embrace me.

Then I found myself wondering why I didn't just take that step into him and touch him.

He made a little *mm* sound, then turned and walked down the hall, leaving me surprisingly disappointed.

What was wrong with me? I couldn't have these feelings for the man. I'd known him exactly one day. I had a farm to run, a grandmother to take care of, a brother to free, and a new House to serve, apparently.

How did any of that, any of the past twenty-four hours I'd been through, add up to the feelings for Abraham Seventh that were taking root in me?

Foolish heart, I thought. *I don't have time for you.*

But my heart, being foolish, did not listen.

Okay. Since I wasn't going anywhere, I pulled the duffel out from under the chair and checked to be sure the scarf was still there. It was half-unraveled and I needed to do something to salvage it before it lost more stitches. I plucked a couple pens off the desktop and used them to knit a few rows, then stared at the clock and pulled the thread back out.

Time did not stop. So this knitting—however Grandma had done it—was a onetime trick. If I wanted to keep the scarf and the time it held near me, or, better yet, on me, I'd need to cut the length of yarn and bind off the edge so no more stitches were accidentally pulled out.

The light coming through the window at the end of the sitting room was already bright. I'd missed dawn, and enough of the day had gone by that it was midmorning. Kiana White had told Oscar that she would send a medical technician over to test to see that I was galvanized— a prospect that made me want to barf.

So that meant I could either pace around the room until the technician showed up, or I could work on the scarf to keep busy.

Scarf it was.

But even though my hands were busy, my thoughts just kept on thinking. Had I made the right choice to sign the contract? Would Oscar follow through with his promise to help me find my brother? Would he let my grandma live on our property without House interference? Would he work to make House Brown legitimized among the other Houses?

Abraham had almost kissed me.

And I'd kicked him in the crotch.

That was a promising beginning to a ten-year work relationship.

I finished tugging the yarn through the last stitch to secure it, then wrapped the yarn around my hands a couple time and pulled until it broke.

I held up the scarf. It was definitely shorter. Probably wouldn't drag the floor when I wore it. But the stitches were all locked in tight until I wanted to unknot them again. No accidentally wasting time.

I tucked the scarf back in my duffel and wound the yarn into a small ball that I also tucked in the duffel.

"Good afternoon!" a woman's cheerful, clipped voice called out from the other side of the bedroom door. "Are you awake, Matilda? There is so much to do."

"Be right there."

The door flew open.

"Nonsense, darling. I shall come to you." The small woman who had served us cookies and ice tea—Elwa—powered into the room. Her straight black hair was pulled back in a tight bun, and she wore a gray jacket, skirt, hose, and shoes all cut in a chic style. She had a bundle of clothes draped over one arm.

A dour-faced man about twice her size, wearing white from head to foot, followed her in.

"I am Elwa," she said as she laid the garments across the foot of my bed in the adjoining room. "No need to worry about packing. It is done. No need to worry about what to wear."

She turned and gave me a sharp eye, then nodded. "Country living agrees with you, Matilda, my darling. Here. This." She pulled away a few hangers, leaving behind a lacy tank top, sweater, and slacks, all in shades of gray. "Perfect for your day. Your travel. But first the blood for tests. Quickly, now."

"What?" I said, my brain not quite up to the speed of Elwa's mouth.

The man in white stepped forward right on cue. "Hold

still," he said with all the bedside manner of an undertaker.

I held still, eyeing him warily. "What are you doing?"

"A scan. Then blood." He slipped the satchel on his shoulder forward and removed a device that looked like a clear, flat screen filled with fluids that shifted with every motion of his hand. He didn't touch me, but used the thing a little like a camera, holding it above my head, pausing, then shifting it in front of my face, then in front of my neck, pausing, and so on, all the way to my bare feet.

I didn't feel anything, didn't hear anything, didn't feel anything, but the liquid moved and changed color as the device scanned me from skin to DNA.

"Now blood," he said after he'd stowed the liquid-screen thing.

Another device, this one the size and shape of a pen. He tapped it against my finger, which hurt a little, held it there until it had sucked up enough blood; then that too was tucked back in the satchel.

"Good day," he said.

"Good day." Elwa bustled over and all but pushed him out the door.

"Now," she said. "Quickly."

"Quickly what?"

"Shower. Dress," she commanded. "Go. I will have lunch brought up. Something light. Something delicious."

"I don't need new clothes," I said. "I packed clothes. My clothes."

She paused and tipped her head so she was looking over her nose at me. "Are they gray?"

"Uh, no."

"Exactly!" she proclaimed. "Go. Shower. Elwa will take care of everything."

So I took a quick shower, then hurried back to the bedroom in a towel. I had no intention of putting on the clothes she'd laid out for me.

"This, my darling." She marched into the room and plucked up the clothes on the bed. She held out the slacks, a lacy tank top, and a pair of my panties.

"I'd prefer to wear my own clothes," I said.

"These are your clothes. I have shopped for you. Planned for you. There is no need to worry." She gave me the down-nose look again. "Do not argue, please. I have been running this House for more years than you have been alive, darling, and there is no argument I lose."

"I thought Oscar Gray ran this House."

She laughed, a musical tinkle. "He only thinks he runs this House. Poor boy. Here now. Slacks. Before you catch cold."

She shoved the clothes into my arms and marched out of the bedroom, closing the door behind her. "I will wait. Ah yes, come in and set the food there." She said to whomever had just entered the sitting room.

I had to admit, the clothes in my arms were soft and fine. Obviously well-made. And if Elwa was someone who ran the House, she would know what sort of clothes were most appropriate for whatever the hell I had to do next.

I sighed and put on the outfit, which covered up all signs of my life stitches, as long as I kept my hair down. I refused to wear the soft gray shoes set out beside the bed and instead put on my boots. Worn, dusty, they were comfortable, strong, and mine.

"Are you dressed?" she called out. "Come out now, Matilda. Before lunch is cold."

I was starving. The last thing I'd eaten was a quick sandwich back on the farm. A twinge of homesickness struck me, and I had to take a breath or two before it faded.

I missed the farm, missed my world making sense, missed Grandma and all the stitched-up beasts. I didn't want to think that it might be a decade before I saw them all again.

Out in the sitting room, Elwa had brought in a table and set it with a lovely gray cloth, against which shone silver cutlery, crisp white china, and sparkling crystal.

It was lunch for royalty, not a country girl.

"What is wrong with your feet?" Elwa exclaimed.

I shot a look at my feet, expecting them to be on fire or covered in spiders or something.

"My boots?"

"You call those boots? My darling, those are a *travesty*. But no matter. This is your first time, after all. And not a bad effort at that. Although your hair . . ." She stopped moving and talking. I found her intense silence even more worrisome than her constant chatter. "Something must be done."

"I like it how it is," I said. "Is that orange juice?" I hoped shifting the subject would keep her out of my hair—literally.

"Yes, yes. Orange juice and a light lunch. Hurry, but don't rush. We'll meet with Oscar Gray in"—she tapped her finger twice in the air in front of her and a half-dozen time readouts flickered there—"seven minutes. Can I help you with that, my sweet?"

I had been trying to unfold the napkin out of the shape of what I could only assume was a Gordian knot, and wasn't having much luck.

"No, I can—"

"Shh. Nonsense," Elwa's tone took on a much softer edge. "Eat, Matilda. I am here to help." She took the napkin gently from me, pulled it easily apart, and placed it in my lap.

All right. If she was here to help, I'd ask some questions. "Do you know what the training is? Abraham mentioned I'd be trained for the gathering." I took a drink of the orange juice, savoring the rich sweetness. I couldn't remember the last time I'd had it fresh.

"Every year, the galvanized gather. What they do is a matter the galvanized do not share." She poured hot tea and honey. "First, you will see Oscar; then you will leave with Abraham Seventh to the training compound. When you return here, I will have everything you need prepared for you to represent House Gray at the gathering.

"I must say I am so pleased you have chosen House Gray to represent. You will be quite the talk, darling. An *exhilarating* wonder."

I assumed that by *representing* she meant *fighting for*.

Great. I could wrestle a feral beast to the ground, but hand-to-hand with another galvanized wasn't going to be easy. My only advantage was that I could make them hurt.

Of course, they could make me hurt too.

"Are there any things you could tell me about the gathering, since this will be my first time?"

"Don't worry. I will collect all the information you need. When you return you will have time to study. So. Now. Enjoy lunch. I will be back soon." She exited the room and shut the door behind her.

I helped myself to the squash soup, salad, croissants, and cheeses, the flavors both familiar and exotic. I wondered if I could get some of the spices used in the meal for the farm. Grandma would love them.

"Tilly?" Neds voice said through the door.

"It's open," I called out.

He stepped in, wearing, I noted with just a tinge of jealousy, his own clothes.

"Help yourself." I waved at the table. "There's too much for me anyway."

"I ate," Right Ned said, but he came over and Left Ned popped a square of cheese in his mouth.

"So, what happened?"

I sighed and leaned back in my chair. "I signed House Gray."

"Tilly . . ."

"I didn't want to, but it was that or be auctioned off. All the Houses were watching."

"All of them?"

"I guess not all. I didn't see House Orange or House Gold. The rest, though."

"Nothing good comes out of drawing the attention of the Houses," Right Ned said.

"Only worse comes of signing with one," Left Ned said. "Stupid choice, Tilly."

"It was the only option I had that outlined anything in my favor."

"What's in the contract? What did House Gray promise you?" Right Ned asked.

"The same as what I told you this morning. Ten years of my life for help in finding and freeing my brother and the farm staying in the family name with Grandma living there."

"What about House Brown?"

"I don't know, but I now have ten years to work on it."

He was silent a moment or two. So was I. I still couldn't believe how quickly my life had changed.

"Come into town with me," Right Ned said. "You can break someone else's arm. That will cheer you up."

I made a face at him. "I can't. There's a training thing the galvanized attend in preparation of the gathering. I'm going to that today. How about you? Did you decide to sign on with House Gray?"

"Have until this evening to decide," Left Ned said. "Thought a walk would do me good."

"You and I could leave now." Right Ned's smile was just a little too tight. "Take some time to clear our heads. We don't have to be under the lock and key of House Gray to still be aligned with them."

"Why, Neds Harris," I said, "it's almost as if you don't like it here."

"Almost is, isn't it? But I'm serious, Tilly. We could leave. I could take us somewhere safe. I know people. People who would take you in. Take us all in."

There was a hint of desperation beneath his words. And I wondered if this was my chance. If I should run with him, hide with him.

But running wouldn't change my problems. I still had a lost brother and a vulnerable grandmother. If I reneged on my deal with House Gray, I'd just be making things worse for all of us.

"I can't," I said. "Too many people I love would get hurt."

"There's always another way," Right Ned said.

"Not this time."

Elwa appeared at the door. "Ah, Mr. Harris. Here you are. Is there something I can do for you?"

"No, thank you, ma'am," Right Ned said.

"Was lunch satisfactory, Matilda, darling?"

"It was delicious."

"Good. Oscar waits for you. Both. Go now. I'll pack your bag."

Elwa marched toward the bedroom. I got up and packed my gun belt into the duffel, then shrugged the bag over my shoulder.

"What about the rifle?" Left Ned asked.

"It's mine, so it goes with me." The rifle was resting near the small couch. I plucked it up on the way out the door.

We strolled out into the main sitting area, where Oscar Gray stood, once again, by the vast windows.

"You wanted to see us?" I asked.

He turned. His gaze took in Neds, me, and my rifle, and his mouth curved in a slight smile. "Yes," he said. "Before you go, I wanted to be sure that you were satisfied with the outcome of the test this morning."

"About that," I said. "I'd like to apologize."

"For what?"

"It was wrong of me not to tell you I had signed the contract before I announced it to all the Houses. I don't think I handled that as well as I could have."

"Apology accepted. The fallout from that particular event is already being dealt with," he said. "The matter with House Red and the Fessler outpost continues to be . . . costly. However, I have already opened an investigation into where your brother Quinten Case may be. By our records, he was last working for House Silver. I'll be speaking with Reeves Silver on the matter this evening."

"Thank you," I said, a rush of hope taking flight in me. "Is there any way I can help?"

"No. As soon as I have news, I will tell you. In the meantime, there is something I would like you to do for me."

I nodded.

"I want you to remain unannounced to the general public. I don't want anyone else to know that you are galvanized or that you are claimed by House Gray until the gathering."

"What does it matter, Your Excellency?" Right Ned asked. "The Houses all know about her now."

"House business is only part of what goes into this position, Mr. Harris," Oscar said. "There is power to be found in bringing honor or unexpected assets into a House."

I frowned, not following his logic.

He must have seen my confusion. He smiled. "I want to reveal you to the public in a very grand manner."

"At the gathering?"

"Yes. It will be a moral boost for all those who claim House Gray. Since we are the caretakers of humanity, you can only imagine how many people will be excited that their House not only found a modern galvanized, but also brought her into House Gray."

I could see how a swell in popularity among the masses would do a lot to argue against his brother's desire to have him removed as head of the House.

"Did I ruin that already? With everything that's happened this morning?"

"Not at all," he said. "The Houses know each other's secrets to an extent. Still, there are certain rules of engagement that are to our mutual benefit."

"I promise I'll keep the lowest of low profiles."

"A talent you certainly have perfected over the years," he said kindly. "Ah, Abraham. I was just explaining to

Matilda that I wish her to remain unseen during your time away."

Abraham strolled into the room from the other hall. "Did she agree?"

"Of course I did," I said.

Abraham wore a plain cotton shirt, open in a V at the neck, but tight enough across his chest to show the muscle beneath. His sleeves were rucked up to his elbows, adding to the casual look, and along with denim jeans, boots, and a belt, he looked like a man ready for some time off. Everything about him was easy, loose, relaxed.

And that looked all kinds of good on the man.

I tried not to think of how good naked would look on him.

"Of course you did," he said with a straight face. "Is there anything else?"

"Neds?" I asked. "Will you be staying?"

"I thought I'd do some sightseeing around town," Left Ned said.

"Have you considered our offer, Mr. Harris?" Oscar asked.

"Yes, sir," Right Ned said. "I'll let you know by the end of the day."

"Good. Well, then?" Oscar raised his brows at Abraham. "Haven't you had enough of me for a while, Bram?"

Abraham gave him a small, almost fatherly smile. That familiarity surprised me a little. But, then, if Abraham was as old as he said he was, and if he had been serving House Gray for much of that time, he would have known Oscar from a young age.

"If anything comes up . . ." Abraham started.

"I know where you are," Oscar said. "Go on now. Enjoy."

"Not yet," Elwa powered into the room, her stride short and punctuated. She was carrying two bags. "Clothing and sundries for Matilda," she said, handing the bags to Abraham. "Are you sure I can't pack for you, Abraham Seventh?"

"No, thank you, Elwa. I already packed."

Elwa frowned, looking disappointed. "Well, I've had the car brought around."

"Thank you." He turned toward me. "Shall we, Matilda Case?"

"Lead the way." I kept one hand on my duffel and the other on my rifle, as we entered the elevator and left House Gray behind us.

22

Millions of people joined their fight. And for fifty bloody years the galvanized tirelessly led that war, that uprising of House Brown.— 2160
                              —from the journals of L.U.C.

We drove through the city to another speed tube. Once Abraham had finished inputting our destination and other information, the pod shot us off at ridiculous speeds while projecting fake pastoral views around us.

"Is it an animal?" I asked.

"What?" Abraham turned so he could better see me. We were both sitting in the front of the luxurious car, our bags in the trunk, my rifle in the backseat, my duffel at my feet.

"I haven't gotten any solid clues out of anyone about the training we are apparently required to attend today. I thought I'd narrow it down a bit. Animal, vegetable, or mineral?"

He grinned and scratched the stubble at his jaw. "You must be a delight at birthday parties."

"So, it's a secret I can't know? That's dumb."

"I didn't say you couldn't know it."

"So? Tell."

"After facing you on the sparring mat? I'm comfortable on this side of caution."

"Are you saying I'm unpredictable?"

"I'm saying you find solutions. You find answers. You don't follow the path that seems the most logical choice. You question . . . *everything*, as near as I can tell. You decide and you act. Rather quickly."

"I'll take that as a compliment."

"You should," he said.

He didn't look like he was going to change his mind about the training, so I changed the subject to something else that was bothering me.

"Before we left, Oscar mentioned something about House Red," I said.

He looked out the window, suddenly interested in the scenery that was filled with quaint cottages and bubbling fountains and moss-covered statuary. I didn't think that idyllic little town existed anywhere in the world.

"He said that calling off the bombing of the Fessler compound continues to be costly."

"Mmm."

"How costly?"

Abraham squinted as if he could see beyond the fake sheep and fake hills and fake world around us. "You do understand what happened there."

"You asked Oscar to call off the people who were trying to level the Fessler compound?"

"Mostly right. I asked Oscar for a personal favor. I asked him to call off the people who were working unregulated, uncontracted night hours on the project for House Red. To do so, Oscar had to halt all workforces for House Red in North America."

"Everyone?" I asked, startled. "That must be hundreds—"

"Thousands."

"—of people. Why?"

He turned back to me. "It was the only fair way to deal with the situation while calling attention to the problem in a manner House Red would respond to."

"Couldn't he have called off that one workforce?"

"Yes. But it would have painted a target on the Fessler compound, on the families who were running for their lives, and on the people who took them in. House Gray oversees people, but every House has ways to make life miserable for those who cross them. People who remain unclaimed, the rebels—House Brown—are uncounted, unnoticed, and, therefore, very easy to eliminate."

"House Red would have been angry enough over stopping one work site that they would have eliminated people? *Killed* people?" I pictured Aranda Red's stern image in the training room, everything about her hard and perfect and edged.

Holy crap, I thought she might be angry enough to do just that.

"Hell," I exhaled. "I made you call off all the workers in North America to cover for one small group of people who should have had the sense to run when they had the chance." I scrubbed my fingers back through my hair.

How many other people had that one small action affected? Would any of them come to harm, or be seen as suspicious enough that Aranda Red would order them eliminated?

"Let's be clear on this, Matilda," he said. "I asked Oscar to call them off. I knew the consequences."

And he'd gone forward with it.

"Because you were that desperate to get me off my property and signed up to your House?"

Something dangerous kindled deep in his eyes. "Because there were children in that compound. Families." His gaze challenged me and my judgment of him.

I finally looked away.

"There is a reason I claimed House Gray," he said. "Reasons I drafted the peace treaty that ended the Uprising between galvanized and the Houses."

"So you could destroy the only chance House Brown had at making the world a different place for people? A better place?"

"So House Brown had a chance to survive. At all. As

long as galvanized fought alongside House deserters, they would remain a target."

"And how did leaving them help? House Brown scratches by on luck and pure stubbornness. If the galvanized had continued to fight for House Brown to stand equal to the other Houses, the world would be a better place."

"One," he said, "House Brown will never be equal to the other Houses, because it is made of people who think for themselves, fight for themselves, and care for their neighbors. It is not a power-hungry monarchy. The day it turns into that is the day it is truly dead. Two, galvanized can't die. Cannot. The Houses knew that. The soldiers knew that.

"If the fight had continued, it wouldn't have been galvanized blood that was spilled, wouldn't have been the galvanized hearts that were stilled. Men, women, and children fell. By the thousand. Too many dead. Far too many."

I knew what he'd bargained away for that peace between House Brown and the other Houses. The right to be recognized as human. The right for the galvanized to be free.

For the first time, I wondered how he'd talked the other eleven galvanized into signing away their freedom for House Brown. I wondered how he'd convinced them to bow to the shackles of the Houses.

"I never looked at it quite like that," I admitted.

"This training is important," he said, changing the subject, for which I was grateful. "We will go over the basics of what's expected of you at the gathering."

"When Oscar announces I'm a part of House Gray?"

"Yes. And when the other Houses verify and give their approval."

"We're still waiting on their approval? I thought we just did that this morning. I proved I was strong in front of everyone. I let them scan me to see that I'm galvanized."

"Yes, but that doesn't mean the Houses will stand by and allow Gray to claim you. The gathering will be their last chance to negate your contract."

"They can do that? How?"

"If you step out of line, if you offend another head of House, if you offend another galvanized or in any other way break the code of conduct expected of you at the gathering, the contract will be voided, your loyalties put into question, and your service will go to the highest bidder."

Hell.

"How long do I have to be perfect in their eyes?"

"Just to be safe?" he said. "I'd start now."

Great. I pressed my lips together and wondered how long it would be before I messed this up.

It took us three hours to reach the west coast. After that, a very short drive took us to a sprawling building lit up with pulsing lights and colors.

"Someone's having a party," I remarked.

"Several someones," he said.

He wasn't kidding. The expanse of parking area around the building was filled with vehicles, and a steady stream of people flowed into the building from streets and skywalks.

"What is this all about?" I asked.

"Let's find out."

He drove the car around to the back, where a door in the side of the building opened up for us. He drove into the very nice garage, parked, then got out of the car and started off toward an elevator.

I got out too, pulled my duffel over my shoulder, and after a moment's hesitation, left the rifle in the car. I had my revolver and a scarf full of time. I figured I could handle just about anything that came at me.

Abraham was waiting in the elevator, so I picked up the pace and joined him there.

He punched the button for the main floor.

"You'll want to hang back a bit, blend in, but don't get out of my eyesight, understand?"

"Sure. Of course," I said.

He didn't buy it.

"Just . . ." He turned and set his shoulders, taking up all the room in front of the doors. "Try not to draw attention to yourself, okay?"

"Like anyone would notice me."

"I don't know how anyone could miss you," he murmured.

The elevator came to a soft stop, a light chimed on, and then the doors opened wide.

Before Abraham had even taken a step, a rise of excited voices got louder. The crowd out in the huge lobby area milled between rows of three-story columns that were lit a vibrant green, washing the ceiling, the reflective floor, and everyone else in that light.

But when Abraham stepped out of the elevator, the columns were washed in a soft gray light, making it feel like early dawn in the room. Hundreds of people oohed; more than a few shrieked. A rising chant of "Seventh, Seventh, Seventh," spread across the room in a rising wave of sound.

Abraham strode out into the crowd, his arms stretched to either side like a beloved warrior returned from battle.

The room erupted in cheers.

Don't draw attention to yourself, he said. Ha! No one was looking at anything *but* him.

I strolled out of the elevator and threaded through the crowd until I was leaning against one of the columns, out of the way of the main flow of people.

"First time?" a woman asked me.

She was about my height and general coloring, maybe a little younger than me, and had dimples and a generous mouth. She wore a white shirt, blue overshirt, green pants, and bright orange shoes. Strips of yellow, violet, and every other House color ringed her arms.

"My name's Listra." She held out her hand.

What was the correct thing to do here? What was the

thing that wouldn't get me kicked out of House Gray? For all I knew, she was a House spy come to check on my behavior.

"Matilda." I took her hand, and when we shook, she tapped two fingers against the inside of my wrist. The House Brown signal. Thank goodness. I tapped the inside of her wrist too, and she grinned.

"I thought so," she said.

"So, what is all this?" I gestured toward the people taking pictures and shouting questions at Abraham.

"The jumble. You know, all the galvanized get together before the big gathering, talk to fans, answer questions, pose for photos."

"Right. I've heard about it, I just didn't think it would be so . . ."

"Noisy?" she asked as a huge cheer went up and all the columns washed with violet.

"Happy," I said.

The cheer went louder and the crowd clapped as a tall, rawboned woman wearing a purple plaid shirt and loose plum slacks walked across the room toward Abraham. Her hair was lavender and cut like a boy's, short and combed to one side.

Abraham smiled, and when she was close enough, they hugged.

The crowd went wild.

"Friends?" I asked.

"You don't know? I heard you went into a House to deal with something." At my look, she added, "Word got out about the Fesslers' place. You know how House Brown is. One person says something to another person, and pretty soon the whole world knows."

I nodded.

"So when you showed up here with Abraham Seventh, I figured it was House Gray you had business with."

"You're right. I'm dealing with House Gray. But I'm still a little behind on all this galvanized stuff."

"Not much to get, really," she said. "That's Clara

Third. Works for House Violet, Faith. Kind of shy, doesn't say much, but Abraham's always been kind toward her. Other galvs already in the building are House Green's Dolores Second, House Red's Loy Ninth, and the three-some from House Blue: Wila Fifth, Vance Fourth, and Obedience Tenth."

"Do all the galvanized show up here and do—this?"

"Every year, for one evening before the gathering. It was their idea, and no matter what's going on between the Houses, they go out and meet their fans. It's nice of them, don't you think?"

I still thought it was weird that the galvanized had fans.

"Yes," I said. "It's nice."

Abraham gave Clara one last pat on the shoulder, then walked away, scanning the crowd for me. He quickly spotted me—so points for the man—and I held up my fingers in a short wave. He nodded toward a door that opened behind him.

"Apparently, I am being summoned," I said.

"Are you all right?" she asked in that House Brown tone that said both *I will help you escape* and *I want info so we can keep an eye on you.*

It was sweet.

"No worse for the wear," I said, because I was not going to screw this up now.

"All right. I just thought the message from your brother sounded like he was in over his head. If you need any-thing, you know how to find us."

"What message from my brother?" I asked.

Abraham had noticed I wasn't following him and threw me a hard glance. Several people around him looked my way, but I half turned with a smile on my face, pretending it wasn't me he was looking at.

"What message?" I asked Listra again.

"It came through yesterday. Didn't you get pinged? I thought Boston Sue would have sent it to you."

"Maybe she did and I missed it," I said. "Basics?"

"*House Orange, hidden enemy,* and coordinates."

"Do you remember the coordinates?"

"No."

"Was his message coded to me?"

"I don't know. I caught it on a half-second scrounge banking off the hub at your place." She glanced over at Abraham. "You'd better go."

I looked that way too. He had moved into the next room, and four people stood at the door, keeping others from entering the room. He was both chatting with a woman with long, light brown hair who had her back toward me and throwing angry glances my way.

Crap.

"If you need anything," Listra said again.

"I'll find you," I said. "May the earth rise to your feet."

"And the wind at your back," she finished.

She faded into the crowd quick as a drop of water in a stream, and I wandered my way through the traffic toward the door.

The lighted columns shifted from violet to white, and the crowd gasped and cheered.

House White galvanized January Sixth sashayed into the room like a celebrity. I caught a glimpse of a knockout figure and long, pale yellow hair before the crowd practically rioted to get closer to her.

No one seemed to be paying me much attention, which was good. The guards at the door ignored me completely, even after I'd politely tried to get their attention.

"Please let her in," Abraham said behind them.

As soon as he spoke, it was like I was suddenly visible. They gave me that up-down look, and one of the men leered at me. "Good luck, sunshine," he said, stepping aside.

They shut the door behind us. The room was nice, just this side of luxurious; couches and chairs coving up the corners, a table off to one side spread with food and drinks so fancy they looked like artwork.

There were also six people sitting on those luxurious chairs and eating those fancy artworks, staring at me.

A woman in her midfifties with long brown hair pulled back loosely from her suntanned, heart-shaped face walked over to Abraham and me.

"Bram," she said, "put on your manners, boy." Green stitches ran along her hairline and down beneath her cheeks, then mouth, giving her a slightly sewn-doll look. "Introduce us to this young lady properly."

Abraham gave her a tolerant smile, then extended his hand toward me. "Matilda Case, I would like to introduce you to Dolores Second, House Green, Agriculture."

"Call me Dotty, honey," she said in a soft drawl. "We're all friends here."

Abraham pointed at the tall, rawboned woman with lavender hair who was curled up in a wingback chair. Her pale purple stitches made a map of her plain face.

"Clara Third, House Violet, Faith," Abraham said.

She nodded.

"That daredevil," Abraham went on, indicating the redheaded man next to Clara, "is Vance Fourth, House Blue, Water."

"Daredevil? I don't know what he's talking about." He was trim, shorter than Abraham and me, and wore a blue shirt. His stitches were dark blue and tracked a diagonal line from the corner of his forehead across the bridge of his nose and down his jaw, neck, and under the edge of his collar. More stitches fanned out from the bottom of his jaw and spread around to the back of his head. His red hair and beard made the blue stitches even more noticeable, and his green eyes shone.

"It's a pleasure to meet you," he said.

"That is the lovely Wihelmina 'Wila' Fifth, House Blue, Water," Abraham continued.

"Well, it's about time we had ourselves a new member of the family," she said. Wila rested on the couch. She was a curvaceous, dusky-skinned woman with powder blue stitches that crossed above her right eyebrow and followed the round of her jaw to scoop at the base of her neck like a necklace. She had massively curly hair, smoothed tight against her skull and left to fall in a tumble of dark curls. "Welcome, Matilda."

"Thank you," I said.

A waif of a woman next to her tucked her honey-brown hair behind her ears and gave me a smile. In her soft blue summer dress, she didn't look like she could be a day over sixteen. Her stitches were blue as the sky, curving in parallel lines across the right side of her pale neck and face.

"I'm Obedience, but you can call me Bede," she said, tucking her hair back again in what was obviously a nervous habit. "Oh, Tenth, I suppose I should say. House Blue, Water."

"Last but not least," Abraham said, "this is Loy Ninth, House Red, Power."

Loy lounged on the other couch, a beer in one hand and a ready smile on his lips. He was square faced, with short black hair and a strong, clean-shaven jaw. His eyes were deeply set. Red stitching licked like fire against his coal skin, down the center of his face and neck to where it split to ride the edges of his collarbone. He wore a button-down red shirt and loose pants.

"*Enchanté,*" he said with a friendly grin. "Beer?"

"No, thanks," I said. What I needed was a minute alone with Abraham so I could find out if he knew anything about my brother's message.

"But I could use a drink of water. Abraham, could you show me where to find that?" I said pointing at the door and hoping he'd catch the hint.

"Don't trouble yourself," Dotty said. "We'll have some brought in." She stepped forward and patted my arm. And just as quickly pulled her hand away.

"Oh," she said, startled. "That's right. Bram mentioned you had that effect on a person." She rubbed her fingertips together. "Aren't you just something?"

"I'm really not. Something," I added. "I mean, I'm sorry that it's uncomfortable."

"Now, don't go on and apologize," Dotty said. "There's nothing wrong with you. I'd just forgotten what full sensation felt like. After all these years, it's a little over-whelming. Here, I'll call you in some water." She patted my arm again on her way past me.

"You two going to stand there all day?" Wila asked. "Come sit and relax."

"Sure." I adjusted my duffel and overswung the bag, getting both it and me in Abraham's way.

"Careful," he said.

"I need to talk to you. Now," I whispered through a clenched smile. Then, louder: "Sorry about that." I pulled my duffel closer to my side. "Um . . . where is the ladies' room?"

"Right out that door," Wila pointed. "It's private, so you won't be bothered."

"Why would anyone bother me?"

"Hon, you're galvanized. That's all anyone is here to bother."

"About that," I said. "I'm supposed to remain unan-nounced."

Vance chuckled while accepting a beer from Loy. "Os-car always had a flair for the dramatic. Is he announcing you at the gathering?"

"I think so."

And that was when I realized maybe I shouldn't have said anything in front of Loy. He was House Red's gal-vanized, and House Red wanted to kick Oscar out of his position.

Loy caught my panicked look and took a drink to cover his grin. "You don't have to worry about whatever is going through your head," he said. "We're friends here, not Houses, no matter the color of the ties that bind us. I don't give a damn about Aranda Red and her lust for power. Frankly, I wish she'd leave poor Oscar alone. He has enough trouble on his hands dealing with Bram."

Vance snorted.

"What he has," Abraham said, "is a friend."

"I know, I know," Loy said. "Practically raised him from a boy, the poor guy."

Bram shook his head. "This way, Matilda."

We walked out of the room into a private hall.

"What's wrong?" he asked.

"My brother sent a message. Yesterday. Why didn't you tell me about it?" I was whispering, but I was also angry. I couldn't believe he'd kept something so important a secret.

He frowned. "How do you know?"

"I know."

"That's not going to be enough. Who told you your brother sent a message?"

"Someone in House Brown."

"And you trust them?"

"Why would House Brown lie to me?"

He took a breath, let it out. "This is humanity we're talking about. Some people prefer the simplicity of lies."

"I trust that a person intercepted a message off a low hack . . ."

He raised an eyebrow, disapproving, or maybe admiring our data-smuggling ways. "Anyway, this person intercepted the message," I said.

"And this person is sure it's from your brother?"

"Um. Yes?"

"And what does the message say?"

"Like you don't know."

"I don't know." He held my gaze, all authority and heat and power. Waiting.

He didn't know.

"It said, *House Orange, hidden enemy*, and gave coordinates."

"What coordinates?"

"I don't know."

"Do you have proof your brother was the one who sent it?"

"No."

"When did the message go through?"

"Yesterday."

"I'll contact Oscar. See if he can have House Yellow run a trace for anything off network."

"Is that all you can do?"

"That's all anyone can do. It's sketchy information, Matilda. But that doesn't mean it isn't real. I'll talk to Oscar. He'll take it seriously and do what he can to track it down. But we'll have to wait until he finds something concrete before we do anything more."

"House Orange. That's not concrete enough for you?"

"Houses"—he glanced down the hall as if trying to put his words together, then looked back at me—"have been known to put out false information for other Houses to find. There are some Houses at odds with House Orange. Blue, for example. Troi Blue believes Slater Orange is jockeying to overthrow her position."

"You think she would send out a fake note from my brother? Does she even know that House Gray cares that my brother is missing?"

"Probably not. My point is, information is easy to fake, and House Orange has its enemies."

"All right, I can see that. I'll do a little looking into it too."

"Don't."

I didn't like his tone of voice. "In case you haven't figured it out yet? You're not going to get very far ordering me around."

"Just . . . let us look into it first. If this came through yesterday, we have some time. Let us double-check the information before we act on it."

"He isn't your brother."

We stood there while that truth and my worry filled the silence between us..

"I'll call Oscar," Abraham said. "Give me this grace at least: let me confirm where the message originated from and what it contained. Then we'll act on it. Will you agree to that?"

I hated the idea of Quinten being held against his will for a minute longer than necessary, but I didn't know if he was being held against his will. He'd been gone three years. It could be because he was so deep in research that time had slipped away from him.

"Okay," I said. "I'll wait until we have more information." Following rules was harder than I expected.

"Good. Anything else?"

"This celebrity thing. That's . . . something."

"Does it bother you?"

"No, I just don't really understand it."

"People need a thing to hold on to. A hope."

"They see you as a hero."

"My hero days are long ago and forgotten."

"I still don't know what I'm supposed to be doing here."

"You're here to meet the other galvanized and see how these things go. Be nice. Or at least be polite." He started back toward the private room. "Coming?"

"I'll be right there. I need to use the ladies' room." I walked down to the ladies' room and pushed through that door into a clean, quiet space. Toilets and sinks to the right; a cluster of couches in the silence of the low-lit room to the left.

I used the toilet, then washed my hands and stared at myself in the mirror. Abraham had good intentions. He'd done right by me so far, including throwing House Gray into conflict with House Red over the Fessler compound.

I didn't doubt his intentions. But I doubted the speed at which he could gather information on my missing brother.

"Sorry, Abraham," I said as I dried off my hands. "I know I promised I wouldn't do anything. But I never promised House Brown wouldn't do anything."

23

No one knows what caused the galvanized to offer a treaty. Some say it was the cost of human lives they could no longer bear. Some say the Houses had threatened global annihilation. —2160

—from the journals of L.U.C.

I had to stand on the arm of the couch in the little side room and press the old walkie-talkie against the wall to catch a spot clear enough to send a signal to Boston Sue.

She finally picked up. "Matilda? Is that you, baby sweet?"

"Yes. I don't have much time. Is Grandma okay?"

"Fine as can be."

"Good. Did you catch that message Quinten sent?"

"No ... should I have?"

"I know you keep your ear to the ground." That was a polite way to put it. Boston Sue was the biggest gossip this side of the Mississippi.

"Nothing came through."

"It was yesterday; bounced off our hub."

Her hesitation was so slight, I almost didn't catch it. "I'm sorry, but there hasn't been nothing but the usual chatter around here. You know I'd tell you if your brother were trying to get in contact with you."

I hadn't told her the message was for me.

She was either a really good guess or she was lying.

"Are you sure you didn't see anything come through?"

"One hundred percent."

"Okay," I said, "if you need anything . . ."

"We're fine here, Tilly. Keep yourself safe."

"I will. I'll call you soon."

"May the earth rise," she said.

"And the wind at your back," I answered.

I thumbed off the walkie-talkie and stuffed it in my duffel.

The door to the ladies' room opened. I jumped down off the arm of the couch, and walked out of the shadows.

Bede stepped through the door and smiled at me before heading into the washroom. "Needed a little time away from all the noise?" she asked.

Polite and nice, polite and nice.

"It's all a little overwhelming."

"I can imagine." She leaned forward at the sinks to study her reflection, tucked her hair behind her ears, then pulled a small sponge out of a pocket in her dress. "You grew up on a farm?"

"Yes."

"In my first life I had a piece of land. Grew squash, corn, beans. And apples, of course. Had a hard cider recipe that would knock your knickers off." She grinned then sponged gently at the blue stitches crossing her face.

"Do you miss it?"

"Every day." She sighed but was still smiling. "It was a long, long time ago. I think my memory has rubbed the dirt off it and made those days shine, but they were nice. Really nice."

"Well, I probably should get back," I said.

"Sure," she said. "Oh, and, Matilda, if you ever want to change Houses, I hope you'll keep Blue in mind. I know Troi Blue can come across as cold and imperial, but she's not unreasonable, like some of the heads of Houses."

"Thanks," I said. "I'll keep that in mind."

I walked out and did some quick math in my head.

I needed to contact someone in House Brown so I could send a message to Neds. He said he knew people who could help me disappear. Maybe they had other resources that could help find Quinten. But Abraham and the others were waiting for me and they'd get suspicious if I wandered away again.

So I pulled the small journal and pen out of my duffel and scribbled a note. When I got my chance to pass the note, I would be ready.

I tucked the note into my pocket and walked back into the room.

The warm roll of conversation and laughter made me pause a moment. Abraham spotted my entrance and stepped away from the stunningly beautiful blond woman he had been talking with.

January Sixth, House White, Medical gave me a cool appraisal and did not seem pleased with the results.

All right. We weren't going to be friends. But I could be polite to her until the end of the world. Or at least until I was announced at the gathering.

"Matilda," Abraham said, as he escorted me over to January, who looked like she could model if she didn't have white stitches running a line up her left cheek. Forget that. She could model even with the white stitches running up her cheek.

"This is January Sixth. She's House White."

She raised one perfectly sculpted eyebrow. "Hello, Matilda," she purred. Sounded like she was hungry for fresh meat.

"Hello," I said with the same I-can-take-you-down tone I used on feral beasts.

Okay, so maybe I was a little rusty on my polite.

Abraham must have noticed the tension, and quickly

stepped between us while guiding me over to the other side of the room.

"You've met Buck Eighth, House Black, Defense."

He was sitting across from Loy and Vance. Just as when I'd first seen him, he wore a black T-shirt and dark denim, both stretched over a lot of muscle. Those light green eyes of his set in a face that was pleasingly angular gave off a big-cat look.

"Nice to be properly introduced," he said, standing up and offering his hand. "Pleased to meet you, Matilda."

"And you," I said, shaking his hand.

He grinned at the contact, which I assume allowed him to feel full sensation. "I was just telling the others about you taking Abraham down with one kick."

"For the love of . . ." Abraham started. "It wasn't just one kick."

"I was there," Buck said. "I know what I saw."

"This," Abraham said, changing the conversation, "is Helen Eleventh, House Silver, Vices."

Helen sat on the couch between Vance and Loy, a beer in her hand. She was compactly built, with a sweep of short black hair ragged across her forehead and just below her ears. Her almond-toned complexion was set off by wide, heavily made-up eyes. Silver threads swirled across her face and down her neck in intricate, lacy patterns, as if stitched there for decoration.

She stood and walked around the coffee table and stopped right in front of me. She was a couple inches shorter than me, but carried herself like she was my superior.

"I've been hoping to get my eyes on you," she said, her smile attached almost as an afterthought.

"Pleased to meet you too," I said.

She put some teeth in her smile. "If you need anything, you remember that my House is always open for business."

"Relax, Helen," Abraham said. "We don't do business here."

She walked back to her place on the couch. "I'm just being friendly. Everyone has their vice, even our little country cousin. Don't you, Matilda?"

"Naw," I said, leaning into my accent. "Clean living and the occasional killing before breakfast keeps me fine."

Buck glanced up at me, then tipped his head down to hide his grin.

Abraham pivoted me around toward the rest of the room, so that Helen was at my back.

"Is this all of us?" Abraham said.

Dotty answered, "Except Robert and Foster."

As if on cue, the door opened and Foster First lumbered into the room. He was just as tall and colorless as when I'd met him on the street, his long black coat lined with yellow that matched the yellow stitches over almost every inch of his skin and scars.

The room went silent.

And then Bede came through the other door. "Foster!" she squealed. "You're here!" She jogged across the room and threw herself into his arms, hugging him tight.

"Bede," he breathed in a voice made of gravel and thunder.

"I am so happy to see you." She leaned back a bit to look up into his red eyes. "Are you happy to see me?"

His mouth pulled up in a crooked smile. "Yes." He patted her back fondly, and she let go of him.

Then each person in the room took turns walking up to him and greeting him.

It was like watching an elder or a holy man come to visit.

I was the last to say hello. Abraham walked with me.

"Foster First," he said. "This is Matilda Case. She is the thirteenth."

Foster searched my face, his own expression blank and unreadable. "Matilda Thirteenth," he intoned. "I have known you as a child."

"Are you sure?" I asked.

But he only bowed to me, then paced over to the

couch they'd left open for him, his footsteps heavy despite the lush carpet and padding.

Dotty handed me a glass of water. "Don't worry about Foster," she said. "Words aren't easy for him. He didn't mean any slight by it."

"Do you know what he meant? How he knew me?"

She glanced over at the big man who was accepting a glass of lemonade from Loy. "Maybe you remind him of a girl from his first life. It's difficult to say. Out of all of us, he has suffered the most."

Even though Dotty didn't say it, I thought I knew why Foster recognized me. I was alive, or at least this body of mine was alive, all those years ago. I wondered whom she had been before she fell asleep, never to wake, until I was stitched into her body and mind.

The conversation geared back up to friendly levels, and just shortly after, there was a knock on the door.

A woman opened it and cheerfully announced that the stage was set and if everyone was ready, it was time to attend. Dotty thanked her and shut the door.

"What about Robert?" Vance asked. "Has anyone heard from him?"

I glanced at Abraham, who shook his head, his hands tucked into loose fists. "I haven't."

Buck pushed up off the couch. "Well, Slater Orange keeps a damn tight leash. He'll be here when he can, I'm sure."

Everyone exited the room through the private hallway. At the end of that hall was another hall, which eventually emptied out into the back of a stage.

There were maybe half a dozen civilians here who looked organized, helpful, and excited at being surrounded by almost all the world's galvanized.

I stayed off to one side, as far away from the entrance to the actual stage as possible while one of the people went over the call-out schedule, which apparently would count down from Helen Eleventh to Foster First.

"Hey," a spiky-haired man shouted at me. "What are you doing here? Galvanized only." He started my way, but Abraham overtook him in four strides and placed his hand on his shoulder.

"She is here at my request," he said.

The man stilled like a rodent in the grip of a hawk.

"Yes, sir," he said. "My apologies."

"None needed." Abraham melted from killer to kindness in less than a second. He smiled and patted his shoulder. "It was my fault. I should have told you I invited a companion this evening."

"No need—no need at all," the man said. "I'll see that she's comfortable."

"Thank you." Abraham glanced over at me, and I was pretty sure that hot smile wasn't just for the civilian's benefit.

Man knew how to handsome up a place when he wanted to.

Abraham returned to the others, and Spiked Hair walked my way.

"I'm sorry to shout," he said. "But you wouldn't believe how many people try to get a little time backstage with the galvs."

"It's okay," I said. "I don't want to be in the way. Where should I stand during the show?" I crossed my arms and tapped two fingers against my elbow. He didn't notice.

"If you'd just step right over here, you'll have a good view." He pointed to a chair set near the door.

"Thanks." I dutifully took my seat.

There was a bit more rushing about and music was building in the room beyond the stage. I tapped two fingers, as if humming along to the song, but none of the workers responded.

So no help here. I needed to get that message to Neds.

Abraham turned to see where I'd gone off to. I smiled and waved my fingers at him. He gave me a "stay there" look and I turned on the "you betcha" smile.

Right. As soon as the show got started and he was busy, I'd sneak out and find someone in House Brown who could run the note for me. If someone noticed, I'd just say I got lost.

"Ladies and gentlemen," the announcer called out. "The moment we have all been waiting for. Please help me welcome our esteemed guests, the galvanized!"

The audience erupted into thunderous cheers, whistles, applause, and stomping. I put my fingers in my ears to take the edge off it.

Didn't help much.

"Helen Eleventh, House Silver!"

Compact, lacy-stitched Helen strode out onto the stage.

From where I sat, the stage stretched out in a wedge beyond the rigging and gear, lights above and around pulsing silver, the audience a dark sea of bodies, noise, and flashes of light. Helen waved at the crowd as one of the multiple screens lit up with images from her life.

Her stitches were brown, white, black, silver as the images flashed by: Helen wrapped in survival gear, dragging half a dozen men out of icy water, a sniper rifle to her eye as she took the shot that ended the Left Street hostage crisis. Helen leading a hundred men, women, and children out of the devastating three-county inferno. Helen standing behind Reese Silver, Vice.

She sat in the chair farthest down the stage.

The noise hadn't lowered but the announcer called out for Obedience Tenth, House Blue.

Spritely Bede hopped out on stage, waving just as Helen had.

Images of her past rolled out under blue lights, stitches fading from brown to green to yellow to blue. Obedience's history involved her world-changing breakthrough in clean-water production, and a haunting image of her running through a cloud of poison gas, her gas mask on the child in her arms. In the last image, she stood beside the regal Troi Blue.

Two more galvanized to go before Abraham took the stage.

Loy Ninth was announced next, and he swaggered out, kissing his fingertips and spreading his arms wide to the crowd.

Lights shifted to red and his past was played out on the screen: Loy opening the water valves of a damaged nuclear power plant, Loy digging through rubble of a collapsed mine shaft to reach trapped workers, and, finally, Loy standing beside the hard-edged Aranda Red.

Buck Eighth strolled out onto the stage and raised his hand to greet the crowd. Lights switched to flood the stage in colorless black and white, and the screens flashed with his life.

Buck's stitches were brown, gray, silver, gold, and black. The screens filled with images of Buck throwing himself in front of an assassin's bullet to save a head of House, Buck defusing a bomb set in the middle of a city, Buck taking down the top ten crime lords in Hong Kong.

Buck standing next to John Black.

Next up was Abraham. And while I was curious about what parts of his past would be put on display, I knew this was my chance to duck out.

The lights filtered to smoky gray and Abraham strode out onto the stage.

That was my cue. No one was paying attention to me. I snuck out the door we'd come in and followed the hallways until I was back at the waiting room. I slipped out that door and into the main lobby of the building.

The crowds had thinned, but there were still plenty of people gathered here, watching the big event on screens placed throughout the space.

I scanned the crowd, looking for a likely House Brown person willing to sneak the message out on the low.

Usually House Brown stayed out of cities and out of sight. But the chance to see the galvanized who had become an icon of House Brown heroism would draw in even the most city-shy person. I was counting on a higher-than-expected number of House Brown people to be among the crowds, especially if any of them were working unsanctioned temporary jobs for local businesses.

A man lounging by the outer door caught my gaze. I tapped two fingers on my thigh, and he nodded.

I walked over to him. "I need a favor," I said.

"All right," he drawled in a slow accent that made me smile. He was probably twenty years my senior, his hair combed back and short, his long face tanned and wrinkled. "What can I do for you, miss?"

"Do you live in city?"

"I spot job. Get home to the wife every three months or so."

"Can you get a message to someone for me? A friend? His name is Neds Harris. Works the Case property. Have you heard of him?"

"Can't say that I have. You know where about Mr. Harris might be?"

"This morning he was in Chicago, Gray Towers. Do you have a way to reach that far?"

"Isn't anywhere on earth House Brown can't reach," he said with a soft chuckle.

"Thank you. Um, I don't have much," I unzipped my duffel, digging through the things I'd stashed there. I pulled out two packets of seeds. "Tomatoes for you. Gladiolas for your wife."

He regarded the seeds like they were made of gold.

"Thank you," he said. "Thank you so much." I handed him the seeds with the note tucked between them, and they disappeared into his pocket.

He, rightly, offered me a trinket in exchange. Every inch of the city was wired with cameras and other recording devices. What they would see was me paying him for a thing, not for running a message.

Out of his other pocket he drew a small cloth. He unfolded it and plucked out a tiny doll. It was made of twine, carefully wound and tied into the shape of a little girl.

"She's good luck," he said.

"Thank you. I think I need her."

"Earth to you," he said.

"And the wind," I replied.

He went back to watching the screens, and I walked away, tucking the little doll in my pocket.

I glanced up at the screen. All the galvanized were on stage, taking questions from the audience. Good. While they were busy, I could do a little more footwork.

If anyone asked, I was just looking around. Enjoying the wonder of it all.

It took me a few minutes, but I finally found the data room on the third floor. I sat in the corner of the room nearest the door so I could dash out if I needed to, and tapped into the screen.

Just because I'd been raised in the sticks didn't mean I was a slouch with modern technology. Far from it, actually. I'd been data smuggling for most my life.

I hitched into the stream, dumped off into a subpar gutter line, and backtracked through enough antiquated systems, I was immediately lost to the noise.

This kind of data mining took longer, but it was as untraceable as a person could be while sitting in the middle of a city network. Minutes slipped past, rolling into a half hour, then an hour.

There was time. I still had time. The event was still rolling. People were still watching.

Abraham hadn't noticed I was missing.

Yet.

That was good, right?

I slipped a frequency, chewed on my fingernail as another twenty minutes ticked away. People came in and out of the room at a pretty steady pace, and I tried not to look up in panic every time a shadow crossed the doorway.

Finally, I got to where I wanted to be: a few hits outside the hub on my property. If I were lucky, there would be an echo of Quinten's message here. If I were really lucky, he would have sent a copy of the message to our brother-sister private off-site pocket.

"Come on, Quinten. Be a brilliant boy," I muttered as I keyed my way into the pocket.

One new message.

Cheers rolled through the building. I glanced at the event feed. The question-and-answer session was done and everyone was walking off stage.

Which meant Abraham was about to find out I wasn't sitting backstage.

Crap.

I just hoped he would have to go straight to autographs and pictures instead of hunting for me. And I hoped the other galvanized did the same.

Just in case I was at the top of his or anyone else's priority list, I quickly pulled up the message and read through it.

I could tell it was from Quinten because it began with the letters: QCTMBMITW, which was the acronym of a title I'd teased him with years ago: *Quinten Case, the most brilliant man in the world.*

Not even the Neds knew I called him that.

My heart was pounding.

The message was coded yesterday and simply said: *House Orange. Hidden enemy. WoM coordinates: 13.09. 2210.2400*

I erased it, backed out of the connection, blowing it as I went, backtracking and scrubbing my trail. I glanced at the clock while the minutes ticked down. To clean up everything, I'd need almost as much time backtracking as it took me to get into the info.

"Hurry, hurry," I whispered.

A half hour crawled by, an hour. I glanced up at the screen. Highlights of the question-and-answer session scrolled across it.

Recorded highlights. They must be done by now. They might even be looking for me.

Fifteen minutes. Fifteen more . . . and . . . yes!

I shut it all down, shouldered my duffel, and hurried out of there. Got down a flight of stairs and one more, then slowed my pace. I needed to find the autograph area, make it look like I'd ducked out to use the ladies' room again, and everything would be gold.

I rounded a corner.

And nearly ran into Abraham.

"Where have you been?" he asked.

"Looking for you," I said, not even lying. "I got turned around."

"For two hours?"

"It's all a little overwhelming."

"You hunt feral beasts in untrackable scrub." Abraham leaned against the wall, mostly in shadow. That didn't stop people from noticing him or from noticing me with him.

"Well, this isn't the scrub," I said. "Also, I'm not supposed to be seen, right?" More than a few people snapped pictures of us. "I was staying unseen."

He narrowed his eyes. I wasn't lying, but I wasn't telling him the whole truth either.

"We might want to move," I said. "Before everyone gets a picture of us. Do you have another event to attend?"

A man pushed past me, brushing against my shoulder as he did so. He whispered, "Done," and moved on.

"Here?" Abraham asked, while I snuck a look at the guy who just bumped into me. It was the man from House Brown who had taken my message out to Neds. Good. Very good.

"No," he said. "It's time for us to go." He nodded toward the nearest elevator and started off that way.

"Where are we going?" I asked.

"Training."

Right. Of course. For the big all-House public gathering I couldn't screw up.

We stepped into the elevator. Even though there were other people waiting, they didn't follow, giving us space and privacy. Abraham pressed a button. The doors closed, shutting away the people, the crowd, and my chance of tracking down anything more to help Quinten.

24

A new human-rights bill, ushered in by a new House Gray, ensured just treatment and fair process to all the people of the world. Except for the galvanized. The twelve bargained for human freedom for House Brown and became slaves once again. —2160
—from the journal of L.U.C.

The house was set on top of a rise, whalebone-gray siding, wraparound decks, and framing that supported more windows than I could count. It had three stories at least, the main-floor windows wrapped around a huge open living space that angled up for two floors of view.

Even though it was night and we'd been driving the streets for over an hour, it felt like we were worlds away from the bright, busy jumble.

"We're training here?" I asked.

"This is where we'll stay for the night."

"Who's place is it?

"Dotty's."

House Green. "And you're sure she's all right with us staying?"

He pulled up to a half-circle enclosure where he parked the car in one of the available stalls. "I'm sure. Did you find anything more about your brother's message?"

"What makes you think I looked?"

He just raised his eyebrow. "Matilda."

"Yes?"

"What did you find?"

I searched his face, and for a moment all the old House Brown secrecy kicked up in me. I didn't want to tell him what the message said if it would hurt Quinten. But it was just as likely that Quinten was already in some kind of trouble, already hurt and in need of rescuing.

I told him what it said.

"How did you find it?"

I shook my head. "You know. Carefully."

"Did anyone see you looking for it?"

"No."

He rubbed his fingers across the bottom of his jaw. "Are you sure it was from your brother?"

"Yes. He used a code that only he and I know. It was from him."

"Do the numbers mean something to you?"

"That's your takeaway? Numbers? What about *House Orange, hidden enemy*?"

"House Orange is an enemy to a lot of people, hidden or not. House Orange also *has* a lot of enemies. But if he felt this was his one chance to pass on important information, why those numbers? *WoM coordinates* doesn't mean anything to me. But the sequence could be time."

I ran the numbers through my head. "Five days from now?"

He nodded.

"Is there anything important happening five days from now?" I asked.

"Your brother must think so, but I don't know what it would be." He opened the door and walked back to the trunk for our luggage.

I didn't know what it could be either. I got out with my duffel and rifle. The air was cool and damp and slightly salty. I wondered how far away from the ocean we were.

"Rifle stays in the car," he said.

I reluctantly set the rifle back in the car but didn't mention I still had my revolver in my duffel.

"Oscar had a meeting with Reeves Silver," Abraham said. "It appears the head of House Vice was unaware Quinten was under his employ."

Since Reeves Silver was the head of Vice—it made sense he might not know the names of all the people working beneath him. Houses were huge, world-sprawling conglomerates, made of multiple companies and industries all held together beneath the House umbrella.

I glanced over at the scowl Abraham was wearing. "You don't believe him?"

"I think there isn't a thing that happens in House Silver without Reeve's knowledge."

"Do you think he's . . . holding him prisoner?" There it was. My fear. That my brother was held against his will, hurt and alone.

"I don't know," he said, then softer: "I really do not know, Matilda. But we can't jump to conclusions about your brother and risk losing you. Things are rarely as they seem between the Houses. Reeves Silver may or may not be involved. He may have your brother working a project he doesn't want House Gray to know about. He may have subcontracted your brother to another House, or there may be a contractual agreement between your brother and him that necessitates secrecy. Quinten could be fine."

From his tone of voice, even he didn't believe that.

"All right," I said. "Let's say it's one of those things. What do we do?"

"We find out who's lying, who's telling the truth, and we find your brother. I'll check in with Oscar again. Tell him what the message you found said. We don't make a move until we have House Gray behind us on this. I need you to agree to that, Matilda. If you want the power of House Gray to help you, if you want to remain with us, do not undermine our efforts to help you."

"Okay," I said, "okay."

Quinten was smart and strong and patient. Plus there was one other thing about the message I hadn't told Abraham. Quinten hadn't said good-bye. If he thought his life was in danger, if he thought he was going to die, I was sure he'd say good-bye to me.

Wouldn't he?

We walked past what looked like a courtyard of flowers and bushes with little paths that led to benches and maybe a pond, then stepped up to the wood-and-glass door. There was a lot of light coming through the windows.

He pushed the door wide.

The room itself was huge, soft lights shining against those tall, tall windows to catch copper in the amber woodwork and white walls. I would have taken a little more time to marvel over the place: the thin sun shades covering the highest windows, the rounded edges of the kitchen that was open to this great room, the tasteful but built-for-comfort couches, chairs, tables, and throw rugs adding pops of color to the place.

But the galvanized, all of them except Foster First and the missing Robert Orange, were lounging around the room, playing cards, relaxing.

"Bram!" Loy called out. "Found her, I see."

"Everything all right?" Buck asked.

"Oh, the poor little thing," January cooed, "I can't imagine how frightened she must have been, all alone in all that fancy light and noise."

Well, wasn't she a peach?

"She's fine," Abraham said, answering Loy and Buck and throwing January a look.

"I'm glad you made it." Dotty wiped her hands on a towel and strolled out of the kitchen. "It's been a long day for us all. Welcome to my home. Let me show you to your room."

"Home?" I asked.

"Abraham's told you why we're here, hasn't he?"

"To train for the gathering?"

Bede and Vance chuckled.

"Abraham," Dotty scolded. "You had this poor girl thinking she was going to be fighting for her life?"

"No," he said. "I just said there'd be training, and there will be. She's never been to a gathering before. I thought we could talk her through it."

Wila *tsk*ed through her teeth. "I suppose all the Houses want to stake claim to you."

"I'm happy with House Gray," I said.

Dotty poked a finger at Abraham. "Shame on you for worrying the girl. Take her luggage to her room. Main floor with the south view."

"Is that an order?"

"Do I need to remind you to mind your elders, young man?"

"No, ma'am."

"Go on, then."

"Yes, ma'am."

"And Matilda?" she said. "Don't worry yourself. There is no training, just a few guidelines for what is expected at the gathering. We're all friends here."

"Thank you," I said.

"Room's this way," Abraham said.

I followed him down a wide hall and past several rooms and through an open door. He dropped the suitcases at the foot of the bed. The room smelled of lavender and mint.

"No training, eh?" I asked.

"Not so much, no."

I grinned. "Jerk."

He chuckled.

"I might need it anyway. Being polite isn't as easy as I'd thought. I'll be lucky to get through the night without January wanting to stab me."

"Don't worry about her. She just doesn't like competition."

"For what?"

"Everything." He strolled across the room, moved the curtain to look outside, then walked back toward the door.

"If I'm the only one who hasn't been to a gathering, why is everyone else here?"

"We all request the time from our Houses every year."

"So you can get a day off?"

"So we can get a day off, together, without being bothered by anyone in the world. It's . . . rare to relax, game, eat, gossip. For a full twenty-four hours, we aren't galvanized. We're just people." He smiled, but old regret shadowed his eyes. One day of freedom wasn't nearly enough compared to years of captivity.

I opened my mouth to tell him I was sorry, or maybe to say something comforting and cheerful, but he shook his head and changed the subject.

"There is something else we should take care of," he said. "I hoped we'd have time to do this in-city, but maybe here is better."

"What?"

He held a small liquid packet the size of my thumbnail in his palm. "Your mother's recording that sent me out to your property, looking for you and your father. I know now that she's gone, but I promised I'd let you see this."

I stared at the drop of liquid. I hadn't forgotten. It seemed so strange that a message from my long-dead mother had mysteriously surfaced and sent him out to my farm. Changing my life so completely.

"Do you know where it came from?"

He shook his head. "We traced it but couldn't catch the origin."

Maybe Quinten had sent it. No, he had worked hard to keep our farm and me a secret. But who else would have access to such an old recording? And who would benefit from House Gray sending Abraham to look for me?

"I never asked," I said, settling on the foot of the bed. "How did you get that gut wound?"

"In a fight."

"With whom?"

"Someone else who intercepted this message. Robert."

"Robert? The galvanized from House Orange?"

"Yes."

"I thought you said he was your friend."

"He is."

"Your *friend* split you open and nearly bled you out."

"True. But he didn't behead me, which I appreciate."

"That is the lowest bar for friendship I've ever heard of."

He chuckled. "Trust me, Robert is a good man."

"Trust the word of a man who thinks a beheading is a flesh wound?"

"I didn't say it wouldn't have been inconvenient."

"Death is inconvenient?"

"Being dismembered is inconvenient. I don't know about death." He crossed his arms and leaned on the wall. "We had to put on a good show so Slater Orange would believe him when he said he tried to stop me, and that I got away with the message before he could."

"Robert wanted you to find me?"

"Robert caught the message and brought it to me. House Orange would not have taken you in with kindness. Slater Orange is a vicious dictator."

"Which makes him so different from the other heads of Houses?"

"Which makes him different from Oscar."

"What about House White?"

"What about it?"

"They showed up on my farm. Looking for you."

"I know. We don't know who tipped them off."

"Maybe your friend Robert?"

"I don't think so." At my look, he shrugged. "It's possible, but I'd be surprised. We go back a long way. So?"

"So?" I echoed.

He held up the drop with my mother's message. "If

you want, I'll leave you alone to watch it. Or I can sit with you."

"I think ... I think I'd rather watch it alone." I got up and he pressed the little packet onto my palm.

"If you need me," he said, running his warm fingers down the outside of my arm, "I'll be right out there on the other side of the door."

"I know. I'll be out soon."

He shut the door, and I sat on the edge of the bed and rubbed my eyes. I felt like I'd been up for days. Considering how little sleep I'd gotten before Neds and I had gone out for coffee this morning, I really had been up for almost two days straight.

At least here in the room it was quiet and quasiprivate. That reduced my chances of saying or doing something stupid in front of the others. I didn't want to ruin my hope of staying with House Gray, even though it meant giving up my freedom.

What I wanted was sleep.

What I needed was to talk to Neds. If he could use House Brown's network to figure out what Quinten's message meant or maybe to find where it originated, I would at least have a trail to follow that might lead to my brother.

I stared down at the drop in my hand.

What I had to do was watch this message.

It had been so long since I'd seen my mom, since I'd heard her voice. It seemed strange I'd be seeing her here, now, so far away from the home and surroundings in which I knew her in most.

I moved to the head of the bed and pressed the drop into the small indent in the bedside table.

An image caught fire on the wall across from me.

A woman's face appeared there, a little out of focus and bathed in a soft green light, but clear enough to make out her features.

I held my breath, memories clutching at me with sharp fingers. She looked older, thinner, her hair cut so short it made her eyes look too wide and robbed her of the softness I remembered. But that was her. Definitely her. My mother.

I exhaled and pulled my shoulders back.

Mom's thumb was pressed against the screen of whatever recording device she was holding. The room around her was dark, just a slice of light coming in from under what must be a door.

"My name is Professor Edith Case," she said in a rough whisper that stilled my heart. "If you receive this message, I implore you take it to House Gray and invoke the decency of jury and trial offered to all human citizens. I believe my husband, Dr. Renault Case, may be alive and on the property registered in the name of Case under House Green."

A shadow broke the light beneath the door and she shot a look over her shoulder.

"Please," she whispered, the image of her shaking as a tear slipping down her cheek. "Save him. And if she's still alive," she bit her lip, and even more quietly said, "save my daughter, Matilda."

The screen went blank.

I wiped the back of my hand over my cheeks, drawing away my tears. I'd never seen her so terrified, so desperate. I wish I could have done something for her. Wish I could have hugged her and told her I was fine. Everything was fine.

Except it wasn't. I'd signed myself into House Gray, Grandma might be in trouble, and Quinten was missing.

How had my life fallen apart so quickly?

I pried the drop out of the indent and the image of my mother faded away. I tucked the drop in my duffel, then dragged the duffel up to the top of the bed with me, crossing my arms over it.

I needed a plan. A way to find Quinten, a way to see that Grandma really was okay and that Boston Sue wasn't lying to me about missing Quinten's message.

I'd seen the surveillance cameras when we'd driven

up to this place. I knew there was no chance I could sneak away.

Yet. I had promised I'd give Abraham time to see if House Gray could do anything to help Quinten. I had promised I wouldn't do something foolish to ruin my chance of staying with House Gray. And I would follow through on both those promises if I could.

I rubbed at my eyes again and pressed my back against the headboard, inhaling the lavender scent of the room. I closed my eyes.

I didn't want to sleep.

Turned out I didn't get any say in that.

A knock on the door woke me.

"Matilda," Abraham said. "Are you awake?"

I pushed up, rubbed my eyes, and stared into the dim light of the room. How long had I been sleeping? No clocks. I smoothed my hair then walked over to the door and opened it. "What time is it?"

"About nine. You've been in here for two hours. Everything okay?"

"Relatively?"

He smiled slightly. "Did you watch it?"

"Yes. It was...." I didn't know what to say. "Thank you for bringing it."

His moss green eyes went soft as he studied me, and I promised myself I was not going to cry again. "Are you okay?"

"She was scared, but it was.... I'm glad ... to see her again, it's just...." I stopped, unable to trust my words for fear that tears would follow.

He paused, watching me for a moment while I tried to smile. Then he pulled me into him, wrapping his arms around me.

I shouldn't do this. I shouldn't want this comfort from this man, but I didn't want to pull away. I pressed my forehead against the hard muscle and warmth of his chest, wishing I could stay there forever. He held me while I gave in to quiet tears. Then he held me a little longer. Finally, he kissed me gently on my temple and I drew away.

"Can I help?" he asked, wiping my cheek with his thumb.

"No," I brushed the rest of my tears away and took a deep breath. "It's old pain. There is no cure." I pulled together a smile. "I'd like to think about something else. Anything."

"Dotty put some tea on and there's dinner if you're hungry."

I was starved. "Food sounds perfect."

"Good. Then come on out. The first game is up and I need a partner."

"Game? There are nine people out there. Ask one of them to be your partner."

"I did. They say I cheat."

"Do you cheat?"

"Of course. But, then, so do they."

"Bram! Do we need to come back there and save you?" someone, I think Loy, yelled from the other room. "Did she kick you again?"

The mingling of voices, good-humored arguments, and laughter filtered down to us. Sounded like a party out there.

"Promise I'll cut you in for ten percent of the take," he said.

"Ten percent? What do you think I am, a rube?"

"Naw, you're all upstage. But you are also hiding in your bedroom, *darb*."

"Darb?"

"Sorry—I was around when that slang was new. It means excellent, top-notch, desirable."

Oh. That was nice.

"Well, aren't you all charm and a half?" I asked. "Also? I'm not hiding in my room. What kind of game are they playing?"

"Probably cards."

"Fine," I said. "Sixty percent." I stepped out and closed the door behind me.

"Thirty."

"Sixty-five," I said.

"Thirty-one," he countered.

We walked down the hall. "How about I cut you in on ten percent since you admitted there is no one else who will play with you?"

"Thirty-two," he said. "You wouldn't be playing without me either."

We had passed through the far side of the sitting room, and the full, delicious smell of fruit pies and something savory wrapped around me.

"There you are," Dotty said. She pulled a pie out of a high oven using two towels as hot mitts. "Wondered if you were going to sleep the whole evening away. Abraham said you needed some rest."

"I just didn't want to be in the way."

She set the pie down and turned to me. "Nonsense. Have you eaten?"

"Not for a while."

"Help yourself." She waved at a pile of fried chicken, a bowl of cooked greens, and a pot of buttery grits.

"I think there's a game . . ." I started.

"Oh, sugar pea, there's always a game," she said.

"There you are, Matilda!" a voice I didn't recognize called out.

I glanced across the room and froze. Welton Yellow, the head of House Yellow, Technology, stood beside the long wooden table in the main room, his galvanized, Foster First, looming behind him.

25

They say those were the peaceful years. Houses and galvanized worked together to create a united front, to settle the unrest, to rebuild the world. The first gathering was held, displaying the prowess and advancements achieved by the Houses and their galvanized. —2175
—from the journal of L.U.C.

Welton wore a yellow T-shirt, this one imprinted with the image of a snail with laser beams coming out of its eyes, torn blue jeans, and a smile.

"Saved you a seat at the game, Bram, my friend," he said, "and I plan to rob you blind."

"How did that plan go last year?" Abraham asked.

"Poorly. You cheated."

"You couldn't prove that."

"This year," Welton said, "I will be winning back my money. Plus interest."

Abraham must have noticed my discomfort. He reached over and gently squeezed my arm. "He's family."

"Mostly because we can't get rid of him," Dotty said, setting a plate of pie and a mug of tea down on the kitchen counter for me. "Annoying boy that he is."

"Please," Welton said. "You love me most of all."

"Well, you have your moments. Like when you're losing at poker."

Welton's gave her a self-satisfied smile, then looked back at me. "Matilda Case. How was the coffee at Jangle?"

"Fine, thank you, sir."

The corner of his mouth quirked up and he leaned forward, resting his elbow on the table, his smooth dark bangs falling to the edge of his heavily lidded eyes. "Here I'm a friend. I suppose you should address me by *sir* anywhere else. But not here. Not at all."

"All right, thank you . . ." I didn't know if I should use his first name.

"Welton," he said slowly, as if I hadn't heard him the first time. "And you . . . you are the mysterious new old. The modern stitched. I've heard more than a few things about you. Come"—he patted the table—"have a sit. Let's talk."

"I promised Abraham a game," I said.

"No rush," Abraham said.

Manners, Matilda, I reminded myself.

I picked up the pie and tea and walked over to the table. I took a seat across from Welton. At the other end of the table, Helen was shuffling cards, but not dealing, and watching me like I was something she might need to tackle.

Vance and Bede were curled up on a couch, talking quietly and Clara, January, and Wila sat on the other couches, rolling dice and scribbling on paper. Beyond them, Buck and Loy were arguing over something that involved throwing coins into shot glasses.

But the figure who drew my eye was Foster First, who moved to stand at the far side of the room, his back to the window, staring at me, or maybe at Welton's back.

Even in this large space, he towered over everyone. From his complete stillness, one might just assume he was dead. But his eyes flicked as he took in all those in front of him, his stony expression unchanging.

"If House Gray hadn't found you first, I would have offered you a place at House Yellow, you know," Welton said.

I drew my gaze away from Foster. "Oh?" I took a bite of pie: apple, cinnamon. Delicious. "I am happy to be with House Gray."

"Why?"

"It seems like a good choice."

"So you can find your brother?"

I was surprised he knew about that. But, then, he was Technology. If anyone could find information, it would be him.

"I saw the message he sent," he continued a little quieter. "We're working on tracking it back. Oscar Gray is a personal friend of mine. I am helping find your brother as a personal favor. You won't owe my House anything."

"There are always debts," I said.

"True," he said. "Some debts are worth getting into, don't you think?"

"Do you have any idea how long it will be before you find something?"

"If we don't have it cracked before the gathering, I'll hang up my hat and hand the House over to my cousin."

"Which one?" Dotty asked, sliding pie down for him, herself, and an extra, then sitting at the table. "Libra?"

"Yes."

"You are a terrible man, Welton," she said as she scooped up a bite of pie.

"Come on, now," he protested. "She has a set of morals. More or less. And her utter love of chaos would make things a little less . . . boring." He grinned at me, and I got the impression he was always on the lookout for things that would keep his life interesting.

"As for settling any debt between us, personally," he said. "I'd like to ask you a few questions. Is it true you have sensation of touch?"

"Yes."

Abraham had walked over to Foster and offered him a mug with what looked like marshmallows floating on top of it. I caught a whiff of rich chocolate. He was giving Foster hot cocoa.

Foster took the mug and his mouth hooked up into a smile. "Thank you, Abraham."

His voice was gravel down a canyon, but his smile contained a humanity I had glimpsed only briefly in him.

"I am curious about the thread that's holding you together," Welton said around a bite of pie. "And most everything else about how you came to be."

Abraham smiled and shook his head. "I thought you wanted to lose some money." He crossed over to the table. "Not grill Matilda on private matters."

"Are these details you don't want to share?" Welton asked.

"No, it's fine. Truth is, I don't know much about the thread. I think my father invented it."

"May I?" he asked, wiping his fingers on his pants then holding out his hand to touch the stitches across my left wrist.

I hesitated. Then put my hand in his.

He gently drew his finger across my stitches and a shiver of goose bumps rippled up my arm.

"Amazing work," he said. "Do you know who made you?"

Here it was, the question of where I'd come from. I'd told Oscar, but I didn't know if he'd told Welton.

If I lied, would it put my claim to House Gray in danger? If I told him Quinten had stitched me together and saved my life, would it put my brother in more danger than he might already be in?

"I don't really know."

Welton tipped his head to one side. "You don't remember?"

"I was young."

"When you were stitched?"

I nodded.

"That's . . . unusual. Very unusual," he said. "There is another thing I'd like to know. Abraham tells me when you touch him, his sense of touch is restored."

"He's told me the same."

"Would you please touch Foster? I'd like to know if certain . . . modifications I've implemented are as pain-free as I'd intended them to be."

"That is not necessary," Foster said in that low growl of his. "I have no complaints."

"For me," Welton asked. Then, with all the maturity of a seven-year-old: "Please?"

Foster sighed and walked over to me, his boots loud and heavy on the floor. He stood in front of me, and I had to tip my head up to meet his gaze.

"Thank you, Matilda Case," he said. He offered his hand, and I took it.

His shoulders stiffened and he sucked in a hard breath. The skin around his neck pulled against the thick yellow threads there, and he moaned softly.

I quickly drew my hand back.

"Does it hurt?" Welton asked, immediately on his feet and moving toward him.

"Not pain," Foster said, as Welton pressed his fingers at different points on Foster's hand, arm, chest, and back. Foster caught the slighter man's hand in the ham fist of his own. "Peace."

"I might ask you to do that again, Matilda," Welton said, not looking away from Foster. "Maybe after the gathering and under more controlled conditions."

"Unnecessary," Foster rumbled.

"That regulator shouldn't be popping like that," Welton said. "And it's something easily adjusted so it won't cause you pain, whether you feel it or not. After the gathering, we will see to it. Please," he added kindly. "For me."

"You are my House," Foster said. "If it is your wish."

"It is my wish." He patted Foster's arm.

"So, what do you think this means, Welton?" Dotty asked. "I suppose a genius such as yourself has more than one theory on Matilda's effect on us."

"And you would be right," he said. "We know each of you lived at the same time, in the same area, before the Wings of Mercury event occurred."

"I've heard of that," I said. "Wings of Mercury. Abraham mentioned it."

Welton nodded. "We have stories passed down from person to person, town to town, or the occasional line in a diary or footnote in a published journal. A scientist searching for the secrets of immortality built a great machine to control time. When that machine was engaged, every living creature in a fifty-mile swath was struck down dead.

"Except for twelve people. Six men, six women. They still breathed, though it was as if they had been sent into a deep sleep. There was also rumor of one child who never woke from that sleep and did not age."

He stopped and watched my reaction. Everyone in the room was watching me.

"I'm that child, aren't I?"

"We can't be sure," he said. "We don't know where any of the pieces of you came from. But all signs point to yes.

"If, however," he went on, "the event was an experiment to control time, the theory goes that it is the reason galvanized brains have survived all these years. Only galvanized brains resist every strain of disease on earth; feel no pain; and are inhumanly strong, adaptive, and infinitely repairable. Only galvanized brains show no sign of aging or decline. Only galvanized are immortal—cheaters of time."

He spread his hands. "The experiment was a story, a legend. The sleeping immortals who would rise and bring about great change. Save the world. Or end it, depending on which story you preferred. Monsters. Saviors. And like all good legends, it had just enough clues and small truths to lead curious people to concoct theories and exhaustive hunts.

"Eventually, the sleeping immortals were found. Taken in by the scientists of the early twentieth century, and the experiments began."

Foster First made a low, quiet sound that was almost a moan.

Welton shifted in his chair and patted the big guy's arm fondly. "Things that will never happen again. Great mistakes were made. But galvanized are strong. The First endured, survived, and eventually fell into much kinder hands."

Foster First turned his head to stare down at Welton, and his expression was grateful. It made me rethink their relationship. Maybe Foster was happy to be with House Technology. If there were any advancements that could make being galvanized more tolerable, House Technology would be on the leading edge of it. And it did not look like Welton wanted Foster to suffer.

Welton pointed at Foster's face. "Cocoa on your cheek."

Foster lifted his huge hand and wiped at the side of his face.

"Right." Welton turned back to me. "The galvanized were brought in, reawakened sometimes decades apart, since there was some shuffling of who really had the claims to the brains and bodies, who had power to do certain procedures, a rise and fall of medical and technological advances, and, of course, the Restructure that set the world under House rule, kicked off the downfall, the Uprising. History—blah, blah, blah.

"But the machine that created the galvanized, if there ever was a machine that altered time, was never found. It has long been assumed the records were destroyed, lost. They've certainly never turned up. And once certain people saw the value in having such powerful creatures on their side"—he lifted his hands to indicate all of us in the room—"everything that could be done to figure out how they were made or how to re-create them was done."

He tipped his head down. "Unsuccessfully. No one has been able to immortalize a brain, nor come up with a fully repairable body. No one. Or so we've thought for many, many years."

He glanced around. "Did I cover it pretty well?"

Dotty tapped the edge of a deck of cards on the table. "Not bad for a kid."

He slid her a grin. "Now do you understand why you are so sought after, Matilda? No one has made a galvanized or discovered a galvanized in a couple hundred years. And if Abraham hadn't pulled you in when he did, you would have had more than one House at your door, claiming you as their own."

"Including you," Loy muttered, as he walked over and took a seat at the table.

"Of course including me," Welton said, his eyes half-closed like a sleeping cat's. "But it only made sense that a galvanized who enjoys conversation and doesn't frighten small children be the one sent to talk to her about her choices. Which ruled me out."

I glanced up at Foster. That stony, almost inhuman expression hardened his face again. I thought he might not really be angry; he just looked that way. All the time.

"Since House Gray and I work very well together . . ." He shrugged. "So little energy and resources from me, and I still get a chance to talk to you. How is that not a brilliant outcome?

"But that thread," he said, staring at the stitches on my wrist. "It isn't anything I've seen in biomodification. Do you have more of it?"

"Yes. On the farm."

I still didn't want to reveal any secret I didn't have to. Like the laboratory beneath the pump house out on my property.

The only reason Neds knew about the lab was because I'd been skewered pretty badly by the pony, and had to have him fetch me the threads since I was losing blood too quickly to do much good for myself.

"What would I have to do to get a length of it from you?"

"Well, you'd have to let me go home."

"I can arrange that."

"Can you?" I glanced at Abraham, who rolled his eyes.

"You rule House *Yellow*, Welton," Abraham said. "Not every House in the world."

"I don't have to rule every House to get what I want," he said.

"What about what we want?" Dotty asked. "We've been waiting for a game of five-card stud for an hour now. Close your mouth and open your wallet, Welly. Who's in?"

Loy, Buck, and Abraham all took to the table. Along with Dotty and Welton, it was a pretty full game.

Helen stood from the couch. "I'm going out for a walk," she announced.

"Want company?" Wila offered.

"No. I just need some fresh air." She threw a look my way, like I was the one stinking up the place.

I did not know what I'd done to get under that woman's hide. We'd barely spoken.

She closed the door behind her, and I headed over to the kitchen to get some tea.

So far, I thought I'd handled myself well, or at least well enough I didn't think I'd be removed from House Gray. If I could just stay out of January's judgmental gaze and not do something stupid like pick a fight with Helen, I might even make it through the night.

I stayed in the kitchen while my tea steeped.

A knock at the door made every face in the room turn in that direction.

"Who knocks?" Welton asked.

"No one," Dolores said. "Helen?"

Every person stood.

Foster First, Abraham, and Buck strode over to the door. Foster opened it, his huge body and coat blocking the entire doorway and the night beyond.

"Aren't you going to invite me in?"

I knew that voice.

Foster stepped aside, and Robert Twelfth from House

Orange walked into the room. Buck gave him one up-and-down look, then shook his head and walked away.

Foster stepped outside, looked at the dark yard, then walked back in and shut the door.

"You knocked?" Abraham asked. "Since when do you think this is a formal affair?"

Robert shrugged. "I didn't want to startle anyone. It is late."

"Never too late for a brother to arrive." Abraham held out his hand, intending to pull him into that half hug they'd done in the abandoned garage, but Robert took his hand instead and shook it.

The last time I'd seen them meet, there had been a lot more smiling, some back patting, and general pleasure in seeing each other.

But now Robert seemed reserved, and maybe even suspicious of Abraham's greeting.

I wondered if something was wrong.

"It is good to see you, Abraham," Robert said with a stilted formality. "It is good to see you all."

A few people waved or called out a hello.

"What took you so long?" Abraham asked.

"There were some House matters that needed my attention," he said.

Still so formal.

"Food's cold, but there's plenty of it," Dotty said. "Help yourself to it, Rob."

"And bring me a beer," Abraham said, slapping Robert on the shoulder.

From where I stood in the kitchen halfway across the room, I saw him scowl, but no one else was paying much attention to him.

He started toward the kitchen and then he saw me.

He stopped, and his body language changed. Robert was just a little taller than me, bald, and sharp featured, with a tight mustache and beard that circled his thin mouth. He wore a pair of rectangular glasses, the lenses of which were orange.

We'd met before. He'd called me sister. But from the way he was looking at me—surprise and a whole lot of what looked like hunger—I wouldn't have guessed he'd ever put eyes on me.

"Matilda," he said.

"Hello, Robert."

"Beer, Rob," Abraham called out. "Anytime now."

And there it was again. The anger, the annoyance. *Weird.*

"Here you go." I handed him a beer from the refrigerator.

The poker game was back on, and the game of dice and paper had been revived by Wila, January, Vance, and Bede.

Which meant besides Foster and Robert, everyone was playing something. Robert reluctantly turned and delivered the beer then settled at a table by the window, watching the room.

His eyes followed me as I walked over to the poker game.

I didn't know what was wrong with him, but he was not acting like himself at all. Or at least not like the man I'd met very briefly once.

Maybe I wasn't the best judge. If no one else thought he was acting strangely, and since they all seemed comfortable with him, I had to assume that was true, then it must just be the way he was.

I stopped next to the game table, behind Abraham's shoulder. He tipped his hand and thumbed the cards so I could see them.

A pair of twos and nothing else.

"Want the next hand?" he asked.

"Sure," I said. "What are we betting?"

"Favors," Welton said.

"It's flexible," Dotty said. "Since you're House Gray, you can bet Abraham's money."

"Hey, now," he said. "Don't go promising my pocket, Dotty."

She chuckled and won the pot on three aces.

Abraham shook his head and pushed away from the table toward the kitchen. "And you all think *I* cheat."

"What did you have in the pot, Bram?" she asked.

"Must be something good." Loy winked at me and took a drink of beer.

"One free month of workforce on one job," Abraham said, "fifty people or fewer."

She plucked a piece of paper out of the pile she'd gathered up. "No, honey, you promised me one free month of workforce on one job, two hundred people or fewer. And I know Feye Green is gonna be happy with that one."

"Oh, I'll win it back," he said.

She grinned at me. "It's cute when he thinks he's in my league."

Welton laughed. "None of us are in your league."

Helen return from her walk, settling on the couch across from Wila and Bede.

Robert crossed the room and stopped next to me.

"Matilda," he said, "I would like a moment with you, please."

"I think I'm in the next hand," I said.

"It is important."

He'd helped Abraham bring us to the city undetected. I supposed I could give him a minute or two of my time.

"Sure, all right. I'll catch the next round," I said.

"Suit yourself," Dotty said.

Robert led me out of the room and down the hallway toward my bedroom. I stopped midway between the living area and the darker reaches of the hall.

He might be Abraham's friend, but I did not know the man.

"So, what did you want to talk about?" I asked.

"You will come with me to someplace more"—he glanced at the living room behind me with disdain—"private."

There was something really off with him. Sure, I didn't

know him all that well, but every instinct in my body was screaming that something was wrong. Really wrong. And, sure, I could take care of myself in a fight, but I was not dumb enough to go somewhere private with a man I'd barely met when my instincts were pushing the needle to red.

"Actually, I'm very tired," I said. "Apologies, Robert, but I'm going to say my good nights and go to bed now."

I took a step to move past him, and he reached out and grabbed my hand.

"You go nowhere without my permission, stitch," he snarled.

26

This, now, is something even the Houses do not know. The Wings of Mercury experiment did more than create the galvanized. It altered time, but not in the way Alveré Case had predicted it would. —2184
— from the journal of L.U.C.

"If you don't let go of my arm, I will break yours," I said calmly.

"You dare—"

"Robert," Welton called out. "We've dealt you a hand. Come on over before we decide your antisocial behavior is because you're trying to hide something. We have ways to get you to talk, you know."

He squeezed my arm a little harder before letting go. "We will speak tomorrow, after you have rested."

"Sure," I said.

No way in hell.

He walked away and I stood there taking ten or thirty breaths to tie down my anger.

He had threatened me. He had treated me like something he owned, called me stitch.

I didn't care that he was Abraham's friend. He was not mine.

I strode down to the bedroom, locked the door, then took a shower, letting heat and water wash away the anger in me. I quickly toweled off, dried my hair, and slipped into the silky gray nightgown I found in my luggage. Just in case, I placed my boots right by the bed, easy to get into, and my revolver on top of the quilt next to me. I wrapped my arm through the duffel.

If I had to run in the middle of the night, I'd be ready.

Even though I was tired, my thoughts raced. It might have been rude of me not to tell everyone I was going to bed for the night, but manners be damned. I wanted as far away from Robert, January, and Helen as I could get. Hell, right now I wanted as far away from here, and anything that had to do with galvanized and Houses, as I could get.

But we still hadn't found Quinten.

"Tilly," a voice whispered.

I opened my eyes and stared straight ahead, shocked into stillness, fear sweat prickling across my face and chest. Someone was in my room. The thin blue light coming in through the window meant it was already dawn.

I had fallen asleep.

"Tilly," the voice whispered again by the partially open window.

Someone wasn't in the room; they were just outside it.

I rolled over and sat in the same motion, grabbing up my revolver, aiming straight at the voice.

Standing just outside the open window with the rising light at his back was a familiar two-headed figure.

"Je-hellzus, Matilda," Left Ned said, backing away from the window. "Put the damn gun down."

"Did you get my message?" I set the gun on the quilt and pushed out of bed. I shoved feet into boots and crossed to the window.

"Yes," Right Ned said. "And your brother . . . he's not safe. But I have an idea on how to get to him."

"Let me get Abraham. Hold on a second."

"No," Left Ned said. "You need to come with us. Now. You're not safe here. Grab your stuff."

"If I leave, I'll lose my standing with House Gray.

Some other House can claim me and my land, and Grandma might not be safe. Have you talked to Boston Sue?"

"Just"—Right Ned held out his hand—"trust me, Tilly. I promise you I can make this all right."

I hesitated. Leaving wouldn't go over well with House Gray. Or Abraham. But if Neds knew where Quinten was and how to help him, well. . . . I'd deal with the fallout after my brother was safe.

"Get in here." I pushed the window open so he could step up into the room. "Let me change." I grabbed my duffel and jogged into the bathroom to get into my pants and shirt.

This was a stupid idea. Oscar wasn't going to be happy about it. But if Neds and I brought my brother back to House Gray, he'd take us in, wouldn't he? Quinten was still claimed by House Gray.

If House Gray wouldn't take me or Quinten, some other House would want us. Who would be powerful enough to claim us? Welton?

No, forget that. If my brother and I were together again, we'd just disappear. Fall so far off the radar even House Brown wouldn't know where we were. We'd stayed hidden for years. We could do it again.

But what would happen to Grandma?

I finished getting dressed and strapped the duffel over my shoulder. "Okay," I said, walking out of the bathroom. "Let's—"

Robert stood in the middle of the room. He had a gun in his hand. A gun pointed at Neds.

"What is this mutation doing here?" he said.

"Mutation?" Left Ned said.

"He's a friend, remember?" They'd met in the parking garage. How could he forget that?

"That's not Robert, Matilda," Right Ned said quietly.

"What?"

Robert lifted the gun even with Right Ned's head. "Leave. Immediately."

"Tilly," Right Ned said. "I promise you, I'm not crazy. Please listen to me."

"You have made a very poor decision in coming here," Robert said.

"Whoa, hold on," I said. "Just settle down. We don't need a discharge of weapons to settle this. I'm not going anywhere. Neds are leaving."

I slowly walked over until I was standing between Neds and Robert.

Neds were holding very still but hadn't raised his hands. If his habits remained true, he had a couple weapons stashed on his body.

This could go so very bad so very quickly.

"Tilly," Ned said.

"There is no fight here," I said. "Nothing is wrong. Do you understand me, Robert? Everything is all right."

"And why," he asked, taking his eyes off Neds for just a moment to look at me, "do you think I would listen to you?"

The chill behind those words was enough to stop me cold.

I was standing so close he could touch me. Which was hopefully close enough that I could stop him from firing that gun on Neds.

He turned the gun on me.

Oh, hell, no.

I grabbed his wrist and swept his foot. The gun fired.

"Go," I yelled to the Neds. "Get out of here."

Robert swung at my head.

I ducked, holding on to his hand and twisting his arm to make him drop the gun.

He yelled, because, hey, one of us was used to feeling things like pain, and that was me. The other one of us had spent years without any sensation.

The gun dropped. He tripped up my feet, and we tumbled to the floor. I hit my head on something, maybe the footboard of the bed, and twisted away from him.

He was shouting nonstop, though I was only catching about every third word.

"Bitch ... will do as I say ... own you ... use you ... throw you away."

I scrambled onto hands and knees, looking for that damn gun, spotted it the same time he did, and kicked it under the bed and out of both of our reach.

I dove for my revolver, pulled it up, and swung it his way.

That's when I realized the room was full of people.

"The hell happened?" Abraham yelled.

"... okay, Matilda?" Dotty asked.

I was shaking and the slick heat of blood coated my throat. Maybe I'd gotten a little more banged up than I thought.

"You're all right," Abraham said, walking toward me with his hands up. "Put down the gun, Matilda. This won't be solved with bullets."

Yeah, I thought that a minute ago too. Changed my mind.

"Matilda." Abraham touched my shoulder gently, his voice calm. "Don't shoot him."

Robert was already being escorted more than firmly out of the room by Buck and Loy.

Dotty and Helen remained in the room with Abraham and me. Helen was looking out the window.

"Was there someone else here?" Dotty asked.

I glanced at the blood on the floor. Maybe mine. Maybe Neds.

"No one out there," Helen said. "You want to try to explain this?" She turned her scowl on me like this was my fault.

"She'll explain in front of Welton," Abraham said. "I don't want any misunderstanding or contention in this." He was back to using his official, I-will-be-obeyed voice.

Helen nodded, and she and Dotty left the room.

I sat on the edge of the bed, feeling a little woozy.

"What happened?" He walked into the bathroom and came back with a white washcloth, which he pressed against my temple.

"Ow," I said.

"Sorry." He backed off the pressure a bit. "What happened?" he repeated.

"Robert came in here with a gun is what happened."

"Why?"

"I don't know. He's your crazy friend. You ask him."

"Is that all that happened?"

"Neds were here."

"And?"

"And he wanted me to leave with him. He knows where Quinten is."

"Is he still here?"

"I don't think so."

"Okay. We're going to settle this in front of Welton. He's head of a House and can absolve you both of any wrongdoing."

"Robert pointed a gun at me. He tried to shoot my friend."

"If this goes public before the gathering, it will negate our claim and paint you as dangerous."

"I hate this," I said, wincing at the throb of pain in my head. "Threats and rules and whatever the hell his problem is, isn't my problem."

He placed both palms gently on my arms. "Welton is a fair mediator. He'll settle this. Then you and I will leave, find Neds, and find your brother."

"We can do that?" It came out a little more hopeful than I'd wanted.

"It's our day off. We can spend it any way we want."

"Good. Let's get this out of the way and go." I pulled the cloth away from my head and strode out of the room. I was bleeding, but I didn't think I was concussed. Yes, I left the gun behind. Right now I'd be too tempted to use it.

"There you go again," Welton said when I walked in. "Adding excitement to our otherwise boring lives."

He sat on the couch and hadn't changed out of his jeans and snail T-shirt. It looked like he'd just woken up. He also sounded a little drunk. "Do tell your side of the story first, Matilda."

Bede walked over and offered me a glass of water. "Is your head okay?" she asked.

"It's fine. Thanks." I gulped the water to get rid of my dry mouth and raw throat.

"Do you want to sit?" she asked.

"I'd rather not."

"Please," Welton said again to me. "Begin."

Foster stood behind Welton's couch, the burning red of his gaze focused on Robert, who sat in a chair, Loy and Buck standing guard on either side. Everyone had changed into pajamas or more comfortable clothing except Foster and Welton. The sun broke the horizon and yellow light poured through the east windows.

"Neds were in my room," I started.

"What's a Neds?" Welton asked.

"Ned Harris. My farmhand," I said. "You offered him popcorn on the street yesterday."

"Two-headed chap?"

"Yes."

"Got it. Go on."

"He asked me to leave with him. I was getting dressed when Robert broke into my room with a gun."

"Lies," Robert said.

"Not your turn to speak," Welton said around a yawn. "But there was a gun fired in this home—your gun, I believe. We need to settle that—between Houses, if needed—before we deal with anything else."

He pushed up off the couch and scrubbed his fingertips over his scalp, pulling his bangs back and shaking them, then letting them fall in a mess. "Coffee?" He shuffled to the kitchen, poured himself a cup, and looked over at me.

"No. What more do you need to know?"

He held the pot up toward Robert. "Rob? Coffee?"

Robert frowned and gave Welton a look of complete distaste.

"What crawled up your ass today, Robert?" Welton asked with a chuckle. "Has Slater been using you as a pillory boy again?"

"I was simply trying to keep Matilda safe from the intruder," Robert said. "I had no intention of using deadly force."

"Which is why you took your nondeadly gun into the room with you?" Welton asked. "I am assuming you're not going to deny that you had the gun. Is this correct?"

"Yes. To defend Matilda from that . . . shortlife."

Welton raised his eyebrows as he took a gulp of coffee. "And I see you've picked up Slater's bigotry too. You really should trade up, man. Come on over to House Yellow. I'm sure Foster would love a fellow galvanized to play with."

Foster was pacing the perimeter of the room. He grunted once, which made Welton grin.

"All right, Matilda," Welton said. "Anything else? Spare no detail."

"Neds asked me to leave with him. He said I was in danger, and then Robert came through the door with a gun. He threatened to shoot Neds. I stood in the way of his shot, kicked him, twisted his arm to make him drop the gun."

Buck, who hadn't taken his eyes off Robert said, "There are no guns allowed here. No weapons allowed, ever. You know that. Why in the world would you bring one with you?"

"I was concerned about Matilda's safety."

"And why would that be?" Welton asked.

Robert just glared at him. "Some matters remain within House."

"That's a dick reply," Welton said with a grin. "All right, let's declare someone guilty of something, mete out a price, and get moving. Robert Twelfth. Did you enter Matilda Thirteenth's room with intent to do her or her House harm?"

"No, I did not," he said.

"Matilda Thirteenth, do you wish to dispute his claim to innocence?"

I glanced at Abraham. He shook his head slightly.

"No. Is this done now?"

Welton held up one finger, so I waited.

"As House Yellow, I declare this a nonevent, of which there will be no legal action or injunctions brought between either House regarding this matter. This matter may be reopened by either involved House, Orange or Gray, if in the future further evidence is brought before a ruling House. Witnessed by Obedience Tenth, House Blue."

"So witnessed," Bede, next to me, said.

"Witnessed by Bernard Eighth, House Black."

"So witnessed," Buck said.

"All right, then," Welton said. "Let's get back to having fun, shall we?"

"Matilda and I are leaving," Abraham said.

"Where?" Robert asked.

Abraham shook his head. "You and I are friends, Rob. But right now I don't want to be in the same building with you."

Abraham took me by the arm and walked with me to my room.

"Get your things."

I still had my duffel, so my things consisted of the revolver which I apparently shouldn't have brought in the house with me. I picked it up, dropped it back in my bag. "Ready."

"Did Neds say where he was staying?"

"No."

"Don't worry," he said. "We'll find him."

27

Alveré Case and his assistant also survived the triggering of the Wings of Mercury. And though Alveré died at an advanced age, his assistant and their children, still live. —2196
—from the journal of L.U.C.

We drove the back roads, starting with those closest to the house, then moving outward.

An hour rolled by. Neds was nowhere to be found.

"Where do you think he would go?" Abraham asked as we drove down the highway for the sixth time, looking for any sign of him. "The farm?"

"I don't know," I said. "I don't think so. He would know that we might expect him to return there, right? And I'm sure he wouldn't just go back to House Gray."

"He was what—House White before working for you?" Abraham said.

"I never asked."

"I think we should go back to House Gray and get records on him. There should be people from his past, family if they're alive, friends. Places nearby where he would think he was safe."

He slowed and pulled alongside a small café.

"What are we doing?"

"Getting some coffee and something to eat. It will only take a minute."

"We need to keep looking."

"I have a feeling if he wants to be gone, he's got a good idea of how to do it. He knows you're going back to House Gray. He will contact you there."

It made sense. Even if I didn't like it.

He ordered coffee and sandwiches, while I stared sullenly at the blue sky.

Abraham handed me my share. Even though I didn't think I was hungry, the coffee was a welcome warmth.

He took a drink, unwrapped the paper off the sandwich, took a bite, and then drove back out onto the freeway to the speed-tube ramp.

"Eat something, Matilda. It will help."

I took a drink of coffee and leaned my aching head on the headrest. I'd stopped bleeding, so that was something at least.

Neds had said that Robert wasn't Robert. I'd sort of lost track of that, what with all the gunfire and wrestling and judgment.

"Is Robert always like that?" I asked after I gave in and took a bite of the sandwich.

"No."

"Neds said that Robert wasn't Robert."

"What?"

I shrugged. "It's what he said. Robert didn't seem to recognize Neds, even though they met in the garage. And when Robert first came to the house, he didn't seem happy to see you. He was so much more . . . formal and annoyed about everything. Could he somehow not be himself?"

Abraham pulled the car into a transfer pod, tapped in our information, destination, and fee.

"He's been under a lot of pressure," Abraham said. "House Orange is a difficult station to hold. But there was no reason to bring a gun to the house. You didn't know that, but he did. Galvanized don't need guns to settle conflicts."

"Maybe he heard or saw Neds outside my window?"

He shook his head. "Still no need for a gun."

"You told me once that scientists and researchers have done experiments on galvanized. And even . . . tortured."

"Yes."

"Do you think someone did something to him? To Robert?"

"No. Not even Slater Orange is that vile. And if anything had happened to Robert against his will, if he had suffered any harm, he would have rights to abandon House Orange. The only time a head of House can physically harm a galvanized is if he or she fears for his or her life, and then the head will use the Shelley dust."

"So he was just being an ass."

"It appears so."

A *ping* on the dash rang out, and he tapped the screen.

"Welton is patching in the security cameras around the town, and"—he touched the corner of the screen—"around the nearest cities, especially the speed-tube exits. Since we have another couple hours to blow before we get back to Chicago, we might as well look through the feeds."

I wadded up the sandwich paper, a little surprised that I'd eaten the whole thing. If someone asked me what kind of a sandwich it was, I wouldn't be able to say, but my stomach was settled and my coffee was still hot.

"At least it will make me feel like I'm doing something," I said.

He keyed up the multiple feeds, and we didn't talk much, watching more than a hundred screens sort and sift through images. If Neds went anywhere near a camera, we'd see him. A two-headed man wasn't such a common sight that we'd mistake him for another.

The hour rolled by, and then the second.

No Neds.

Abraham paused the feed.

"I thought Welton's cameras were everywhere," I said.

"Neds could be going overland on foot." He rubbed

at his eyes. "He could have taken side roads, avoiding cameras. Or . . ."

"Or?"

"Or he could have thrown in with a House who is covering his tracks for him."

"What House has the power to do that? And why would they?"

"Any of the Houses can make someone disappear," he said. "On their own or in concert with another House. And to answer your second question: to get to you."

I pressed my palms over my face and exhaled into them. "I am beginning to seriously regret coming to the city."

He drew my hair away from the side of my face, where it had fallen in a heavy curtain.

"We'll find a solution. There isn't any problem we can't solve as long as we don't stop trying to solve it. Trust that, Matilda. And if not that, trust that you are strong enough and resourceful enough. You'll find your way through."

I pulled one hand away from my face and let it fall in my lap. "That's nice of you. But if we don't find Neds, if we don't find Quinten . . ."

"We'll find them."

He finished tucking my bouncy hair behind my ear, which I knew revealed the line of stitches down my jaw and neck.

I turned to look at him. Concern kindled in his eyes, shifting into heat and desire.

He held very still, maybe waiting for me to say something. Maybe waiting for me to say no. I raised one eyebrow. I wasn't saying no.

He bent and covered my mouth with his own.

I made a small sound in the back of my throat, surprised, but not in a bad way. Not at all in a bad way.

His soft, warm lips moved over mine with a slow

intensity, as if every inch of me should be savored, tasted. I inhaled and let him devour me. Heat pooled in my chest, pouring down my stomach and spreading across my thighs.

Oh.

I drew my thumb and palm gently across his rough jaw and smooth temple, and then buried my fingers in his hair, resting my palm across the back of his neck so I could hold him closer to me.

He gently opened my mouth with his tongue, and I gratefully let him in.

It was his turn to moan a little.

Slowly, we drew away from the kiss. His hands remained on my back and at my hip. I wasn't ready to let go of him either. I pressed my lips together, already missing the taste of him.

"Are we going to talk about that?" I asked.

"Do we need to?"

"Most people would."

"What would most people say?" He drew his hands back slowly, fingers slipping across my ribs.

I reluctantly released my hold on him. "I don't know. That relationships aren't easy. And we don't even know if I'm staying in House Gray—"

"You're staying in House Gray."

"—much less if you and I are going to work well together."

"I don't see why we wouldn't."

"Your friend tried to shoot me today, Abraham. Maybe we should hold off on whatever this"—I pointed my finger at him, then at me—"is. At least until things are less complicated in our lives."

"Lives are always complicated, Matilda. Happiness doesn't seem to care. But, then, I am so much older than you."

"You're older than almost everyone."

"That doesn't bother you?"

I shrugged. "I think I'd like an experienced man."

"You say this because of all the experienced men you've had in your life?"

"No. I say that because I haven't had any experienced man in my life. Or," I said, "any man in my life."

His head pulled up and he leaned back on an exhale. "You've never . . . had a boyfriend?"

"Hello? Living on a farm, staying off grid and as far away from civilization as possible. Also, stitched, so even if I did meet someone, I'd be a monster. Not human enough for that sort of thing."

The chime of exit warning rang out and Abraham tapped the screens, closing the camera feeds and preparing to take over the driving again.

"You are not a monster," he said, giving me a smoldering gaze. "Not even close."

"That's nice of you to say so. But look who's talking."

That got a smile out of him. "The voice of experience," he said. "You should listen to it."

"Should I?"

"I promise I'll make it worth your while if you do."

And there it was again, that smile, that heat. A blush crept across my face and neck, which only made Abraham smile wider.

"Is that a yes?" he asked.

"It is," I said, while my heart pounded too hard for just those simple words. "Yes."

"Good."

Then the pod deposited us in the queue to the exit ramp, and a call came in.

Abraham shifted, his shoulders pulling back and his hands gripping the steering wheel tightly. He drove the car down a side alley and opened the message.

"Who is it from?" I asked.

"Slater Orange." He frowned.

"House Orange? What does he want?"

"For me to attend him. Immediately." He closed the

message and swore, scowling out at the city and shifting crowd of people who moved by, paying our dark-windowed car no attention.

"Do you think it's because of what happened with Robert?" I asked.

"Probably."

"When does he want you there?"

"Immediately. The moment the message is sent, a countdown begins. If it takes me a minute more than allowed to reach him, there will be tension between our Houses. Debts owed."

"That's a stupid rule."

"It's there for a reason. We cut corners in the old days," he said. "Took our time doing service to the Houses. Sometimes it would take us decades to following through on their summons. So the countdown was implemented."

He rubbed at his jaw, then brushed fingers through his hair, making a decision. "I'll take you to House Gray before I go."

"I could go with you to House Orange."

"No. He wants to see me alone."

"All right. How long will it take you to drop me off at House Gray?"

"Ten or fifteen minutes."

"Just let me out here. I can walk."

"I don't think you should be left unprotected."

"I'm not made of glass," I said. "There are signs posted everywhere to guide me and a million cameras watching. I couldn't get lost if I wanted to. It's in walking distance right? Plus, you were just saying I am resourceful and strong. Don't go making me doubt your pretty words, Abraham Seventh."

"Fine." He bent and pointed out the window. "Do you see that building with the spiral at the top?"

"Yes."

"That's Gray Towers. Oscar will be there. He will know about my summoning and is probably already waiting for you. Someone at the door will let you in. Oscar will allow you up the elevators to the suites."

"Good. That's settled." I reached into the backseat and picked up my duffel, slinging it over my shoulder. I thought about taking my rifle too, but decided it might cause more attention than I wanted. I still had the revolver in the bag anyway. I put my hand on the door handle.

"Matilda," Abraham started.

"I got it. Don't cause problems, don't insult other Houses, and don't get lost."

"Yes," he said, squeezing my arm, "but most importantly, be careful."

"I will be fine," I said. "I'll go straight to the tower. I've faced a lot deadlier things than what roam these streets."

"I know." He hesitated, looking like he wanted to say something more.

"You are going to be late. Go." I got out of the car, glad for the cool breeze on my warm face, and made sure to hide my stitches with my hair before I started off at a long stride toward the spiral building.

Abraham revved the engine and drove in the opposite direction.

I tried not to make eye contact as I strode down the street, but shouldn't have worried. No one would look me straight in the face unless it was behind dark glasses. People standing alongside buildings or lingering in alley openings or dancing on street corners waved whatever they had in buckets, pockets, carts, telling me to buy, telling me it was good, the best, telling me they had no food and sickly children and no House to claim them.

The throb and noise of the place took up an ache in my head. Just like any other great beast, the city rumbled and roared and moaned in a language of wants and needs and pain, built out of a million voices, machines, and minds.

I looked for Neds, but the crowds were filled with strangers. I had never felt so alone in my life.

I crossed the next intersection, weaving between people, and glanced up at the spiral building now and again to make sure I was keeping my bearings. I reached the other curb, and a woman in a hooded coat bumped into me.

"Sorry," I said.

Her hand caught at my arm and did not let go. I took a closer look at her. Short black hair, and a whorl of silver stitches laced across her cheek.

Helen Eleventh. "I know where your brother is," she said. "Come with me."

She strode down the sidewalk, swallowed by the crowd.

I waited, tracking where her pace should be taking her. Caught sight of her almost a block off.

I shouldn't follow her. She was from House Silver, Vice, and could be using my missing brother as a way to try to claim me. Or maybe she knew where he was and I was letting a perfectly good lead get away.

"Dumb, dumb, dumb," I muttered as I hurried up and followed her. I'd promised Abraham I'd walk straight over to Gray Towers. Oscar was waiting for me, right?

Still, if she could give me answers, it would be worth being a little late.

I paid attention to street names so I could navigate my way back. She was another block ahead of me, waiting next to a car. I looked around for guns or other signs of ambush. Didn't see any.

Every fiber of my body was tense. This was probably a trap. But I had a gun in my duffel and it wasn't there for decoration. I stopped a few yards away from her.

"You know where my brother is?" I asked. "Prove it."

She gave me a look, one that said she didn't like it when I asked questions.

Then she reached into her pocket and pulled out Quinten's pocket watch. I knew it was his, just like it had been Dad's and Granddad's and Great-Grandad's, all the way back to the early twentieth century. Quinten always carried it and wouldn't have given it up easily.

My heart sank and then started pounding its way back up into my throat.

"Where is he?" I asked.

"Get in." She pointed at the open car door. "I'll take you to him."

Bad idea, I thought. But that didn't stop me. I got in the backseat, expecting the car to be crowded with muscle and threats. But it was clean and empty.

Helen got in the driver's seat and started the engine.

"Sit back. Relax," she said, pushing the hood away from her face now that she was safely hidden behind the darkened windows. "Have a drink if you like—there's a small selection of spirits in the center section of the seat."

"Where are we going?"

"It's not far."

House Silver. Abraham told me House Gray had contracted Quinten to work for House Silver. Oscar talked to Reeves Silver about it. Maybe Quinten was still there.

"Is he okay?" I asked.

"He's alive."

Relief hit me so hard, I almost went light-headed. "Are you holding him prisoner?"

Helen laughed, and it was the sort of low, sexy sound that makes men cut off their wedding rings.

"That's a question for Reeves to answer."

"Is that where you're taking me?"

Her black-lined eyes shifted to look at me in the rearview mirror. "Yes. To meet the Saint of Sin."

28

*The Wings of Mercury device still exists, filled
with the pulse of a long-dead comet. —2196
—from the journal of L.U.C.*

Helen navigated the streets to a downward ramp and
then drove through a series of tunnels lit with alter-
nating yellow and red lights. We emerged into daylight
and eventually turned down another street, and climbed
up that to a huge mansion on top of a hill that over-
looked the entire town.

She parked the car beneath an awning, turned off the
engine, and paused before opening the door. "I'll take
you in. You can keep the gun in your duffel, but my ad-
vice? Leave it stashed, sugar. You don't want to play
hardball here." She checked her lipstick in the mirror,
then put on a smile and got out of the car.

She opened my door.

"I want my brother's pocket watch," I said.

She shrugged and handed it to me. I tucked it immediately into my duffel.

"This way," she said.

I followed her to the door beneath the awning and
into an elevator. We didn't say anything on the short ride.

When the elevator opened, she waved her hand, indicating I should step out into the room.

I did so.

Plush was the first word that came to mind. Plush furniture, plush blinds framing the windows that looked over the city that rolled out at its feet. Plush greenery and flowers. Plush carpet. Even the fireplace crackling away with real wood was polished marble and gold.

Plush.

Helen strolled past me. She was my height in the heels she wore, her dark straight hair cut in chunky bangs that highlighted the heavy makeup around her eyes. She'd taken off her coat and wore a fitted silver tank top that enhanced her toned arms and the silver stitches down them.

"I hope you aren't too disappointed with me," she said without a lick of sincerity. "But orders are orders."

"Did you take my brother?"

"That's a question you can ask Reeves. Or I suppose you could have asked Neds years ago."

"What? What does Neds have to do with this?"

"You didn't know?" she asked with a cruel twist of a smile. "He's been working for us all these years. Spying on you, out on that dirty little farm of yours."

That couldn't be true. Not Neds.

"You didn't think he was working that farm for the money, did you?" She raised one eyebrow and gave me the up-and-down. "Or the company? One late-model stitch and her crazy grandmother? I'm surprised he lasted as long as he did."

She could bad-mouth me all she wanted. She could bad-mouth Neds. I knew him. I had lived with him for years. I'd seen his good days and his bad days. And no judgmental galvanized was going to make me change my mind about his character.

If he told me everything over the past two years had been a lie, that he'd been spying on me for House Silver or whatever, I'd believe it. But only when those words came out of his mouths.

"Is my brother here or not?" I asked calmly.

She glared at me. What had she expected? Hysterics?

Yeah, well it took more than a few accusations to ruffle my feathers.

"This way."

She crossed the carpet, making no sound over the thick fibers. To all appearances, she didn't care if I followed her or not.

I took note of all the windows, halls, doors, and anything I might be able to use as an escape route if I needed one.

"Here." Helen stopped outside a sleek silver-plated door. "Reeves is waiting for you."

She opened the door but did not enter the room.

I pulled back my shoulders and walked right on in. I'd faced down nearly every kind of dangerous beast the scratch could cook up. I could handle one overly entitled man.

"Hello, Matilda. Please have a seat."

I'd expected the room to be dripping in silver. Not only was it smaller than I'd thought it would be, it also leaned toward dark leather and rich redwood in the desk, wall shelves, and carved ceiling tiles. The carpet was a tight black-and-silver-checked design, and a bank of three door-sized windows to my left looked over a balcony and the city in the distance. Cloth-shaded lamps on the walls made the entire space feel comfortably intimate and warm.

The man, Reeves Silver, stood behind the desk, pouring two tiny cups of coffee. His hair was startlingly white, cut short and clean, no beard. He had the build of a swimmer: wider shoulders and a long, lean torso. He wore a silver sweater and slacks.

Since I hadn't moved, he glanced over his shoulder at me. "Please. I thought you and I could have a cup of coffee and get to know one another."

He placed one cup on his side of the large redwood desk and the other nearer me, in front of the two pale wood-and-silver-cushioned chairs tipped invitingly toward the desk.

"I've come here to get my brother, Your Excellency," I said. "I don't want to take up any more of your time. If you'll just tell me where he is, I'll be leaving."

"I assure you, he is fine," he said, as he pulled out the dark leather chair behind the desk and sat. "Didn't Helen tell you he is fine? This won't take but a moment, Matilda. You have my word on that."

I didn't believe him. I sat anyway, hoping it would hurry things along.

He took a sip of coffee from the delicate china, his eyes the color of arctic ice.

I took a sip of my coffee. Rich, warm, and sweetened with dark sugar. It was the finest I'd ever tasted.

"I do want to apologize for this invitation," he said. "Stealing you off the street. But I wanted a chance to meet you without interference."

"You mean without anyone at House Gray knowing?"

"Anyone at House Gray or any of your galvanized friends. I prefer uninterrupted time when I'm first meeting someone with whom I assume I will be doing business."

"Business?"

"Have you been informed of the gathering tomorrow?"

"Yes."

"I brought you here before that event to make you an offer that would benefit us both."

I shook my head. "I'm not interested in moving to any House. I'm claimed by House Gray and I'd like to stay that way."

He just smiled. "Why don't you listen to my offer, and then make your decision? Tomorrow all the Houses will gather. What I want is for you to let things play out as they may."

"What does that mean?"

"Your presence is already drawing lines between the Houses. But the game the Houses play is a very old one.

The pieces have been in place for more years than you have been breathing. You, Matilda Case, are fate's twist, chaos' card stacked in the deck between the Houses. We all want you. We all want to use you."

"Why?" I breathed. My heart was starting to pound again. He wasn't talking to me in a threatening way. If anything, he seemed more amused than angry.

"Everyone has their reasons," he said with a smile. "I will tell you mine. You are the key to a very old story. One that most people do not believe. But, then, I enjoy getting to the root of stories. Especially if there is a profit to be made."

He waited, drinking his coffee.

"What story?" I asked.

"The end of the world. The fall of the Houses. And all that entails. Everything has its end. It is the cycle that allows for new beginnings. New opportunities. In this story, you are the one who will decide the fate of the world."

"There isn't a story with me in it," I said. "I think you're reading into me much more than you should. All I want is my brother returned to me and both of us returned to House Gray. I promise you I have nothing to do with anything else."

"No piece knows its place on the game board, nor its future," he said. "It knows only the square it occupies and the touch of the hand that controls it. I want a promise from you, Matilda Case, daughter of Dr. Renault Case and Professor Edith Case. Whatever happens tomorrow at the gathering, do not get involved. Let the game play out as if you were not a part of it. Watch, but do not act. If you can promise me you will not interfere with my story, I will give you a great gift."

"What gift?"

I didn't believe he was really going to give me anything. I'd seen more than my share of salesmen in the past, and Reeves Silver was just a salesman who had all the power and all the time in the world to make people buy what he was selling.

"I know where your brother is."

"So I've been told," I said. "Where is he?"

"I will show you, though if you speak of it, Matilda, I will change my mind as to which piece you are playing on *my* game board. You will fall from rook to pawn." He tipped his cup, took another drink. "Betray me, and I will remove you from the board completely."

I wasn't an idiot. I recognized a death threat when I heard one. I nodded.

"House Orange holds him prisoner."

I heard him—really I did. But the tightness in my chest wouldn't allow me to answer. Hope was a painful thing.

"Why should I believe you?"

"Because I make it a priority to uncover the yearning of every sinful heart," he said. "I do not promise what I cannot deliver."

I stood. "Then deliver. Take me to him."

Pure delight glinted in his eyes. He'd gotten what he wanted out of me. And while it rankled, I didn't care what I'd have to do to save Quinten.

He stood and stretched out his hand, palm upward. In his palm was a silver coin with the image of wings pressed into it. There was a small hole at the top of the coin, as if it were intended to be worn on a chain.

"This is a personal token. It entitles the owner to one favor granted unconditionally by me, House Silver. You can use it now or keep it for the gathering. People want you, Matilda. People will do anything to have you. While I, on the other hand, am offering you my assistance."

He tapped his wrist.

The wall behind his left shoulder became a screen.

An image of a white-walled room pulled into focus, though the recording was shaky.

"This is a room in House Orange," Reeves said, as he watched me. "A room Slater Orange thinks is unable to be tapped by any House or device. He is wrong, of course."

The recording device panned from the ceiling down to the center of the room.

"Oh," I said, the sound escaping me as if I'd been punched.

My brother sat on the edge of a bed, cuffs on his wrists and ankles connected by chains to the walls. He was tapping his fingers, two fingers together in the signal for House Brown. Morse code.

S.O.S.

He really was in trouble. A prisoner.

"Do you know where that room is?" I asked, my mind racing through solutions, options, resources.

"I do."

"Can you get to him? Can you free him?"

He hesitated. "It wouldn't be easy."

I met his gaze and held out my hand. "I won't get in the way of your House games."

He tipped his hand and dropped the silver coin into my palm.

I stood and pushed the coin across the desk with one finger. "Free my brother and bring him to House Gray alive, by the time the gathering is over."

His eyebrows shot up.

"That is the personal favor I want from you, Reeves Silver. If you want me to stand aside and let your games play out, you bring me my brother."

"If I agree," he said, not touching the coin yet, "you will say nothing of our agreement. You will say nothing of anything that has transpired between us."

"And if I do?"

"I will tell Boston Sue to kill your grandmother, Lara Unger Case."

His smiled like a fox that had just caught dinner by the throat.

Boston Sue was working for him too. My stomach hit my knees, but I didn't let it show.

"I agree to say nothing of our agreement to anyone."

"Good. I will see that Quinten is returned, alive, to

you immediately after the gathering," he said. "Look for him there." He plucked up the token with long fingers.

"And my grandmother?"

"As long as our agreement stands, she'll come to no harm. Helen will drive you back to the city. It was a pleasure doing business with you, Matilda Case."

I walked out of the room, wanting to be as far away from him as quickly as I could. If he owned Boston Sue, who else did he control inside House Brown? I didn't know who I could trust anymore.

Helen was on the other side of the door. "This way."

We strode back to the same elevator.

"Why do you care for him?" Helen asked when we were alone.

"Quinten?" I asked. "He's my brother."

"You were made of dead people," she said. "You aren't really Dr. Case's child. You aren't really his sister. You're nothing more than just a chunk of medical waste that didn't have the good sense to die."

I reached over and grabbed her wrist, squeezing just a little harder than necessary.

"Flesh and blood doesn't have anything to do with family and belonging. Not that you would ever understand that. If you ever let your House hurt my family again or if Reeves Silver betrays me, I will reach down your throat and pull out your pretty guts. And I can make sure you feel every single second of it."

Her eyes widened, then narrowed. She felt my hand on her arm. She'd feel anything I did to her.

I let go and we rode in silence back down to the car.

29

*Alveré Case and his descendants swore to sac-
rifice everything to correct their mistakes.—
2197*
                        —from the journal of L.U.C.

Helen dropped me off a block away from Gray Towers.

I made my way down the sidewalk, watching for hos-
tile movement.

When I was just a few feet away from the slick glass
front of the building and the doors that I hoped would
let me in, Neds shouldered out from a shadowed over-
hang and fell into step beside me.

"I'm angry and sick, Ned Harris," I said. "You don't
want to talk to me."

"Tilly," Right Ned said. "Let me explain."

"All right." I stopped in the middle of the crowded
street. More than one person cursed as they were forced
to squeeze past us. "Explain to me why you lied to me
for two years, ate my food, worked my land, and falsified
our friendship so you could spy on me for House Silver."

"It isn't," Right Ned said, his eyes tight with anger or
pain. "That isn't how it happened. I mean, it happened,
but that's not why. I answered your ad for House Silver.
But I stayed—I *wanted* to stay for you."

"She won't listen," Left Ned said. "You're a part of

House Gray now, aren't you, Matilda? Working your deals, playing the game. Just like a low-class citizen. Just like us. So before you go judging us off something some dick of a House said we did, get your facts, and get them straight."

"Were you spying on me?"

"We were," Right Ned said, putting his hand on his brother's shoulder. "But we were trying to keep you safe. I understand if you won't trust us. But we've never wanted you hurt or used or involved in this mess. We tried to do right by you, Tilly."

"What about Quinten? You call that doing right by me?"

Right Ned frowned. "No. We know we failed you. But we'll do what we can to fix that. To help him."

If I told Neds what I'd done, the deal I'd made with House Silver, all bets and all favors would be off.

"I hate this," I said. "I hate this place and I hate these people. You were right, Ned. I should have run when I had the chance. The things they do. The things you've done . . ."

And then, before I knew what was happening, he stepped right up to me, brushed his bare hand down my bare arm and pulled me into a hug.

"For all the—" Left Ned muttered, but I wasn't listening to him.

"I'm sorry, Matilda. Please believe that," Right Ned said. "I never wanted to hurt you."

And then he stepped back and walked away, swallowed by the jostle of humanity.

"Matilda! Matilda!" Elwa pushed her way through the crowd, her sharp, short steps puncturing the roiling mass and thrusting her through the crowd like a needle.

"We've been looking for you," she said, catching hold of my sleeve as if to keep me from drifting away. "Abraham said he dropped you off an hour ago. Where have you been?"

She hadn't waited for my answer, but was already tugging me up to the front door of the building, her steps still brisk enough to make me jog a bit to keep up.

She waved a hand impatiently at whatever camera or scanner or other identification device lingered in the clear glass, and the doors opened for us.

I'd never come into the building this way, but Elwa didn't give me time to take in any details. Maybe marble, certainly clean, unfailingly gray. And then the elevator opened and I was pushed inside and whisked to the upper floors.

"Have you seen him?" she asked.

"Who?"

"Abraham." She shook her hand like swatting a fly. "No matter. He will arrive in time. Abraham is a warrior, a soldier, a liberator. He knows how much punctuality matters."

I was ushered out of the elevator and then off to my room, where Elwa grilled me on if I needed food or if anything was wrong, and if I had packed yet, and when I was going to take time to prepare for the gathering.

I finally got her to leave by promising her I just needed a little time to collect myself.

After she left, I pulled a chair up next to the door and sat there with my handgun in my lap.

I was numb, my thoughts scattered and raw. I didn't know what to do. Didn't know how to keep Grandma safe. And I most certainly didn't know whom to trust.

House Orange had Quinten captive. My brilliant brother would have gotten free if there had been any chance to do so.

Abraham was there now meeting with Slater Orange.

But whose side was Abraham on?

Neds were spies, Boston Sue a hired thug.

All I wanted was to get away. But if I broke my deal, Reeves would kill the people I loved.

There was a soft knock at the door.

I got up, stiff from what must have been hours sitting utterly still. I held the gun ready and opened the door.

"I brought you a late supper," Elwa said, letting her-self in, despite the gun in my hand. "And a few things you need to study for the gathering. We'll be leaving tonight. Soon." She set a tray with silver domes over the plates down on the table. "Here is information about the gath-ering and how you will represent House Gray."

"Wait," I said, rubbing at my forehead and trying to track her words, which seemed to tumble together too quickly. "What do I need to do?"

"Read this." She pointed at the thin screen. "You are galvanized. Important, valued. You will stand in the great arena as the pride of House Gray. Your name and face will be projected across all the breathing world. And since you are the unexpected discovery, there has al-ready been speculation. People are curious. People are placing odds...."

"There are wagers being made? On what?"

"If you'll be pretty, strong, ancient, young. If you'll be advanced or a throwback like the First. And, most of all, who made you and why have you been a secret for so long. What is your purpose? Why have you emerged now, of all times? Isn't that exciting?" She clapped her hands once and laced her fingers together.

"No. It's not," I said. "Will all the heads of Houses be there?"

"Yes, of course. Here is your schedule, some history of previous gatherings, a list of things you will be expected to do, a list of mistakes that will cause our House grief and therefore you will be expected *not* to do, etiquette guidelines, current House loyalties, current House stand-ings, current House projects under negotiation. Tell me you know how to operate chopsticks and walk in high heels."

"At the same time?"

"If necessary."

"I've never used chopsticks, and I've never worn heels."

She made tiny shakes of her head, then pressed the

screen into my hand. "I'll have your gowns brought by. Eat. There are chopsticks on the tray. Use them. Read as much of this as you can. We will go through walking lessons in an hour. I will test you on your knowledge. You will do brilliantly, I am sure. But you must begin now. We have no time. No time at all."

She clapped again, then turned and stomped her way out of the room, pausing at the door to give me a conciliatory look. "You will have to put the gun away, however. There are no weapons allowed in the gathering."

Then she shut the door.

I stood there feeling like I'd just been buffeted by a tiny, demanding whirlwind.

Her visit had done me some good, actually. It had shaken me out of my wallow enough to clear my head.

Time to make a plan. I ate while I thought things through, doing my best with the food sticks. Turned out I wasn't half bad with them, and by the end of the meal—vegetables and meat over rice and noodles—I had gotten more food in my mouth than on my lap. Good enough.

I wanted to get a message out to House Brown to look out for Grandma, but doing so might bring her harm. There had to be a way to save Grandma, get Quinten away from House Orange, and deal with the gathering.

I just didn't know how.

Yet.

I pulled out the screen and information Elwa wanted me to learn. I read through schedule and history of past gatherings, looking for when I might have a chance to be unobserved. Because any plan I came up with would need to be handled House Brown's way: off grid and out of sight.

A curt knock on the door pulled me up out of the information.

Elwa didn't wait for an invitation; she waltzed right in, a man dressed all in gray following her with an armful of clothing.

"Take it to the bedroom, please," she said to him. "How was your meal?"

"I practiced with the chopsticks."

"Good, good. Now let's get you in your gown and heels so you can practice your walk."

"Does it matter how I walk?"

"Yes. Every galvanized has been tutored in proper presentation. It is ceremony, Matilda. Pomp and performance. Theater. It won't take long, but it must be given proper attention. You'll be fine. Go. Change into whichever dress you wish. I'll wait here."

She made shooing motions with her hands, and I walked to the bedroom while the man who had accompanied her walked out.

"All my life going to hell, and I have to walk the right way and look pretty," I muttered through clenched teeth.

I shucked out of my slacks and T-shirt, then looked at the three dresses laid out on the bed. Strapless or nearly so, cut to show neck, arms, and a good portion of leg. Any one of these would make me feel like I was parading around naked.

"Are you dressed?" Elwa asked. It had been exactly one minute since I'd shut the bedroom door.

"No." I shrugged into the thick, soft gray bathrobe hanging on the hook by the bed and had just gotten it closed around me when she burst through the door.

"What is the trouble?" She looked at me, then at the dresses, then back at me.

"I'm wondering which order to put them on," I said.

"Any order. I'd like to see you in all of them."

"But which one goes on the bottom?"

She did that short head shake again. "I don't understand."

"All together, they're enough material to make a dress. Which layer goes on first?"

"Oh no. No, darling. One dress. One layer." She reached over and pulled the second dress off the bed, unzipped the side of it, and held it open for me.

It wafted there as if made of spiderwebs.

"You have got to be joking."

"What is the problem?"

"My arms will be bare. My legs, my neck."

"Yes, of course. You are galvanized. Every stitch is your strength, your pride. In this gathering, you must be seen, your stitches revealed. Next gathering will be different. But for this, you stand with head high. Unafraid of what you are. Strong for your House. Here. Try this."

She lifted the dress toward my head and I shrugged out of the bathrobe and into the soft gray material.

I'd expected it to be a disaster, but the dress floated down around my body, not too tight and with a lot more modesty than I'd expected. Both my arms were bare, ribbon straps covering just the crest of my shoulders, and while the back plunged enough that I could feel a breeze, the skirt fell to my feet, allowing the cleverly placed slits to give a glimpse of my leg up to my thigh when I walked.

"Yes," she said, zipping up the side and steering me by the shoulders over to the full-length mirror. "I think this will do. So pretty."

It had been years since I'd stood in front of a full mirror. It had been never since I'd worn a dress. So the woman who stared in mild shock back at me from that mirror was a little unfamiliar.

The dress fit perfectly, and the soft gray of it, along with a barrage of cleverly placed jewels, brought out the silver lines of my stitching that crossed beneath my collarbone, curved above my breast, and looped around my arms and wrists and hands.

Elwa pulled back my hair so the stitches down my cheek and neck were revealed. "Beautiful and strong," she said.

I never much cared how much stitch I was showing out on the farm. After all, it had just been Grandma, Quinten, Neds, and me. But I had always been meticulous to hide my life stitches from anyone else.

Standing there in that dress didn't make me feel vulnerable or exposed. I felt strong. Like I was getting all gussied up to go hunting for a different sort of feral beast.

"I can do this," I said. "I can wear this one."

"Good, good. Now we try on the shoes."

That turned out to be more of a problem. I was not made to be balancing on stilts, and nothing Elwa did could convince me otherwise.

"I'll just wear my boots," I said for the hundredth time.

Elwa frowned. "No."

"Then I will go barefoot. Listen, I'm letting you put me in frills, I'm letting you pull my hair up and stick pins and nonsense in it, but the high heels are never gonna happen."

"Boots," she muttered. "Show me."

I pulled my boots out from under the edge of the bed, and she took them out of my hand like she was holding a dead rat. "I will see what can be done."

"Wait—you can't take them."

"We have only a few hours before we leave. And if it must be boots," she shrugged, "then it will be boots. But better than these."

She clipped out of the room, and I changed back into my jeans and T-shirt. All this nonsense had shaken loose a small plan. A way to get Quinten out of the city as quickly as possible. A place for him to stay.

I didn't dare write anything down or scan for information. If Reeves Silver had cameras hidden away in House Orange's most private rooms, I could only assume he had done the same to House Gray.

Any plan I was going to try would have to be constructed solely in my head.

So I got busy constructing.

A couple hours later, there was a knock at the door.

"Matilda," Oscar Gray said. "May I have a word with you?"

I hadn't expected him to visit. I answered the door.

"So good to see you," he said. "I hope your training wasn't too strenuous?"

"Training?"

"With the other galvanized." He had a sparkle in his eyes. He must have known that there wasn't really any training, and that it was actually just a chance for the galvanized to get together and relax.

"It was fine," I said. "Educational."

"Good, good. Can you tell me when you last saw Abraham?"

"Early this afternoon."

"And what did he say when you were with him?"

"That he had been summoned by Slater Orange. He said you'd know that."

"I do. Did he say anything else about that meeting?"

"Nothing I remember."

"And how long did it take you to navigate your way here?"

"I got lost." I couldn't mention Reeves Silver. I couldn't mention the deal and Quinten. I couldn't mention Grandma or Neds or anything.

But I didn't have to be completely silent. "Do you have any news on my brother?" I asked, even though it made my stomach cinch into knots.

"Nothing yet," he said. "I'm sure we'll know something soon. You'll need to pack your things. We'll be leaving in a few minutes."

"To the gathering?"

"Yes."

"Where is it being held?"

"Hong Kong," he said with a smile. "Vibrant city. I think you'll enjoy it."

"What about Abraham?"

"I'll worry about Abraham. You just follow Elwa's instructions and everything will fall together. The woman's maddening, but she does run a tight ship. House Gray wouldn't be the same without her."

I nodded, my thoughts running too fast. "Do you

think Abraham is safe? With Slater Orange?" I couldn't tell him what Vice had shown me, but I couldn't just stand here if Abraham might be in danger too. Unless he and Oscar had double-crossed me too.

No. There was no use seeing evil in every shadow. I had to trust someone. Oscar had earned my trust.

"Why would you ask that?" Oscar said.

Abraham had said Oscar was a good man, a moral man. I hoped to hell he was right.

"Robert Twelfth was acting very strangely at the training. There was an . . . altercation."

"Altercation?"

"He came into my bedroom, waving a gun. He said he thought I was in danger, but . . ." I bit my lip. Shook my head.

"What else, Matilda? Why are you crying?"

I pushed the tear away with the back of my hand and whispered, "I think House Orange might know what happened to my brother."

"Oscar, darling," Elwa chirped as she ducked by him and into the room. "Don't worry an inch. I'll have Matilda ready to go in just a shake. Your face is splotchy, darling," she said to me. "No need to get worked up about a little trip overseas."

"I'm sure that's it," I said. "All the excitement." I sniffed and wiped at my face again, making sure there were no more tears to betray me. "Don't mind me."

Elwa had already powered her way across the room and was muttering to herself in the bedroom as she unlatched suitcases and began piling in clothing.

"Well, then," Oscar said, everything about him seeming calm and upbeat, but sharpened somehow. "I'll leave you in Elwa's capable hands." He reached over and took my hand for just a second, and nodded.

He had heard me. I knew he was going to make sure Abraham was okay. Maybe even find out that Quinten was trapped at House Orange.

It wasn't much, but it might be enough to tip the scales in our favor.

"I will see you at the gathering, Matilda Case." He squeezed my hand gently, then walked away.

"What happens if Abraham doesn't arrive at the gathering in time?" I asked Elwa.

"It would be scandal. *Scandal.*" She chuckled. "But we would recover. If we made a showing with no galvanized presence, that would be a much harder hit to our House reputation. I am certain Abraham will be there. And even if he is not, you will be. So. Worry not, darling. You may even find the event filled with excitement and delight."

Delight was pretty much the opposite of what I was feeling, but I put on a smile for the cameras, hefted one of the bags, and then followed Elwa to the car.

30

HOUSE ORANGE

Robert Twelfth woke in a body filled with searing pain. Every breath stabbed and caught, every movement crippled. It was such a strange experience, after all the years of being galvanized, that he had thought it was a dream.

But now he knew it was no dream. He was dying. No longer in his own body. Trapped in the failing body of Slater Orange. Barely strong enough to speak.

Robert was strong enough to know that as long as he was in this body, he was the head of House Orange. And his commands would be obeyed.

So he had commanded Abraham Seventh to be brought before him.

And now, finally, his old friend had arrived, walking into the room where he sat in the austere but expensive bed, breathing his last breaths.

"You summoned me, Slater Orange?" Abraham asked, crossing the room with the confidence that had led men into battle and eventually into peace.

"Bram," Robert said. "It's good to see you, my friend."

Abraham paused midstep. He tipped his head down and gave him a long, considering gaze.

"I do not think we have ever been friends, Your Excellency," he said evenly.

"Not Slater," Robert wheezed. "I am not Slater."

Abraham walked closer and stood beside the bed.

"He's dying, Bram. This body. I'm dying. He traded, he took . . ." Robert inhaled too quickly, desperate to get all the words out, to let Abraham know what kind of danger he was in.

Every muscle in his body cramped and he coughed weakly, unable to get enough air into his lungs to do anything more.

Abraham waited, his expression unreadable.

The coughing eased, leaving Robert light-headed and exhausted. "Water, please," he whispered.

Abraham poured water from a crystal decanter by the bedside, and then offered the glass to Robert. He had thoughtfully filled the glass only half-full, so it wouldn't be too heavy for him to lift, and Robert took a sip, amazed at the smooth, cool edge of the glass against his fevered lips. He closed his eyes to savor the cold wash of water down his throat, as it spread across the inside of his chest like a soothing wing of shade.

"Would you like me to call your medical care?" Abraham asked.

Robert rolled his eyes. He didn't believe him.

"You aren't alone," Robert said. "You'll survive this because you have family."

"What?"

"That's what you said to me. When we met. After the scientists had brought me back to life. You came to see me in my private room. No recording devices. Full privacy."

"And what did you do when I said that?" Abraham asked.

"I wept. And you promised never to tell anyone that I did. You never have."

"One secret between two men doesn't prove anything," he said, narrowing his eyes.

"I covered for you when you went out to get Matilda on that farm," Robert began slowly. "I warned you about that assassination plot back during the Uprising, which you ignored."

He paused for breathing again, and tried to work moisture into his mouth. "You warned me not to date that House Green woman, Blythe, which I ignored. I told January not to date you, which she ignored, and one time you told me"—he paused again—"when you were very drunk, that you regretted signing the treaty with the Houses to end the Uprising, because while it stopped the innocent bloodshed and saved House Brown, it sentenced every galvanized—your family—to a life of slavery."

"Rob," Abraham breathed. He believed him, and for that Robert was grateful.

"We need to get you out of here," Abraham said. "Now."

"This body won't last much longer."

"Like hell," Abraham pulled the coverlet away. His eyes widened at the sight of his wasted, broken, and rotting body.

"We can do something," Abraham said. "We can save you."

"No, Bram," Robert said softly, "we can't. Whatever disease it is, it's advanced. Beyond repair."

Abraham closed his eyes. After a moment, he nodded. He drew the covers up around Robert and sat beside him on the bed. "How did he do this? How did he take your body and brain for his own?"

"A man was there. Unfamiliar equipment. The man was a prisoner."

"Do you know who the man was?"

"Quinten Case. Matilda's brother."

"Do you know where he is? He might know how to reverse this. He might know how to return you to your own body."

"Please, Abraham Seventh," another voice said. "There is no need for questions and plans. I have taken care of all that."

Robert glanced across the room. His body stood in the doorway, a gun in his hand. It was beyond strange to see himself standing there, more whole than he'd ever really considered himself to be.

It was beyond strange to see that the orange stitching that crossed his face and head brought out the blue of his eyes, and somehow made him look strong.

But the strangest thing was to see the alien intelligence behind his eyes, and to hear words spoken in a cadence he had never used.

"Step away from the bed," Slater said. "The bullets in this gun are filled with Shelley dust. One shot, and your stitches will begin to dissolve. Two shots, and you will be unconscious. If I empty the clip, you won't wake for years."

Abraham looked down at Robert, saying good-bye. Saying more than that, as only a brother could. Robert nodded. It had been a long and ultimately good life. He had no regrets.

"What do you want, Slater Orange?" Abraham said as he stood. "What is your play in this game?"

"Immortality, which this body provides. Power, which I will obtain after your House is brought down by your actions, Abraham Seventh."

"Where is Quinten Case?" Abraham asked.

"Nowhere you'll ever find him." Slater squeezed the trigger. One shot, two, three. He unloaded the clip into Abraham, even as the bigger man threw himself to one side.

Slater might be new to the body, but he was not new to killing. His shots struck true, and Abraham fell to his knees, then to the floor, unconscious and bleeding on the plush carpet.

Robert couldn't move. He could barely breathe.

"And for you," Slater said, strolling over so he could look down upon his own image. "A mercy. I will put you out of the pain I know so well."

"Why?" Robert asked. "Why kill me when soon I would die?"

"Your death will be on Abraham Seventh's hands. Your death will fall on House Gray. I will rise in your absence, I will speak for House Orange until your successor is secured. And I will take from House Gray all the knowledge and things that I want. Including Matilda Case."

The gun he raised was of a more standard design. Bullets to kill a more standard man.

Robert did not look away. If this was death, his final death, he wanted to see every moment of it.

The gun fired. The bullet bored through his brain. And then there was no pain.

31

*Some say Alveré Case and his descendants
knew exactly the day the world would end.
They are not wrong. —2198
　　　　　　—from the journal of L.U.C.*

Delightful was not the word I would use to describe
Hong Kong. *Huge, bright, noisy,* maybe, but so beyond anything familiar to me, I found myself wishing I'd
kept the gun in my jacket pocket instead of back in my
duffel at Gray Tower.

No matter. I didn't need a weapon. I was a weapon.

Plus, I'd packed my hunting knife. And I was wearing
the time scarf Grandma had knit.

The city rocketed past us as we traveled the glass
speed tubes that blossomed above, through, and around
the buildings like the petals of a massive flower pulsing
with golden light.

House travel meant there was nothing to stall us—no
checkpoints, no searches, just a clear drive, private flight,
and private tubes. It was surreal to find myself here. Just
a couple days ago, I'd been hiding on the farm, killing
crocboars for the lizard and tossing apples into the pond
for the leapers.

Now I was going to not only attend the gathering of
the most powerful people in the world, but I was also
going to have to represent one of those powerful

Houses. And reveal that I was a stitch. For all the world to see.

That wasn't what mattered to me, though. Reeves had promised I would get my brother back. As soon as that happened, I'd find a way to make sure Grandma was safe from House Silver and all their damn spies.

Abraham still hadn't checked in.

Oscar tried not to look concerned about that when he bid me good night, leaving me to my ultramodern and ultraluxurious room in the corner of the entire floor of the hotel that had been reserved for House Gray. But he was concerned. And so was I.

It was late afternoon, and the gathering was tomorrow morning at dawn. I should have slept, but nerves kept me on my feet, pacing and reading through the information Elwa had given me.

The galvanized would be announced from one to twelve and take their place inside the huge coliseum. The heads of the Houses would walk out with their galvanized and stand beside them. Security was ridiculously high, and every eye in the world would be tuned in.

Reeves said he'd bring Quinten to me after the gathering and that I could look for him there. I didn't know how I'd get away from everything and everyone to be with him. What I needed was luck and a little time. I drew my fingers over the soft beige scarf I was wearing. Time I could manage; luck was going to be harder to come by.

I watched afternoon fade to evening beyond my suite's window and then the night pulled fire out of the streets and buildings until the city glowed in dazzling shades of luminosity. From here I could see the building where the gathering would take place tomorrow: a spiraling pinnacle with a globe balanced at the top, rising above even the tallest building in the city, the coliseum at its feet.

If Reeves Silver was true to his word, I'd have my brother back in just a few hours. Whatever happened after that, I would just find a way to handle.

And even though I wasn't tired, I crawled into the bed that was big enough to sleep a dozen, and waited for dawn.

Before sunrise, Elwa powered into the room with an entire entourage of stylists, assistants, and I didn't know what all else, who saw that I was fed, dressed, and fancied up to acceptable standards.

They went with the gray dress I'd tried on, pulled my hair up into curls and swirls to show my stitches, and then applied makeup and shading to better highlight my best features, which, in their opinion, appeared to be the stitches that held me together.

"I bring you a gift," Elwa said, placing a box on my lap and shooing away the woman who was still fiddling with the ends of my hair, even though it looked fine an hour ago.

"What's this?" I asked.

"Open." She glanced at the small screen in her hand where a million messages, images, and announcements for the gathering buzzed, flickered, and chattered.

I lifted the lid on the box and pushed aside the soft, thin paper there.

"Boots," I said. "They're . . ."

"Magnificent," Elwa provided. "Yes, they are. Put them on. Go."

I pulled one up out of the box and could not argue with her. They were magnificent, made of a sturdy leatherlike material, gray, with grommets and buckles and a second zippered layer that all came together in a graceful symmetry. But under all the good looks was a sturdy heel that was not too high, and the waffled sole of a work boot.

I slipped them on and one of Elwa's assistants laced them up.

"Stand, and let's see what you have become," she said.

The cluster of people around me all took a simultaneous step backward, leaving me room to stand, and clearing a pathway to the full-length mirror.

I had insisted I wear the scarf. For hours. Undaunted, Elwa had reknotted and wrapped the scarf across my shoulders so that it actually looked stylish, then pinned it in place with a fist-sized pendant set with a smoky gray stone that probably cost half a year's wage.

"See now, here is the pride of House Gray," Elwa said from where she stood at my elbow.

I finally glanced in the mirror.

I didn't know how they'd managed it, but somehow I didn't look like I was wearing a layer or two of makeup and a coating of hair products. My hair was pulled back away from my face to show all the angles of my features, then wrapped into a loose bun.

The feminine cut of the dress was offset by the hard slashes of my stitches, the slit in the skirt kicked open to show boots I could wear into battle. Put a gun or sword into my hands, and I looked like someone who could wade into the fray and come out stylish on the other side.

"Is that even me?" I asked.

Elwa squeezed my arm gently, her gaze holding mine in the mirror. "This is you. This has always been you. But there is no more hiding, no more fear. You are House Gray. You are immortal. Strength. Protection. Wisdom. Warrior."

And when she said it, I almost believe her. But she'd left out one word that described me: *vengeance.*

Because once I had my brother back safe, and once I knew I could keep Grandma away from the manipulation of other Houses, I was going to make someone pay for all this.

I was going to make Slater Orange of House Orange pay.

Elwa waved hands and barked orders, clearing out all the people and their equipment. It gave me just enough time to smuggle my knife into my boot.

As soon as she shut the door behind them, she strode over and dropped a small electronic device into my hand.

"Place over your ear, and you will be in the loop for the entire event. You will hear the public commentary and you will hear my instructions. It is like having a tiny Elwa on your shoulder. Nothing will go wrong."

"Thank you," I said.

"Thank me tomorrow morning when all this is done. We will be *exhausted*, darling. Come. It is time."

She hustled me toward the door as I affixed the earpiece to my left ear, where it settled in snugly. "What about Abraham?"

We made our way to the private car and private tube that would take us to the gathering.

"Do not worry," she said. "Everything will be fine."

And since that wasn't much of an answer, I figured that no, he hadn't checked in.

Three soft chimes rang out in my earpiece, and suddenly a flood of music and noise and voices poured out as clearly as if I were standing right in front of them.

I was shuttled, ushered, and hustled into lifts, moving walkways, and a car. Finally, I was left alone in a small private room attached above the arena, waiting for my cue to walk out into the main gathering.

I'd read up on this. I knew what I had to do. Wait for Elwa to tell me I should walk down the hall and then through the door, out into the arena, where I would take my place on the raised platform. Images of me would play across screens, and the history of my work and success . . . whatever that might be . . . would be broadcast to anyone in the loop.

Since I was thirteenth, I would go out last.

Oscar, and the other heads of Houses, would follow just behind me.

The room was decorated in shades of gray, and while it wasn't anywhere as luxurious as our hotel, it was still very nice. I made a cup of tea and moved the plush chairs to one side, so I could pace in front of the window while I watched the arena and crowd of people below me.

"Now," Elwa's no-nonsense voice chirped in my ear.

"First there will be galvanized and you. Then the heads of House will walk the field and the great spectacle begins—each House declaring their new advancements, projects, and allegiances.

"They say House Blue, Water—the strongest of all— will announce a breakthrough in life expansion. They say Troi Blue has now genetically regressed to twenty years old, the youngest regression ever preformed. We shall see with our own eyes, won't we?"

I'd read all this too, but it was nice to have Elwa's voice reminding me of what I'd need to do.

I stood in front of the window that looked out over the coliseum and sipped the tea. Elwa's voice was gone, replaced by a male and female voice that announced how excited the world was now that the gathering was here, and speculated on what new advancement each of the Houses might be bringing to the event.

The chime rang in my ear again, and the gathering began. The announcers switched over to historical bits about Foster First. A door opened on the field and Foster First walked through it. He stood while the cheering people gathered in the arena, chanted his name, and flashed yellow shirts and screens, and threw yellow ribbons.

He was grim and arresting, and no longer wore his long dark coat. A sleeveless vest the color of saffron covered his torso, spread open down the front. The huge screens around the arena flashed with images of him, his heavy scars knotted and twisted across his flesh, held together by thick yellow stitches across his chest, stomach, arms, neck, and face.

As he walked around the track to his platform, the screens lit up with older pictures of him, stitches in black, white, red, and brown, each adding new scars, new lines to his already monstrously scarred body.

The pictures flashed by: a smoke-covered battlefield, the dead spread out in a gruesome carpet of blood and bodies, with only one figure standing: Foster. Foster in a jungle, wielding a machete; leading men across a mine-field; carrying a child out of a fallen building. Foster drag-ging a ship to shore with a cable slung over his shoulder. A lifetime—two—flashed past, until the pictures of Foster standing beside Welton Yellow paused on the screen, then faded.

The crowd cheered, and the camera swung to capture audience members with hair dyed white and styled like Foster's. They even had fake pink eyes and fake yellow stitches on their faces, necks, and hands like Foster.

I scanned that crowd, looking for Quinten, but didn't see him.

Foster took to his platform, which caught yellow light around him, bringing out the stony edges of his face and body and making his yellow stitching glow neon.

Before the cheering died down, another chant rose from the crowd: "Second."

Dolores Second walked through the door, wearing a flowing green, sleeveless blouse and wide-legged forest green trousers, her hair pulled away from her face but falling in waves down her back. The crowd went wild. Green ribbons wrapped around leafy branches fluttered down through the stands, as green shirts, screens, and stitches stood up and cheered.

Where was Quinten? Reeves had said to look for him, but there were almost two hundred thousand people here.

Images from Dotty's past flashed on the screen, her stitches in white, gray, blue, brown, and green as she shoulder-carried a man out of a fire, swung an ax to cut a ship free from the rocks, stacked boulders against a raging river that had burst its dam, and wielded a flame-thrower to burn the plague-carrying crops. The announc-ers listed her accomplishments until she stood on her platform, lit in a green light.

The camera swooped through the crowd. Still no Quinten.

The introduction for the next galvanized, Clara Third, began.

Despite the fact that it was a spectacle that took place every year, the crowd hummed with excitement. It was a sportslike atmosphere as the crowd tried to outcheer each other when their favorite galvanized took the field.

Clara was serene and graceful in a sleeveless lavender dress that draped her lean body in gauzy Grecian gathers, lace cutting thin floral designs over the violet stitches on her legs and arms. Her history showed only violet stitches in her pale skin. There was one image of her on a battlefield, wearing the white band of House Medical on her arm as she tended a wounded woman while bullets fell all around her, but the rest of her images were of her helping the poor and rebuilding disaster-ravaged lands.

Purple scarves of every shade rained down out of the stands like soft petals.

Next up was Vance Fourth, who strode onto the grounds in a blue military-cut, short-sleeve shirt that accentuated his compact, muscular build and the blue stitches tacking his skin.

His history played out, stitches flashing brown, yellow, black, and silver as he piloted experimental jets, broke the land speed record, and manned an exploration vehicle through the ocean's deepest trenches. Sprinkled between those deeds were images of him carrying wounded out of the ash-clogged streets of burning London, and the famous shot of him throwing himself without a parachute to catch and save the little girl nicknamed Rose Blue.

The crowd shouted even louder and tossed blue roses onto the field. He scooped up one rose and tucked it into the buttonhole of his breast pocket as the images stilled on him standing beside Troi Blue.

Wilhelmina Fifth strolled out next, her pale blue skirt and blouse all the colors of the ocean. Her hair had been braided back into ropes that looped up in intricate curls pinned in place with sapphire flowers. The soft blue of her stitches looked almost like feathers against her skin.

The crowd cheered and sent little folded paper cranes down upon the field.

Images of her history flashed across the immense space: Wila's stitches in brown, gray, green, and red. Wila taking down the warlords in Africa, Wila pulling people out of the great oil-line explosion, Wila carrying food and medicine through the two-year blizzard, Wila overturning train cars in the bridge collapse of '93.

And the last image: Wila standing next to Troi Blue.

January Sixth was the next to arrive, but I was scanning the images of people in the crowd.

"Quinten," I breathed. For a flash, for a moment, I saw him, standing between two large men with silver bands on their arms.

And I knew Reeves Silver had placed him there, in that exact spot, knowing I would see him.

He was on his feet—that was good. But he was pale and thin. I think if the two men hadn't had their hands on his arms, he might not be standing.

He was alive. He was breathing. Reeves had come through with his part of the deal.

So far.

I clenched my hands into fists. I wanted to run out there, up into the stands, and take my brother away to safety. But right now, that was the worst thing I could do.

January Sixth was already gliding out onto the field.

She was the image of wealth and couture. Tall and beautiful, her white dress slicked over her perfect body like a silken glove, glittering with diamonds. Her hair fell in soft waves against her bare shoulders where white stitches laced her skin.

The crowd flashed white lights and roared even louder. They threw white feathers tied to glass jewels onto the field until the ground seemed to be covered in snow.

Her history rolled, showing stitches of brown, silver, black, and white.

January leading an army of medical staff into the walled-off city of Mumbai, January climbing bombed-out signal towers to patch communications, January digging through ancient ruins, diving for wrecks, and recovering the lost Leonardo. January smiling and posing with heads of Houses, famous stars, scientists, and children.

And, finally, January standing next to Kiana White.

Abraham was next. The crowd cheered, "Seventh, Seventh, Seventh." The door opened.

I rocked up on my tiptoes, held my breath, and searched for him in the shadows.

The announcers paused. He should be walking through the door; Abraham should be on the field.

The screen filled with his image, a warrior leading the other galvanized across the rubble of a city, and then it froze.

"Elwa," I said, wondering for the first time if the earpiece worked both ways. "Can you hear me? Is Abraham here? Should I do something?"

The chanting faded, the cheering faltered. Voices rose into a buzz of concern. The screen went blank and the announcers in my ear rattled on about how unusual this was, and they were certain the situation would be solved soon.

"Elwa," I said again. "Can you hear me?"

"Yes, darling," she said. "Stay where you are."

"Can I help?" I asked. "Should I go down there?"

No answer.

The crowd had worked itself up. The announcers continued with their soothing commentary, but even up this high, behind glass, I could feel the crowd shifting.

Someone booed; more people joined in.

"Brace yourself, Matilda," Elwa said, sounding rattled.

A movement in the shadow behind the door caught my eye.

I must not have been the only person who saw it. The cameras zoomed in and the blank screens were filled with that door, those shadows, and the figure who walked out of them.

Abraham Seventh. He wore a long gray coat covering him from neck to boot. The only stitches visible were those edging his face, and they were dripping in blood.

The crowd exploded in a cheer and the announcers started into their prewritten speech about Abraham's exploits. The screen flashed with images of him, but I could not take my eyes off the man who walked the field.

At first I thought he was taking his time around the field for show. But after he had crossed a short distance, he began limping.

The crowd noticed it too. Cheers shifted again to strained muttering.

Before he even reached halfway around the stadium, he stumbled and fell.

No.

I didn't pause, couldn't stand aside. My heart was pounding with fear.

I ran out of the room and down the hall, jogging the switchbacks that took me down and around the underwork of the stadium, to the door that emptied out onto the field.

He had to be alive. Galvanized couldn't die, right?

Even before I reached the field, I saw the galvanized from the other Houses running to help Abraham or already at his side, doing what they could to shield his body from the cameras while they helped him sit.

He was unconscious. But there was something else wrong with him. Something much worse.

He didn't seem to be tied together right, as if pieces of him had loosened, been torn away. They were propping him up to sitting, but one of his arms was too low, not just dislocated out of the shoulder socket, but no longer attached to him at all. His torso sat wrong on his hips; his legs weren't moving.

If they weren't holding his head, I thought it might fall off his shoulders.

He shuddered, convulsing.

The crowd gasped, screamed.

I ran for him.

Voices yelled in my ear, voices yelled around me. I didn't listen to any of them. Abraham was falling apart. Dying. Had this been Reeves' plan? To kill Abraham?

I had promised to stand aside while the event played out. But I couldn't let this happen.

"Let me through. Let me see him."

Dotty stood in front of me and pushed her palms against my shoulders to make me stop.

"Listen to me, Matilda," she said, low and quick. "He's hurt. He's falling apart. That means he's been attacked by a House head with Shelley dust. We are going to take care of him as best we can."

"Let me touch him," I said, "I can help."

"If you touch him, he will feel his body dying. He will feel his skin tearing, his bones breaking. If you touch him, you will bring him agony. Do you understand what I'm saying?"

I nodded, the shock and reality of what was happening mixing up with all the confusion and raw fury in me.

Foster was doing the most to support Abraham, and Clara was on her knees, a lavender-robed angel talking to him, comforting him.

I would make it worse, make him worse.

"Matilda!" Elwa's voice screeched in my ear. "Get off the field now."

I jerked my head up, expecting death to be riding down on me.

The crowd was silent. They were on their feet, and my startled face was on every screen around the arena.

The announcers in my ear called me the woman in gray. They couldn't believe I was galvanized. They thought I had to be a fan, that my stitches were so fine and beautiful that they would not be strong enough to hold a real galvanized together.

"Off the field," Elwa said again. "Matilda, darling, now."

I pulled my shoulders back. Yes, I'd revealed myself,

but if my getting off the field would make it so Abraham could get medical attention, then that's what I'd do.

The crowd cheered. I glanced over my shoulder.

Somehow, impossibly, they had gotten Abraham onto his feet.

He looked over at me, his gaze pleading me not to go.

Hell to everything. If I stayed, was I breaking my deal with Reeves Silver? If I left, was I breaking the deal?

Which action would keep my brother safe, my grandmother safe? Leaving Abraham? Leaving House Gray?

Reeves hadn't asked me to leave. He'd just asked me not to get in the way of whatever happened today. I glanced up, looking for Quinten. He was still there, still standing between the men in the stands.

So maybe I hadn't blown this deal yet.

I took a step toward Abraham.

"Stop this event." A voice echoed across the arena, silencing the crowd, silencing the announcers. "I am Robert Twelfth, the galvanized of House Orange. As of this moment, I am also standing as head of House Orange. Stop this event. Immediately."

Screens filled with his image. Robert Twelfth, Abraham's friend who had been acting so strangely. Abraham's friend whom Neds had said wasn't who he appeared to be.

"Slater Orange has been murdered," he said.

A cry rose from the crowd, drowning out the voices in my ear.

"His blood is on the hands of House Gray."

A second cry rose from the crowd.

Abraham weakly pushed away from the others. Even though he should have fallen, he remained standing. I didn't know how he did it.

"What proof do you have against House Gray?" he asked, his voice picked up and amplified by the recording devices.

"My eyes, my word, and my witness." The screen flickered, and Robert's image was replaced by a recording of

Abraham walking over to the bed where Slater Orange sat. In one smooth motion, Abraham pulled a gun and shot Slater Orange.

The crowd screamed and cried out.

Men and women dressed in House Black flooded the field. House Black, Defense, coming to arrest Abraham. Coming to take him away.

Buck was already on the field, heading toward Abraham.

And then another voice called out: Oscar Gray.

"The accusation of House Gray will not be tolerated." There was no need for the camera to search Oscar out. He strode onto the field through another door, wearing a fine-cut gray suit and coat.

The forces from House Black paused and created a ring around Oscar and the galvanized, facing outward to halt the restless crowd that looked ready to jump the stands.

Every person in the stadium was on their feet.

"Robert Twelfth," Oscar said, as he strode toward Abraham, "House Gray does not recognize your right to speak for House Orange without the proper procedures in place. This matter will be brought into the private audience of the Houses immediately. Remove yourself from this arena and join us there."

"Agreed and accepted," Welton Yellow's voice said over the speakers.

Eight other voices—the heads of the Houses—including Reeves Silver, also agreed and accepted Oscar Gray's request for a private audience to find out what was going on.

The crowd's voices rose in heightened chatter. If I ran now to find Quinten, would anyone miss me?

"Matilda." Oscar waved me over, then turned to Abraham, helping him stay on his feet. Abraham looked even worse than a moment ago, as if standing on his own had taken the last of his strength.

Too late, I saw the figure in black step in front of me. She was compact, her silver stitches glinting in the shadow of the black hood she wore.

Helen Eleventh? Why was she wearing black? Too late, I saw the gun in her hand. Too late, I saw her aim.

In less than a second, she unloaded the bullets into Oscar Gray.

32

Edith Case sent the encoded message. She begged House Gray for help. They must find her husband, Dr. Case. They must find her daughter, Matilda, hidden away on a strange little farm that appeared on no map. They must hurry, while there was still time to save the world. —2199
— from the journal of Lara Unger Case

Chaos.

Helen ran as the arena filled with screams and shouting and people. Buck Eighth pounded after her and took her down, holding her pinned to the ground.

More people were filling the field, screaming, panicking. Over it all, an announcer's voice told people to stay calm, to file out in an orderly manner, and that the situation was under control.

Only the situation very much wasn't under control.

I ran to Oscar, to Abraham. The galvanized were trying to help them both, and hold off the panicked crowd that had jumped the barriers and were running across the field. A dozen or so people dressed in white—House Medical—were half a field away and pushing to get through the confusion of people to Oscar.

House Black did all they could to hold the human wall around the wounded, standing shoulder to shoulder and facing outward, to keep Oscar and Abraham from being trampled.

"Please," I said. "I'm House Gray. Please let me see them."

Two people shifted enough I could slip between them. Clara and Vance knelt beside Oscar, performing CPR.

Abraham lay unconscious a few feet from where Oscar had fallen. His skin was a sickly mottle of black and yellow, his features swollen and bruised.

My heart was pounding so hard, my head buzzing.

They say galvanized are immortal. But I didn't know how Abraham could survive this.

I hurried over and knelt beside Oscar.

Clara was doing what she could to compress the bullet wound, and Vance was pumping Oscar's chest to try to keep his heart beating.

But neither of them were speaking.

I gently touched Oscar's cheek. "You're going to be all right," I said. "Everything's going to be fine."

His glassy eyes rolled and focused on me kneeling over him. "Save . . ." he breathed, "Abraham . . ."

"We will," I said, trying to smile though tears filled my eyes. "He's fine. Just keep breathing, Oscar. We need you. We need you to just keep breathing."

His mouth worked around words, but no sound came out. Then he smiled, as if trying to reassure me that he was okay.

"Oscar?" I said. His eyes rolled back into his head and a sudden and complete stillness spread over him.

Vance cursed, and Clara quietly prayed.

The world blurred through tears. He couldn't be gone. He couldn't be dead. Oscar was too kind, too good to be ended by petty violence.

Killed while I stood by and let it happen.

Dotty was suddenly behind me. She put her hand on my shoulder and helped me to my feet.

"What can I do?" I asked Dotty. "Can they save him? Can they bring him back?"

"We won't give up on Oscar until it is medically impossible to revive him. I'm sorry, Matilda, I don't think he's going to make it."

"Abraham?" I asked, looking wildly for him.

"Abraham can't die, no matter how badly he's injured. But there has never been a House assassination," she said. "Not in all the time since the Restructure. For two to happen in one day?" She shook her head and swallowed hard.

"What now?" I asked.

"I don't know. If the allegations are proven true against Abraham, he will not be allowed to survive. His brain will be locked away in storage, his body dismantled." She nodded, her lips white at the edges, her eyes wide with fear.

But her voice didn't betray the horrors she was so matter-of-factly telling me. "The Houses will demand justice. I believe things will become very dark for the galvanized and for you. At the best, at the very best, you will be claimed by House Orange in payment for House Gray killing Slater Orange.

"There will be a testimony and trial, but the Houses err on the side of brutal punishment when it comes to the galvanized, and I am sure they will do so now. Even if Abraham is innocent, Helen is not. It is possible we will all bear their guilt."

"Everyone? All the galvanized will be punished?"

"Our treaty with the mortals, our trust with the Houses, has been gravely damaged. Under no circumstances— none—are we allowed to injure a head of House. I don't think anything will be the same again. Our world is gone. It is too late now. Too late for all of us."

She gave me a sad smile, then turned to help the other galvanized with Oscar and Abraham.

The medical people pushed into the circle, hurrying over to Oscar with cases of equipment.

I had lost Oscar before really knowing him. I had lost Abraham and this new life that I might have learned to love. I wanted to fall on my knees and sob.

There was no time for that. But there was plenty of time to fight, to survive.

What resources did I have?

My strength, my brother in the stands, and the scarf around my shoulders.

It wasn't much.

It would have to do.

I unpinned the scarf, my fingers fumbling through the clasp as more medical people slipped through the ring of House Black around us. Finally got the clasp free. I quickly unknotted the end of the yarn and pulled. The yarn ticked as it slipped free of each knotted stitch.

Time slowed, stopped.

My heart was beating the same, well, faster now since I was facing a future of pain and punishment and might, by these decisions, be sealing my grandmother and brother's death.

People around me froze in place.

Even the slight breeze and sounds ground down to a halt. Except for me.

I pulled the stitches as slowly as possible as I walked over to Abraham. I bent and deadlifted him into a fireman's carry. I pulled yarn while I hurried out of the stadium. I set him down outside. I only had two feet of scarf left.

"I'll be right back." I ran into the stadium, then up the stairs, only pulling on the yarn when I thought I saw someone move. I needed time. Much more than I had.

Quinten was easy to pull away from the two men who guarded him, lift, and carry outside. By the time I made it clear of the stadium and around the corner to where I'd left Abraham, the scarf was gone.

The world suddenly snapped back into motion. The earth shook beneath me as if a giant had struck it with his fist and the sky cracked with thunder and copper lightning.

I stumbled. Fell onto my knees with Quinten, the

smells, sounds, and motion slamming into me all at once, overwhelming and painful.

"Matilda?" Quinten said, startled. It took him half a second to grasp the situation: me on my knees, him on the ground next to Abraham, who wasn't moving.

"We have to get out of here," I said. "Can you walk?"

"Yes," he sat, brushed his coat, and got on his feet, pulling me into a rough hug. "I thought I'd never see you again, little sister. What took you so long? No, never mind. We need to go." He released me, then took a step, his hand held out for me.

"I won't leave him."

Quinten looked down at the mess that was Abraham.

"We can't take him."

"He'll be tortured."

Quinten frowned, then pressed his fingers against his lips the way he did when he was thinking through possibilities.

"They'll know he's gone any second now," I said.

"Carry him. Can you?"

"Yes." I picked him up again, and this time he groaned. Since time wasn't paused, my contact caused him pain.

I knew galvanized couldn't die. I was just hoping he might go unconscious and spare himself some suffering.

We started running.

"Money?" he asked.

"Nope."

"Weapons?"

"Knife. You?"

"No."

"Boston Sue is working for House Silver," I said as we jogged down an alley to a street and another alley. "She's looking after Grandma."

"That's delightful," he said. "Why did you claim House Gray? Why did you even leave the farm?"

"To find you. To save you. They had already found me anyway. And Neds were spies too."

"Neds?"

That's right, they hadn't met. "Farmhand I hired when you went missing so long. What were you doing? Why were you gone so long?"

"I was looking for a way to change the world. To save Mom and Dad."

I stopped, not because I was out of breath — I'd lugged crocboar that were heavier than Abraham — but because Quinten was making no sense.

"Mom and Dad are dead."

"I know," he said. "But there is an event. A loop in time that according to my calculations will hit in four days. Well," he added, "less than that now."

"The date in your message?"

"You got that?"

"Yes."

"Wings of Mercury. It's a ... break in time triggered three hundred years ago by our grandfather several generations removed. Dr. Alveré Case. His experiment created a ... think of it as he shattered a moment in time. One piece of time broke away and is now boomeranging back to that break point. Those who survived the ground-zero blast of time breaking became the galvanized. Immortal."

"Wings of Mercury."

He nodded. "Exactly. I was looking for a journal — it belonged to our grandmother — that contains vital information. The key to controlling the experimental machine. The key to controlling time."

"Grandma doesn't keep a journal."

"They took it, along with the rest of Dad's research."

"Did you find it?"

"No."

"So, what's going to happen in less than four days?"

"Nothing if we get home before then."

"Quinten," I said in my not-one-more-step voice. "What's going to happen?"

"The galvanized are living on borrowed time. Quite

literally. And when time mends, when that broken piece snaps back into place, the galvanized will die."

"All of us?"

"All." His eyes were dark with a sorrow and guilt I could not bear to see. He had saved me years ago when he'd put me in this stitched body. And now I had only a few days left to live.

It was hard to take in all at once.

"Gold," I said, because I had no other words in me.

"I think I can fix it," he said. "I might have enough information to be able to change it. We just have to get home. As quickly as we can."

I glanced back at the stadium.

Getting home was not going to be easy. Already waves of people were pouring onto the streets. A good deal of them wore Black, Defense. They knew this city a lot better than we did. They probably had weapons. They were probably looking for us.

But none of them were running for their lives.

"Do you have your breath?" he asked.

"Yes. Go."

We bolted down several more streets, putting a solid mile between us and the stadium, but there were cameras everywhere. It was only a matter of time before they caught us.

We ducked into a pocket of shadow and I crouched there, catching my breath. Abraham needed medical attention, and soon. He might not be able to die, but his life stitches were pulling looser and looser. Pretty soon there wouldn't be enough of him in one piece to carry anywhere.

And, yes, that horrified me.

"We'll wait until dark," Quinten said quietly. "Let me see his injuries."

I set him down as carefully as I could, then leaned my head back against the dirty alley wall, running through our options. Our farm was a continent away. We couldn't trust House Brown, or any other House for that matter. We had no vehicle, no money, no weapons, and no time.

"Matilda?" a familiar voice called out softly.

Quinten pivoted where he was crouched to look out at the mouth of the alley.

"I know you're there," Right Ned said. "And I know we're not square. But I brought you this."

Something soft fell into the middle of the alley. My duffel.

"I have a car and I can take you back to the farm. You and Quinten if he's with you."

"Who are you working for this time, Neds Harris?"

"You," he said. "Only you. And you have my word on that, not that it holds much worth anymore."

I didn't say anything. He had probably brought House Black with him, or Silver or Orange or whoever he was working with now.

"Do you want to know what I see when I touch you?" Left Ned asked as they walked up to the mouth of the alley and looked right at me.

There was no use hiding anymore.

I moved out into the light. "What do you see?"

"I see this," Right Ned said. "Always this one moment. I ask you to trust me. I tell you I'm going to take you home with your brother and Abraham. I tell your brother I know what's in that journal because whenever I've touched your grandma, I've seen the things rattling in that old head of hers. The time loop. The Wings of Mercury project, how she knits up time with those ridiculous little sheep. I know we have only a couple days to get you all back home."

"And what do I say?" I asked.

"I don't know," Right Ned said.

Left Ned was silent, but he wasn't scowling. If anything, he looked worried, just like Right Ned looked worried.

I'd known those boys for some time now. They'd lied to me. But right here, right now, they were not lying.

"You know about the time loop?"

"I know what your grandmother knows," Right Ned said. "Most of it anyway."

"Did you tell anyone? Helen Eleventh? Your boss at House Silver?"

"No," Left Ned answered. "I was spying on you at the start, Matilda. Then when I got to know you, well . . . neither of us have said a word about this to anyone. Time isn't something we think the Houses should rule."

"I'd be a fool to trust you," I said. "Again."

"We know," Right Ned said.

"Maybe I should have sent you packing when you first showed up on my land," I said.

"Always told you strangers weren't nothing but trouble," Left Ned said.

"Strangers, maybe," I said. "But not you, Neds Harris."

They waited.

"Her trust was broken, and now it's mended," Quinten said as he stepped out of the shadows. "Can we settle this while we're running for our lives? You did say you had a car?"

"Yes," Left Ned said. "You must be Quinten?"

"I am. Help me with Abraham." He and Neds got to work carrying Abraham, and I picked up my duffel, glanced through it—everything was there, including my handgun and Quinten's watch.

"You decided I trusted him?" I said to Quinten.

"You would have gotten there eventually." He flashed me a smile as he and Neds carefully deposited Abraham into the backseat of a car with just enough room for him to lie in.

"Best if you drive, Mr. Harris," Quinten said ducking in the back. "Since you don't have a price on your head. Either of them."

Neds got into the front, and I got in next to Quinten.

"He's not going to make it," Quinten said as Neds drove the car down the alley, toward another street and the airport. "His stitches are dissolving."

"Here," I said. "Try this." I dug a jar of scale jelly out of my duffel and handed it to my brother.

He grinned. "You are such a clever girl, Matilda. Have I told you that lately?" He unscrewed the lid and applied jelly to Abraham's stitches.

"You haven't told me anything lately. You left me and disappeared, remember?"

"Not my intention—you know that. This seems to be helping. Did you happen to pack a needle and thread?"

I held both out for him.

"That's my girl. Never misses a step." He grinned and climbed back next to Abraham then methodically stripped him down.

There was an awful lot of blood, but Quinten didn't seem worried as he applied the scale jelly, and started in on stitching Abraham back together.

"We'll be at the plane in five minutes," Right Ned said. "I have a friend who will take us out without records."

"Thank you, Mr. Harris," Quinten said, as if Ned was a personal chauffeur.

"Just Ned," Right Ned said, taking us down streets at speed.

"Tell me everything that's happened since I left," Quinten said.

"Everything?"

"Yes."

"Other than my life has fallen apart and you and I are wanted criminals?"

"Tell me the things I don't know."

So I told him. Everything that had happened in the three years since he'd been gone, and especially everything that had happened since Abraham had showed up bleeding on our kitchen doorstep.

Neds stopped the car.

"This isn't the airport," I said, looking out the windows.

"We don't want the airport," Right Ned said. "Give me a second. I'll be back with help to move him."

Quinten tied off the last knot at Abraham's neck and sat back a bit to consider his handiwork. "Satisfactory," he declared.

I wanted to touch Abraham, to comfort him, but I couldn't even do that much.

The back of the car opened and Neds stood there next to a woman and a man. Even in the dark of night, I could see the woman had an extra arm on one side, which was currently holding a medical stretcher, and the man next to her was built to mammoth proportions.

"Sadie, Corb," Right Ned said, "This is Matilda Case and her brother, Quinten. The stitch is Abraham Seventh."

"Pleased to be of help," Corb said in a low but pleasing voice.

"Thank you," I said. "We'll repay you in kind."

"No need," Corb offered his huge hand to help Quinten exit the car. "Any friend of a Harris is a friend of ours."

"We'll want to hurry, though," Sadie said. "I'll warm the engines."

I gathered up my duffel and got out through the passenger's door.

In that short time, Corb and Neds had helped Quinten settle Abraham on the stretcher, and then they carried him at a jog off toward a floating dock.

That was when I realized where we were.

"We're going out by seaplane?"

"Not a bad idea," Quinten said, walking quickly beside me and already out of breath. "Less regulated. All the smugglers do it."

We had made it to the door of the little plane, and Corb somehow folded down into the thing. He helped first Quinten, then me onto the plane and into our seats. Neds and Corb were sitting in the cargo area just behind us, strapping Abraham in securely.

Corb reached over and locked the hatch. "Take us up, Sadie," he called.

She gave a thumbs-up from the pilot's seat and eased the little craft out across the water. The engine grew louder; the night whisked past the windows. The little plane bobbled slightly, straining for her wings. Then she lifted into the air, heading for the distant sky.

"Is Abraham going to be all right?" I asked Quinten.

"He'll need blood," he said. "And a chemical wash to try to neutralize the Shelley dust. It won't kill him not to have it, but he won't be conscious until he does."

"Blood," I said. "Sure. I'll just put it on my to-do list." I rubbed my fingers through my hair, only to find the pins and jewels there. I began plucking them out and dropping them into my duffel. I hoped they were real. We could use the money.

Quinten shook his head and smiled. "Don't worry, little sister. We'll get through this."

"Because we're House Brown and so terribly resourceful?" I asked.

"No," Quinten said, settling back in his seat and closing his eyes. "Because we are Cases. And we are going to change the world."

ABOUT THE AUTHOR

Devon Monk has one husband, two sons, and a dog named Mojo. She writes the Allie Beckstrom and Broken Magic urban fantasy series and the Age of Steam steampunk series, knits silly things, and lives in Oregon. To find out more about her novels or short stories, visit her online.

CONNECT ONLINE

devonmonk.com
twitter.com/devonmonk

Read on for an exciting excerpt from the
next book in the
House Immortal series
by Devon Monk,

INFINITY BELL

Coming in March 2015 from Roc.

Abraham was sitting, covered in sweat, his hair finger-combed off his forehead. He had on pants and boots. Quinten was just tying off a knot in a bandage he'd wrapped over both Abraham's shoulders and around his chest and stomach.

Gloria looked up from where she was putting things away onto a shelf.

"We've been made," Left Ned said. "In the shop. Domek. Assassin. Run. Now. You want to get out of here quick, Gloria. He's armed."

"Domek?" Abraham said. "Are you sure?"

"More than."

"How long until he can get back here?" Quinten asked as he quickly shoved medical supplies into a duffel Gloria had tossed to him.

"Can't get in from the front," Gloria said. "Did he come into the shop?"

"Yes." Neds glanced around the room and stuffed his pockets with a couple jars of pills.

"He'll realize there's no access in five minutes or less," she said. "How quickly he gets in here depends on how much firepower he's packing."

I jogged over to Abraham and helped him into a shirt, flannel, and jacket.

His hands were trembling. He was kicking off an awful lot of heat even though he was shivering.

Fever.

"Can you stand?" I asked as I helped him up off the table. "Can you run?"

His eyes tightened, and he hissed air between his teeth. "I'm fine," he gasped, one arm pressed against his stomach. "Let's move."

"Any other doors in here besides the one to the parking lot?" Right Ned asked.

"Basement," Gloria said, pulling a coat off a shelf and pulling into it. "This way." She ran off toward the hall Neds and I had just come in from.

"Hurry," Quinten said, throwing the duffel over his shoulder and following Gloria.

Abraham took one step, then another. From the way his body stiffened against each movement, it looked like it hurt like hell.

If he was already feeling everything, then I didn't see how my touching him could make it worse. "Here," I said, sliding my arm around his back and drawing his arm over my shoulder. "Lean if you need it."

He leaned.

I helped him take the next few steps and wanted to scream for how slow we were moving. But with each step, his body seemed to come back to itself, seemed to remember how to move as one whole.

And then it remembered how to move smoothly and quickly, until we were moving at a fairly fast pace.

"Faster, faster," Left Ned chanted behind us.

Gloria and Quinten were dragging a heavy cabinet away from the end of the hall and shoving it up against one wall. Gloria crouched down and pressed a button in the floorboards. A hatch popped up, and she pushed it to one side where it slid seamlessly into the floor itself.

"Watch your step." She started down a ladder, Quinten hurrying after her.

I looked up at Abraham. This wasn't going to be pretty.

He scowled at the ladder. "Go," he said, pulling his arm away from me.

"I won't leave you," I said.

"Down. I'll be right behind you."

I didn't waste any more time arguing. I sat and slipped my boots down to the first rung, then scurried down as fast as I could.

Not a lot of light at the bottom of the ladder, but it smelled of damp and mold and rot.

"What's taking them so long?" Quinten whispered from somewhere in the shadows to my right.

Abraham's boot—first one, then the other—pressed against the ladder rungs. He climbed down methodically, but not nearly as slowly as I'd expected, which was good.

Neds scrambled down almost on top of him.

As soon as Neds' heads cleared the floor above us, the hatch closed, snicking into place, then sealing with a thud of metal sucking down vacuum tight.

The darkness was complete now.

"This way," Gloria said. She shook something and a soft yellow glow appeared in her palm.

I heard Quinten shake something too, and then the little packet strapped to the back of his hand glowed.

"Do you need assistance?" he asked Abraham.

Abraham was leaning against the ladder and breathing hard. Sweat caught in small droplets at the ends of his hair over his eyes, and his clothes were soaked with it. He looked like he'd just run a marathon, not walked down a simple ladder.

"We'll catch up," I said.

Abraham pushed away from the ladder. "We'll keep up," he said.

Neds swore softly, probably Left Ned. He stood next to Abraham and wrapped an arm around him.

I came up on the other side and did the same. I'd expected Abraham to argue, but from how much he was leaning on us both, I didn't think he had the air for it.

"Don't like ladders?" I asked.

Abraham breathed for a bit, as if just trying to keep

his lungs and feet moving at the same time was taking all his concentration.

"Most. Repairs," he said, one word on each exhale. "Days. To recover. Coordination. Difficult."

"It's coming back to you pretty quickly," I said.

"Wouldn't hurt to step it up a bit," Left Ned said.

The glow of Quinten's and Gloria's lights was moving ahead of us faster than we were keeping up.

"Think you can?" I asked Abraham.

Instead of wasting breath, he just put a little more effort into walking. He had longer legs than either Neds or me, but I was wishing he were moving at about twice the speed.

"Do you think Domek will find the hatch?" I asked Neds.

"Yes," Right Ned said.

"How long?"

"Hopefully not before we're out of this tunnel," Left Ned said. "We're fish in a barrel down here."

"Where do you think this empties out?"

"No idea," Right Ned said.

Abraham was doing what he could to stay breathing and moving. Even wounded, fevered, weak, and hurting, he didn't complain.

"Hold up here," Gloria said from a little way ahead of us. "I'll see if we can cross."

"Just a little more," I said. We finally caught up to Quinten at a place where the tunnel widened a bit. The walls were a rough mix of dirt and bricks, the ceiling supported by wooden beams. Gloria's light bobbed ahead, casting yellow over more bricks and more beams; then she took a sharp right and was gone.

"Let's lean for a second," I suggested. Neds and I guided Abraham to the wall and leaned against it.

We were all sweating and breathing a little hard. Abraham closed his eyes and worked on getting his breathing under control.

Quinten squinted at the shadows that filled the tunnel

where Gloria had been moments before. Then he dug in the duffel over his shoulder and pulled out a soft canteen. "It's water," he said offering it to me. "He should drink as much as he can."

I took the container, a waterproof fabric with a hard nozzle and cap at the top. I unscrewed the lid and held it up for Abraham. "You should drink," I said. "Doctor's orders."

It took him a moment, but he opened his eyes and tipped his head down again. He shifted and pulled his arm off from around my shoulders, then did the same with Neds.

He locked his knees to hold him up against the wall and held out his hand for the water.

I gave the canteen to him, and he tipped it up and drank several long, deep swallows. He pulled it away from his mouth, paused to get his breath again, then drank.

While he repeated this, his breathing getting better and better after each time he drank, I glanced around the tunnel, trying to set its location in my head.

"Do you have any idea where we are?" I asked Quinten.

"Other than under the city? No. She always told me she had a way to get out if she was ever discovered by a House."

"I think I love her a little for that," I said.

He smiled, the shadow and light carving his profile as if he were made of wax. "There's a lot about her to love," he said quietly.

I walked the short distance to my brother and leaned in close. "I need to talk to you about Abraham."

"Matilda and I will go partway down the tunnel," he announced to Neds and Abraham. "See if we can see or hear Gloria."

Before Neds could argue, Quinten took my wrist. We walked about halfway to the junction Gloria had taken to the right.

"What?" he whispered.

"He feels. Pain," I said. "I think it's the thread you

used on him. My thread. And the scale jelly. Whatever it is, he can feel now."

Quinten frowned, glanced back over his shoulder, then back at me. "Are you certain? Did he tell you that?"

"Yes. I don't know how painful that procedure you just did on him is, but from the sound of it—"

"It would be excruciating for a normal human." Quinten wiped at his mouth with his nonglowing hand. "He shouldn't be walking. Matilda, we need to find a safe place to leave him. He won't be able to keep up, and running, now, will only do more damage to him."

"I won't hold you up," Abraham said. He walked on his own toward us. I had to admit he seemed to be carrying himself better.

Neds followed behind him. I couldn't see their expression in the darkness.

But Abraham looked calm, confident, and collected.

Yeah, I'd seen him put on that act before. I knew he was weak, wounded, and hurting.

"If you care for your well-being," Quinten said, "you'll allow us to find a safe place where you can recover fully."

"There's a price on my head," Abraham said. "There is no safe place for me."

"Then if you care at all about my *sister's* life," Quinten said, "you will put her safety before yours and leave this group behind."

"Hey, now," I said. "Stop it. Both of you. This won't help anything."

I may as well have been scolding a wall.

Abraham advanced on Quinten and glowered down at him. "I care very much about your sister. Do you understand me, Quinten Case? I know what you've done to make her. I know what you've done to keep her hidden. But she is no longer your secret alone.

"The Houses know about her; the world knows about her. And they know about you. If you think you can outrun them, you are a fool with a fool's pride."

"She was safe until *you* put her in danger," Quinten

snapped. "She would have stayed safe if *you* hadn't stepped into our lives. I blame you, Abraham Seventh, for all the damage done to her. All the damage done to my family."

"I will only tell you this once, Mr. Case," Abraham said in a low growl. "You don't want me as your enemy."

"Enough!" I pushed my way between them, grabbed the sleeves of their jackets and physically pulled them apart.

Yes, I'm strong enough to do that. "We are all going to get along. Do you both understand that? I do not care one bit about who thinks they have or haven't done enough to keep me safe. For one thing, keeping me safe is *my* job. I will not be argued over like I'm a fragile knickknack someone dropped and chipped.

"Right this second, I could wrestle you *both* to the ground and make you cry uncle, so do not even *think* of testing how serious I am about this. We travel together. Period. We keep the hate, blame, and anger where it should be kept: against the Houses who have sent assassins to kill us, and anything and anyone else who gets in our way. Are we gold?"

Neither of them said anything.

"Gold?" I repeated, shoving back my sleeves so I'd have better reach to wrestle them.

"We're gold," Abraham said.

"Fine," Quinten said. "We travel together. If Abraham falls, we all fall. That should be a familiar refrain to you, Abraham Seventh, now that all the galvanized are falling because of your actions."

Abraham lifted his head and forced himself to take a couple steps away. I noted it put him out of strangling range, which was pretty much what it looked like he wanted to do to my brother.

"We haven't told you," Quinten said, "but we are trying to get back to our property."

"Why?" Abraham asked me.

Quinten answered him. "Because if we don't, the time

anomaly that has given the galvanized such a long life will end, killing all galvanized instantly."

Abraham was silent for a moment. Just a few hours ago, I'd told him his friend Oscar was dead. Just a few hours ago, he'd found out my brother had killed his friend Robert. And now he was being told his own death was just days away.

"You have a way to stop the anomaly?" he asked with far more calm than I was feeling.

"Yes. It's a theory, but there is a way."

"How?"

A blast ricocheted through the tunnel. A bomb? Who was throwing bombs at us?

"Go," Left Ned said, grabbing Abraham's arm and helping him past us down the tunnel. "Domek must have blown the hatch. He'll be on us."

I jogged after them, caught up, and took Abraham's other side.

This time, Abraham held more of his own weight, and his breathing was steady. He'd gotten enough water and rest back there that we could sprint for it.

So we ran.

Down to the end of the tunnel. Hard right following where Gloria had gone.

Could be a dead end.

Could be a trap.

Could be that Gloria had been captured and we were running to our doom.

Could be that none of that mattered because Domek was behind us, and he would kill us deader than dead if he caught us.

A light ahead of us descended from the ceiling. This tunnel ended in a shaft.

"Hurry!" Gloria pulled a cage door to one side and waved us in behind it. "Where's Quinten?"

I pulled out from under Abraham's arm, leaving him to lean against the back of the cage—maybe an elevator—

and looked out into the darkness and dust behind us for Quinten.

I couldn't see him, but the light he carried arced and then hit the ground. He'd thrown it away. I didn't know why.

"Quinten!" I got three steps out of the elevator into the dust when a hand shot out and grabbed my wrist.

"Run, run!" Quinten said.

We hauled it into the elevator and Gloria worked the controls. It was an old freight lift, mechanics and gears, pulleys and chain. It clattered and rumbled, starting up.

"Did you see him?" I asked Quinten.

"Cover your ears," he said.

Which was a weird answer, but then it all clicked. He had a lot of different medical compounds and chemicals in that bag he'd packed. If he didn't have something that was already a bomb, he was sure to have packed something that could pretty quickly become a bomb.

I covered my ears.

The blast hit. Sound and impact almost simultaneous. Dust and rock smothered out the air, stung my eyes, and covered me in grit. I prayed the mechanics would withstand it. The elevator shuddered like an animal that just had its jugular cut.

But it kept rising, grinding, cranking up and up.

Quinten was saying something, but I couldn't hear him after that blast. Gloria shook her head at him, pressing her fingers over her lips. Quinten shut up.

Neds and Abraham were covered in a thick layer of dust. I supposed we all were, but they had seen Gloria's signal and weren't talking.

The elevator hopped to a stop. Gloria pulled the cage door open and walked out into a concrete enclosure with a single steel door at the end of it.

She took a second to bat the dust off her shoulders, head, face, and hands.

We all stepped out of the elevator, Abraham under his own power.

"Which wire do I cut?" I asked Quinten.

He glanced at me, then at the elevator gears that were exposed. He pointed. "That should work."

I nodded, reached over, wrapped my hand around the cable chain, and pulled.

Not as easy as it looked, but I am an uncommonly strong woman. It finally gave under my insistence.

"It won't stop him," Left Ned said. "He'll keep coming until he's dead."

"Just trying to buy us some time," I said as we jogged to where Gloria was picking the lock on the steel door.

"No key?" I asked.

"Never had one," she said.

"Let me." Right Ned flicked a ready-all out of his pocket and a slim knife out of the other.

Gloria moved aside and Neds got busy with the lock. Right Ned gave a little "aha" and had it sprung in less than three seconds.

"Three seconds? You're losing your touch, Harris," I said.

"Want me to reset it so you can give it a try?"

"There's no time for this, children," Quinten said.

Neds stepped back and pulled his jacket hood up so that at a casual glance, you wouldn't suppose he had two heads.

I adjusted my scarf and took a look at Abraham. He had his hands in his pockets and, with the dust and scruff, even the stitches on his face were difficult to see unless a person got close enough.

Quinten and Gloria left their heads bare, which was a good move. Five people all hooded up might be more than a little coincidental.

She opened the door and we all stepped through.

The light wind and clear, sunny day made me want to gulp down big lungfuls of the cleaness of it. I'm not claustrophobic, but that run through the tunnels had my shoulders creeping up.

The elevator had left us in an alley between two

buildings—one must be a restaurant from the smell of hot oil and fish that was coming from it.

Right or left? Left was darker, leading to a narrow cross street and another jag of alleys. Right was light, a busy street, maybe a park beyond it.

Abraham strode off to the right.

"He'll see us," Quinten said.

"He'll expect us to hide," Abraham answered.

"What about cameras?" Gloria asked.

"I know someone who will help us with that," he said. "Hurry. He'll find a way out of that tunnel, even if he has to climb the elevator shaft."

"Who?" I asked. "Who do you know who can help with the cameras?"

But by then, he was at the end of the alley and striding out into full and open daylight.

ALSO AVAILABLE
FROM
Devon Monk

STONE COLD
A Broken Magic Novel

Marked by Life and Death magic, Shame Flynn and Terric Conley are "breakers"—those who can use magic to its full extent. Most of the time, they can barely stand each other, but they know they have to work together to defeat a common enemy—rogue magic user Eli Collins.

Backed by the government, Eli is trying to use magic as a weapon by carving spells into the flesh of innocents and turning them into brainless walking bombs. To stop him, Shame and Terric will need to call on their magic, even as it threatens to consume them—because the price they must pay to wield Life and Death could change the very fate of the world... and magic itself.

Available wherever books are sold or at
penguin.com

facebook.com/acerocbooks